I0822507

HER CONFESSIONS COLLECTION

Kirsten S. Blacketer

CONFESSIONS OF A FANGIRL
CONFESSIONS OF A GAMER GIRL
CONFESSIONS OF A GLAMOUR GIRL

Printed in the United States of America.
First Printing, October 2025
ISBN: 9781966905189

Written by Kirsten S. Blacketer.
Published by BlackShip Press
Kirsten.blacketer@gmail.com

Cover Illustration: **V. Miller Artist**

https://kirstensblacketer.com

Dedication

To all my fellow Fangirls. Though our paths may be different, we will always have our fandoms.

To all the gamers who just want to escape for a bit.

To all the *good girls.*

I see you.

Table of Contents

CONFESSIONS OF A FANGIRL

CONFESSIONS OF A GAMER GIRL

CONFESSIONS OF A GLAMOUR GIRL

Kirsten S. Blacketer
Confessions of a Fangirl
KORBIN RANSOM

CHAPTER ONE

STAGE ONE: DISCOVERY

Everyone thinks they've got their shit figured out until they don't. Somewhere between my first cup of coffee this morning and the afternoon staff meeting, my mind decided to take a leisurely stroll down Fantasyland Avenue. Unfortunately, I need to get it back in familiar territory so I can focus on the words coming out of my boss's mouth.

But that will never happen. Thanks to the new guy sitting across from me in his well-tailored suit and rocking dark, wavy hair a tad too long to be fashionable. I bet it's soft. His attention shifts away from the boss, and I catch his penetrating gaze. A half-smile forms on his lips. *Shit.*

I readjust the notebook in front of me and scribble a few incoherent phrases down to make it look like I'm doing something productive. My heart slows to a normal rhythm, and I curse myself for not paying closer attention to Mr. Roberts who's rambling about quarterly reports.

Normally, I dread this monthly meeting when all the department heads gather. I'm flattered my supervisor is considering me to step in while she's on maternity leave, but it's been hell getting over this feeling I'm pretending to fit in instead of actually being part of the team. This opportunity will give me a shot at the promotion I've been hoping for—if I can focus.

When I glance up at Mr. Roberts, the new guy sits perfectly in my peripheral vision. And like that, my mind is cruising down Fantasyland Avenue again with Mr. Tall, Dark, and Handsome riding shotgun. I glance at the pad again in defeat.

"That should do it for the moment." Mr. Roberts gathers his files into a pile. "Before you go, I'd like to introduce you to the newest member of our staff." He gestures to the new guy

I've been eyeing for the last hour. "Mr. Shaun Townsend. He's transferred in from our Denver office to give us a hand in Marketing."

My gaze shifts to Mr. Townsend who glances around the room with a pleasant smile. His gaze lingers on me for half a second before drifting back to Mr. Roberts.

"Thank you. Glad to be a part of the team."

Oh, man. His voice. I could sit and listen to him read me the phone book.

"That'll be all. Enjoy your weekend." Mr. Roberts dismisses us, and I'm out of my chair in an instant.

I edge toward the door with the rest of my coworkers. Part of me wants to introduce myself to Mr. Townsend, but I remind myself to be professional. Work isn't an appropriate venue for flirtation and romance as Pamela down in HR reminds us in her memos constantly.

Once I reach my desk, I settle in to work on the orders I started before the meeting. Not even five minutes later, Lily appears around the corner making a beeline for my desk. I envy her ability to rock vintage styles without effort. She slides into the chair beside mine, tugging her polka dot wiggle skirt down her stockinged thighs.

"Hey, Jen, did you see the new hottie in marketing?" She fans herself with dramatic flair.

"Mr. Townsend," I inform her. "And yes, he was at the department heads' meeting."

"Isn't he gorgeous?" She plucks a candy from the crystal dish and unwraps it.

My mind replays the fantasies I indulged in during the meeting. "Yes. He is."

"Think he's single?" Lily's eyes sparkle.

"I doubt it." I sigh and pout for her entertainment. "He's probably married."

"I didn't see a ring." She pops the candy in her mouth with gusto. "Means he's still fair game." She pauses. "Unless you want a shot at him."

"Geeze, Lily, give the man a chance to breathe. He just got

here. I'm sure he's already got half the single ladies on staff drooling over him, not to mention the married ones." I chuckle.

"You're right." She stands and smooths her hands over her hips. "Hey, are we still on for movie night this weekend?"

"Yeah, my place. Six o'clock. The new *Space Vendetta* movie is on Prime, I think."

Lily bounces on her toes and claps with excitement. "Yay! I've been dying to watch it, plus I need some girl time. My roommates are great, but they don't seem to get me. Ya know?"

"Why are you living with three guys again?" I lean back in my chair.

"I went to school with them." She shrugs. "They needed a roommate, and I needed a place to live."

"Any of them single?" I wink.

Her eyes go wide. "Trust me. You don't want to involve yourself with these three. I've seen the train wreck dates they bring home." She mimes gagging and laughs.

"Point taken."

"I'll see you after work." She waves and saunters down the hallway toward her own desk.

My first day at Valentina's, I ended up with a mud stain on the hem of my brand-new cream skirt. I couldn't start my new job at a trendy, upscale department store looking like a hobo off the street. Without a word, a gorgeous woman who looked like a pinup model from the fifties took my hand and pulled me into the nearest restroom. Within twenty minutes, she'd worked her magic on the stain. Lily saved my ass, and I'm forever in her debt.

Three years later, we're best friends. She grew up in Manhattan but lives in Brooklyn now. My family is from Staten Island, but I live in a small apartment in Brooklyn not far from Lily's place. We commute together because single city ladies stick together.

I shake off the slump I feel sneaking up on me and dive back into those reports I promised myself I'd finish before the weekend. I hate having a pile of work waiting for me on Monday mornings. I focus on the screen and drown the office noise into the background.

Two hours later, I hit send on the final report and glance at the clock. Nearly four. I power down my workstation and tidy up before gathering my things and heading for the elevator. I pop by Lily's desk on the way, but she's nowhere in sight.

I glance around and then check my watch again. Five after four. Where is she?

As I wander the floor, I pull out my phone and send her a text. I stumble back when I collide with a solid warm wall, dropping my phone and my bag.

A pair of hands grab my arms and steady me. "Are you okay?"

Once I find my footing, I glance up to meet the piercing gaze of Mr. Townsend. My face warms and I curse the natural blush God blessed me with.

"I'm fine. Thank you."

"It's dangerous to text and walk, you know." His lopsided smile makes my stomach flip.

"So I've been told." I pick up my phone as he bends to retrieve my purse. Once we both rise, I offer my hand. "I'm Jen. I work in acquisitions for women's wear."

"Nice to meet you." His warm hand nearly engulfs my own and a spark of need envelops me.

"And you, Mr. Townsend."

His grip tightens. "Call me Shaun."

I swallow the lump in my throat. "Shaun." With reluctance, I release his hand.

A strained pause pulls tight between us, until he smiles. "I don't want to sound presumptuous, but are you free tonight?"

My heart pounds. Free? Me? Are you kidding? "Yeah, why?"

"Would you like to have dinner with me?" He chuckles and the sound reverberates through me. I'm smitten with the sound of it.

"Sure. I know this great place in Brooklyn if you're craving pizza."

"Sounds perfect." He laughs. "You read my mind."

Oh crap, I'm beyond smitten. I'm half in love with him. I

shake my head when I remember Lily. "Give me a minute and we can head out."

"Sure. I'll grab my coat." He disappears down the hall.

I slump against the wall and text Lily. *I'm going out to dinner with a friend. Catch you tomorrow.*

After I send it, I close my eyes and lean against the wall. Did I just fall in love with a stranger? What the hell am I doing? I must be insane.

CHAPTER TWO

Within thirty minutes, we're in Brooklyn, standing in front of the pizza place I told him about. Mario's neon sign glints from inside the front window. My apartment is in the building above the shop, but I don't mention it to Shaun.

He opens the door and gestures for me to enter. Butterflies take flight in the pit of my stomach when he smiles. Oh man, I need to pace myself with this one.

I slip inside the door and wave at Johnny working behind the counter. The middle-aged pizza slinger with slicked black hair and a thick Brooklyn accent is like the older brother I never had since I eat here at least twice a week. I can feel his curious gaze sizing up the man entering the shop behind me.

I snag the booth in the corner facing the front window. It's comfortable and familiar, and yet with Shaun sitting across from me, it feels new and exciting.

My coat is too hot. I tug it off my shoulders and set it aside as Johnny comes up and puts two menus on the table.

"Hey, Jen, how's it goin'?" He tosses an easy smile at me before eyeing my dinner companion.

"It's goin'." I return his smile and smack my lips. "Can I get a Yuengling?"

"Yeah, sure." Johnny turns to Shaun.

"Same for me." Shaun leans back with a casual indifference that seems to say *you're driving this car.*

"Want the usual, Jen?"

"You particular about toppings?" I ask Shaun before making my decision.

"Nope. I'm game for anything."

I swear there's a double meaning behind those words, but before I can chase the thought, Johnny mumbles under his breath.

"The usual is fine. Thanks, Johnny."

"You got it, kid." He shoots a glance at Shaun before retreating behind the counter once more.

"I don't think he likes me much." Shaun's crooked grin makes my heart thump against my ribs.

"We're practically family. I mean, I eat here more than I eat at home, so..." I shrug and my face heats at the confession of how much pizza I consume on a weekly basis.

"Ah." He nods as Johnny returns with two frosted mugs brimming with lager. "Thanks."

Johnny shoots me a sidelong glance as he sets the mug down with a look that screams *if he tries anything stupid, let me know.* It's nice to know someone's looking out for me. Once we're alone again, I take a sip of beer and relax.

"Nice place." Shaun's gaze strays for a second taking in the small shop. When it meets mine, my whole body warms through like I took a shot of whiskey.

"So." I shift in my seat under his perusal. "How was your first day? I'm sure our office is quite different from Denver."

"It is. But that's not necessarily a bad thing. I'm excited for a new challenge."

"Are you from Denver originally?" I dig deeper wanting to know more about him.

He shakes his head. "No. I was born in Davenport, Iowa."

I blink at him drawing a blank. "Where's that?"

His eyes sparkle when he laughs. "Not many people can point it out on the map. It's right on the Mississippi River. Just find St. Louis and follow the river north, you'll run smack into Davenport."

My face warms. "It's been years since I've been anywhere farther than Pennsylvania. Guess it shows, huh?"

He shrugs it off. "You grow up here?"

"Staten Island. I mean, it's still one of the boroughs, but it's a bit more spacious than Manhattan." I take another sip of the cool lager.

"But you're a Brooklyn girl now, huh?"

"Yeah. I mean, my apartment's not much, but it's in a

decent neighborhood." I gesture to the room. "And the food's great."

We sit in silence for a moment, and I can't help but wonder what's going through his mind. I mean, I don't know this guy. But being with him is comfortable and his warm charm makes me trust him. Maybe that's why they chose him for the marketing director position. His charisma will go a long way in bringing in potential clients.

"You okay over there?" He rubs his thumb across the frosted mug as he watches me.

"Yeah." I shuffle off whatever doubts remain and remind myself we're still coworkers.

"You look worried." He's intuitive. Damn, that's kind of hot.

"I don't want you to get the wrong impression." I twist the mug in my hand searching for the words. "I don't normally..."

"Jen." He interrupts me with a gentle tone. "You're showing the new guy the best pizza joint in town. It doesn't have to be anything more than that."

I groan and hide my face behind my hand. *But what if I want it to be more?* "Sorry."

"Why are you apologizing?" He chuckles. "I asked you to join me for dinner."

"I know." Open mouth, insert foot. "But I'm still trying to figure out why?"

His eyes darken the slightest fraction, almost as though I'd imagined it. "Because I wanted to get to know you."

Years of telling myself not to get involved with a coworker fade into a distant oblivion with those simple words. "Do you use that line often?" I tease, unable to stand the tension pulling tight between us.

"I've never used that line." He laughs and the tension eases back into comfortable companionship. "In fact, I've always made it a point to avoid mixing my personal life with work. It's cliché, I know, but it's true."

"So you never went out with your coworkers for pizza in Denver?"

"Never." He scoffs. "What about you?"

"Oh, I hang out with my coworkers all the time outside of work."

His brow arches, and I kick myself for not being clearer.

"I mean, I have a lot of friends at the office." *Yeah, keep putting your foot in your mouth.* I groan. "Maybe I should shut up now. I sound like an idiot."

"No, you don't." He leans forward resting his elbows on the table. "I want to be honest with you."

Johnny arrives with a steamy, delicious supreme pie laden with veggies, sausage, and pepperoni. He slides it onto the table between us. "Enjoy."

"Thanks." I flash him a smile as he walks away. When I turn back to Shaun, his intense expression steals my breath.

"I've never broken my rule about dating a coworker." His focus hones on me like a laser, and I freeze mid-reach for a slice of pizza.

"Dating?" The word feels foreign on my tongue.

"Is that a problem for you?" He reaches across the table and takes my hand. Those soft fingertips brush over my skin making me shiver with need.

"I mean if we were in the same department, maybe, but I don't know. I've never dated anyone from work before. Holy shit. I wasn't expecting this." My heart thunders in my chest drowning out the sound of my own thoughts.

"Neither was I." He squeezes my hand gently and then lets go. "If I'm going too fast, tell me. We can take it slow. I've always been told I'm too direct for my own good."

My hand tingles where he touched me. I miss the warmth already. "Knowing what you want isn't a bad thing."

"The question is, what do you want?" His gaze bores into my soul.

"As long as it doesn't affect work, I'm game for anything." I throw his own words back at him in an effort to play it cool regardless of the simmering attraction steaming up the window beside us. *Oh, no, that's from the pizza.* I reach for a slice giving my hands something to do other than reach for him.

Shaun grins and grabs a slice for himself. "Sounds like a plan."

We eat in relative silence and hang out to chat over another mug of Yuengling. He's sweet and conversational. The topics range from his childhood in Iowa to my adventures in Brooklyn and beyond. He asks about my parents and my interests. I reciprocate the inquisition, and we laugh at how different yet similar we are.

When Johnny finally kicks us out at eleven, I'm stunned at how quickly time passes in Shaun's company. Finally, a man who doesn't make me feel inept or defensive. It's so refreshing. We exchange phone numbers before pulling on our coats.

We stop outside the shop so I can pull on my gloves.

"Can I walk you home?" Shaun asks, his eyes glinting under the streetlights.

"I thought you said we were gonna take this slow?" I sway against him with a nudge of my elbow.

"You're right." He grins. "I wanna make sure you make it home safely."

"That's quite chivalrous of you. It's not far. I'll be okay." I squeeze his hand. "Thanks though."

His gaze searches my face like he's trying to decipher a code beneath the surface of my skin. My whole body ignites and I'm melting regardless of it being a chilly twenty-five degrees in the middle of February.

He steps closer and cups my jaw in his hand smoothing his thumb across my lower lip. My breath catches as he lowers his head and kisses me. The soft brush of his mouth on mine is a welcome invasion. I grasp his lapel and pull him closer. His warm, spicy scent envelops me, tugging at the back of my mind. *Gucci Guilty*, I think, subtly buried beneath the fresh scent of linen and what I can only assume are his natural pheromones.

Shaun pulls me against him and teases my lips open with the slightest press of his tongue. I'm lost in the kiss, in his arms, drowning in a sea of unexpected bliss, I barely hear the sound of someone coughing behind me.

"All right, you two. Get a room."

I pull away from Shaun with a start, and he laughs. I turn to see Johnny standing in the doorway with his hands on his hips.

"This ain't that kind of establishment. Go home, Jen." He jabs a finger at Shaun. "Don't mess with her."

"Sorry, Johnny." I turn back to face Shaun. "I'll see you later."

"Yeah. Sleep well." He reluctantly drops my hand and retreats down the street.

I watch until he disappears around the corner. With a sigh, I head toward the entrance beside the pizza parlor. My mind spins over the impossibility of the day's events. If someone would have told me I'd meet the man of my dreams at work today, I'd have called them crazy.

Maybe I'm the one who's crazy. Either way, I can't complain. Crazy is feeling pretty damn good right now.

CHAPTER THREE

"Hot! Hot! Hot!" I juggle the hot cookie sheet between my mitt-covered hands. I seem to forget to buy new ones until I pull something from the oven and the heat seeps through the thinning fabric. Once the tray is safely on the stovetop, I pull off the offending mitts and set them aside. The sweet aroma of fresh-baked chocolate chip cookies fills the apartment.

Where are they? I pick up my phone and check to see if I missed a message from the girls. Nothing. Only five after six. They should be here any minute.

My fingers hover over the messages button. Shaun's name on the screen hypnotizes me and in a flash, I'm back in the pizzeria, just the two of us. I want to send him a message, so he knows I'm thinking about him. But maybe that's too weird. I mean, we only met this week, and already it feels like whatever sparked between us the other night is barreling toward a raging inferno at critical speed. I shake my head and set the phone aside. No. I'll wait for him to text me.

I mean he spoke to me at work yesterday, so there's something there, right? Before the seeds of doubt can burrow into my soft, anxious brain, the doorbell rings.

Pushing thoughts of Shaun aside, I rush to open the door.

Lily and Maggie's grinning faces greet me.

"I thought you forgot about me." I pout and step aside.

They push past me and drop their bags on the table.

"Oh honey, I wouldn't miss this for the world." Lily turns with a cherry-lipped smirk. "You refused to dish on your impromptu dinner the other night." She winks. "Was it the new guy?"

My face warms. Betrayed by my own body. I sidestep into the kitchen to get plates out of the cabinet. "His name is Shaun."

"I knew it!" She bounces up and down. Today she's sporting a cute pair of navy trousers and a warm, deep red cable knit sweater. Vintage, all of it, I'd put money on it. This girl and her classy style put us all to shame. "So," she pushes, practically salivating, "What's the deal? You two hook up?"

I avoid eye contact and set the plates down.

When my back is turned, Maggie chimes in. "Wait! Hold the phone. Who's Shaun?"

Lily's animated chatter sparks to life. "He's the new Head of Marketing and a stone-cold fox. Oh my god. Seriously. So hot."

Maggie's expression vacillates between surprise and hurt. "Why am I only hearing about this now?"

"Jen's holding out on us." Lily pouts playfully and opens the Chinese food container with those perfectly manicured hands.

Maggie grabs a plate, but her gaze remains fixed on me while Lily starts doling out servings. Her piercing stare could level a grown-ass man. I wonder if she ever uses this glare on her bosses at Solus? She's talked about her single bosses, Mr. Ben Statler and Mr. Evan Waldorf, but neither Lily nor I had the pleasure to meet them in person. But we knew all about their reputations as Mr. Grump and Mr. Sunshine thanks to Maggie. Judging from the pictures on their website, they fit those monikers perfectly as well.

We often tease her about snatching one of them up to which we're immediately interrupted with an ever-growing laundry list of reasons why neither man is worth her time. For a personal assistant in a multi-million-dollar company, diminutive Maggie packs a mean punch with her purple and teal highlights and don't-bullshit-me attitude. Most people find her cute and often make the mistake of treating her like one would an unruly child or rebellious teenager. That's their first mistake. Now she turns her intense stare on me.

I exhale in defeat knowing I will get no peace until their curiosity is sated with every juicy detail. "Fine."

We load our plates with our favorite assortment of foods and retreat to the small living room. I take the oversized chair while Lily and Maggie sit on the narrow couch. Between bites, I tell them everything from the moment Shaun collided with me in the hallway to his friendly greeting yesterday morning in the break room.

Their rapt attention is punctuated with random questions. At this point, I can't tell whether they're impressed or concerned by the speed at which this whole relationship is hurtling like a bullet train into the great unknown.

"When was the last time you heard from him?" Lily sets her plate on the coffee table, picks up an empty glass, and pours the wine I put on the table in preparation for movie night.

"Yesterday at work." I ignore the urge to pull out my phone and skim through the messages again. "Should I text him?"

"Yes," Lily responds just as Maggie says the opposite.

"No," Maggie repeats. "Don't push it. Let it play out."

Lily looks torn. "I mean, it is moving fast but don't be too distant. I know there are a lot of girls at the office who are dying to get their hooks into him."

I groan at the uncertainty driving a wedge between my common sense and my desperation to make it work.

"Jen, you two will be banging by next weekend." Maggie grins. "Then you'll be all about Shaun and forget all about us."

Lily nods, her curls bouncing and eyes wide.

"You know me. I would never put a guy ahead of my friends." I smirk. "Even if he is handsome and charming."

"I am glad you finally found someone worth investing time in." Maggie pours herself a glass of wine. "Those last few were losers."

I wave my hand as though trying to chase away any possibility of the horrific memories of the last handful of idiots I went out on dates with. "Can we not talk about it? You promised you wouldn't bring up my shame." I pour myself a glass. "Besides, your track record isn't the best either there, honey."

Maggie shrugs. "I've given up all hope of finding someone worthwhile."

"It'll hit you one day when you're not expecting it." Lily nods sagely.

"Don't jinx yourself, Lily." I chuckle.

She sighs wistfully. "Someday my prince will come."

"Dude, you sound like a fairy tale princess, knock it off." Maggie jabs her with an elbow nearly spilling Lily's wine.

Lily sticks out her tongue, which Maggie mimics.

"Okay, children, can we watch our movie now?" I grab the remote on the stand and turn the power on.

"Yes, please." Lily claps and pulls a blanket across her lap.

Maggie leans back and sips her wine. "Proceed."

I turn on Prime and find the movie we agreed upon. *Source of Destiny*. A newish science fiction spin on the superhero genre one of my other coworkers, Mike from supply, recommended a few weeks ago when he overheard me and Lily talking about movie night. Once I find it, I hit play and settle back in my oversized comfy chair.

Movie night with the girls is my favorite night of the week. It's relaxed and comfortable. Yeah, we banter and argue about stupid shit while drinking wine and watching ridiculous movies. Sometimes we even get in debates about how hot an actor is or how idiotic a plot turns out to be. But that's half the fun of it. Nothing's too serious and in the end, we're just friends spending time together and having a blast.

"What's this about again?" Maggie wrinkles her nose as the movie starts dark and ominous.

"It's a superhero flick set in space." Lily's voice cuts through the increasing tempo of the music.

"Who's in it?" Maggie asks.

"I have no idea." I shake my head.

"Looks like a B-rated space opera." Maggie giggles.

"Shhh." Lily jabs her with a finger.

Twenty minutes into the film, and we're all sucked into the action. Then it happens.

The villain reveals himself, and suddenly I can't think of anything but how sexy he is. I shift in my seat and my body warms at the deceptively seductive monologue surrounding me. His dark charm. A sinful voice. It burrows beneath my skin. How is any of this logical? Getting all worked up over a fictional character.

I shove it aside and focus on the story. But as the film continues, I find myself cheering for the villain. He's tortured and brooding...which does not make him a suitable candidate for a relationship, I remind myself.

The rest of the film passes in a blur of action and cathartic release. There's obviously room for expansion with more films. I'm curious to see if there are more with the villain since he wasn't defeated in this one.

"Well, that was interesting." Maggie stands and carries dishes into the kitchen.

"How exciting!" Lily takes the empty wine bottle and puts it in the recycling can. "I wonder if they made a sequel."

"Look it up." Maggie's voice carries over the sound of running water. She washes the dishes as I put away the leftovers.

"I'll check it later." I place the containers in the refrigerator.

We make quick work of cleaning up. Maggie and Lily grab their coats.

"Thanks for coming over, guys." I open the door for them.

"Of course." Lily hugs me. "See you on Monday."

"Unless I don't survive dinner with my family."

"Oh, I forgot about that. Your place tomorrow, isn't it?" Maggie wraps a scarf around her neck.

"Yeah." I shrug. "It'll be okay, as long as Mom doesn't freak about the mashed potatoes and Dad doesn't remind me for the twentieth time to install a security camera outside the door."

"Awww, he's just worried about you." Lily grins.

"Your parents are being little shits," Maggie adds with a wink. "Tell them to get over it. They're in your house now."

I shake my head. "Do you two want to run interference tomorrow for me then?"

Both girls shake their heads vehemently.

"I didn't think so." I laugh. "Good night."

"Night." Lily bounds down the stairs.

"Later, doll." Maggie follows suit.

Once the door is locked, I grab my phone. No new messages. Damn. He's probably busy getting settled in. I head for the bathroom and flip on the shower.

After a warm, aromatic soak, I curl up under the covers and open the internet browser on my phone. In the search engine, I type the name of the movie and add villain to the end of the proffered search. Enter.

In a flash of pixels, I'm sucked into his world and I want to know everything about him. I scan through the articles and see the character's name, *Captain Korbin Ransom.*

I click on the IMDb listing, curiosity coursing through my every fiber, and find the actor's name.

Nicholas Hughes.

Down the rabbit hole I tumble.

CHAPTER FOUR

I finish whisking the gravy and pull it from the stove when the doorbell rings. Wiping my hands on my apron, I make sure I turned off the stove one last time before darting across my small apartment and opening the door.

"You didn't even ask who was at the door before opening it." My dad scowls.

"Hi, Dad." I hug him and he pushes through into the kitchen to grab a beer from the fridge.

"Don't listen to him." Mom steps over the threshold and wraps me up in a warm hug. "Dinner smells wonderful."

"Thanks, Mom."

"Jenny, where's this new man of yours?" Grammy shuffles forward and pulls me into a bear hug. Even though she's petite, her hug is ferocious. I groan inwardly at her question.

I made the mistake of mentioning Shaun to Mom yesterday afternoon, making a point to assure her there's nothing serious between us. But it seems this information is lost on Grammy who is bound and determined to see me settled with some strapping young man before I hit spinster age. Which I've already reached years ago if we're going by Regency standards.

"He's not my man, Grammy." I close the door behind her and take her coat.

"You need to snatch him up before some other woman sinks her claws into him." Grammy winks. "Just like I did with your Grandpa."

I roll my eyes and chuckle. I've heard the story a hundred million times. "Yes, I know. You stole him away from those hussies down the street. I remember."

"Damn skippy." Grammy straightens to her full height looking like a general preparing for battle. "When you know what you want, you don't beat around the bush. You strike first.

Strike hard. No mercy!"

I pinch the bridge of my nose and glare at my father. "Dad, stop watching *Cobra Kai* with Grammy. It's rotting her brain."

"She's a grown woman. What am I going to do? Kick her out of the room when I watch it?" He shrugs and takes a swig of beer.

Before I can reply, Grammy gets this dreamy look in her eyes.

"Johnny." A wistful smile tugs at her lips. "He's easy on the eyes. Looks a lot like your grandpa did back in the day."

Great. Now I won't be able to watch *Cobra Kai* without imagining Johnny as my grandpa. "Stop. Grammy. Just stop."

She scoffs. "Oh, admit it. He's a hunk."

"Okay, yes, Johnny is a hunk. Great. Now that we have that settled, can we eat?" I head into the kitchen and grab silverware out of the drawer. Mom has already set the plates out and starts pouring drinks.

"When I was young, I couldn't get enough of Elvis." Grammy sits down in her seat and chuckles. "I even saw him in concert once. Stood in the front row. We had a moment."

Mom shakes her head. "He sang one line while holding eye contact with you, Mom. You and Elvis didn't have *a moment*."

Grammy sips her tea. "We most certainly did. Brief as it was, I remember it like it was yesterday. It was like our souls spoke to each other."

Mom and I share a glance before biting our tongues. We know better than to rain on Grammy's reminiscences of her younger years.

I finish setting the table, but I can't shake the thoughts haunting me after watching the movie last night with the girls. Nicholas Hughes. I'd never seen him in anything before and I certainly haven't met him. But part of me longed for the connection like Grammy said she shared with Elvis. What would it be like to catch the eye of someone like him? Handsome, charming, and famous. I shake my head at the ridiculous thought.

"I see the gleam in your eye, Jenny." Grammy chuckles.

"Who are you thinking about?"

I shake my head. "No one."

"That young man of yours?" She nods knowingly. "You're smitten."

Part of me is embarrassed she called me out, but I can't tell her the truth. I wasn't thinking about Shaun. I was thinking about Nicholas Hughes, a man I've never met and probably never will.

"His name is Shaun, Grammy." I sigh at her persistence. "And he's not my young man."

"Are you dating?" Mom asks taking a seat beside Grammy and across from Dad.

"Yeah." I pull the roast from the stovetop where it was resting and put it on the table. "I mean, Thursday was our first date, I guess." I shrug.

"You guess?" Mom ladles potatoes onto everyone's plates.

"He just moved to the city and wanted to find a good pizza joint." I place the pot with the gravy on the table. "I took him to Mario's. We hit it off."

"Did he make a move on you?" Grammy asks her eyes glittering with mischievous interest.

"Mom, really?" My mother glares at her.

"What?" Grammy puts some gravy on her potatoes as Dad cuts the roast. "We're all adults here. I think we can handle a little sex talk."

My face heats. "Yes, okay. He kissed me. But that's it. I don't know if it's serious and I have no idea what's going to happen tomorrow at work."

"Office romances can be dangerous, honey. Just be careful." Mom accepts a slice of roast and puts some veggies on her plate.

"Yes, Mom. I know." This was not the conversation I wanted to have with my parents over our weekly Sunday family dinner.

"Speaking of dangerous." Dad clears his throat. "Why didn't you call Art and have a security system installed like I told you to?"

I give dad a grateful smile for coming to my rescue and cut

my roast. "Actually, my landlord said he's going to install a surveillance system with a video doorbell next week."

Dad nods. "Good. I'll feel better knowing you've got a little better security in this place." He points his fork at me. "I don't like you living here all alone."

"Oh, Mike. Let the girl alone. She's been living in the city for years."

"I'm not allowed to worry about her safety?" He bristles. "Excuse me. I'm not the one who asked the poor girl about her sex life at the dinner table."

I hang my head as my parents launch into a debate about my personal choices across the dinner table. When I look up, Grammy meets my gaze and grins before shoving a spoonful of potatoes in her mouth.

My. Loving. Family. I love them. Yes, I do. I repeat this over and over until it starts to sink into my brain.

Instead of interjecting my own opinion about my personal life, I join Grammy and enjoy the food I spent the afternoon preparing. Finally, Mom and Dad lapse into silence and decide to eat before their food gets cold.

Scattered conversation during the rest of the meal is more subdued. My parents like to burn hot when they get into a debate, but it fizzles out pretty quickly. I'm thankful for small mercies.

After the meal, Dad and Grammy clear the table while Mom and I do the dishes. I glance at the clock and nudge Mom.

"It's after eight. You guys should get home." I turn and see Grammy leaning against the sofa her eyes fluttering. "She'll fall asleep on the way home I bet."

"You're right." Mom dries her hands and kisses my forehead. "Thanks for dinner, pumpkin. It was delicious." Her smile warms me.

"Thanks, Mom." I hug her and then give Dad one. "Drive safe."

"Always do. Call if you need anything." Dad kisses my cheek.

"Bye, Grammy." I hug her tight.

She squeezes me. "Remember what I told you. Snatch that man up."

"Oh, you can invite him to dinner next week," Mom offers as she pulls on her coat.

"It might be a bit soon for that, but we'll see." I open the door for them.

"Okay." Mom blows me a kiss. "Love you."

"Love you too." I wave as they file out the door. "See you next week."

"Don't rush me." Grammy snaps as they descend the stairs to the ground floor.

Mom's heavy sigh echoes in the hallway as I close the door.

Without the chaos of my family, the apartment seems so lifeless. Maybe I should buy some posters or plants or something and liven it up. I've lived here for a few years, but I've never been one for interior design. It's been livable, and that's fine with me.

I turn on some music and finish cleaning up the kitchen. Maybe I should text Shaun. I don't want to seem too eager. I mean, I'll see him at work tomorrow.

My fingers hover over the text messenger app. I debate for a moment and instead open the internet explorer. The Nicholas Hughes search results are still there from last night. I click on images and slide through the results.

On autopilot, I turn off the lights in the apartment and lock the door. In my bedroom, I flip on the light and boot up the computer. I wonder what other films he's been in. Are they on Netflix?

Chapter Five

I should have texted him after our first date at the pizza place. But honestly, I worried it was just a fluke and if I played my hand, he would realize he made a mistake. After a few weeks on the job, Shaun would soon wise up to the fact I'm an introvert with few hobbies and zero cool points. Barely anyone recognizes me at work. I literally blend in with the wallpaper most days. But he's the only one anyone can talk about.

The latest and greatest addition to the team.

When I wake up Monday morning, I dread the thought of going to work. It was a fluke. Had to be. I haven't heard from him all weekend, and I don't have the guts to be the one who sends the desperate first text.

I walk into the office at half-past seven. There's a group of women chatting in the hallway outside the break room. Their voices carry when I walk past and I hear exactly how much attention Shaun attracted when he started last week. They all want a shot at the sexy new guy.

I can't say I blame them. The memory of our date last week feels like a far-off dream. And the kiss...I shove the thought away. I can't think about it now.

Lily bounds over when I reach my desk. "Hey, hon. How was dinner with the fam last night?"

"Good." I hang my jacket on the back of my chair. "Awkward. Grammy and Mom decided to discuss my non-existent sex life over dinner, right after Grammy tells me all about the *moment* she had with Elvis at a concert back in the day."

"Sounds like I missed out on a good time." Lily's laughter makes me smile. "Your Grammy is by far the coolest person on the planet. I wanna be her when I grow up."

"She'd be honored to hear you say that."

"Oh, did you hear anything from—" she drops her voice

low so no one can overhear her "—you know who?"

"Nothing." The anxiety descends once more.

"I'm sure he was busy."

"Yeah." I catch a glimpse of her victory red-tipped nails when she waves her hand. "But..."

"Stop that thought right there!" She grasps my arm. "Listen. Give it time. This is all new, for everyone, but don't you dare sell yourself short." Lily's encouraging smiles bolster my confidence.

"You're right." I hug her. "Thanks, Lily."

"Any time." She grins and saunters back to her desk her black and white polka dot skirt swaying beneath the red cardigan.

I sit down at my desk and pull up the files for the latest orders. Two minutes into my groove, my phone pings. I glance at the screen.

Hey, gorgeous. Look up.

When I glance up, Shaun is leaning against the wall near the conference room. He smiles and resumes texting. Another message comes through.

I missed your smile. Busy this weekend?

I unlock my phone and type out a response. *Actually, yes. But I'm free the weekend after, why?*

Dinner and a movie. My place.

My heart damn near floats out of my chest, and I can't stop grinning. When I peek at him again, he's waiting expectantly. *Sure. It's a date.*

He glances at the phone before locking the screen and slipping it into his pocket. With a wink, he crosses the room, tapping on the edge of my desk as he passes.

The rest of the week, I'm floating on air. We speak in passing at work, and as promised, he keeps it professional. Most of our conversation comes through texting while in the office. He calls me every night to make sure I get home okay. Normally I would find it intrusive, but his midwestern charm reminds me he's just being a gentleman.

Upon outward appearances, no one would suspect we even show any interest in each other. Well, except Lily. She shoots me looks when he walks into the room. I can trust her not to say anything about whatever this is, and better yet, she encourages it.

By the time Friday rolls around the following week, I can barely contain my excitement. Shaun texts me his address and tells me to show up at seven. That doesn't give me much time to change and head across the borough to his apartment.

It's a classy little joint in the Heights. The neighborhood is quiet and well-kept. I'm kind of jealous, if I'm honest, a smidgen intimidated.

I double-check the address before I ring the doorbell. When the door swings open, the warm smell of freshly baked bread encircles me. Then I see Shaun wearing an apron with small images of spaceships against a midnight sky.

"Hey, come on in." He steps aside.

"Hi." I venture into the entryway and take off my coat. "Oh my God, what is that heavenly smell?"

He hangs up my jacket and leads me down the hallway. "Oh, I made some fresh bread to go with the lasagna."

I stare at him in shock. "You made fresh bread? And lasagna? From scratch?"

"Yeah." Shaun notices my expression of surprise and chuckles. "What? Like it's hard?" He opens the oven and pulls the loaf pan out setting it next to the casserole dish already resting on the stovetop.

I lean against the counter and watch him in fascination. "I mean, no, it's, well, I don't know a lot of men who can cook." I narrow my gaze. "Wait, when did you find time to make this? We get off work at five-thirty?"

He winks and tosses the oven mitts on the counter. "You expect me to share all my secrets on the second date?"

"Not all of them no. But I'm definitely interested in learning your magical time management skills." My heart warms. I guess he's still counting pizza at Mario's as a first date. "Teach me the ways, master."

Shaun pauses as he unscrews the cork from a bottle of wine. "Did you just drop a *Space Vendetta* reference?"

I bite the inside of my cheek. "Maybe."

"Wow." His smile makes my stomach do a little roller coaster swoop dive. "You're full of surprises, aren't you?"

"Aren't we all?" I laugh and try to stomp down the excitement from bubbling from my pores. "Are you a fan too?"

"Yeah, I guess I am." His laugh makes the roller coaster in my stomach do a corkscrew. Damn him. "Of course, I started as a fan years ago when it was only a novel series."

"It started as a book series?" I ask, cursing my incomplete research. I'd been so distracted by Nicholas Hughes, I never dove into the actual history of the source material for the films that made him famous. I push away the image of him clad in red silk and black leather this direction of thought has conjured in my mind.

Shaun pours two glasses of wine and hands one to me. "Cheers."

"Cheers." I toast him and we drink. How strange we both seem to gravitate toward similar things.

"Yeah, the books started back in the mid-nineties. They ran for a decade or so before they even discussed making it into a film."

"Do you collect them?" I follow his movements as he pulls a knife out and cuts the lasagna.

"I used to be religious about collecting anything *Space Vendetta*." He shrugs and plates two large slices of hot, melty lasagna. "But I stopped around the time I graduated from college."

"Can I help?" I offer as he tries to balance both plates and carry his wine.

"Here, you take the wine. I got the food." Shaun leads me to the small eat-in dining room table.

There's a lovely red tablecloth and a candle in the center of the table. He sets the plates down and I deposit the wine glasses next to them.

"Have a seat. I'll get the bread." I sit and admire the little romantic meal before me. No one I've ever dated took the time for ambiance let alone cooked for me. A girl could definitely get used to this.

"This looks delicious." I inhale deeply noting the rich familiar scents of tomato and rosemary and melted mozzarella.

"Thanks."

I watch as he slices the bread, careful not to crush it. Steam rises up and my mouth waters. The only person who makes fresh bread in my life is Grammy. It looks like Shaun may give her a run for her money. He places the slices in a basket and brings them to the table along with a plate of softened butter.

"You thought of everything. Color me impressed."

He smiles, his cheeks pinkening at the compliment. "Eh, what can I say? I aim to please." He picks up his fork and gestures to mine. "Dig in."

Following his lead, I take a bite. It's heaven. The perfect balance of meat sauce to noodles with a hint of garlic and spinach to change up the flavor.

"Oh, my God. This is amazing." I take another bite. "Where'd you learn to cook?"

His grin widens. "My mom. She was determined her son not rely solely on junk food and take out alone."

"Smart woman." I toast her with my wine.

"I'll pass along the compliment."

We lapse into silence as we eat. Every now and then Shaun asks me a question about my family and where I went to college. When I finish my last bite, I push the plate aside and sigh.

"Amazing." I pat my stomach. "I don't think I've had a lasagna that good...well, ever."

"I'm glad you liked it." Shaun laughs, his eyes twinkling. "Hope you saved room for dessert."

I groan. "Oh, have mercy. I'm about to pop."

He lifts his hands. "If you don't have room for tiramisu, that's fine. More for me later."

"Please don't tell me you made it from scratch." I pinch my eyes closed.

"Okay, I won't." He collects the plates and carries them to the kitchen.

I follow him into the kitchen and bump his hip with mine. "You cooked. Let me do the dishes."

Shaun nudges me aside. "No. You're my guest. Let me spoil you."

The thought of him spoiling me has my mind overloading. I feel my face heat and nod. "Fine."

"Why don't you turn on the TV? I have a movie in for us to watch." He winks. "I think you'll enjoy it."

I narrow my gaze. "Is it inappropriate?"

Shaun's eyes widen. "What would give you the impression I would dare cross that line? We've only known each other for two weeks."

"True."

"Normally I let crazy out of the bottle after the third date, never before then."

I spin around to face him. "I knew it."

He doubles over the sink laughing. "Just turn on the TV, Jen."

When I turn it on, a familiar song comes through the speakers. I grin like an idiot when I see the familiar logo. "*Source of Destiny*," I mutter under my breath.

"Good thing you're a *Space Vendetta* fan, huh?" He dries his hands and joins me.

My face heats. "Actually, I'm a newbie to the whole thing. We watched it the other weekend for movie night. It was the first time I'd ever heard of the series."

"Oh, so you had your SVS cherry popped recently, huh?" Shaun sits on the couch next to me and takes the remote from my hand.

"I guess you could say that." I bite my tongue knowing he doesn't mean anything by the comment, but it leaves me a bit breathless.

"I guess it's not your typical movie night choice then."

"No. One of the guys in the mailroom suggested it when he heard Lily and me discussing ideas in the break room."

"Lily." Shaun thinks for a moment. "Oh yes, the classic vintage aficionado." He nods sagely. "She always looks stunning. It's a great style on her."

"Right?" I push away the twist of jealousy. "I envy her style.

She looks so put together."

"You do too." He grabs my hand and laces his fingers with mine. "It's what I noticed first about you."

There goes the damn rollercoaster again. "Really?"

"Yeah." He squeezes my hand.

I turn my head away to hide the flaming blush I know has consumed my face. My gaze rests on the TV and the logo on the screen.

"Shall we start the movie?"

"Sure." He presses play and pulls me against him, draping his arm around my shoulder.

We've both seen the film before, but within moments we're both drawn into the story on the screen. My body tenses in anticipation. I know what's coming, and I brace myself for it.

Captain Korbin Ransom appears on the screen on queue. An ache settles in my chest. Guiltily, I glance at Shaun, who's entranced by the film. My gaze drifts back to the movie.

This inexplainable gravity draws me into the story. A closeup of the villain's profile has my heart racing. My fingers dig into Shaun's thigh. He shifts and pulls me closer.

What the hell is wrong with me? My second date and I'm swooning over a man on the screen when I should be all over the warm, solid man beside me. He made me dinner. Made me feel special. Hell, he made me tiramisu!

As the movie continues, I hold my breath for the moments Korbin Ransom appears in all his leather-clad wonder. The character's brooding darkness and sexy swagger have me on the edge of my seat. I'm drawn to this villain in ways I can't comprehend.

I like good men. Honest men. Men who make me dinner and treat me like a queen. But deep in the dark recesses of my mind, my imagination flirts with something I've never allowed into the light. I'm aroused and ashamed. I shove these fantasies of a tempting villain aside and focus on enjoying this moment with Shaun, a good man of flesh and blood.

When the credits roll, I slowly shift from beneath his arm and stretch. "That movie gets better every time I see it. I mean, it's like I catch details I missed before."

"Yeah, happens to me too." He stretches his arm out and grabs my wrist, pulling me back against him.

I'm breathless, caught in the haze of his blue eyes. My heart's racing.

"Jen...am I going too fast for you?" There's hunger in their depths.

I swallow. "No."

"If I ever make you uncomfortable, tell me." A soft smile curves his lips. "I like you."

"I like you too." My fingers brush his cheek. I lean in and kiss him.

His soft lips part beneath mine and he pulls me closer. "You can stay tonight if you want," he whispers between passionate kisses.

"As much as I would love to take you up on that." I sigh against his lips. "I can't."

He nods. "I understand. Sleeping together on a second date feels like we're going at hyperspeed."

I chuckle at the *Space Vendetta* reference. "Yeah, it does."

"I'll leave it up to you." He kisses the tip of my nose. "When you're ready, let me know."

I wrap my arms around his neck. "A couple more dinners ought to do it."

"You're on." He grins and kisses me firmly once more before helping me get to my feet.

While I straighten my shirt and fix my hair, Shaun heads for the kitchen. He returns with a small bag. Inside is a Tupperware container with tiramisu.

"Figured you'd want some for the road since we never got around to dessert." He leans against the counter and licks his lower lip.

"You sure know how to show a girl a good time." I kiss his cheek, and he grabs my waist, holding me against him.

"Need me to walk you home?"

"Nah, I can handle it."

He releases me with reluctance and retrieves my coat. "Text

me when you get there."

"Of course." I bundle deep in my winter coat and step outside.

The chill of the night air revives me from my stupor. As I weave down the streets towards home, my phone pings. I pull it from my pocket.

Thanks for tonight. Miss you already.

Even though it's below freezing, my body is on fire. How the hell did I win the freaking jackpot? Shaun is almost too good to be true. I pray it lasts.

CHAPTER SIX

"Jen, seriously, it's been two months already." Maggie pours the margaritas with almost exact precision. "When are you two gonna seal the deal?"

I nearly choke on a jalapeno popper. "Geezus, Maggie. Tell me how you really feel."

She eyes me suspiciously and pushes the top-heavy glass of frozen liquor in my direction. "What's the hold-up? You two have hung out every Friday night for the last month and a half."

I shrug and take a sip of the margarita.

"I think it's sweet they don't want to jump into bed together right away." Lily takes her glass and plops a tiny umbrella in it. "It's classy and romantic."

"It's suspicious as fuck is what it is." Maggie props her hand on her hip. "What did you two lovebirds do last night then?"

"Had dinner and then watched a movie." My weekly dates with Shaun have become a staple to my routine. Just like Saturday girls' night and family dinners on Sunday afternoons. It's my turn to host, but Maggie is in charge of drinks.

"No making out or heavy petting?" Maggie studies me closely.

"We kissed a little, but it wasn't a full-on Olympic sport racing for the finish line."

Maggie shakes her head. "Why are you two stuck on first base after two months?"

"Because Shaun is a gentleman," Lily adds with a forceful nod making her well-set pin curls bounce.

"That's what you tell me, but I haven't met him. So, I'll withhold judgment for now." Maggie doesn't seem convinced. "Why don't you invite him over?"

Lily chokes on her drink. "It's girls' night."

Maggie waves her hand. "I'm okay with breaking the no-men rule this one time." Her smile terrifies me. "I have some questions for lover boy."

"I'm not inviting him into this viper pit." My stomach clenches at the thought.

"That's a bit dramatic, Jen." Lily chuckles. "He already knows me from the office. But if you don't feel comfortable inviting him to join us, then don't." Her smile soothes my anxiety a fraction.

"He's probably already got plans." I pull my phone out.

"Text him." Maggie's eyes bear a mischievous glint. "The worst he can say is no. Won't hurt my feelings if he doesn't want to meet your friends."

"No, you'll just break his kneecaps in some abandoned alleyway for being rude." I roll my eyes.

"Wrong. That's only if I find out he's cheating on you." Maggie shakes her head. "The punishment must fit the crime."

I'm not sure how breaking kneecaps is equivalent to cheating on someone, but I'd rather not chase the conversation any further. Holding my breath, I type out a quick text and hit send.

"There." I set the phone aside. "Like I said, he's probably already got..." My phone pings.

Sounds fun. Give me twenty.

"Holy shit." Lily glances at the text over my shoulder. "He's coming over."

"Noice." Maggie imitates Jake Peralta and takes a sip of her drink.

"Please, don't ask him why we're not having sex." I pin her with my most serious pleading stare. "I'm begging you."

"I won't ask him." Maggie leans on the counter, holding my gaze steadily. "If you admit to me right here and now why you're not climbing that man like a tree and riding him into the goddamn sunset."

Why am I not riding him into the goddamn sunset? Well, if that isn't the million-dollar question, I don't know what is. I steal a sip of my drink and use those stolen seconds to think of an excuse, any excuse. But the reality is, I don't have one. Not a good one anyway. Lily and Maggie watch me expectantly, their attention riveted.

I groan and push the drink aside. "Fine. I told him I wanted to wait."

"Wait?" Maggie crinkles her nose as though catching wind of something rank. "Wait for what?"

Lily rolls her eyes at Maggie. "Will you let her speak?"

Maggie gestures with her hand in a regal you-may-proceed motion.

"Shaun's a great guy. Everyone at the office loves him, and by everyone, I literally mean *everyone*." I shrug. "I didn't want to ruin anything by jumping into a purely physical relationship."

Lily nods with understanding, but Maggie's shaking her head vehemently. These two are at polar opposites of the spectrum.

"What's wrong with enjoying the physical side of this? He's a flesh and blood man standing right in front of you practically throwing himself in your bed." She shrugs. "I don't see the point in putting off the inevitable."

"And what if it blows up in her face, huh?" Lily counters. "There's nothing wrong with approaching a new relationship with a bit of caution. They're allowed to take their time if that's what they want."

"Thanks, Lily."

She rests her hand on mine. "I understand completely. There's no reason to rush into anything."

Her words reassure me at least for the moment. "I really like him, and I want this to work. I'm scared, you know."

"Scared it's too good to be true?" Maggie asks.

I nod and my throat constricts. "I don't want to fuck this up."

"Literally." Maggie teases me. "*Ba-dum-tish.*" She mock drums on the countertop.

The joke makes me laugh.

"While I'm glad you're being honest, I also think you're being a bit hard on yourself." She lifts her glass in salute. "Don't take life too seriously. You'll never get out alive."

Lily and I groan at the corny line Maggie always seems to throw around when one of us is in a rut.

"Groan all you want. You know it's true." She winks and takes a huge gulp of her drink.

"Promise you'll behave when Shaun shows up."

Maggie crosses her heart. "I will do my best."

"From what I've seen at work, not much intimidates Shaun." Lily nudges me in the side with her elbow. "I think he can handle Maggie."

We both watch as Maggie pours the rest of her drink down her throat in one fluid motion.

"Sober Maggie, yes. I'm not sure about drunk Maggie." I grab another popper and nibble on it.

Five minutes later, the doorbell rings. I check the screen for the door camera grinning like a fool when I see Shaun on my doorstep. I unlock the door and let him in.

"Hey." He pulls off his coat and hangs it on the rack. "Thanks for the invite." When he pulls me in for a kiss on the cheek, I can feel Lily and Maggie's gazes burning a hole in the back of my head.

"Of course. The girls wanted a chance to get to know you." I gesture to the two women nursing margaritas in the kitchen. "We were planning on watching the new release for *Space Vendetta.* Just came out today. I know you said you've been wanting to see it too."

"That's sweet of you." He smiles. "I brought some snacks too. I wasn't sure what you guys liked, so I brought a few things."

I grab the bag from his hand and carry it to the kitchen. Inside are some chips and salsa along with some homemade queso dip.

"This will go perfectly with the margaritas." Maggie pours a tall glass for Shaun. "Here."

"Thanks." He shifts the drink to his left hand and extends his right. "Shaun. Nice to meet you."

"Maggie."

The two face off and I cringe waiting for Maggie to open her mouth and insert her size five platform shoe. The greeting ends, and I'm almost stunned at how painless it was.

Shaun turns to Lily, who's wearing a pair of black leggings and a maroon wrap-around vintage sweater. "And Lily. It's nice to see you outside of the office."

"Likewise." Lily shakes his hand. "I'm so glad you could join us." She beams at him like he's just hung the moon. "You're *a Space Vendetta* fan too?"

He shrugs. "A bit. I read the books as a kid. Have quite a collection back home."

"Oh, so you're an old school fan," Maggie says leaning on the counter. "What do you think of the films so far?"

Shaun swallows the mouthful of margarita and clears his throat. "Wow, that's strong."

Maggie laughs. "You're welcome."

"Well, the first film followed the books pretty faithfully, so it'll be interesting to see what they do with the rest." He grabs a popper. "I think they're trying to make a ten-film run out of this series."

I grip the counter. "Ten movies? All the same characters?" Part of me hopes they are all the same because I need some more of my sinful space pirate.

"Well, most of them." He winks. "I don't want to give any spoilers or anything. If they decide to stick with the source material, then we'll lose a few major players before the end."

No. No. Don't you dare kill off my captain! I bite my lip to keep from making an idiot out of myself. Since when have I gotten all worked up over a fictional character. I brush it aside and refocus on the conversation.

"Who's your favorite character?" Lily seems genuinely curious, but I'm hanging on like it's the most important question in the universe.

"When I was younger, it was Commander Colton but now I'm older and more jaded, I relate more to Ransom. He's got all the moves and most of the best lines in the series."

I swear, I could kiss him right now. "Yeah, I agree. He's my favorite too."

Shaun glances at me with an arched brow. "Really? You

prefer villains across the board or only Ransom?"

This is a loaded question, isn't it? I shrug and play it off, ignoring Lily and Maggie's stares. "Well, it depends, honestly. But in this case, I think there's more to Ransom than most people see. He doesn't see himself as a villain. In his mind, he's a hero."

"Anti-heroes are so hot right now." Lily nods solemnly. Her face turns pink when we all face her. "What? My kindle is full of sexy anti-hero romance novels. That inner turmoil makes for great conflict and amazing sex."

Maggie coughs mid-sip and sputters margarita all over the counter. I glare in her direction as I grab the paper towels from beside the sink.

"Bad boys are better in bed, is that what you're saying?" Shaun dives into the conversation headfirst without hesitation.

I'm going to kill those two if they take this conversation any further.

Lily glances at me and her eyes widen. "Well, I mean. I don't have any personal experience with bad boys per se. But I do read a lot of romance novels, and I know alphas, bad boys, and anti-heroes are popular."

"Your personal preference too, I take it?" he asks clearly amused by the direction of the evening.

"For reading, yes." Lily grins. "I blame Jen."

Now it was my turn to sputter. "What? I didn't do anything."

Maggie smothers a laugh behind her hand and Shaun is outright grinning. They're both loving how uncomfortable I am right now.

"Yes, you did." Lily waves a chip around wildly. "You told me to read that completely irreverent novel about a wicked prince who likes to..."

"Oh, my God, Lily! Seriously. No kink shaming here." I snap in an effort to save myself from embarrassment.

"I wasn't kink-shaming! I was explaining the plot of the book you recommended." She pouts.

"Okay, ladies." Shaun holds up his hands in surrender.

"How about we take this party to the living room and put the movie in?"

We all nod in agreement.

"Maggie, bring the margarita pitcher with you." I nudge her as the rest of us carry snacks a few steps to the left into my small living room.

I only have one couch and a small recliner. Maggie snags the recliner while Lily, Shaun, and I squeeze onto the narrow couch, shoulder to shoulder and thigh to thigh. Shaun takes the far-right side against the arm and pulls me tight against him.

Once the movie starts, we're all riveted by the film. None of us had a chance to see it in the theater, so we don't know what to expect. Except for Shaun and his book spoilers.

He pulls me close to his side, and I'm distracted by the scent of him. Whatever soap he uses in combination with the heat of him sends my head into orbit. I lean against his chest and enjoy the movie.

When our favorite character appears, my fingers flex against his thigh.

Shaun shifts and takes my hand. He leans down and whispers in my ear. "I guess bad boys are your thing, huh?"

He has no idea. None at all. And I hope he doesn't uncover how much I enjoy watching Captain Korbin Ransom and the actor who plays him.

Later that night, after Shaun and the girls leave, I pull open my laptop and do another search. This time I'm on the hunt for a clip from the film we finished watching. Korbin traded in his red silk for green and I'm one hundred percent here for it.

I find the photograph and the link leads me to a blog site called Tumblr. The page loads and I tumble headfirst down another, more dangerous rabbit hole.

Chapter Seven

The following week is a blur. Between the insanity at work and my newfound love affairs, I'm pleasantly exhausted. Shaun takes higher priority than sinful Captain Ransom because real men should have precedence over fictional ones. Of course, Shaun and I haven't had sex yet, but after Saturday's little get-together with him and the girls, I'm confident we're one step closer to sealing the deal, as Maggie would say.

Fortunately, Maggie kept her promise and didn't outright interrogate Shaun after the movie. I'm waiting for the events of that whole evening to come back and haunt me.

I drop my purse on my desk and slip off my jacket. As I settle in my seat and power up my desktop, Lily appears beside me wearing a cute swing dress covered in lemons with a dark green cardigan.

"Hey, Lily."

"Morning!" She beams. No one should look as fresh and chipper as she does every morning. It must be the clothes. "Do you have plans tonight?"

"Um, not that I know of, but Friday night has become our standing date night." I drop my voice in case all the single ladies on the floor overhear us. They've pulled out all the stops trying to get Shaun's attention over the past few weeks. So I make a conscious effort to avoid mentioning his name because it draws them all in like strays catching wind of a bag of catnip. "Why? What's up?"

"Well, my roommates are having a video game tournament this weekend." She rolls her eyes. "Instead of doing movie night at my place tomorrow, I was hoping after work tonight we could check out the new vintage bar they opened last fall in Greenwich."

"Changing things up." I nod in agreement. "I like it. Did

you already talk to Maggie?"

Lily nods, her pin curls bobbing. "Yeah, she said she's game for whatever."

"Okay. I'll see if he's willing to move our date to tomorrow night."

"You could invite him to join us." Her grin is saccharine. "It would be nice to have a guy around to help weed out the unwanted male attention."

"Not interested in looking for a man of your own?"

She laughs. "In this city. No way. I need to find someone far removed from this rat race."

"I don't see you as a country kind of girl, Lily." I organize the files on my desk to prepare for the meeting I have at nine with the department heads.

"I love the country. My heels don't." She pouts those cherry red lips. "But I've always had a thing for the rough and tumble types." The sudden image of a pin up sex kitten Lily wrangling herself a cowboy out in the middle of bum-fuck America pops up in my mind. Funny enough, it suits her.

"No dapper dudes for you, huh?" I tease her.

"Country boys clean up the best." Lily winks.

"I'm not even going to ask how you know that."

"Good. A girl has to maintain some mystery." She primps her hair with her palm and bats her lashes. "Seven o'clock at Ginger's Lounge. Don't be late." Lily returns to her desk.

While Lily's entrances are angelic, her exits are damn near Hollywood gold standard. How does she channel a classic, chic vibe so effortlessly? I shake my head and focus on gathering the information for the meeting.

My phone pings. I smile before I even look at it because I know it's my morning message from Shaun.

Hello, gorgeous.

I glance around, but he's not in the common area where my desk sits. I type out a quick response. *Hello, handsome.*

Same time tonight?

Can we do tomorrow night instead? The girls want to hit up Ginger's Lounge over in Greenwich.

Of course. He adds a winking emoji. *Tomorrow is fine. Enjoy girls' night out.*

Want to join us?

Two weeks in a row crashing girls' night? I don't want to make enemies with Lily or Maggie.

Their idea actually. Interested? I chew on my lower lip waiting for his response.

What time do you want me to pick you up?

I send him a good time to stop by my apartment and set my phone aside. It'll be nice to get out and try something new tonight. Suppressing my excitement, I focus on work.

At five to nine, I grab my phone and files before heading to the conference room. Fortunately, I don't have to present anything, just take notes for the head of the department while she briefs the vice president.

A notification pops up on my phone for Tumblr. I stare at it dumbfounded. After discovering the microblogging platform, I spent nearly all the free time of my last week scrolling through profiles dedicated to not only the *Space Vendetta Series* but Nicholas Hughes and his other roles. I downloaded the app the day before, and it's been difficult to stop myself from endlessly scrolling through my feed.

Once I take a seat in the conference room, I click on the notification. A private message. I stare at the little mail icon. Who could have messaged me? My blog consists of like two dozen gif images I reblogged from other sites.

Half of them were from a page called Ransom's Wicked Whispers. The moment I saw the page, I fell in love with it. Whoever was behind this genius deserves all my admiration and thanks. I said as much in a private message on Monday night. Honestly, I never expected a response.

But here it is.

*Thanks for the support! And welcome to the fandom. * Winking emoji* I'm glad you like my page. Are you a fan of only Ransom or all of Hughes's work? You can follow my other page if you want to check out some other good fandom pics. Madre Fiero. Chat soon.*

I stare at the message in awe. There was a moment in my

life when surfing the internet and interacting with strangers was considered dangerous and highly discouraged. Have we reached the point where we can connect so easily with other like-minded individuals without fear of being kidnapped and sold on the black market?

"Jen. The meeting started." My superior, Sherry, jabs me in the side.

I focus on the VP, Mr. Roberts, speaking at the head of the table. I slip my phone on silent and tuck it in my pocket. While I take notes, my mind drifts back to the message waiting for my response.

After the meeting, Sherry takes me aside in her office. "I'll be starting maternity leave in a few weeks. I've talked to the other department leaders, and we'd like for you to step up and fill my position while I'm gone."

"Really?" I shake her hand. "Thank you. I appreciate the opportunity."

"You've been working hard lately, and we're excited to see what you bring to the table." Her smile leaves me lightheaded.

"Thank you again. I'm honored."

Flabbergasted, I head back to my desk and eat my lunch. It's not until after I get home I realize I haven't responded to the message from Madre Fiero.

I type out a quick response and change for a night on the town. At six-thirty, Shaun rings my doorbell. On time, as usual.

"You look amazing." He pulls me in for a soft, lingering kiss.

I'm half tempted to send a message to the girls telling them I'm staying in tonight. I know they'd approve of my reasoning, but as soon as the kiss starts, Shaun pulls away.

"Don't want to keep the ladies waiting."

Shaun takes my hand and we push through the rush hour hustle. It's five after seven when we finally reach Ginger's. The 1920's art deco décor gives the lounge a classy ambiance. I almost wish I'd have worn a beaded flapper dress instead of my best pair of jeans and a silk top.

"There they are," Shaun says in my ear countering the jazz

music filtering through the speakers and pointing across the room.

Lily and Maggie wave. We approach the table and I feel severely underdressed. Of course Lily is rocking a glittering beaded dress with a matching headband. Maggie must have come directly from the office. She's rocking a black and gray pinstripe power suit and teal blouse.

"You both look amazing!" I tug at my silk top with a frown. "That suit makes you look like you eat men for breakfast, Mags."

"I know." She winks taking a sip of her gimlet. "I wore it special for today's meeting. Ben wasn't amused with my statement, but Evan thinks it suits me better than the platform heels and leather."

"Who are Ben and Evan?" Shaun asks.

"My bosses." Maggie fills him in.

"Where do you work?" Shaun seems intrigued.

Oh, if he only knew half the story. Maggie's bosses are sinfully hot. One dark, one light. Both are one hundred percent fuckable. I've only seen photographs of them, but from the stories Maggie tells me, they're both extremely eligible bachelors with deep pockets. Whoever catches their attention and is able to pin them down are going to be set for life.

"I work for Solus Incorporated." Maggie slides closer so she doesn't have to shout.

I move beside Lily and scan the drink menu while Shaun talks to Maggie. I'm glad they're hitting it off. It warms my heart to see him bonding with my friends so effortlessly.

"I'm surprised he came out with us," Lily whispers in my ear.

"He's a glutton for punishment." I shoot a sly glance at Shaun who's engaged in an animated discussion with Maggie. "Or he's just comfortable."

"Either way." Lily winks. "He's definitely a keeper."

"Yeah, he is." My face warms when Shaun looks up and grins.

"Girl, if you two keep making eyes at each other you might as well head home now." Her breathless assertion makes me hide my face. "You're going to set this place on fire with those heated exchanges."

"Oh, God, Lily." I whimper. "What if I fuck this up?"

"There's always a chance something will go wrong in a relationship." Lily pats my shoulder. "But you can't hide from it forever. Sooner or later you're going to have to take the next step."

"I know." My conscience nags at the fraying edges of my mind.

"You'll figure it out. Just relax. When the moment comes, you'll be ready." She sips her drink.

I nod and try to push away the anxiety. My phone vibrates in my pocket. I pull it out and check my notifications. Two unread messages on Tumblr.

"Anything important?" Maggie rejoins us and glances over my shoulder.

"Not really." I shrug and slip the phone back into my pocket. I'll read the messages when I get home.

"Is Shaun sending you dirty pictures?" Lily teases.

"No." I whip around looking for him. "Where did he go?"

"I sent him to the bar to get you some beverages." Maggie grins. "I approve of Shaun." She toasts me with her half-empty glass.

"Thanks," I reply with an edge of sarcasm.

"I saw Sherry pulled you aside after the meeting today." Lily takes a sip of her drink.

"Yeah, she asked me to fill in for her while she's on maternity leave."

Lily squeals. "I'm so excited for you. What a great opportunity."

"Yeah. It will definitely look good when I apply for a promotion."

"So, who's sending you messages?" Maggie finishes off her drink.

I sigh. There's no way to avoid this, not when both Lily and Maggie are more observant than they have any right to be. "Oh, someone I met online."

Maggie and Lily stare at me in equal parts horror and surprise.

"Are you stepping out on Shaun already?" Maggie growls in my ear.

"No. I'm not...It's nothing like that, okay?" I groan. "After our long discussion about *Space Vendetta* last weekend, I did some digging and found some blogs." I wave it off. "One of the contributors and I have been messaging back and forth. She's a fan of the series too."

"She?" Maggie asks, incredulous. "How do you know it's not some pervert jacking off in his mom's basement?"

Acid stings the back of my throat at her statement. "First off, ewwww. That's a visual I didn't need. And second, I don't know. We're fans of the same series, and I respected her commentary on it."

"Uh-huh." Maggie nods, but I can tell she doesn't believe a word of it.

Shaun appears beside me carrying two drinks. "I wasn't sure what you wanted, so I made an educated guess." He hands me a gimlet similar to Lily's. "It's called the Stucky Special."

"Thanks." I take a sip. The rich flavors are strong but not unappetizing.

"Did I miss anything?" Shaun asks, sipping his drink, which looks like an Old Fashioned.

"Looks like your girl's found herself a new hobby trying to impress you." Maggie nudges me. "She's been researching *Space Vendetta.*"

My face must be the color of a boiled lobster. I press my hand to my cheeks.

"Is that right?" He leans against the table with casual interest and studies me. "What'd you find?"

"A few blogs with some...interesting theories and photos from the films." I laugh it off. "Nothing exciting. I wanted to dive into the series a bit more."

"Interesting. What kind of theories?" Shaun's got eyes only for me, but I can't shake the feeling he's silently judging my life choices.

I launch into a brief summary of what Madre posted bout Captain Ransom's role in the larger picture. Shaun listens intently and a smile tugs at the corner of his mouth.

"What? I know. It's ridiculous. Forget I said anything." I try to shift the topic feeling like I'm dominating the conversation.

"No. I like the theory. It's solid. But I can't give any more information without inadvertently spoiling the arc of the story." He slides closer and whispers in my ear. "But if you're rooting for Captain Ransom, you're in for a wild ride."

Shit. It shouldn't be hot he's teasing me with information while overtly flirting.

"We're gonna get some more drinks." Maggie tugs on Lily's sleeve and they disappear into the crowd.

Shaun rests his hand on my hip and pulls me against him. "You're not doing it to get my attention, are you?"

"Doing what?" My voice cracks.

"Researching *Space Vendetta*." His fingertips burn my skin through the silk top.

"No, I enjoy it. I'm curious." I lick my lips. "About how it's going to play out."

"Well, I can tell you, but I don't want to ruin the experience." His breath ghosts over my neck, making me shiver.

"Shaun."

"Yes, baby."

"When you tease me, I can't think." I turn to face him and see the same hunger I feel reflected in his whiskey gaze.

"Good."

"Why is that good?"

"Because sometimes you need to throw caution aside and let yourself feel instead of think."

I chuckle. "Are you trying to seduce me?"

"Is it working?"

"Possibly." I glance toward the bar where Lily and Maggie are talking to two men. "I shouldn't leave them."

"Maggie told me if I don't take you home with me tonight, she's going to burn down my apartment with me in it."

I snort-laugh. "Oh my God. She didn't."

"She did." He smiles, and I'm swept up in the heat of it. "But honestly, I had every intention of working my seductive charm on you tonight." He leans close and brushes his lips against my ear. "I've been hard for you all week."

I whimper, unable to form coherent sentences.

"Don't make me break out my Ransom smolder."

Heat curls in the pit of my stomach and radiates through me. He can't possibly be using my affinity for a certain dark, charming villain against me. Is he?

"What makes you think that will work on me?" I press my hand against his chest, putting some distance between us.

"Let's find a quiet spot, and I'll prove it works," he growls.

Without hesitation, I down the rest of my drink. "Let me tell the girls, then we can leave."

The wicked glint in his eye tells me I'm in for it now. And my body is one hundred percent ready for whatever he has to offer.

CHAPTER EIGHT
STAGE TWO: OBSESSION

Between the alcohol simmering in my blood, the heated glances and gentle brushes of his fingertips against my skin have me teetering on the edge during the entire trip back to my apartment.

As I fumble with the key in the lock, Shaun's hands settle on my hips. His mouth ghosts across my neck. I nearly drop the keys.

"If you keep it up, we won't make it inside." My throat is hoarse and the words tangle together in a jumbled, breathy exhale.

His hand covers mine, taking the key. In two seconds, he has the door open and pushes me through it. It slams behind us with a force that shakes the building. Shaun pins me against it and covers my mouth with his.

I'm drowning in sensations. He deepens the kiss, darting his tongue between my lips. I'm completely at his mercy. I've wanted this, him, for weeks. But until this moment, I wasn't able to give in to the temptation. My own insecurities, maybe. Truth is, I'm still terrified this will change everything. Sex always does, and not always for the best.

He slides his hands beneath my jacket and under the silk top. The press of his hot fingertips against my skin drives my need higher. When he rocks his hips against me, I groan.

"You taste so good." His words make my face warm. "You drive me crazy. Do you know how hard it is to see you at work and not touch you?"

"It's torture." I rest my hand against his chest. "I know."

"I've been tempted to call you into my office a few times," he whispers against my throat.

"That would definitely cause some talk." I release him so he can slide my coat down over my arms. It drops to the floor.

"Maybe the rest of the women in the office would stop hitting on me if they knew I had my hands full already." A wicked grin curves his lips as he grabs my ass with both hands.

Need courses through me, and I know if he touches me, he'll see exactly how much I want him. I've never been so wet. His teasing words set me on fire.

"Shaun..." I stumble over his name because his hands are on a mission to distract me from everything but the heat building between us.

"Do you want me to stop?" He pulls back but doesn't stop touching me.

"No. Don't stop." I grab a fistful of his shirt and push his coat over his shoulders.

He shrugs it off and tosses it aside. We stumble back and start pulling clothing off. He slips the green silk top over my head. I grab his belt and unfasten it. He rips off his sweater and the shirt beneath in one fluid motion. On it goes until both of us are standing in my living room in our underwear panting.

Shaun tugs me by the hand and motions toward the couch. I turn to the door on my right leading to my bedroom, but he stops me with a tug of my hand. When I turn back, he wraps his arm around my waist and pulls me against him. His cock is hard against my stomach.

Shit, it's been so damn long since I got laid. I don't remember it being this scattered like I can't find direction in an open sea. I focus instead on the man holding me. His gaze penetrates the haze clouding my floundering mind.

"What do you need, baby?" His hands never stop moving. They caress my spine, my hips, sliding beneath the fabric of my panties.

"My bed. In there." I sound like a babbling idiot.

He grins. "Is that where you keep all your toys?"

I blink at him in disbelief. "Toys?" I don't think of myself as a prude. I have a vibrator, yes, but do I keep a treasure trove of sex toys hidden in my bedroom? Hell no. I wouldn't know where to start with that whole...lifestyle.

His throaty laugh sends a pang of lust straight to my core.

"I'm teasing you, Jen."

"Are you into that...kind of stuff?" I swallow the lump in my throat.

"Not really." His sexy smirk tells a different story. "I've dabbled, but honestly, life is complicated enough. I like to keep sex simple."

"Simple?" I gape at him as he slowly backs me toward my bedroom. "Like casual or like vanilla?"

Shaun cocks his head. "Which worries you more? That sex with me will be boring or that everything will change afterward."

My heart stops. How the fuck did he know? "I...uh." I drop my gaze.

He hooks a finger beneath my chin and forces me to meet his intense whiskey stare. "I get it. This is new for me too. I gave you time and space because I didn't want to ruin this." He gestures between us.

I can't form words around the lump in my throat. He reads me like a book, and for once, I'm relieved. "You're perfect. I didn't want to fuck it up."

He chuckles. "I'm not perfect. Not by a long shot."

"You know what I mean." I run my hands over his chest. His heat sinks into me and those intoxicating eyes darken with need.

He wraps his hand around the nape of my neck. "Tell me what you want, kitten."

The pet name stuns me for a moment, but I can't deny it leaves me drenched and desperate. "You."

"You'll have to be more specific, Jen." He teases me. "What deep dark desires do you have hidden away? What turns you on?"

"I..." My tongue darts out to wet my lips as my mind spins unable to get traction. His scent, his tone, his presence overwhelms me. "I don't know."

His deep chuckle melts over me. "Then I guess we should find out."

Shaun reaches behind me and opens my bedroom door. Inside, he steers me toward the bed until I fall back and collapse onto my oversized comforter.

"Condoms?" he asks simply.

"In the drawer." I gesture to my nightstand.

He opens the top drawer and finds the box I picked up two weeks ago on a whim at the market. "I see I have competition."

My face heats. He found my vibe next to the condoms.

"Not competition." I tease him, pushing down the covers to the end of the bed.

Shaun rips open the box and pulls the foil packet out. He sheathes himself, and I won't lie, it's hot as hell watching him roll his hand down over his cock. I imagined him naked and in my bed so many times over the past few weeks, this feels like a dream. I can't even remember why I put it off so long. He climbs onto the bed and over me, pushing me down onto the soft mattress.

"Do you use it every night?" He kisses my neck and palms my breast through the thin fabric of my bra.

"Yes." I gasp and scramble to unclasp the hooks and pull it free then wiggle out of my panties with his assistance.

Shaun growls and takes my nipple in his mouth. Pleasure shoots through me. "What do you think about?"

His question swirls around in my mind. I hesitate because the first image popping into my mind isn't Shaun. Hell, it's embarrassing.

He tugs with his teeth, and I hiss at the sting. He releases my tender nipple and grins at me. "Whatever you were thinking right now...tell me."

"I...can't." I grab a pillow and bury my face in it.

Shaun snatches it from my grip and throws it to the floor. His hand smooths over my hip and palms my pussy. I arch against his touch. His fingertips slide along my clit and between the folds.

"Promise..." I gasp at the pressure building inside me and the bliss radiating from his touch. "Promise you won't laugh."

"Promise." He slides a finger into me, making my hips arch off the bed. "Tell me." He rakes his teeth gently over my breast allowing his gaze to drift to mine between bites.

Pleasure pulses through me as he moves a single finger along my inner walls. "Ransom."

Shaun stills, and I wonder if my confession broke him. Before I can open my mouth, he removes his finger and settles his whole body over mine. He captures my mouth in a bruising kiss while he parts my thighs. In one fluid motion, he thrusts deep filling me completely.

My whimper mixes with a groan as he moves his hips, pushing deeper. Every sense is heightened, every fraction of my body sings with desperate need. I want more, and Shaun gives it to me without even needing to ask.

The punishing kiss breaks, and he draws back enough to rest his forehead to mine. I grasp his hips in my hands and urge him faster. He draws my thighs up and I wrap my legs around him giving him the perfect angle to pound harder, deeper, faster.

"Is this what you wanted?" He nips at my ear lobe.

I nod, drawing my lower lip between my teeth to keep from crying out.

"Let me hear you, kitten." He growls against my throat. "Purr for me."

"I don't want the neighbors to hear." I gasp the words, punctuating each thrust of his hips.

"I don't care about the neighbors." He reaches between us and rubs my clit in urgent circles.

A keening moan escapes from deep in my chest. The blissful spiral of need climbs higher and higher with every stroke. I'm going to explode, and he knows it.

"That's it, kitten." He draws my skin into his mouth and pulls long and hard never wavering in his rhythm. "Come for me."

The pressure increases and I buck my hips against him. "Oh, shit...oh, please, don't stop."

Shaun doubles down on his efforts and it's enough to tip me over the edge and headlong into abandon. I come hard, stars flashing behind my eyes when they drift closed. A glimpse of a blinding, cocky smile and bright blue eyes fill my vision for half a second before they're replaced by Shaun's lust-filled gaze and satisfied grin.

He kisses me, deep and slow as we ride our orgasms down from those dizzying heights. Our breaths mingle while our heart rates gradually slow to a sensible, steady beat.

"Wow," he whispers against my mouth. "That was...wow."

"Understatement of the century." I chuckle.

Shaun collapses on the bed beside me and draws me against his chest. I rest my head on his shoulder and trace my fingers over his bare skin.

"Why the hell did I wait so long?" I murmur, nuzzling deeper into his warmth.

He laughs and it reverberates through me. "I don't know. But it was worth the wait." He kisses my forehead tenderly. "You were worth the wait."

"Thanks." I sigh and a soft contentment settles over me.

"Better than your battery-operated Captain Ransom, huh?"

"You said you wouldn't tease me." My face heats.

"I promised I wouldn't laugh." He kisses me gently. "Not that I wouldn't tease you."

"Great. I set myself up, I guess."

"Don't worry." He smiles with sincerity. "It will be our little secret."

"How kind of you." I jab him in the ribs with my fingertips.

"Would it make you feel better if I tell you who does it for me?" He chuckles. "Fantasy-wise, I mean."

I prop myself up on my elbow and stare down at him. His hair is mussed, his mouth twisted in a teasing grin. "Who?"

"Lynnea."

"Really?" I can't stop the laughter. "The bad-ass ranger?"

He nods. "Yup. Now you know my Vendetta crush. See, yours doesn't seem so crazy now, does it?"

"No." I rest my hand over his heart. He covers my hand with his. "So, is it the character or the actress who does it for you?"

"The actress, Tina James, is gorgeous to be sure, but I think I prefer the character." He cups my face in his hands. "But I'd take you over Lynnea any day of the week." Shaun draws me into a deep kiss that leaves me aching and ready for round two.

When he pulls away, we're both breathing heavy.

"Hold that thought." Shaun slips from the bed and disappears into the bathroom.

When he returns, he draws the covers up over both of us and takes me in his arms. We make love once more before the daze of sexual exhaustion and orgasmic bliss claims me.

As I drift easily into sleep, I'm wrapped tight in Shaun's embrace. But it's Ransom waiting for me in the dark expanses of my dreams.

Chapter Nine

I can't remember the last time I had a Friday off. Mom asked me earlier this week if I could take Grammy to her physical therapy appointment. Not that she needs my help, Grammy is perfectly capable of going to and from her appointments without assistance. But after the old trickster skipped the last two, Mom wanted to be sure she made it to this one.

Grammy insisted her crocheting group was more important than physical therapy. I assured her this was incorrect, but while we were at her appointment, I made sure to change her standing therapy sessions to a different morning so it wouldn't create a conflict in her busy social schedule.

It was nice to have a day out of the office outside of my regular routine. I took the peaceful moments in the waiting area at the physical therapist's office to read the new messages from Madre on Tumblr.

Did you read the new one-shot JustMyStarShip posted on FicArchive?

I stare at the screen in stunned silence. "What the hell?" I mutter under my breath.

Unfortunately, my response garners a huff from the octogenarian sitting two seats over. I ignore her. Not all old ladies are prudes, I remind myself remembering Grammy's weekly suggestions on how to spice up my relationship with Shaun.

It's been a month since we crossed into physical relationship territory. The world didn't explode in a ball of fire and ice. Actually, if anything, our relationship got better. We alternate apartments for our weekly sleepovers after Friday date night, but for the most part, we keep our routines as they were before, with an added bonus of sexy-fun time. He certainly keeps things spicy. I like spice. Spice is good.

I refocus my attention on the open message box and type

out a reply to Madre. *Okay, you're going to have to back up a step or two. First of all, what's a "one-shot," and what's FicArchive?*

Madre replies almost instantly. She must be awake. We're still relative strangers, but I know she's from the Midwest, only one hour behind me, and she knows I'm on the East Coast. That's as far as we've allowed ourselves to go when it comes to personal information. Honestly, I kind of like it this way. No judgment. No personal details mucking up a perfectly good conversation about the merits of leather and villains who are too sexy for their own good.

Her response pops up on the screen. Damn, girl, write a book why don't you.

I keep forgetting you're a newbie. Feels like we've been friends for ages talking about Space Vendetta and the incomparable sexiness that is Nicholas Hughes.

Okay, so FicArchive is where I go for all my fanfiction needs. They have a solid platform to upload fanfics and their search feature makes finding specific tropes a breeze. You'll definitely have to check it out, just use the advanced feature for specific keywords and pairings.

A one-shot is literally that. It's a self-contained scene. Most of them are PWP (porn without plot).

I glance around the waiting room with a guilty flush warming my cheeks. Porn? Really? Oh lord, what the hell have I gotten myself into? I shift in my seat angling away from the old woman glaring at me over her magazine. My attention refocuses on the message.

There are hundreds of thousands of fics on the Archive. It can feel impossible to navigate. I'll send you a few of my favorites featuring our favorite space pirate. What ships are you into? Do you have an OTP? NoTP? Specific tropes you avoid? Give me a direction, and I'll make some recommendations.

My mind spins. OTP? NoTP? What the hell are these? Words? Acronyms? Code? Trope sounds familiar, but I can't seem to remember what it means. I rub my hand across my forehead and take a deep breath. Have I dived into the deep end? I suddenly forgot how to swim.

I type out my reply. *Newbie overload. I'm assuming ship means relationship, but what are OTP and NoTP? And remind me what tropes are? I feel like an idiot for not knowing this stuff.*

After I hit send, I stretch my arms over my head and arch my back. Maybe I should take a long walk in the park since I have the day off.

Grammy appears in the doorway. "You ready to go, kiddo?"

"Yeah." I gather my purse and tuck my phone inside.

Together we head out. As we walk down the street, Grammy points to the corner on the opposite street.

"Let's get a cappuccino and one of those fancy pastries." She's pressing the crosswalk button before I can stop her.

An hour later, Grammy and I are well-caffeinated and stuffed full of flaky pastries. We hobble down the street toward the station contented with light conversation and enjoying the lovely spring weather.

When we reach my parents' house, Grammy kisses me on the cheek.

"Do you want me to hang out with you until Mom and Dad get home?" I ask half-heartedly hoping she says no.

"No. You're free as a bird." She winks. "I have some ladies coming over at one. We're going to play Gin Rummy and eat all of your father's cookie stash."

I laugh. "Grammy, you're a horrible influence. But I can't say I blame you. Seize the day."

"Damn skippy." She pats my cheek. "Enjoy your afternoon. Maybe rest up for your date tonight with your young man." Her bawdy wink has me blushing.

"Grammy." My stern tone melts into laughter.

"Why don't you bring him to dinner on Sunday? I want to meet this stud."

Did Grammy call Shaun a stud? I cover my face with my hand. "We'll see."

She shuffles inside the house and turns to face me. "Love you, kiddo. Be safe."

"Always, Grammy. Love you too."

As I walk back toward the station, I send a text to Mom letting her know Grammy is home safe. I see a response waiting for me from Madre.

Once I'm on the train heading back toward Brooklyn, I open Madre's message.

Don't worry about it. We've all been there, sugar. Okay, here's your crash course. Buckle up.

OTP – One True Pairing (the couple you want in a solid relationship)

NoTP – No True Pairing (the couple you never want to see in any relationship)

3TP – Threesome True Pairing (pretty self-explanatory, typically rare)

Ship – Relationship

Canon – holds true to the source material and is recognized as truth by the original creators.

Non-Canon – deviates from the source material and is not recognized as truth by the original creators.

CrackShip – A pairing that doesn't exist in canon, relationships of characters from different fandoms or characters from the same fandom that never meet and/or don't have a relationship

Tropes – cliches used in writing...for example: Enemies to Lovers, Forced Marriage, Brother's Best Friend, Alternate Universe, etc. There are sooooo many. It's good to know which ones you like and which you don't.

That's a brief introduction to fandom lingo. If you have any other questions, ask. No judgment here. Send your OTP and trope preferences. Here are a few fics I had bookmarked you might like. Let me know what you think. Off to work now. Chat later.

I glance up at the station sign as the train pulls to a stop. One more until mine. Madre's fire hosed me with information. I send a quick thank you message and log off.

When I get home, I grab a sandwich from the fridge and boot up my laptop. Madre's right, FicArchive is easy enough to navigate. I click the links she sent for the recommended fics.

The first two are pairings between Ransom and characters who do nothing for me. The third is a modern, contemporary alternate universe (AU) with what the author calls an OFC. I read the text behind it. Other Female Character. Okay.

It's a one-shot. So it takes all of five minutes to read. Steamy, sexy but it leaves me a bit unsatisfied. The female character wasn't well-rounded. I make notes on a sticky pad and move on to the next story.

This one is a bit longer, but it pairs Ransom and Lynnea.

My mind drifts back to Shaun's confession the first night we had sex. On-screen Ransom and Lynnea haven't shared a single scene, although the way the story is written, I know it's inevitable. I wonder if Shaun already knows what happens between these characters. My curiosity is piqued.

One chapter in and I'm hooked. I devour the rest of the story quickly and pull up my Tumblr messages.

Ransom and Lynnea are my OTP. I need more recommendations if you have them. I'll search for more, but you seem to be a reliable source of smut.

I chuckle and hit send.

After grabbing a drink, I move to the couch with the laptop. I do a couple of searches and sift through the results. Most of the stories have a good premise, but they just don't capture my attention. I get it. Most of the authors on this site are fans with little or no experience with writing. They're fans filling in the gaps of the stories with their own fantasies. Nothing wrong with that, but I'm hungry for more.

I change tactics and search to the backlist of the author Madre recommended. *JustMyStarShip*. They seem to have multiple ships they write for multiple fandoms. Fortunately, they also prefer the Ransom/Lynnea pairing affectionately dubbed RanLyn. I grin at the absurdity of the name. It's cringey like those cutesy combo couple names celebrities use, but in this instance, it's not the couple using it. The fans create it as an homage to their favorite pairing.

Four hours later, I've devoured all of her backlist and move on to her bookmarked recommendation list. I take a break between fics to grab a drink or go to the bathroom, but it's not until darkness has completely settled on the city I pick up my phone to check for messages.

Five missed texts, two missed calls. Shit. I forgot to turn on my ringer after Grammy's appointment. I slide the tab up and open messages. Lily sent me a reminder for girls' night at her place tomorrow. Maggie wants to know the number for the masseuse I used last November. And three messages are from Shaun.

I check the clock. Holy shit! Eight o'clock! No way. I shove the laptop aside and type up a response to his last message which was a frowning emoji and the words *where are you?*

Sorry. I lost track of time. I hit send and head into the bedroom to change.

The doorbell rings, making me jump ten feet in the air. I run to the door and glance at the security screen. Shaun's on my doorstep with a pizza box in his hand. I unlock the door and let him in.

"Sorry about that. I completely lost track of time."

"It happens." He sets the box on the coffee table. The scent of fresh pizza has my stomach growling.

"I'm starving." I wrap my arms around him. "Thanks for thinking of me. I'm sorry, I got distracted."

"When you didn't show up for dinner, I got worried." He holds me close and captures my lips in a tender kiss. "It's all good. I'm glad you're okay." He brightens. "How was your day off?"

"Good. I spent the morning with my Grammy. She's been skipping her physical therapy appointments, so I had to chaperone." I shake my head. "Then she roped me into cappuccino and pastries afterward."

Shaun laughs. "She sounds like a riot. I'm glad you spent the day with her."

"Me too." Guilt pricks my conscience. I can't tell him the real reason I missed our standing date tonight. Instead, I clear my throat and get plates out of the cabinet. "How was work today? I miss anything fun?"

He launches into a short recap of his day while we eat. Afterward, I put in a movie, one we haven't seen before but I know it has Nicholas Hughes listed on the cover. I've been wanting to watch it all week.

I fiddle with the television. Shaun's low chuckle draws my attention away from the screen.

"What?" I ask, half-listening.

"Her Wicked Pirate."

I whip around in horror. Shaun has my computer on his lap reading from the screen. I pinch my eyes closed in mortification. Shit. I forgot to close the damn thing and now my boyfriend has discovered my new addiction to *Space Vendetta* fan fiction.

"I didn't know you were into fan fiction." He teases me. "Oh, and from the ratings on this one, looks like it's mature." A sinful smile curls on his lips. "Have you been reading smut all afternoon?"

Guilt pours through me. I don't have to respond; my flaming hot face says it all.

Shaun reads through the tags. "RanLyn. Ransom/Lynnea. Enemies to Lovers. Hate Fucking. Spanking. Possible Non-con." He turns to face me and I can't tell if he's horrified or aroused, pretty sure it's a mixture of both. "Did you write this?"

"No." I steal the laptop from him and close the cover. "I did not write it."

"Just reading it." He wraps his arm around my waist and pulls me against him.

"Yes." I sniff and tense under his touch. He's judging me, I can feel it. Shame washes over me. "There's nothing wrong with reading sexy fan fiction."

"I never said there was." He kisses my cheek and tightens his hold on me. "We've all been there, kitten. Sexy fan fiction comes with the territory. Be careful. Rule thirty-four can be detrimental to your health."

"What's rule thirty-four?" Hasn't my curiosity had enough today? I guess not.

"If it's out there, there's pornography for it."

I recoil in horror. "What? Oh my God." A series of realizations hit me at once. One, there are children's shows with inappropriate material twisted from it. Followed by, how the hell does he know about this? I ask him.

"I have friends who are bigger fans than me. I've heard some crazy stories."

"Good to know." I wiggle out of his grip and snatch up the

remote. “Can we forget this conversation happened and watch the movie?”

“Only if you let me hold you.” He pulls me back against him and kisses my neck. “I missed you this week.”

I turn the movie on, but we end up getting distracted in the sexiest way.

CHAPTER TEN

Spring has finally embraced the city. It's quite refreshing to have daylight after I get off of work. Lily stops by my desk on her way out the door.

"Hey. Don't forget. Game night at my place. Six."

"Got it." I pull on my coat. "Are you sure your roommates are cool with this?"

Lily waves her hand. "James and Mike are out of town for an expo in California. Gavin's looking forward to it."

"Really?" That piece of information stuns me. "He's so reserved. I don't see him enjoying game night with a group."

"Trust me. If he didn't want to be there, he would find an excuse to be out of the house." Lily giggles and adjusts her bag on her shoulder. "You invited your man too, right?"

My gaze drifts to the hallway leading to Shaun's office. "Yeah."

"Good." She beams. "Okay. Well, I'll see you tonight."

I wave and collect the last of my stuff. This week has been a whirlwind. There's a stack of orders sitting on my desk I need to get done as soon as possible. Filling in for Shirley certainly has shown me a whole different side of the job. I feel like my workload has doubled in the past three weeks. But it's good. I need the practice if I'm going to apply for a promotion this summer.

On my way to the elevator, my phone pings. I smile when I see the message. Madre and I have been chatting daily for the past few weeks since she introduced me to the glories of fan fiction. Shaun takes every opportunity to tease me about it. Not in a brash, rude way, but in a simple, are-you-learning-any-new-kinks way. I try not to bring it up when we're together.

Madre sends me all the latest information on our favorite space pirate and his real-life counterpart. I feel guilty dedicating this much time to a person I've never met and will probably never meet. Some people follow sports teams, I follow Nicholas Hughes. Nothing wrong with that.

When the elevator reaches the lobby, I tuck my phone in my pocket and head out. Within thirty minutes, I'm standing on my doorstep staring at three boxes stacked in front of my door. I do a little dance and carry them into my apartment.

It seems between my internet searches and Tumblr the algorithms uncovered my secret obsession with *Space Vendetta*. I've been bombarded with ads for months. At first, I was able to resist, but the farther I fell into the fandom the more my restraint crumbled.

I open the first box and find a journal with a pretty embossed photograph of Ransom on the cover. The second package has a few Pop figurines including Ransom and Lynnea. I set them on the shelf, side by side. The last box has a Sherpa throw blanket with Captain Ransom in bright bold colors. I drape it over the back of the couch.

After putting the boxes in the recycling, I change and grab the board games for tonight.

Halfway through changing, my doorbell rings. I pull on my sweatshirt and run to the door. Shaun greets me with a lopsided smile and a bouquet of daisies.

"Awww. Thank you." I kiss him and take the flowers.

"You're welcome." He steps inside and lingers in the living room while I put the flowers in some water. "Are you sure this is okay? I hate to keep crashing your girls' night."

"Trust me, if Lily and Maggie don't want you there, they wouldn't invite you." I set the vase on the table and smile. Anyone can buy roses, but he buys me daisies. They're my favorite. I wonder how he figured it out since I never told him.

Shaun's inspecting my new figurines on the shelf. "These are cute. Although if you're needing visuals for writing your fanfic smut, you're going to need the fully posable action figures."

I slap his arm. "You promised you wouldn't tease me about that."

He wraps his arms around me and kisses me, stealing all the fight right out of my body. I cling to him tighter.

"We can stay here and have our own game night." He winks. "Roleplay maybe. I'll dress up as Ransom and you can be my Lynnea."

My face heats at the thought. As hot as that would be, I can't cancel on my girls. Lily's been looking forward to it all week.

"Raincheck?" I grin.

Shaun nods. "You ready?"

I lock up the apartment and we make our way to Lily's spacious building. She has a whole brownstone. Granted, she has three roommates, but her dad owns the building. He's a banker in the city with money coming out of his ears. While her dad is quite wealthy, Lily never flaunts her connection or the fact she grew up on Park Avenue.

Maggie answers the door. "Hey, lovebirds. We were taking bets when you two would show. If you came at all."

Shaun and I share a look. Ever since we did the deed, Lily and Maggie seem convinced we'll abandon them completely and stay locked up in the nearest bedroom.

"Jen was busy with her new toys." Shaun teases as he hangs up his coat and takes mine.

"Stop." I elbow him in the side.

"I don't want to know," Lily adds, walking by with a tray of snacks.

"I do." Maggie grins. "Are we talking floggers and nipple clamps here or a new vibe?"

Shaun bursts out laughing and leans against the door frame.

"None of the above." I groan and hide my face behind my hands. "Seriously, Maggie. All you think about is sex."

She lifts a shoulder without a care. "You knew this about me for years and never made a stink about it before."

"Well, that's because you weren't talking about my sex life," I growl.

"She's bitter because she's not getting any." Gavin appears behind her. He resembles a young Shemar Moore with his

Criminal Minds confidence mixed with his trademark swagger. He's handsome and typically quite reserved. This is certainly an interesting development.

Maggie's face turns pink and she throws her elbow back. It barely grazes him.

"Hi, Gav." I chuckle at their byplay.

"Hey, Jen." His attention shifts to Shaun. "Gavin."

Shaun reaches out and shakes his hand. "Shaun."

The two men nod as though sealing an unspoken agreement. I shake my head. "Okay, game night. Hope you're ready for a little inappropriateness."

"A little." Maggie snorts. "Bring on all the inappropriateness."

"Oh, did you bring the expansion pack?" Lily calls from the dining room where she's set up the table for our evening.

"Yes. And the nineties one too."

"Wicked," Gavin says before joining Lily. Maggie follows behind him.

I round on Shaun. "You, be nice."

He lifts his hands in supplication. "I'm always nice."

"You know what I mean." I drop my voice low. "Don't mention..."

Shaun kisses my forehead. "I promise."

We dive into the game, and after two rounds we're all laughing so hard, no one can breathe properly. This game is so inappropriate, but hot damn is it fun.

My phone keeps vibrating against my hip. I pull it out and see notifications from Madre. She must have found some good fics to be blowing up my phone right now.

"Jen. You're up." Gavin nudges me.

"Oh, yeah." I set the phone on the table and focus on my cards.

Maggie's gaze narrows. "Who's got you so distracted?" She grins. "We know it's not Shaun. That's why I made him sit over here instead of beside you."

"Ya gotta keep 'em separated." Lily singsongs before falling into a fit of giggles. Looks like her homemade sangria is stronger than she thought.

Amusement dances in Gavin's eyes. Shaun's hiding his face behind his cards, but I see his shoulders shaking with laughter.

"Who's blowing up your phone?" Maggie arches her brow.

"No one." I lie.

As I reach for my phone to put it back in my pocket, Maggie snatches it and reads the notifications. "Oh...and who is Madre?"

Lily wrinkles her nose in thought. "Isn't she the moderator of the *Space Vendetta* blog you emailed a few months ago?"

"Yeah." My face heats. Even though I'm among friends and they know I like the show, I can't help but feel they're judging me right now. "We chat once in a while."

Maggie's eyes widen. "There's like twenty missed messages here."

"You're into *Space Vendetta*?" Gavin asks.

"Yeah. I mean. Not deep into it, but I enjoy the films." I motion to my boyfriend. "Shaun's read the books."

"Have you played the video game based on the series?" Gavin's eyes glisten with interest.

"There's a game?" I glance at Shaun.

He nods. "Yeah. PlayStation, I think. I never got into it, but it's supposed to be good."

"Can we get back to this Madre person?" Maggie asks, her brow folding in concern.

"What about her?" I lift my shoulder trying to be nonchalant but my heart is hammering inside my chest.

"Honey. You're spending an awful lot of time chatting online with someone you never met." She leans on the table. "Do you need an intervention?"

I laugh. "Come on, Maggie. Like none of you have ever had extended conversations with someone on the internet." My gaze drifts over their guilty faces. "Exactly. This is the digital age."

"Just be careful, okay." Maggie slides my phone back onto the table in front of me. "It's easy to get caught up in the online drama."

My heart twists with uncertainty, but I push it aside. "Thanks for the warning, but I got this covered."

"What app do you use to chat?" Gavin asks.

"We started on Tumblr and then moved to Twitter." I tuck my phone in my pocket.

"You should try Discord. All the gamers use it. There are groups for everything on there. It's like Reddit, but more conversation-friendly." Gavin taps his fingers on his glass before taking a drink.

"Thanks." I shift in my seat and refocus on the cards in my hand. "Now, can we get back to the game?"

"Yes, please." Lily wiggles in her chair making her curls bounce playfully.

"You're cut off." Maggie grabs her drink and Lily pouts. "Drink some water."

Lily sticks out her tongue.

"Okay, children." I clear my throat. "There's one *blank* in the *blank*. Make it count."

Gavin and Maggie lay down their cards first and we gradually shift our attention back to the game.

As the evening continues, I can't shake the conversation from my mind. How dangerous can a fandom actually be? What kind of drama could they possibly mean? Madre is harmless. I enjoy our discussions. After making a mental note to download Discord and send a message to Madre, I refocus on the game and spending time with my friends.

Balancing my life with this newfound love is proving tricky, but I've never had a problem finding balance before, why would this be any different?

Chapter Eleven

The deeper I venture into these uncharted waters, the more I realize I'm out of my depth. It takes me half an hour to drag myself from bed and get ready for work. When I finally arrive at my desk, I'm five minutes late. All eyes are on me as I settle behind my desk.

I drink lukewarm coffee and focus on the order forms on the computer screen.

A month into filling in for Shirley, and I honestly don't know how she maintains her sanity. My workload has doubled in the office. Never mind my typically relaxing weekends have now been commandeered by a plethora of paperwork I'm unable to finish during the workweek. It's the other distractions that prove to be the biggest time suck. They slid their slimy tentacles into my weeknights stealing what little time I have to myself.

I rub my forehead. Other distractions. I laugh because I do it to myself. It's like an addiction. I can't stop myself from opening the apps and checking for updates and messages whenever I unlock my phone. I groan and ignore the urge to check it even now.

Like last night. I meant to send a quick message to Madre and ended up spending half the night in a chat forum arguing with a half dozen other fans who are as obsessed, if not more so than I am. The argument began over an article published by a fansite over the perceived direction of the new film now in production.

I should have walked away. Closed the app and went to sleep. That's what a smart person would have done. But when I saw them gang up on Madre, who had a valid point about Colton's dynamics with Lynnea, I couldn't stay silent. The forum exploded with impassioned opinions and spiraled into chaos quickly. Gavin deserves a piece of my mind after his recommendation. Discord was aptly named. I should delete it. But I won't.

An hour into work, Lily stops by my desk on her way to the ladies' room. "Hey. Are you feeling okay? I saw you come in late."

"Yeah. Rough night." I stretch and fake a smile. "I'll live."

"Let me know if you need anything." Lily encourages me with a warm grin and heads off down the hall.

I refocus on the numbers littering the screen. Not even five minutes later, my phone pings. I ignore it, thinking it's Madre with a message about last night.

My desk phone rings. I answer it with my standard work greeting.

"Good morning, Miss Ashcroft." Shaun's voice echoes through the receiver. "Will you be joining us for the meeting?"

I glance at my calendar and all the blood drains from my head. I clear my throat. "Yes. One moment, just finishing up a quick note."

Once I hang the phone up, I scramble to gather the information needed for the monthly sales meeting. I completely forgot about it. Shoving away the exhaustion and panic, I hurry down the hall to the large board room near the vice president's office.

Quietly as I can, I slip in the door and take the empty seat toward the end of the table. The meeting started, but I can tell by the gazes shifting covertly in my direction there's no excuse for being tardy.

As the heads of the other departments give their reviews, I haphazardly organize my notes. My fingers fumble with the papers. Shit. Where is it? There's a page missing. Panic claws at my throat.

When my turn arrives, I muscle through it using what I have to show the fluctuation in the department's orders over the past year compared to this last month. It's the worst presentation I've ever given. And the fact it's my first in this temporary position reflects poorly on me as a professional.

After the meeting, I slink out the door amid my coworkers

clutching my notebook containing all my files to my chest. Could this day possibly get any worse?

"Miss Ashcroft, would you mind staying for a moment? I'd like a word," the vice president, Mr. Roberts, calls from the doorway.

"Yes, sir." I return to the board room and stand at attention trying to project confidence I don't feel.

Once the room is empty except for the two of us, he sits at the head of the table. "Please, have a seat."

I select the one close to him even though I'm terrified this isn't going to end well.

"Miss Ashcroft, I noticed you were late to the meeting this morning." He leans back in his chair studying me.

"Yes, sir." I pick at the hem of my skirt before I meet his gaze. "I apologize. I lost track of time."

He rubs his hand over his jaw. Mr. Roberts is handsome and quite shrewd. I can see why many of the women in the office congregate in small groups just to catch a glimpse of him in the hallway. I've heard their whispered fantasies when he walks by. He's got that old Hollywood style and charm with a CEO no-nonsense attitude. This is the first time we've ever shared a conversation in private and my hands can't stop shaking.

"Shirley assured me you were up to the task of filling her position during her absence." His gray eyes pierce me. "Do you feel this is still accurate?"

"Yes, sir." I nod a bit too vigorously and my head spins.

"Your report had some noticeable omissions." He taps his fingers on the table. "Please have a report drawn up and on my desk by the end of the day."

"Of course, sir." I bow my head for a moment, unable to take the intensity of his gaze.

"Is everything all right at home, Miss Ashcroft?" The question seems to arise from a place of genuine concern.

"Oh, yes." I offer a shaky smile. "No problems at home."

"I trust Shaun is treating you well."

I blink twice before I'm able to form a response. "I...Yes, he is."

"I typically don't approve of office relationships." He strokes his jaw and shrugs. "But Shaun assures me you are both able to maintain a balance with your relationship in the workplace."

He did? I open my mouth, but Mr. Roberts continues.

"He informed me of your relationship a few months ago, Miss Ashcroft." A knowing smile transforms his face into a dichotomy of power and sincerity. This is a warning as well as an acknowledgment. "So long as it doesn't affect your work, I see no issue with it. Thank you for maintaining professionalism."

"Of course, sir. I appreciate the concern, but you have nothing to worry about on that issue."

"Very good." He slowly rises to his feet and extends his hand.

I quickly rise and take it in a firm handshake. "I'll have my report to you by the end of the day."

"Keep up the good work, Miss Ashcroft." And with those words, he escorts me from the room.

The rest of the day, I'm hyper-focused. I ignore everyone and everything except the report I should have had prepared for the meeting this morning. I fucked up, and I'll be the first to admit when I do. I even skip lunch with Lily.

By four o'clock, I'm completely dragging. I still have a few details to polish before I can hit print and put this report on Mr. Robert's desk.

A hand appears in my peripheral vision bearing a coffee cup. I glance up.

Lily smiles, her cheeks as pink as the little strawberries on her swing dress. "You looked like you could use a boost of energy."

"Thanks." I take a sip and savor the rich caramel macchiato. "You're the best."

"Don't thank me." She winks. "I'm only the delivery service."

"Who?" Her chuckle makes me pause. I glance around the room but Shaun's not there.

"He slipped me a note earlier and told me to keep an eye

on you. Oh, and make sure you're well-stocked on caffeine." Lily sighs wistfully. "He's a keeper, that one."

"Yeah, he is." I cradle the cup in my hands and sigh.

"I'll let you finish up your report." Lily pats my shoulder and retreats to her desk.

Renewed by the kindness of my friends and the caramel macchiato, I finish the report and hit print. I put it in a folder and place a sticky note on the cover.

Once I drop it off, I can get back to what I should have been working on today. Pushing the internal irritation aside, I head down the hallway and pass Shaun's office.

He's on the phone but smiles when he sees me. I mouth *thanks for the coffee* and wave.

Shaun winks and continues with his conversation.

Mr. Robert's secretary stops me outside his office. "He's in a meeting, hon."

"Can you make sure he gets this, please?" I hand her the file.

"Absolutely." She sets it on top of another file on her desk. "Have a good night, dear."

"You too." I exhale as I walk away feeling a fraction better than I had all day. But I know there's still a mountain of work waiting to be completed. I return to my desk and pull up the spreadsheets for this week's orders.

"Working late?" Shaun's voice startles me.

I press my hand to my chest. "Yeah. What time is it?"

"After seven." He shoves his hands in his pockets.

"Shit." I rub my eyes and turn off the computer.

"Everything okay?" His kind eyes search my face. "You seem a bit out of it lately."

"Yeah, I'm good." I stand up and pull on my coat.

"Want me to escort you home?" he asks with a hopeful grin.

"Always a gentleman." I laugh. "Thanks. But no. I'm gonna crash hard when I get there."

"Make sure you eat something." He brushes a strand of hair away from my face. "Check your messages then."

Even though the office is completely empty, I feel guilty

pressing a kiss to his soft lips. "See you tomorrow."

He walks back toward his office, and I take the elevator down to the ground floor. When I board the train, I open my phone. There are a dozen missed messages from Madre and some texts from Lily and Shaun.

I read through Shaun's texts. *I miss you.*

My heart melts at the words. I type back. *I miss you too.*

Once I get home, I skim through Madre's messages and respond showing support for the continuing battle on Discord. I make sure to put the phone on silent after I eat dinner and curl up in bed with my Ransom figurine keeping watch from my dresser.

CHAPTER TWELVE

Summer is right around the corner. Finally, I have a Saturday morning free. I should use it to do something fun for myself, but there's that pull demanding I check the fandom social feeds or read through the Vendetta Vixens chat group. And I know where it leads. To a wasted day and nothing accomplished. No. Today, I'm going out.

After making a cup of coffee, I sit down at the table and make a list of things I need to accomplish. For work and myself. It helps to have a list.

I've finally found my footing at the office even though the workload hasn't decreased. I honestly don't know how Shirley does it. The time I've spent catching up hasn't left me with much of a chance to spend time with the girls or Shaun. Even my weekly Sunday dinners have taken a hit.

I can't completely blame work. Part of it has been my newfound online community. I love it, most of the time. Then there are moments I feel so emotionally drained I don't want to deal with anyone. Not my family, not my friends, and no, not even Shaun. Ninety percent of the time I'm exhausted after chatting in the group or scrolling through fandom news updates.

Truth is, I can't talk to them about it. My family doesn't understand. Maggie and Lily try to understand, but the conversations seem strained after a few minutes. It's hard not to bring it up frequently because I spend so much time in the chat group and on Tumblr when I'm not with them. I don't want them to worry I've been sucked down this multi-dimensional wormhole.

Shaun. I sigh. Well, he gets it to an extent. He's part of the fandom even if he doesn't participate in any online forums. But even his gentle teasing about Ransom over the past few weeks has me on edge. It's his way of connecting with me, but I feel guilty. Insanely guilty.

I shouldn't be thinking about another man, even a fictional one when I have such a wonderful boyfriend. He's amazing. Thoughtful, caring, and supportive. I love him. We haven't reached that point in our relationship where I can tell him this. It still feels too fragile and the last thing I want to do is ruin it by bursting in like the Kool-Aid man with a declaration of love.

My phone rings. It's Mom.

"Hey, Mom. What's up?" I put the phone on speaker as I finish my list.

"Hi, honey. Grammy and I were going to do some shopping and get lunch. Do you want to join us?" Her voice filters through the room.

I stare at my list and ponder the request. "Yeah, that sounds great."

"We were thinking King's Plaza. Do you want me to pick you up?"

"No. Don't worry about me. I'll meet you there." I draw a small heart on the edge of the paper.

"Perfect. Ten o'clock enough time for you?"

"Yeah. See you there, Mom."

"Love you."

"Love you too." I end the call and glance at the clock. It's eight twenty now. I have plenty of time.

Reading through the list, I see there are a few things I can take care of while I'm out today. Good. Maybe I need to unplug for a bit.

Once I take a shower and throw on some comfortable clothes, I grab my list and head out the door. Using public transportation never phased me before, but on days like today, I wish I had a car. It'll take an hour to get to the mall.

I settle on the bus and pull out my phone taking advantage of the long ride to catch up on the latest fandom drama. I shouldn't, but I do anyway out of habit. It's become part of my commute routine.

As I scroll through the chat, I notice a few of the members commented on a theory I posted. Most of the responses were positive and showed total agreement, but there were a couple who did not. Their abrasive comments settled like a brick in the pit of my stomach.

MistressViper: Anyone who knows anything about this fandom knows this is impossible according to the canon. Even the creators have addressed this. Fucking noob. Do some research before posting.

I swallow hard trying to ignore the bite of her comment. The name calling was uncalled for. I might be new to the fandom, but it doesn't give her the right to police the group like she's the authority on everything *Space Vendetta.*

Some of the comments below it are in my defense. I'm thankful there are a few who understand. Even Madre left a stinging response to Viper's comment. My heart swells at the show of solidarity.

The bus comes to a stop. Shit. This is me. I close out the app and get off. Once I board the train taking me to the mall, I find an open seat and check my email. There are a few newsletters and some spam. There's a notification from FicArchive.

You have three comments on your post.

I blink rapidly and my heart rate speeds up. After devouring every fan fiction I could find, I decided to try my hand at a one-shot. Even as I wrote it, Shaun's surprised expression at finding fan fiction on my laptop lingered in the back of my mind.

What would he say if he found my fic? I shove the thought aside and open the website.

The first two comments are encouraging. They both loved the premise of the fic and want more. I grin and continue to scroll down to the third.

This fic is a waste of time. Don't quit your day job. There's no way Ransom would be this sentimental. Read the fucking books.

I want to reply, but I don't. Instead, I close the window and write up a little note to Madre telling her what I found. I hate running to her every time someone shows their ass like this, but honestly, I feel like she's the only one who understands.

There's no one else I can talk to about it. Not in my real life anyway. With a sigh, I put my phone away and stare at the floor trying to ignore the prickling unease at the scars those comments left behind. I wish I could shove them aside, but they fester instead.

When I finally arrive at the mall, it's difficult to shake the cloud hanging over my head. I spot Mom and Grammy waiting by the entrance and wave.

"Everything okay, honey?" Mom asks her brow furrows as she looks me over.

"Yeah." I force a smile. "I'm good."

Grammy narrows her gaze at me. "Well, I don't know who pissed in your Cheerios, but it's time to turn that frown upside down."

I chuckle at her unwavering optimism. "Where to now?"

Grammy and Mom outline their itinerary, and I can't help but smile. I'm along for the ride, it seems. So I follow their lead and carry bags while listening to their chatter and adding my opinion when allowed to do so.

Three hours pass in a blur and my stomach growls.

"Mom, I need to eat. I'm gonna pass out." I shift the bags in my hands feeling like a pack mule rather than a daughter.

"You shouldn't have skipped breakfast then." She eyes me. "Fine. Let's go."

We find an open booth at one of the burger joints, and I order the fattest bacon cheeseburger on the menu. Mom stares at me horrified when I take a massive bite.

"Do you eat that way in front of your boyfriend?" she asks before taking a dainty bite of her pasta.

Grammy chuckles and sips her soup.

"Shaun doesn't judge my healthy appetite, thank you." I take another bite.

Mom tuts her disappointment in my manners. "So is the cow still giving the milk away for free then?"

"Mom!" I shout with a mouthful of food garnering stares from nearby tables. I swallow and round on her. "Really, Mom? Did you call me a cow?"

"Not at all. I was using an analogy."

"That's not what it sounded like," I grumble.

"She's worried she'll never get any grandkids at this rate," Grammy adds pointing her spoon in my direction.

The thought of marrying Shaun and having his babies makes my whole body melt into a puddle of hormonal slop. I shake my head. "We've only been dating a few months, Mom."

She waves her hand. "That doesn't mean anything. Your father and I were engaged within two months of meeting. Married within a year."

"I know, Mom." I dip a French fry in ketchup and take a bite. "But things are different now."

Grammy pshaws with her elegant flair. "Times change, yes. Situations change, true. But if you know, you know." She pins me with her best stare over her glasses. "Is he the one?"

The chaos of the last few months hasn't given me a chance to consider this. Maybe I didn't want to ask myself this for fear I'd fuck it up somehow and chase him off. I shrug noncommittally.

"Bullshit." Grammy snorts. "Tell me what's going on in your head."

I stare at Grammy in surprise my jaw opening and closing a few times before words finally form on my tongue. "Shaun's amazing. I care about him...a lot. But, I don't know."

"Has he said I love you yet?" Grammy asks.

"No." I take a lackluster bite of my burger. My stomach churns at the conversation, and instantly, my hunger disappears. I shove the plate away.

"Hmmm." Grammy nods. "And you haven't told him how you feel yet either?"

"What if I fuck it up?" I swallow the lump in my throat and drop my gaze to the salt shaker.

"You'll never know if you don't try, honey," Mom adds, taking my hand. "Sometimes you need to take a chance. The risk is worth the reward."

I nod, unable to trust my voice.

"Why don't you invite him over for the family dinner?" Mom smiles. "We'd love to meet him."

I chuckle. "I'm sure you would, Mom."

"We promise to be on our best behavior." Grammy's eyes sparkle with mischief.

"Somehow I don't trust you." I laugh out loud this time.

Grammy shifts in her seat and sniffs with indignance. "I'm always on my best behavior."

Mom rolls her eyes.

"I'll see when he's available," I say and take a sip of my iced tea. "But I won't promise anything."

We finish our meal, and I lug all the bags to mom's car. She gives me a ride home.

Once I'm safely hidden in the comfort of my apartment, I collapse on the couch. The cloud hanging over my head all day opens up and a torrential downpour engulfs me.

I send a message to Lily telling her I'm not feeling well and can't make it over for girls' night. Then I turn off my phone. Today should have recharged me, but it only left me floundering in uncertainty.

Grabbing my Ransom blanket and pillow, I curl up on the couch and turn on *The Raven Comes*, a period film set in the early nineteenth century staring Nicholas Hughes.

I drown in his expressive blue-green eyes. His deep, commanding voice soothes my frazzled nerves. His smirky grin lures me deeper into the abyss.

I'm in love with two men. Guilt consumes me. I shove it away with both hands and focus only on Nicholas while wrapped in Ransom's warmth.

CHAPTER THIRTEEN

The following Friday, I'm almost relieved at the text message I get at lunch. Shaun has a dinner meeting with the corporate office tonight and has to cancel our date. I finish the rest of the day and slip out the door before Lily can stop by my desk.

This past week hasn't done much for my mood. I spend most of my time on work, and the rest of it is dedicated to this new project I'm working on with Madre. We're writing a fanfic together. I enjoy the challenge and the break from work-related stuff.

It's getting harder and harder to spend time with Shaun and the girls without bringing up the fandom or Madre. They humored me in the beginning, but now the glassy-eyed stares I get in response to my excitement relating to anything Vendetta or Nicholas Hughes leaves me deflated. So I've been avoiding it.

Unfortunately, that means I've been avoiding my friends too.

Lily sends me a message. *Hey, where'd you go? Want to get dinner?*

I chew on my lip as I wait for my train and ponder how to respond. *Not feeling great. Gonna crash on the couch and take it easy this weekend.*

When I reach my front door, my phone pings.

*I'm worried about you. *Sad emoji face** Lily's message only twists the guilt deeper in my gut.

I push it aside and toss my bag on the table. After I change into my trusty yoga pants and oversized Vendetta sweatshirt, I settle on the couch and pull my laptop open. Madre should be home from work soon, and I promised I would have the latest chapter of our fic ready so she could write her response.

We've found a nice rhythm. She writes as Lynnea and I write as Ransom. We alternate chapters building off the other's scene. There's no outline, no stress, no expectations. It's fun and helps me purge the fantasies rolling around in my mind. I like writing as Ransom. He's wicked and devious while being charming and using his seductive wiles to get what he wants. It's so freeing.

An hour later my fingers are flying across the keyboard and I'm pouring my goddamn heart into this fic. It's getting steamy. I lick my lips and finish a particularly dirty line when my phone dings with a message notification.

I glance at the screen and open Discord. It's Madre. *I'm home from work, how's the chapter coming?*

Almost done. Brace yourself, it's definitely NSFW. I'll send it over in a few minutes. I hit send and finish the last few paragraphs before saving the document and emailing it to Madre.

Too late, I realize I sent it from my personal email account and not the one I created for fandom-only interactions. Shit.

I got it. Madre's messages slide onto the screen in rapid succession. *It took me a minute to realize it was from you. Is this your personal email?*

Yeah. I guess I got carried away with the story I forgot to switch to my other account before I sent it. I groan. *Now you know who's behind HoldMeRansom.*

An email appears in my inbox a few minutes later. I don't recognize the account. "Who the hell is Bonnie Reynolds?" I open it.

Hey, Jen. I figured it was only fair to reveal who's behind Madre since you revealed yours. I'm a Midwest mom, wife, and badass baker. My kids are hitting their teen years, so that should give you an idea of how old I am. Hint: over thirty. I've been married for fifteen years and this fandom is my only escape. LOL. Now since we've been unmasked, I want to say it's been a pleasure connecting with you. I've made some great friends through the fandom, but not many of them know the real me. So count yourself among the few and the privileged. Hugs. I'll work on my response to Ransom's chapter now. Chat soon. ~Bonnie

I chuckle. Wow. I forget there's a life behind the username, not only a fan. Honestly, I'm relieved. For a while, I wondered if I was going crazy bonding with someone who's just a username over a fictional character tangled up in a fictional universe. I type up a response.

Bonnie. It's nice to finally meet you. Thanks for the email. As for me, I'm a single working woman living in Brooklyn. That's about it. I'm not married. No kids. Hell, I don't even have any pets. But I have some great friends and a handsome boyfriend. So, that counts for something, right? Anyway, it's nice to know there's a real person on the other end of the screen. Hugs. I look forward to your chapter. ~Jen

The moment I hit send the doorbell rings making me jump three feet of the couch and nearly toss my laptop to the floor. With a racing heart, I set the computer aside and check the monitor next to the door.

Lily and Maggie stare straight into the camera. I sigh and unlock the door.

"What are you doing here?" I ask as they make themselves at home.

Lily sets the two bags she's carrying on the table and gets some bowls out of the cabinet. "Oh, well you said you weren't feeling well, so I stopped by the Starlight Diner and got some soups and sandwiches."

"Then she called me and told me you've been acting suspicious all week." Maggie flops down on the couch and scans the room. "Where the hell did all this stuff come from?" She lifts the Ransom throw pillow and stares at it for a long moment before arching her brow in my direction. "What the hell is this?"

I snatch it from her hands and hold it against my chest. "What? It's a pillow."

Her lip quirks. "Do you sleep with it too?"

"I'm not going to dignify that with a response." I sit down and clutch the pillow against my heart. "If you're going to judge me, then take your soup and leave."

Lily slaps Maggie's shoulder. "I told you to tone it down." She returns to the kitchen to finish putting the soup in bowls.

"Fine." Maggie rolls her eyes. "So, what's the deal, Jen? You cancel on us last week and now you're dodging Lily at work. Poor Shaun hasn't heard a peep out of you all week either."

"We texted him," Lily adds from the kitchen. "Cause we

were worried."

I hide my face in the pillow. Shame washes over me.

"You two have a fight or something?"

"No." I groan lifting my head from the fabric and meeting Maggie's gaze. "It's complicated."

"How complicated can it be?" Maggie asks. "I mean Shaun's like the magical fucking unicorn of boyfriends. You'd be crazy to fuck it up. Is there someone else?"

"No," I reply honestly.

Her attention shifts from me to the room skimming over every surface where I have memorabilia of *Space Vendetta*, Captain Ransom, and Nicholas Hughes. "Are you sure about that?"

"What?"

Maggie spots my open laptop. Before I can reach it, she snatches it up and flips through my open tabs. "Girl, you're obsessed. Seriously. Tumblr, Twitter, Discord, and holy hell, are these *Space Vendetta* fan fics?"

"Maggie," I growl in warning.

Her expression shifts from disbelief to complete and utter shock as she reads. "Lily, you need to read this."

"Come on, Maggie. That's enough." I try to grab the computer, but she dances out of reach.

"Ransom's hand glides along the inside of her thigh. He's wanted to taste her since the first time he saw her on Nova Prime, but now he has her right where he wants her and he fully intends to taste every inch of her body before he releases her from his captivity." Maggie coughs and stops reading aloud.

My face flames red hot. I pluck at the seam of the pillow unable to meet her eyes.

"Whoa, this is hot," Lily says leaning over Maggie's shoulder and reading. "Did you write this?"

I nod, unable to breathe.

"It's good." Lily takes the laptop from Maggie and goes to the kitchen table. "Really good."

"Is this what you've been doing with all your free time? Writing smutty fan fiction?" Maggie props her hand on her hip.

"Not all my time, no." I shrug feeling the pain of my exposed secret ripping open further with her invasive questions.

"Does anyone know about this?" Her eyes widen. "Does Shaun?"

"My friend Madre knows. She writes fanfics too." I hang my head. "Shaun knows I read it, but not that I'm writing it. Please don't tell him."

"Madre? The chick you met on Tumblr a couple of months ago?"

I nod.

"I won't tell Shaun. But you should be honest with him." She shakes her head. "I mean I'd want to know if my girlfriend was writing vivid sexual fantasies about a fictional character instead of spending time with me."

"Actually, you should show this to him," Lily says from the kitchen, her voice husky. "Reading romance and erotica has been proven to increase intimacy between committed partners."

Maggie waves her off. "What I want to know is, how is this infatuation with a fictional character better than the flesh and blood stud muffin you've got eating from the palm of your hand?"

Her question pins me in place. I have no response.

"Jen." She reaches over and takes my hand. "I know you're still freaking out about this whole relationship. You were worried sex would ruin it. It didn't. Now you're freaking out and pushing him away filling the void with some space pirate played by an actor who doesn't even know you exist."

Her words sting, but I know she's right. I nod.

"Let's eat. Then Lily and I will leave you alone." She pats my hand. "You should call Shaun. I know he's worried about you too."

We join Lily at the table and my stomach growls at the sight of the Starlight's famous homemade chicken noodle soup. The three of us eat in silence, but a sense of peace settles over me. Even though they've uncovered my secret, they still love me.

I hope Shaun is as understanding as they are. Before I can overthink things, I send him a message inviting him over for dinner tomorrow night. I guess I'll find out.

CHAPTER FOURTEEN

STAGE THREE: THE FEELS (FRUSTRATION)

By four o'clock, I'm convinced the dust bunnies in my apartment do nothing but reproduce in multiples of ten. No amount of dusting and vacuuming seems to wrangle them into submission. Finally, I concede my defeat and take a shower.

Shaun should be here at five, and I want to start dinner before he arrives. I picked up some steaks to pan sear and finish in the oven. The Polish deli had some fresh pierogi this morning. I don't know if he's ever tried pierogi, so I figured this was a good opportunity to introduce him to one of my favorite foods.

A ten-minute shower rejuvenates me. I throw on a Vendetta T-shirt with a pair of my nice jeans and pin my hair up in a loose bun. It's a casual night in with my boyfriend, right? Then why do I have butterflies twisting in my stomach?

I pull the seasoned steaks from the fridge and let them sit at room temp while I chop some mixed veggies for a side.

My phone pings on the charger. I glance at the screen and see a message from Madre. After popping a piece of pepper in my mouth, I scan the contents.

Hey, Jen. Love the new chapter. Just sent you my reply. Sorry, it took me so damn long to respond. My kids are driving me crazy this weekend. Ugh. Anyway, I saw they're having comic con in Philly next month. Are you going? They announced Nicholas Hughes will be there. I'm trying to sweet-talk my husband into letting me go. We should meet up! Let me know what you think. ~Bonnie

Multiple realizations hit me simultaneously. One, what's a comic con? Two, Hughes is going to be there! Swoon. And three, meet Madre in person. While I process all the information, I do a few quick searches. Sure enough, Hughes signed up to appear at the con in Philly for two days. He's offering photo ops and autographs.

My heart flutters at the possibilities. How awesome would that be? Meeting him in person. Touching him. Talking to him. Oh God, smelling him. I'm a weirdo, I know. What can I say, I appreciate a man who smells good.

I click on the link and read through the options and frown. They're only offering the VIP Gold package which includes photo op and autograph.

"Holy shit!" I click on the price link and damn near choke on my own spit. "Five hundred bucks! Are you insane? Who the hell has that kind of money lying around?"

I chew on my lip and read through all the other options before returning to the main screen to see what other actors and artists are going to be there. It looks like there are quite a few actors from the franchise who have signed up.

From what I've read in his interviews, Hughes doesn't do a lot of public events. Especially fan-centered events. Wow. I can't believe I haven't heard any of this on the blogs I follow. I log into Tumblr and see the posts flooding my wall. The event announced his attendance last night.

"Well, that explains why it's plastered all over the fandom sites now," I mutter to myself.

I finish cutting veggies and pull out Grammy's iron skillet while the possibilities of comic con flash through my mind. Getting to Philly wouldn't be a problem. I could easily take the train. I wonder if Lily and Maggie would go with me. No, they wouldn't get anything from it, plus I don't think I could handle Maggie tormenting me all weekend.

Madre might be going. It would be fun to meet her then spend the whole weekend fangirling with someone who understands. I won't lie. It worries me meeting someone in person when I met them on the internet under a pseudonym. She could be a serial killer luring me into a trap.

Maggie would flip her shit if I met up with a total stranger. But what if Shaun went along? I mean, it wouldn't hurt to ask if he's interested in attending with me.

I heat up the oil in the skillet and drop the steaks in to sizzle.

A few minutes on each side and I tuck them in the pan side by side before sliding the skillet into the oven.

The doorbell rings. I glance at the clock. Five to five. I shake my head. He's so prompt.

"Hey, you." He grins and hands me a bouquet of fresh gerbera daisies.

"Hi." I take his offering and invite him in. Once I close the door, he wraps his arms around me and kisses me.

All the thoughts swirling in my mind fly right out the window at the insistent heat of his mouth on mine. I cling to him and melt.

"I missed you," I murmur against his mouth.

His lips quirk in a half-smile. "I thought you forgot all about me."

"Not at all." I squeeze his hand. "It's been a rough couple of weeks."

"I understand." He tucks a lock of my hair behind my ear. "You can always call me if you need anything."

"I know." Guilt digs its claws into my mind.

"Dinner smells fantastic." He moves toward the kitchen. "Need any help?"

Grateful for the shift in conversation, I instruct him to chop an onion while I heat up a skillet with butter. In another pot, I steam the veggies I chopped earlier.

Shaun falls into a companionable banter with me as we cook. I like this. Working alongside him on something we both love...something domestic. As I figured, he's never heard of a pierogi and is fascinated by the concept of mashed potatoes and cheese tucked inside a pasta shell. Carb on carb, or as I like to call them, little slices of heaven.

Once the food is ready, he helps me set the table. I'm so glad I spent the morning getting my apartment in order. I hate having to clean a week's worth of accumulated junk off the table for a meal.

He praises my steaks and devours a half dozen pierogis. I wish I would have bought two bags seeing how much he enjoys them. I make a mental note for next time and smile. Yet another thing we have in common. It warms my heart.

"Oh, man. That was amazing." He pushes his plate away and sighs with contentment.

"I have some chocolate chip cookies for dessert." I collect our plates and put them in the sink.

He comes up behind me and wraps his arms around my waist. "You definitely know how to sweeten me up."

I try to shove him out of the kitchen, but he insists on helping me with the dishes. I take the opportunity to ask him the question that's burned in my mind all evening.

"Have you ever been to a comic con?" I ask, scrubbing a plate.

"Yeah, a few times, mainly Chicago and Denver. Why?" He takes the plate and rinses it.

"Well, I saw they're having one in Philly next month. There are going to be quite a few of the actors from *Space Vendetta* there." I glance at him out of the corner of my eye trying to gauge his interest without seeming overeager.

"It sounds like it would be fun. What weekend is it?" Shaun takes the glass from my hand and rinses it.

"The last weekend, I think." I act casual, but inside I'm dancing around in circles at the possibilities. "I'll double-check once we finish cleaning up."

Once we have the kitchen cleaned. I curl up on the couch beside him with my laptop. Together we scroll through the convention itinerary. He seems as interested as me, which shouldn't be a surprise because he's also a fan. Clearly, I'm the only one who doesn't understand how to control myself when I get excited about something.

He checks his work calendar on his phone and groans. "Damn it. I have a conference for work in Chicago that weekend."

"Damn." My mood dips into a mire of disappointment. "I was hoping we could have cosplayed too."

"Trying to get me into Ransom's tight leather pants, huh?" He teases me and kisses the corner of my mouth. "I mean, you can ask me nicely. I don't need a comic con to put on some hot pants for you, baby."

The thought of Shaun wearing Ransom's costume makes my blood heat. I lick my lips and laugh it off. "I don't think I could fit in Lynnea's costume anyway."

"You'd look amazing." He whispers in my ear, "It would be on the floor pretty damn quick anyway."

Heat pulses between my thighs. I'm speechless.

Shaun leans back and traces his fingertips along my neck. "If you want to go, why don't you ask Lily and Maggie? Make it a girl's getaway weekend."

I chew on my lip. "I don't think they'd enjoy it."

"You never know if you don't ask." His touch makes me ache for more.

"I'll ask, but I may end up going by myself." I don't have the guts to mention Madre will be there along with some of the other fangirls I've met online.

"If you feel comfortable with that, then I trust your judgment." He smiles when I stare at him open-mouthed. "What?"

"You don't care that I want to attend to a comic con in another city alone?"

He shrugs. "You're an adult, Jen. You've survived as an independent woman this long. In New York City, no less. I think you can handle comic con without me hovering over your shoulder."

As much as it thrills me to hear him say this, I still feel guilty about leaving out key details. Finally, I cave. "Well, Madre is going. She wanted to meet up."

He arches a brow. "Madre? The fangirl you've been messaging for the past few months?"

I nod. "Yeah. Her real name is Bonnie. She lives in the Midwest with her husband and two kids."

"Bless her heart. No wonder she wants to get away for the weekend." He grins. "Honestly, if you're comfortable with it, then I trust your judgment."

"Really?" I beam at him. "No lecture on meeting strangers on the internet and traveling alone as a single woman?"

"Not from me." He cups my cheek in his palm. "I know better than to tell a woman what to do. I have three sisters. It never ends well."

"Three sisters?" I gape at him. "How come this is the first time I'm hearing this important fact about you?"

He chuckles. "We may have been officially dating for close to four months, but there's a lot you don't know about me."

"I know, but why haven't I heard this specific tidbit before?" I smack myself mentally.

"Well, I never mentioned it." He nuzzles my neck, and his hot mouth on my skin makes me gasp. "Besides, we only get to spend one day a week together, if that, and I don't want to spend it talking about my sisters when I could be doing this."

Starlight infuses me. How is this man real? I cling to him as he pulls me across his lap and kisses me hard. Desperately, passionately, thoroughly Shaun claims my mouth and then the rest of my body until nothing exists in my mind but him and his talented mouth.

"I love you," I murmur when he draws the first orgasm from me.

"Is that the orgasm talking?" he asks with a smirk.

I shake my head. "No. But maybe we should try again and see if it happens twice."

Twenty minutes later we're both naked and sated lying on the couch our heads resting on my Space Vendetta pillows. He draws my Ransom blanket around us and kisses my cheek.

"Definitely not the orgasm." His soft chuckle tickles my neck. "I love you too."

I snuggle closer to him. How did I get so lucky? And why does it make my heart ache?

CHAPTER FIFTEEN

A rush of relief washed over me when I returned to my apartment. After another insane week at work and the chaos of fandom chatter, I need some time to myself. I try to plug back into reality by taking the morning for myself.

There were a handful of boho shops and small businesses I wanted to check out. So I did. Then I splurged on lunch at the café near the harbor. Maggie told me about the place a few months ago, but today's weather proved perfect for sitting outside and enjoying the skyline in the distance. It was exactly what I needed to recharge.

Up until this moment, I was able to suppress the need to check my phone every five seconds. The weight of it in my purse gave me a gentle reminder I had my lifeline, but when I catch myself reaching for it, I make a conscious decision to let it go. Why is this so damn hard?

I try desperately to ignore the pull, the need to check in with my girls. The desire to reblog gif posts or make notes for my next fan fiction. I fucking try. In the end, I can't stop myself. I have to know. I have to see him.

I slip the phone from my purse and see notifications scrolling down my screen. When I open Tumblr, I see the headline for a new article. My heart sinks to the pit of my stomach where it burns in acid and bile, threatening to make me heave my lunch all over my living room.

Nicholas Hughes has a girlfriend. A new one. Some musician I once enjoyed. Well, there goes that playlist.

I click the link and cringe at the photographs. There is a series of images lined up with captions. Them holding hands, walking side by side on the beach, him leaning close to her whispering sweet nothings and secret promises. My vision blurs at the images poisoning my mind.

I want to throw the fucking phone. I bite my lip to keep from screaming the agony clawing at the inside of my chest. I'm home, I can make a scene if I want and no one will see it. I can throw a goddamn temper tantrum right now and no one would know.

The world stills around me. I stare at the screen in shock and disbelief.

Why the hell am I acting like a jealous girlfriend who caught her man with another woman? I have absolutely zero say or control in anything he does with his life. He's an adult and can make his own damn decisions. He's not mine. He never was. Nicholas Hughes is a complete stranger with his own life. I'm a fan with a serious crush.

I shake my head. What the hell is wrong with me? I have a wonderful boyfriend, one who treats me with love and respect. Guilt twists in my chest. I push it away and take a sip of my iced caramel macchiato.

Fangirls. Why do we even exist? What does it mean? I feel the weight of the world bearing down on my soul. I toss my phone on the couch and head into my bedroom.

A poster of Captain Ransom hangs on my wall. A high-quality photograph sits framed on my nightstand. It's got a black scribble on the bottom of it. His signature. I picked it up cheap at one of the comic shops downtown. There's a small collage of his characters framed in the bathroom complete with cutesy hearts and ridiculous memes. It always made me chuckle, until now. Now it makes me miserable.

I grab my laptop from my dresser and head back out to the couch.

Frustrated, I toss the Vendetta throw pillows to the floor and flip the blanket around so I don't have to see his face. Looking at it now only triggers images of him and her on the beach making googly eyes at each other. Makes me gag.

His image stares back at me from the round pillow on the floor. I kick it over with my foot. Fury replaces this unreasonable sense of loss and disappointment. I want to beat the hell out of the pillow, shred it, light it on fire, throw it in the street, and let the dogs piss on it. Transference much?

Instead, I boot up the laptop and log into my email. I need to purge this...whatever this is, and the only person who will understand is fifteen hundred miles away. My curiosity burns bright and hot, itching for me to check updates.

I want no part of it.

My phone pings and I pinch my eyes close. *Damn it.*

I snatch it from between the cushions where it fell earlier. A notification from Madre. I open the app and read through her personal message sent for my eyes only. I'm glad she did it away from the group. I don't want to hear their bullshit. Not now.

Did you see the Hughes news?

I sigh and respond. *Yes. I saw it. When the fuck did this happen?*

She responds right away. *I guess they've been together for over two months. They've been keeping it quiet. I guess the paparazzi finally caught a whiff of their whirlwind affair.*

This is so stupid. They have literally nothing in common. He's so sophisticated and level-headed. She's...well, she's not his type. At. All.

I switch to my laptop and open Tumblr. There's a private message from one of my followers. She thought she could soften the blow by letting me know before I saw it plastered all over social media. Too late. Too fucking, goddamn late.

She's not a fan of his, but she tries to understand. How could she really? Truth is, she can't, no one can understand the internal agony twisting in the pit of my stomach. I close the window without responding and instead read Madre's reply.

No. She's not his type, I agree. The fandom is blowing up over it right now. Half of them are excited about the news, the other half are in a rage and blowing up social media. Sigh. I'm going to keep my head down and avoid all the drama right now.

Madre has a point.

*Sounds like a good idea. I think I'll take a week or so and see if the fandom calms down before logging on. I can't even bear to look at the photographs of them together. Makes me wanna puke. *gags**

Agreed. It feels like an ad for a new cheesy rom-com. Haha. On a side note, are you still interested in going to comic con at the end of next month? My husband gave me the green light. I'm going to book my flight and hotel this week. I've already bought my passes for the con. Her response makes me smile. *It'd be great to finally meet you in person.*

As long as I don't have to deal with fandom drama, I'm game. I'll order my tickets next week after payday. I hit send and the unease I felt at seeing Nicholas with his new girlfriend pulls at my conscience. Do I want to deal with that?

If it gives me a chance to see him in person, yes, it's worth it. Even if I can't afford the VIP Gold package, I may be able to catch a glimpse of him.

Awesome. Madre responds after a few minutes. *If you need a place to crash, you're welcome to stay with me. Promise I'm not a creepy old man who's luring you to his hotel room in order to steal your kidney. Seriously, it might be easier for us to split the cost of the room.*

I laugh out loud. *Sounds good to me. I'll be tapping my savings account to come, so it'll be nice to save a few pennies. If you book the room, I'll send you half once I get paid.*

*Perfect. I've had my eye on the hotel across from the convention center. If we're lucky, we may run into some famous peeps staying in our hotel. *wink**

I stare at Madre's message. "Wait, there's a chance we could see him outside the con?" Hope blooms inside my chest, then I remember. He has a girlfriend now. What if she goes with him? Hope sours into bitterness and I slide right back into a shitty mood.

Madre sends another message. *I need to take my son to his baseball game. I'll send you the details later. Xoxo. Chat soon and don't forget. No social media all week. I'll let you know when the fandom chills out.*

Thanks. I respond before taking my phone into my bedroom where the charger is.

When I plug it in, a message comes in from Lily asking if Shaun will be coming to game night since her roommates decided to invite themselves tonight. My shoulders slump. I don't know if I can deal with people right now. Part of me wants to curl up in a ball under the blankets and sleep for a week.

But if I bail on them tonight, I'll never hear the end of it. I text Shaun and extend the invitation. When he finally responds, yes, I relay the message to Lily.

Stripping as I walk, I head into the bathroom. Nicholas's gaze follows me from where his picture is taped to my mirror, right next to a photo booth series of pictures of me and Shaun. I touch his face, but my gaze lingers on Nicholas. I turn away, unable to look at either of them. Unable to stomach my own fucking reflection.

Something's wrong with me. I know. I'm overreacting. Nicholas Hughes has never been mine, and he never will be. So why the hell does it matter if he found happiness in the form of a tall, leggy blonde with more money than brains?

It shouldn't. And still, the image of them together flashes in my mind again. I lean my head against the wall and reach inside the shower to turn on the water. *Leave me alone. I hate you. I fucking hate you.*

Why? Because someone I've never met has the audacity to find happiness and love? Yes, damn it, because it's not me in those photographs.

I step under the spray and hiss at the sting of the heat biting into my skin hoping it will wash away the shame of these thoughts. Shame because I already have a wonderful man in my life. I shouldn't be upset over this. I should focus on my own relationship. The man who goes out of his way to make me feel wanted and desired.

What if Shaun knew? What would he say? Would he call me obsessed and leave with a disgusted look on his face? He knows part of my fascination but not the depth of my fantasies. I can't bring myself to tell him. He would leave and never return.

The thought sobers me quickly. Would I throw away my relationship with Shaun for some adolescent crush on a man I could never in a million years hope to even meet?

I soak up the heat of the water letting it burn the ache from my mind. I wash again, even though I took a shower this morning. I feel dirty. Ashamed, angry, and frustrated. I want to rage against something. Maybe I should write before I go to Lily's. I can't face them like this. I need to purge these thoughts in my mind.

Am I one of thousands of fangirls with a broken heart right now? Dreams shattered for a romance we will never experience. A fantasy that will never become a reality.

I shut off the water and step from the shower. I can't go out like this. But I can't stay home either, tempted to log online and see this train wreck again, even by accident. No fics, no binge-watching his movies. No. I need to unplug.

I need my friends. I need Shaun. But even more, I need to get a grip on this chaos threatening to take control of my brain. Nicholas Hughes does not belong to me. He doesn't owe me a damn thing, and I must remember this before it's too late.

CHAPTER SIXTEEN

Come the following Monday morning, I'm emotionally exhausted from hiding my fangirl disappointment from not only my friends and family but my boyfriend too. Somewhere along the line, I crossed into some deep waters. Now I'm drowning, and I can't reach out to anyone around me.

I drag myself into the office, barely making it in time to clock in. Lily waves from across the room. I shoot her a half-hearted smile and return the wave.

Instead of hunting down a cup of coffee, I dive right into my inbox knowing I have a ton of work to get done before the quarterly meeting next week. If I'm going out of town at the end of June, then I need to get my priorities straightened out before then.

I slog through about four emails before I can barely keep my eyes open. Stifling a yawn, I wander toward the break room. I'll probably have to make a fresh pot of coffee; hopefully, Niki brought in some of the good shit her family sends from Hawaii.

The breakroom is empty and so is the coffee pot. I frown and rifle through the cabinets. In the back of the third cabinet, I find a half-empty bag of Sumatra. Coffee is coffee at this point, and I can't complain if it's not what I was craving.

Once I get the coffee brewing, I lean against the counter and pull my phone out. There are a few notifications on Discord. I ignore those. Madre sent me something via Tumblr. I open the link and scan through the headline.

A fic? I scan through the summary and cringe. Pairing: Ransom/Colton. In the past few months, I've seen some interesting pairings, but nothing with these two. They're polar opposite. Colton is the quintessential hero archetype while Ransom is his nemesis. I read through the tags. Angry sex. Hate fucking. Genderswap. Tentacle porn. Undersea AU. What the ever-loving fuck?

Why the hell would Madre send me this? There isn't a single tag that fits my typical reading preferences. Even the pairing is way off. I scroll down further and find the picture. The image burns into my retinas.

"Oh my God." I gag and throw the phone.

"Good thing you have a sturdy case on this thing." Shaun picks up my phone and inspects it. Then he sees the picture.

I bite back the whimper coagulating in the back of my throat. My moment of judgment has arrived. Of course, he would see this. All the shit he could find in my search history, this is where it lands at his feet. Literally.

His eyes widen as he scrolls up and then back down. Finally, he laughs.

"Rule Thirty-four." He shakes his head and hands me my phone.

We're a foot apart now. Even though there's no one in the room, anyone could walk in at any moment. The last thing I need right now are rumors flying around the office. His voice drops low enough to keep our conversation somewhat private.

"I tried to warn you." He chuckles. "Is this what you've been doing with your free time?"

"No." I lock the screen and return my phone to my pocket. My tone is defensive. I shouldn't be. He's been a fucking saint with my yoyo mood lately, and I already feel guilty as hell.

"Is something wrong?" He grabs an empty cup and pours a cup of fresh coffee.

When he hands it to me, I take it without a word. How can I even answer that question? I add some creamer while he pours some for himself.

"You've been distant lately." His fingers brush mine when he takes the creamer. "I don't want you to think I'm prying, but I am worried about you, Jen."

The soft sweetness in his tone jabs a painful shard of guilt through my chest. I have been a shitty girlfriend. Hell, I've been a shitty friend. I owe him and the girls an apology for how off I've been lately, but why should I feel guilty for enjoying something and spending time on it?

I shrug. "Nothing's wrong. It's..." I bite my tongue not wanting to lie, but not ready to tell him the truth and sound like I'm losing my grip on reality. "Work has been kicking my ass lately. I guess it's more than I thought it would be."

"You're doing the job of two people right now." He smiles. "Give yourself some credit. You're practically a shoe-in for the upcoming promotion."

"Thanks. I can't seem to make any headway with the orders and organizing the data in the system." I scoff. "One step forward and two steps back."

"If you need help, you can ask the rest of your team to take a little bit off your plate and make it more manageable." Shaun takes a sip of his coffee. "No one would fault you for asking for some help."

"I would." I groan. "But there's no reason I can't do this." Deep inside I know the real reason I can't get ahead with my paperwork at the office. I'm distracted when I'm off the clock. Adventuring through fantasies with Nicholas Hughes provides such an alluring alternative to stats and numbers and orders and logistics.

"You can do it." He rests his hand on my shoulder and the innocent gesture ignites need inside me. I miss him. I do. I miss his warmth, his kiss, his touch. "I have faith in you."

"Thanks."

He leans close and whispers in my ear. "Saturday night. You're mine. No excuses."

Heat infuses my veins. His simple words flip a switch somewhere deep in my subconscious, and I'm inundated with images of him wearing leather, his hand wrapped around my throat, whispering wicked words against my skin.

Shaun takes his coffee and leaves me standing boneless in a pool of my own need in the breakroom. How the hell am I supposed to work now?

After a few deep breaths, I'm able to compose myself into some semblance of a dutiful employee and return to my desk. It's difficult to shake the tantalizing thoughts from my mind, but somehow I do.

Before I realize it, Lily's tapping my shoulder. "Hey. Want to grab some lunch in the café?"

"Damn." I glance at the clock on my screen. Noon already?! Wow. I guess I must have finally found the zone. "Yeah, sure." I nod and turn off my monitor.

Lily's animated chatter dominates the ride in the elevator. We put our order in at the café and find a small table near the window.

"You doing better?" Lily asks, sipping her water. She adjusts the lime-colored scarf tied prettily around her neck. "You seemed off on Saturday night?"

"Yeah. I'm good." I crack open my soda.

"Good." Lily shifts in her seat and smiles. "If you need to talk, call me, okay. I don't care if it sounds stupid or you think I wouldn't understand." She rests her hand on mine. "You can always come to me. No judgment. Promise."

"Thanks, Lily. I appreciate it." I cover her hand and squeeze. "You're too pure for this world. The sweetest cinnamon roll."

"Cinnamon roll?" Lily chuckles and tilts her head in confusion.

"Yeah, it's a fandom word used to describe a character who deserves the best things, selfless and sweet, but always seems to catch the short end of the stick."

"Yeah, that's me." She wrinkles her nose. "I attract the strangest men. They don't appreciate this vintage goddess."

"Have you stepped out in the dating pool again?" I ask and take a sip of my drink. The fizz tickles the back of my throat.

"Kinda." Lily shrugs a shoulder. "I downloaded the app Gavin told us about. I figured there had to be some vintage groups or something. There's a group for pin-ups. Super fun, actually. There were a couple of guys in the group, but they keep to themselves."

"Have you been getting unsolicited dick pics in your personal messages?" I frown trying to tamper down my rage. How dare they soil my pretty, sweet Lily with their nasty sausage selfies?

"No. Nothing that bad." She sighs. "Just some internet catcalls. Nothing I haven't heard before. It's exhausting."

"Well, if they give you any more shit, send me their name and I'll light up their DMs."

"Awww, defending my honor." Lily laughs. "How cute. You know I'm not as innocent as I look, Jen."

"I know. It's fun to pretend there's one of us in the group who isn't a kinky freak." I wink.

"I'll let you have your little fantasy, but there are some things you can't unsee should you choose to pry into my sex life." Lily winks.

"Oh God, that reminds me." I launch into the story of the fanfic and the picture Madre sent me this morning. Lily doubles over laughing when I tell her Shaun caught me in the middle of this realization.

"Whoever this Madre is, she certainly has a great sense of humor. I like her."

"Me too." I hedge around the idea of telling Lily about my plans to attend the comic con and finally give in. "I'm planning on going to comic con in Philly at the end of June. We're going to meet up there."

Lily's eyes widen. Fortunately, the waiter interrupts us with our lunch. Once he disappears, Lily rounds on me.

"Is Shaun going with you?" she asks.

"No. He has a conference that weekend." I take a bite of my sandwich.

"You're going alone?" She squeals this time.

"That's the plan." I shrug. "What's the problem? I've traveled alone before. Not a big deal."

"Yes, but you're planning on meeting up with strangers you met online." Lily bites her lip. "Why don't I go with you? At least then we could keep an eye out for each other."

"Lily, I don't want to put you out." My heart softens even as the guilt wraps around it. I should have asked her, but I wanted this to be just for me.

"If you don't want me to come, I understand." She takes a

bite of her panini and pouts. "But you need to have a safety plan in place."

"I will, Lily. Don't worry. And please don't tell Maggie. I don't need a lecture on internet safety and making good choices."

Lily laughs. "I won't tell her. Your secret adventure is safe with me."

"Thanks."

The conversation shifts back to Lily's foray into the Discord chat groups. She tells me about the different styles she's seen and some new ideas for dresses their discussions inspired. One of the men in the group has a cowboy hat as his icon and it's inspired a whole outfit.

It's nice to see Lily's passion invested in her clothing and style. I wonder if I'm nearly as cute when I fangirl over Nicholas Hughes. Probably not. I look like a stalker with no life. Ugh, something has to give or I'll end up as desperate as those men who send unsolicited dick pics.

Once I get home, I send Madre a message berating her for sending me something so Not-Safe-For-Work when she knew I was at work. The immediate response is a picture of a bottle of bleach with the words Brain Bleach across the label. I laugh out loud.

With friends like these, who needs enemies. I love them all equally.

CHAPTER SEVENTEEN

Lily practically bounces on her tiptoes beside me. "Thank you for letting me do this. You're like the perfect candidate."

"You mean Maggie wouldn't let you give her a makeover," I tease her as we walk down the sidewalk heading toward the upscale boutiques.

"Well, that, but honestly, it needs to be themed. You're the only one I know who would even be game for it." Lily grins and winks. "Plus, it'll be a nice touch for your hot date with Shaun tonight." She fans herself dramatically. "He won't know what to do with all this sexiness."

I scoff. She's optimistic, which is typical for Lily. The pin-up community group Lily joined a few months ago issued a challenge to create the most creative pin-up ensemble based on a character from a book or film series. Of course, Maggie has no lingering interest in either pin-up couture or *Space Vendetta.* She only has eyes for her video games. It would be a lie for me to say I'm not excited at the prospect of channeling my inner Vendetta vixen.

We slip into an innocuous shop with a red fox over the door. I hang back and let Lily work her magic. This is her world. I'm letting her do the talking.

The shop bursts at the seams with a plethora of vintage garments. I run my hand over the rack inside the door feeling the textures of the fabrics. The patterns range from paisley to stripes to polka dots to bold solids. Every now and then I catch a glimpse of more modern designs, but before I can reach for them, Lily grabs my arm.

"Vikki will be our stylist. I've told her what I'm looking for and she's pulling some dresses for you." Lily drags me in front of a tri-fold floor-length mirror.

I cringe at the jeans and T-shirt combo I'm wearing beside

the vintage casual Lily rocks so effortlessly. Today she's wearing a teal wiggle dress with white polka dots. God, her curves look amazing in it. I know if I try on the same dress, I'll resemble an overbaked potato.

"As soon as Vikki returns, you can start trying on dresses. I'll sit over here and text Armando." She grins. "He's my stylist. I'm calling in a favor. He's the only one I know who can do the curls right."

I shake my head in a panic. "No, Lily. Don't call in any favors for me. I don't need my hair done. Seriously. We can do something simple."

Lily tuts. "No. You're getting the full workup. I've also asked Marco to meet us in the park by the bridge at five so we can snap some pics." She does a little excited wiggle. "This is gonna be so good."

I can't bring myself to ruin her good mood. This is her artistic project. I'm merely the medium. When Vikki appears, I select one of the dresses and disappear into the changing room.

Most of the dresses are bold colors or patterns. She selected the swing styles instead of the form-fitting wiggle dresses. Thank goodness. I'd be way too self-conscious with all my curves on display.

After a half dozen vehement noes from Lily, defeat settles over me. I slip on the dark green swing dress with leather accents. I'm not sure I can even discern the shape of the dress until I finally fasten it around my throat. A halter-style swing dress. The cold air conditioning brushes my arms making me shiver. I step from behind the curtain.

Lily's eyes narrow and she slowly rises from her seat. "Yes." Her gaze skims down the length of me and back up again. "That's the one."

"Really?" I turn and examine my reflection. For a moment, I'm stunned. The cut of the dress hugs my natural figure adding enough to flatter my curves without distracting from the flow of the fabric. I do a little twirl in the mirror and the skirt fans around me flashing a glimpse of my thighs amid green petticoat ruffles. Damn. I catch Lily's approving nod and grin.

I spend the next thirty minutes trying on shoes and settle on a pair of strappy kitten heels in black leather. Lily selects a few accessories while I gather my clothes from the dressing room. She even insisted I put on some sexier lingerie. Honestly, I feel like I'm going to burst out of the skimpy lace garments she chose. But there must be something to it because I feel ten times hotter now than I did earlier.

She's waiting at the counter for me. The cashier slides her Am Ex Black card into her hand.

"Wait. You can't buy this for me. Seriously," I protest, but Lily holds up her hand.

"My treat. You're my friend, and this is my project. So I'll take care of expenses." She chuckles. "Besides, I rarely use this card."

"Dare I even ask why you have a Black Am Ex?" I mutter beneath my breath.

"Oh, well, Dad insists I carry it." She laughs but it sounds forced. "For emergencies."

"This isn't an emergency, Lily." I glower as I pick up my bags and follow her out of the store.

"I know, but I need to use it once a month, or Dad calls me in a tizzy." She shrugs. "Not a big deal." She links her arm with mine, and together we teeter down the sidewalk in our kitten heels looking like we stepped from the pages of a vintage fashion magazine.

We hail a cab and take it to the salon where Armando is waiting with his small makeover army.

I shoot Lily a death glare as we settle into our seats for an afternoon of pampering and primping. This is definitely not something I'm used to. As Armando assesses his canvas, aka my hair, I finally relax. Lily would never lead me astray. If I could trust anyone with a makeover, it would be her.

Armando and his assistants give me the five-star treatment. When I finally leave the salon two hours later, I swear the whole experience is better than sex. I love having someone play with my hair, but I can't afford to have a stylist on call let alone see one for a trim every eight weeks. Being pampered like this could spoil me.

Lily squeals when we settle in the cab. "You look amazing! Shaun's going to freak out."

"I'm freaking out. You certainly have an eye for this style, Lily."

"We have one more stop before we meet Marco." A wicked gleam sparks in her eyes.

Uncertainty fills my gut. "Whoa, where are we going?"

"It's a surprise." She presses her finger to her pursed lips.

Anxiety twists in the pit of my stomach as the cab takes us deeper into the city. Finally, it pulls to a stop in front of a small row of shops.

"Come on." Lily pulls my hand.

Together we step out onto the street. That's when I see it. JD's Comics and More. It's one of the more famous comic shops in the five boroughs. I've been meaning to check them out for months, but it seems Lily knows exactly what I'm thinking. She tugs my hand.

"He's waiting for us."

He. Who's he? My heart stops when we open the door and step inside. I can't stop myself from spinning around trying to take in the whole shop at once. There are comics, floor to ceiling, around the whole shop. Cases of figurines and games litter the main floor. A man behind a glass counter looks up from the comic he's reading.

"Lily!" He comes around the counter and hugs her.

I stare at the two of them and wonder what I missed. How does she know him?

"Jen, this is JD. He owns the shop." Lily beams. "JD, this is Jen. She's a huge fan of *Space Vendetta*."

"Really?" He shakes my hand. "Nice to meet you. Have you gotten hooked on the books?"

I shake my head. "Not yet."

"Well, let me know if you want to start. I can hook you up." He winks. He's in his mid-thirties with salt and pepper hair, a crooked smile, and warm blue eyes. Handsome, but not in a traditional way.

"Thanks. I'll keep that in mind." I glance at Lily who's turned her attention to the contents of the glass case.

"What can I do for you today, ladies?" JD leans against the case.

"Well, I'm trying to get a Vendetta vixen vibe going for my friend." Lily bites her lip. "Do you think you have a piece or two that could enhance this gender-swapped Captain Ransom?"

JD strokes his chin while he appraises me from head to foot. I resist crossing my arms and hiding from view. This was the whole point of the makeover, to make a statement. Instead, I rest my hand on my hip and give my best sassy pose.

He laughs. "Yeah, I think I have something that will work."

Lily motions for me to join her when JD retreats behind the counter. He shuffles inside a cabinet before pulling out a leather box. An expensive-looking box. I swallow hard and try not to think about the cost of the contents.

He opens the box and pushes it closer for our inspection. "What do you think?"

Inside the box is a leather choker with a silver medallion encircling a dark green gem. A pair of leather cuffs and matching earrings lay inside the box.

"Perfect," Lily says before I can stop her. My voice dies in my throat. "I'll take them."

"You got it." JD takes the Black Am Ex and rings up the sale while Lily turns to me.

"Let's put these on and make some magic." Her excitement is infectious. I relent if only to keep from killing the mood. I can't let her foot the bill for this. There's no way.

After she's fitted the jewelry and paid the bill, Lily leads me back to the waiting cab. As soon as we're in motion, I round on her.

"I can't accept these. It's too much, Lily." I beg feeling guilty.

"You can and you will." Her gaze softens, and she takes my hand. "I don't often splurge like this. You gave me a reason to get out and enjoy the benefits of having a rich father who doesn't give a shit how much money I spend."

"You never told me how rich your dad is." My voice is soft.

"I normally don't tell anyone." She shrugs. "But you've been working so hard at work and you needed a morale boost." Her hand squeezes mine. "I've seen how hard you've been struggling lately. You needed something special. Something just for you."

Tears threaten to ruin my perfect winged liner and thick mascara. I blink them away and smile. "Thank you, hon. I appreciate it. Although you didn't have to buy me anything. Being with you was enough to boost my spirits."

Her red lips quiver. "I know. I wanted to do it. Plus, I want to hear all about Shaun's heart attack when he sees your sexy pin-up makeover."

I laugh out loud. "I imagine we won't make it to dinner. He may drag me right to the bedroom."

"Good." She winks. "At least one of us will get some tonight."

With a laugh, I pull her into a hug. "You're the best. Thanks again, Lily. I owe you."

"I'll remember you said that." She smooths her skirt and crosses her ankles. "Now, lay out your plans for comic con. I want to make sure you've got your shit together."

As the cab weaves through traffic, I tell Lily my plans for comic con and vow to keep her in the loop via text the whole time. I even allow her to track my location because that's what friends do when they're overly paranoid.

When we reach the park, we find Marco waiting for us. I pose for some sexy pictures against the skyline and then head home, bracing myself for Shaun's reaction when he arrives at seven. I can only hope he appreciates the temporary transformation.

CHAPTER EIGHTEEN

Shaun will be here any minute. I take one last glimpse in the mirror and smooth my hand over the sexy curls Armando wrangled into submission earlier. Butterflies take flight in the pit of my stomach.

With the hair and makeup, it's a stunning transformation. I hardly recognize myself. The whole ensemble is beautiful and artistic, but it's not a style I would wear often. Only once in a while, maybe. I honestly don't know how Lily can pull off this level of sophistication on a daily basis. It truly boggles my mind.

Judging from the photos Marco took, I unleashed some deep part of my ego or subconscious. I hope they earn Lily first place in their little Discord group competition. I did my best to channel my inner Ransom vixen. She promised to email me the photos as soon as Marco touches them up.

The doorbell echoes through the apartment. The butterflies take flight again, and I smooth my hands over the skirt before I open the door.

Shaun's soft whiskey gaze transforms into molten chocolate. "Holy shit, Jen. You look good enough to eat."

"Thanks." My whole body warms. I spin in a slow circle giving him the full three hundred-and-sixty-five-degree tour of my transformation. "Lily outdid herself."

"Remind me to thank her on Monday morning." He steps forward and snatches me by the waist. I feel his hard length pressed against me. He holds me close and presses his lips to mine.

I melt into his touch, into his kiss. It's been too long since we've been alone together. His hands grip my hips and fist in the fabric. I'm drunk on him. Any longer and I doubt either of us will be willing to leave the apartment for the rest of the night.

When he finally breaks the kiss, we're both breathless.

"We should go if we're going to make our dinner reservation." He licks his lips. My red lipstick leaves traces on his mouth. It makes me smile seeing him so undone by a kiss.

"You're right." I grab a tissue from inside my purse and wipe away the evidence of our kiss from his mouth. "Is my makeup okay?"

He runs his thumb beneath my lower lip and nods. "Perfect."

I grab my bolo wrap and we head out into the warm evening air. We grab a taxi to the restaurant. When it stops in front of Star Shanty, an upscale seafood restaurant on the bay, I clap with delight. I've wanted to try it forever but could never justify the cost.

"How did you know I wanted to try this place?" I whirl around and catch Shaun staring.

"I know things." He winks then bursts into laughter. "Actually, I had to ask Maggie and Lily for suggestions. They both said this place was number one on your list."

"That's the sweetest thing." I lean over and kiss his cheek. "Thank you."

"Don't thank me yet," he whispers in my ear. "It could be absolutely horrible food. Let's reserve judgment until after the meal."

"Maybe we should do pizza at Mario's," I reply in an equally conspiratorial way.

"Nothing quite tops the first date, huh?" He chuckles.

We walk toward the entrance and I sway into him. "Sometimes it's the simple things that make the biggest impact."

"Agreed." He holds the door open. "After you, my Lady Ransom."

Inside the restaurant, the hostess seats us and I can feel people's curious gazes on me as I pass their tables. We take a small table toward the back of the restaurant with a perfect view of the bay and the skyline. Shaun orders drinks for us and an appetizer.

"Your outfit is certainly drawing a lot of attention." His gaze drops to the choker around my neck, and a blush steals across his cheeks.

"Yeah, I know." My fingers brush over the velvet at my throat. I'm a little more self-conscious than usual. "Something wrong? You keep looking at my choker."

He shakes his head. "It's unique. Where'd you find it?"

"Oh, Lily took me to a comic shop across town today. JD's Comics and More."

Shaun sputters midway through taking a sip of water. "You're serious? I've been meaning to stop there. It's the most popular comic shop on the east coast."

"Yeah. Lily asked JD for something special to give me a more Vendetta vibe for the outfit." I glance at the menu in my hands.

"I figured that's what you were going for." He chuckles. "You look like a pin-up version of a gender-swapped Captain Ransom."

"Exactly what Lily was hoping for." I beam. "She joined a pin-up makeover challenge in this group she's involved with." I downplay my excitement. "I guess she took my fangirling to a whole new level."

"She did an amazing job." He lowers his voice. "I almost didn't want to take you out in public like that in case someone got ideas about stealing you away."

I laugh. "No one is stealing me away. I promise." I ponder the possibilities of wearing the dress again and the idea sticks. "I was thinking of wearing it to the comic con."

His gaze darkens. "Don't."

My laughter dies in my throat when I see his serious expression. "Why not? Are you afraid someone will steal me away in Philly?"

The waiter appears and takes our order. Once we're alone again, Shaun turns pensive, a muscle ticking in his jaw.

"Shaun." I reach across the table and take his hand. "I won't wear it to comic con. Okay?"

He relaxes beneath my touch. "Sorry. I...I don't want to control you or dictate what you can and can't do. But if you wear that, it will garner unwanted attention." He smooths his fingers over mine. "I won't be there to protect you."

"Do you think I'll need protection?" I tease him.

"Dressed like you are right now, yes." His frustrated exhale punctuates his internal struggle. "Men are idiots, and I don't trust they won't act like assholes. It's certainly not a reflection on you."

"I understand. I've seen a lot of posts lately about cosplay and consent and all kinds of drama." I squeeze his hand. "It's more drama than I'm prepared to take on anyway. Although, I do like dressing up."

"I think you look amazing. The spin would be a huge hit at comic con, but I won't be there to show everyone this gorgeous woman is already taken."

His words turn my insides to mush. "You're my hero."

"You'd rather have the villain, admit it." Shaun's smirk makes my stomach flip. He has a point but before I can answer the waiter brings our appetizer.

"Depends on the villain." I take a bite of the crab legs dripping with seasoned butter. The meat melts on my tongue. So delicious.

Shaun takes a bite and moans in appreciation. How is that sexy? I shake my head and focus on the glass of wine instead of the wicked ideas in my head.

"I know. Captain Ransom has your heart." He points the fork in my direction. "It's hard for me to compete with a fictional character, Jen."

His statement seems innocuous enough, but it sends a pang of guilt straight through me. The delicious crab turns to sawdust on my tongue. I reach for my wine and my mind spins. How do I respond without sounding like an absolute nutcase?

"I don't expect you to compete with a fictional character." I keep my tone light and playful. "Your personality is completely opposite of Captain Ransom anyway."

"What are you trying to say?" Mischief sparkles in his eyes.

"You're not selfish or vindictive. In fact, you're pretty damn perfect." I pop another bite into my mouth before I insert my foot instead.

Shaun scoffs. "I'm far from perfect."

"Really?" I cock my head and study his handsome features. "You're handsome, successful, charming, witty, thoughtful, and chivalrous without being overbearing. You get along with everyone, and I've never heard you raise your voice, not once."

He takes a long sip of wine. I can almost see the wheels turning in his mind, but he doesn't respond. The silence torments me. I take another bite of appetizer to keep my hands occupied.

"When did we meet? February?" Shaun sets his glass aside.

I think for a moment. "Sounds right."

"Do you think five months is enough time to know someone well?" he asks.

"Not really. I mean, I've known some people who've been married for years and still don't know everything about their spouse." I see where he's going with the conversation.

"Exactly." He leans closer. "I'm not perfect. You haven't spent enough time with me to see the darker side of my personality."

A laugh escapes me. "You have a dark side?"

"We all do, Jen." His gaze pins me in place. "Some of us hide it better than others."

"Are you saying I have a dark side?"

"Yes."

"And you see it?"

A wolfish smile curves his lips. "Yes."

"Care to enlighten me?"

"Later." He leans back when the waiter appears with our entrees.

I stare at my shrimp scampi, but my thoughts are fixated on Shaun's words.

"How are your parents?" he asks, shaking me free from my own head.

The conversation takes a dramatic shift to lighter topics. Shaun tells me about his family and being the only boy with three sisters. I tell him about my parents and Grammy. The rest of the meal passes with anecdotes of childhood and bad job experiences.

He takes me home and even though it's late, I invite him in. I need him.

The moment the door closes behind us. He pushes me against it and slides his hand along the inside of my thigh. When he reaches my lace panties, he growls and kisses me hard. He trails bites along my throat teasing the edges of my velvet choker.

"This." He slides his lips over my throat where skin meets fabric. "Has been driving me insane all night."

My mind can barely string together two coherent thoughts with his hands teasing my thighs and his hot mouth tormenting me. "Why?" I gasp through the haze of desperate need.

He chuckles and the vibration sends my body into overload. "You have no idea, do you?"

"What am I missing?" I moan when his fingers brush against my wet panties with enough pressure to make my legs tremble. "Tell me."

"Spoilers, love. Spoilers." He nips at my lower lip.

"Fuck spoilers, tell me." I'm panting now.

"In the last book, Ransom steals the rarest jewel in the galaxy. He hides it inside a worthless glass gem and has it fashioned into a gift for his woman." He smiles against my mouth.

"Lynnea?" I arch my hips against his hand.

"She has no idea of its true value, but he trusts her implicitly even though she hunted him to the ends of the galaxy."

"Why? They've hated each other for years." It's getting harder for me to focus on the words through the intensifying sensations.

"That's enough spoilers for now, kitten." He slides his fingers beneath the fabric and strokes my soaked folds before slipping deep inside me.

I grasp his shoulders tight. "Shaun, please."

"So needy. Aren't you, sweetheart?" He removes his hand and steps back.

Loss surrounds me. Before I can protest, he guides me into my bedroom and unzips my dress, unwrapping me like a present on Christmas morning. Once he slides the shoes from my feet and discards my thigh-high stockings, I'm left with only my lace panties and bra.

He regards me for half a moment before reaching for his own belt. "Take it off."

The heat in his gaze stuns me. I unfasten my bra and let it fall to the floor. Then I slide my panties off.

Shaun strips his shirt and points to the bed. "Lie down. Legs spread. I want to see all of you."

Uncertainty makes me hesitate for a fraction of a second, but I'm desperate for release at his hands. I do as he bids.

"Touch yourself."

His command sends a bolt of lust through me. I stroke my fingers through my arousal getting hotter with every pass.

"That's so fucking hot, kitten." He tosses aside the last of his clothes and climbs onto the bed. His heavy cock presses against my thigh as he kisses me.

When we break apart, I'm breathless and arching my body into him. I need him inside me. I want him now. My fingernails scrape against his back.

"Impatient, are we?" He reaches for the nightstand drawer and growls when he fishes in the drawer. There's a repeated slam of metal on wood.

I glance over and see him overturning my photographs. Not all of them. Just Nicholas. Just Ransom. Before I can ask him what the hell's going on, he tears open the condom, slides it over his cock, and settles himself between my thighs. He drives deep with one thrust.

"Shit." I grasp his arms and dig my nails into his skin.

He moves frenzied and desperate driving into me. "Is this what you wanted?"

"Yes." Instead of sweet lovemaking, he takes me. Relentlessly. Passionately. And I love every second of it, rocking into his thrusts for more friction, more everything.

Shaun's hand wraps around my throat enclosing the choker. He's gentle, but the pressure only amplifies the heat coursing through my body with lightning speed.

"Tonight, you're mine." He growls against my ear and tugs

the lobe between his teeth punctuating his words with the thrust of his hips. "Mine."

The intensity of his words sends me to the brink of orgasm. I'm so close I may explode. My fingers circle my clit while he drives deeper. His panting breaths against my ear echo my own. The moment my orgasm peaks, Shaun grasps my chin.

"Look at me when you come." His fathomless eyes draw me in.

My climax rips through me, and I cry out. He kisses me hard and doubles his pace drawing every drop of pleasure from me until I'm left trembling beneath him. His climax pulls him under, and I wrap my legs around him.

Shaun collapses against me. Our breaths mingle in the aftermath of pent-up frustration. He rolls to the side and draws me against him. We lay still until our heartbeats slow and our overheated skin cools.

"Damn." He mutters in surprise. I'm not sure if he's talking to me or himself.

I kiss his shoulder. He pulls me in for a lingering kiss and then slips from the bed to clean up.

Shaun flicks on the bathroom light, and I admire his broad figure in the doorway and the way the light highlights the curve of his ass. How did I get so damn lucky?

As he turns to close the door, I catch a glimpse of his profile. He doesn't look happy. Not at all.

Alone and naked, post amazing sex, I start questioning myself. Did I do something wrong? Is he upset with me? I chew on my lower lip and draw the blankets up over myself.

The toilet flushes and water runs beyond the door. My mind races. Do I say something? I brace myself when the door opens.

Shaun slides beneath the blankets and pulls me against him. He holds me close and peppers kisses across my forehead. My anxiety stills.

"You okay?" I mumble against his chest.

"I am now." He kisses me. "I love you, Jen."

"I love you too." Whatever fears I had moments ago fade away and we drift off to sleep.

It's not until after he leaves the next day I notice my photographs of Nicholas/Ransom taped to the bathroom mirror are gone without a trace.

CHAPTER NINETEEN
STAGE FOUR: DENIAL

When I round the corner, the Philadelphia Convention Center fills my view. My heart races. I see people wearing costumes and lanyards milling back and forth around the outside of the building. Excitement bubbles up inside me.

The moment I arrived at the 30th Street Station, I sent Madre a message letting her know I would meet her in the hotel lobby in an hour. The hour and a half train ride from New York to Philly gave me ample time to work on my next chapter of the fanfic, but honestly, I needed something to distract me from the nerves twisting in my gut.

I made sure to take Friday off and book the afternoon train so I didn't have to deal with rush hour and weekend traffic between cities. The convention starts officially at four o'clock. I glance at my watch. It's almost three.

The hotel is a few blocks from the convention center, which is fine. I walk down the opposite side of the street, stealing glances at the building where I know he's going to be. Oh. My. Freaking. God. I'll get to see him in person. *In freaking person!*

I take a few deep breaths. The map on my phone pings telling me to turn at the next street. I cast one longing glance at the convention center before heading down the indicated street. Within five minutes, I'm standing outside the Loews.

Inside, I head to the bar area and find an empty table near the window. I order a water and check my phone. Nothing.

After a quick message to Lily and Shaun assuring them both of my safe arrival at my hotel, I shoot off a message to Madre letting her know I'm in the hotel bar. Sipping my water, I watch the people pass outside the window and try not to overthink the insanity of what I'm doing in Philadelphia.

"Jen?" A slow, sweet drawl pulls me from my thoughts.

I spin around and see a curvy redhead with bright green eyes and a Space Vendetta t-shirt grinning at me. "Madre? I mean, Bonnie?"

She nods and wraps her arms around me pulling me into a warm hug. "Oh, it's so good to finally meet you in person." She releases me and gushes. "I mean, I know we've only known each other a few months, but I have to tell you, you're like my sister from another mister."

My face heats at the compliment. "I feel the same way. Sit down. Tell me about your trip."

Madre slides into the seat across from me and waves her hand. "Nothing much to tell. I flew in this morning and took the hotel shuttle. Here I am." She ends with a flourish. "What about you?"

"Took the train in from New York City." I shrug. "Pretty straightforward."

Once we get through the friendly small talk, she launches into the itinerary. "You have the pass for Friday and Saturday, right?"

"Yes, ma'am." I pat my purse.

"Did you buy any photo ops or autographs?" She pulls out a map of the convention center.

"No. The one I wanted was way too expensive." I wrinkle my nose and tamper down my disappointment.

Madre gives me an understanding nod. "Yeah, I was pissed when I saw that. Total bullshit. I mean, I know he doesn't do a lot of public appearances, but to gouge fans with a five hundred dollar price tag for a quick photo and a signature." She sniffs with distaste. "Total fucking rip off. The cost to fly here and the hotel alone is astronomical. Some of us live on a budget and had to make sacrifices to even get this far."

"Agreed." I sigh. "But maybe we'll get a glimpse of him at some point?"

She studies the map for a moment and nods. "It looks like this area is open for people to walk around. You may be able to see him while he's signing autographs."

The thought of seeing Nicholas Hughes in person has my

stomach twisting with anticipation and excitement. "Did you get any ops?"

Madre shakes her head. "No. I'm in the same boat as you. We'll have to admire from a distance."

I take a sip of my water and her face lights up.

"Oh, by the way, I forgot to tell you. There are a few other fangirls from our group here."

Surprise grips me. I mean I figured there would be fans here, but not any I would actually know. "Seriously? Who?"

"JustMyStarShip, NoticeMeSenpai, IDreamofVillains, StarShipper." Her eyes sparkle with excitement. "They're excited to meet you too."

"Are you freaking serious?" I nearly squeal. "Those are all my favorite fic authors."

"I know. Mine too." She bounces in her seat. "They invited us to join them for dinner tonight after we hit the con."

"Oh, my God. This is insane. I wasn't expecting this at all."

"I debated on telling you when I found out this week, but I wanted to see the look on your face when I told you." Her smile fades. "Heads up, Viper is here too. I just found out, otherwise, I would have warned you."

There are a handful of opinionated fangirls who believe they know everything there is to know about the fandom and make it a point to criticize any and all who join the fandom and aren't *true fans*. That being they haven't read every single book, seen every documentary, ingested every piece of canon material verified by the creators, blah, blah, blah. I swallow the news with a bitter smile.

"Sorry. I know she's not your favorite person after she trashed your fanfic. But we all gave her shit for it." Madre takes my hands and squeezes. "We've got your back. If she starts shit, we'll tell her to fuck off."

The anxiety constricting my chest eases at her words. I laugh. "Thanks."

"No problem." She motions to my bag. "Now, let's put this in the room, and then we can get over to the center. The doors open in fifteen minutes."

Her enthusiasm infects me. The room on the fifteenth floor gives us a great view of the city. I can see the convention center clearly. There's a line already starting outside. The thought crosses my mind before I can stop it...I wonder where Nicholas is?

Three hours later, I'm overwhelmed by the amount of excited, uninhibited fans and the endless amounts of fandom memorabilia. The convention center is divided into two parts. One has all the booths with artists, sellers, creators, and vendors hocking everything from custom portraits to Lego mini-figures and beyond. The other side has the autograph booths with roped-off sections of space designated for each celebrity. Behind that is the huge sign directing anyone with a pass for a photo op.

Madre and I try to get a better glimpse of the photo area, but it's completely sectioned off. Only those with passes can even get close to the photo area. We do notice, however, the autograph area doesn't have this restriction and it's fairly easy to see the celebrities signing autographs even if you don't have a pass. But no cameras are allowed in this area.

So I may be able to see Nicholas tomorrow during his scheduled signing, but I won't be able to snap a picture. Damn. Oh well.

We wander back to the vendor booths and check out all the amazing artists. I see quite a few items I want to buy, but my apartment is already brimming with *Space Vendetta* memorabilia. Plus, my bank account is already taking a hit with this trip, so I refrain.

The two of us cover about half the vendor area before we decide to head out to meet up with the other fangirls for dinner. We'll hit the rest tomorrow in between sneaking over to see some famous faces and, of course, Nicholas Hughes.

As we walk out of the convention center, I admire the creative cosplay costumes while Madre pulls up directions to the restaurant. Together we wander a few blocks and find the quaint Irish pub the girls decided on.

Inside the dim restaurant, I can hear female laughter echoing from the back of the pub even over the typical bar noise.

Madre leads the way.

"Fellow, fangirls!" Madre announces when we reach the table. "We have arrived."

"Madre Fiero!" One of the girls stands up and raises her glass. The rest of the women turn to face us.

"This is HoldMeRansom." She introduces me with a loud flourish.

The petite brunette woman in the seat beside me stands. "I love your one-shots." She hugs me tight. "I'm JustMyStarShip."

My inner fangirl freaks the fuck out and I hug her even tighter. "I love your fics too! You're the reason I started writing fan fiction."

She releases me and pats the chair next to her. "Sit. Want a drink?"

I take a seat and slowly relax as the chatter resumes at the table. Madre orders a berry mixed concoction. I stick with a Yuengling lager.

Conversation revolves around the con and who's splurged to get a photo op with Nicholas Hughes. I sip my drink quietly and listen. Three of the ladies came together for a group photo with him. Only one of the fangirls splurged for a one-on-one photo package. I restrain the jealousy pulling at the back of my mind.

The more I listen, the more I learn. These fangirls are so diverse. Every corner of the country, as well as one originally from Canada and another spent time in the UK, with varying backgrounds, educations, cultures, and relationship statuses. It's eye-opening. When I first met them, they were usernames on a website dedicated to one sole purpose, celebrating the Space Vendetta Series. Now I have real names, faces, and lives to go with their online personas and fan fictions.

Vicky, also known as JustMyStarShip turns and grins. "So, are you going to meet Nicholas tomorrow too?"

I push away the disappointment. "No. It wasn't in my budget." I shrug. "I'll try to catch a glimpse of him tomorrow while he's signing autographs."

Her gaze softens with understanding. "Yeah, I'm with you

there. I was going to, but then my car needed new tires." She sighs heavily. "Adulting sucks."

I like her. She's sweet and down-to-earth. Her fanfics are sinfully steamy and wicked. They've kept me up late and given me tons of lucid dreams. Actually talking to her in person and seeing the real Vicky takes away those remaining reservations. She's human, like me. Knowing that makes a world of difference because a few hours ago, I viewed myself as an impostor faking my way through the fandom.

Several hours later, a small group of us make our way back to the hotel. It seems most of the girls picked the same one. We take the elevator back to our room. Vicky and Jessica, also known as IDreamofVillians, join us for a couple more drinks. This devolves into a ridiculous giggle-fest where Vicky retrieves her cardboard cutout of Captain Ransom from her room for us to make silly videos. I only pray if these videos make it online Nicholas Hughes never sees them.

I honestly can't remember what time we crash. When I wake up the next morning, Madre's already in the shower. I drag myself from bed and walk around the corner. Once the smell of coffee fills the air, my energy levels rise.

I turn and scream when I see the figure half-obscured by the curtain.

Madre opens the door dripping wet and draped in a towel. "What happened?"

"That fucking Ransom cardboard cutout! Scared the shit out of me." I press my hand to my racing heart.

Madre's laughter fills the room. "Damn near did the same thing to me. Vicky said she'd pick it up this morning before they head to the con."

"Good." I glare at the offending, but sexy, cut-out. His perpetual crooked smirk mocks me.

"I'll be out in a minute." Madre shuts the door.

I pour a cup of coffee and stare out the window overlooking the city. Today I'll finally share the same space with him. This may be the closest I'll ever get, and that knowledge wrecks the piece of my heart he occupies.

An hour and a half of primping and preparation passes in a flash. Vicky retrieves her Ransom cut out and then returns with Jessica. The two of them join up with Ginger, while Madre and I hang back to grab her forgotten purse before heading toward the convention center. Madre chatters with excitement, but I'm trapped inside my own mind. All I can think of is him.

Ronnie joins us and pulls me into a huddle with Madre while we stand in line. "Okay, so according to the itinerary, he'll be doing photo ops from eleven until two, then sign autographs at two-thirty." Her gaze lingers on me. "The best chance of seeing him will be then. Shall we meet up at two near the autograph booth here?" She points to a block on the map.

"Sounds good to me. I want to finish looking at the vendors first." Madre nudges me. "You coming with me?"

"Yeah." I nod focusing only on our two o'clock meeting time.

Ronnie splits off to find the other fangirls, her sights set on finding Michael DeHart, the author of the *Space Vendetta* novels. The gaps between vendors are full to bursting. It's more difficult to wander through the area today than it was yesterday.

As we wander, we stop a few cosplayers and complement their creations. A few of them agree to pictures with us. Some of them I recognize from Tumblr and Twitter. They're famous in the world of cosplay. When we cross paths with the most infamous Ransom cosplayer, a dead ringer for Nicholas Hughes, I balk.

"That's IAmRansom!" I squeal under my breath.

Madre grabs my arm and pulls me toward him. He's snapping selfies with a few other fans. When he sees us, his smile widens.

"Hello, ladies." He uses his best imitation of Captain Ransom's charm adding a bit of smolder on the end of it.

"It's so great to see you here!" Madre treats him like they're old friends, and they fall into a conversation without effort.

I listen, starstruck and speechless. His profile is different from Nicholas, but he has the same coloring and crooked smile. The costume he's wearing looks accurate, although I'm not an expert on costuming or cosplay. But I appreciate the work that must have gone into being this painstakingly accurate.

His gaze shifts to me, and I notice the difference in the color of his eyes compared to the real Ransom. "I love your shirt." He gestures to my T-shirt displaying a RanLyn ship logo.

"Thanks." I tug on it aware of his intense, but kind, attention.

"Can we get a picture with you?" Madre asks.

"Absofuckinglutely. I'd love to have a picture taken with such beautiful ladies." He wraps his arms around my waist and Madre's pulling us against him.

His friend takes Madre's phone and takes a few pictures.

Madre elbows me in the side. "Get in there, just the two of you." She winks.

IAmRansom pulls me against him, his warmth enveloping me. He smells good, and his touch is polite regardless of there being no space between us. We pose for a few pictures, and he releases me, taking my hand in his and kissing the back of it.

"A pleasure, my lady." He winks.

"You're damn good at this." I laugh.

"Just doing my part to bring pleasure to the masses." He slips a card in my hand. I glance at it while he hands one to each of the other girls. It's a link for his cosplay website and an email address.

"Thanks." I tuck it in my pocket.

"Enjoy the rest of the con." He bows deeply and wanders off in the opposite direction.

"Holy shit, did that really happen?" I whisper to Madre.

"Yeah, it did." She claps her hand on my shoulder. "Welcome to comic con, love."

As we wander through the rest of the vendor area, I soak in the vivid art and cosplay, and the unlimited creativity overwhelms me. Even though this event isn't limited to only *Space Vendetta*, it is a popular fandom. The other fandoms are represented to varying degrees. Some of them I recognize, but there are others I don't. Madre introduces me to a few other fangirls I've interacted with on Discord.

Mistress Viper, whose real name is Beth, appears from behind a booth flanked by Ginger (StarShipper) and Ronnie (NoticeMeSenpai). Beth is the only one who's ever posted anything even remotely negative or discouraging on my stuff. I've learned to ignore her, plus it helps Madre and the other girls have my back.

Beth chats with Jessica and Vicky, pointedly ignoring me. Which is absolutely fine. I have no interest in befriending someone who's openly hostile to someone who doesn't view the fandom the way they do.

Madre links her arm through mine and we wander to the next booth. She glances at her phone. "You hungry?"

"A little. What time is it?"

"Almost one." She taps her chin. "I bet we can slip out to the Reading Terminal Market and grab something quick before we have to meet the other girls at two."

"Sounds good." I walk beside her while she types out a quick message to the other girls.

"Okay, let's go." She takes charge without hesitation. I admire this about her. What little time I've known Madre, she's definitely not afraid to embrace what she wants and seems to have her shit together.

At lunch, we chat about our lives back home. She tells me about her husband and kids, her job at the local bakery, and the small-town life she's grown up with. I quickly realize how different we are and yet how connected I feel to her.

When I tell her about my family and friends and my job in the city, she's riveted. I personally don't see what's so fascinating, but she asks me a million questions.

"I'd love to visit one day. I've never seen New York City." She sips her soda.

"You're more than welcome to visit any time." My heart swells at this strengthening bond.

"And if you ever want to escape to the country, you're always welcome in Iowa." A grin splits her lips. "My sister from another mister."

Stomachs full and bond strengthened, we head back to the

convention center with five minutes to spare before the designated meetup time. Vicky and Jessica are waiting for us.

They show us their purchases and we chat for a while until Vicky notes the queues have fully formed in front of several of the booths. Nicholas Hughes's included. We shift our position to give us the best view of the table beyond the crowd waiting to get their autographs.

I'm fifty feet away with a perfect view of the table. My stomach twists in knots with every passing second.

Two thirty arrives and Nicholas still hasn't appeared. The crowd is restless and impatient. According to Vicky, for some, it's already been a long day of waiting in line for their photo op and other engagements. She says one of the girls told her it was a two-hour wait for a five-second photo where she barely exchanged two words with Nicholas before she was shuttled through like cattle off to slaughter. Definitely not worth the five-hundred-dollar price tag. I would have been pissed.

The crowd erupts into cheers and applause. I spin around to see Nicholas waving to the crowd of adoring fans. He takes the seat at the table beside his assistants. Security begins to admit the fans one by one.

Nicholas is all smiles for his fans. There's no way to know what he's saying to them, but I watch his mouth move with each exchange. Jealousy and disappointment curl through me like a viscous smoke staining my mind. That could be me. My heart drops to my feet. Even at this distance, a part of me longs for him to glance my way, to form a connection without a word.

"Hey, we're gonna hit the bathroom. You coming?" Madre sways into me breaking the spell.

"Oh, uh, no, I'm gonna hang out here for a bit."

Madre hugs me. "Okay. I'll be back for you."

I nod, and they leave me to stare at Nicholas in peace.

The chaos of the comic con fades into the background, and for twenty minutes, I watch from the sidelines as fans get their opportunity to talk to Nicholas Hughes. But not me.

Look at me. Look! I beg silently.

Nothing.

I've come this far, and it's still not enough. Fifty feet of empty air, and not a single chance of him noticing me. The emotional shit storm brewing inside me only intensifies. Why would I even think anything would happen? I lean against the concrete post and wonder if maybe this whole trip was a bad idea.

When Madre retrieves me, I go willingly with one final longing glance at Nicholas. An hour later, I escape to the hotel and pack my stuff. After writing a note for Madre and the other girls, I pack my suitcase and head to the station.

I save my tears for the train.

CHAPTER TWENTY

It's Sunday. Comic con feels like the distant past, but it's only been twenty-four hours since I stood outside the autograph booth and watched Nicholas Hughes from a distance.

After a flurry of messages from Madre, I sent another apology and turned off my ringer. The moment I got home, I sent a message to Lily and Shaun telling them I was safe at home. I didn't even wait for a response; I turned off the phone and went to bed.

Chaos and confusion spun a tangled web in my dreams. I woke up several times through the night. Nothing calmed my mind. I finally took some melatonin and crashed hard. When I woke at nine, I crawled from bed and made coffee.

The desire to check my phone drives me insane. I refrain, knowing it'll only spike my blood pressure and give me a migraine. Instead, I pull out the documents for the presentation I need to give next week. Since I wasn't supposed to return from Philly until this afternoon, I told my parents I wouldn't be around for the family meal today. I'm glad I canceled because, honestly, I'm not in the mood for their questions.

By noon, I push them aside and open a blank Word document. I pour my heart into a new fic, writing what I wish would have happened at comic con. A fantasy bordering dangerously on reality, enough to send my mind into a distracted state.

I'm a few thousand words into it when the doorbell rings. A quick glance at the clock makes me jump to my feet. It's nearly four o'clock. Shit, where has the day gone?

The monitor is filled with daisies. I smile and unlock the door.

"Hey."

The bouquet blocks Shaun's face. He drops them to his

chest. I chuckle at the ridiculous pout on his lips. "Hey, you." He pauses. "I tried to call."

"I must have forgotten to turn the ringer on." I lie and take the proffered flowers into the kitchen. "How was your trip?"

Shaun comes up behind me and wraps his arms around my waist pressing a kiss to my neck. "Boring. I would have much rather been with you at comic con."

"I'm sure." I put the flowers in a vase full of water. Once my hands are free, he spins me around and kisses me.

"Seriously. It was boring as sin." He kisses me softly, and I melt into him. "How was your first adventure to comic con?"

I shrug my shoulder and drop my gaze. "It was good."

"Did you meet your fellow fangirls?" His question is sincere, but I bristle at it.

"Yeah. Madre is great. There were a few others we hung out with too." I don't offer any details. I'm sure he doesn't care.

"Get to meet any celebs?"

"Not really. A few popular cosplayers and YouTubers, but that's about it."

His brow furrows in thought. "Everything okay?"

"Yeah. I'm fine. Just tired."

"I was going to take you out for dinner, but I can order pizza for delivery too." He winks. "Good thing you live near the best pizza place in town."

"Pizza sounds good." I grab my phone and clear all the unread messages before finding the number. "Here. Call it in. I'll pop in the shower quick."

"The usual?" he asks.

"Works for me." I close my bedroom door and strip.

The shower revitalizes me. Slowly I let the events of the past few days fade into the background and instead focus on the upcoming week. I have multiple meetings and my parent's anniversary dinner to plan.

Fifteen minutes later, I'm wearing my RansomMe tank top and a pair of boxer shorts. The pizza should be here any minute. The doorbell rings as though on cue. I tie up my hair and rejoin Shaun in the living room. The smell of pizza hits me first, then I see Shaun standing between the dining room table and the couch.

Shaun glances up. No smile, not even a flicker of emotion. I freeze in the doorway. His gaze skims down my length and back up.

"What's wrong?" Then I see my phone in his hand. "Did you find my new one-shot?" I stick out my tongue playfully.

"No." He crosses to where I'm standing and spins the phone around. "Who is this?"

My heart drops through the pit of my stomach and hits the floor at terminal velocity. "Babe."

The photograph of IAmRansom holding me close fills my vision. *Goddamn it, Madre.*

"Is this one of the cosplayers you met up with?" Shaun's jaw ticks. He's livid. Can I blame him?

"Yes. His name is IAmRansom. It was just a quick photo." I attempt to defend myself.

Shaun cuts me off. "Looks a little cozy here."

My gaze fixes on where the cosplayer rests his hands on my waist. From this angle, he looks like his fingers are brushing the underside of my breast. I cringe.

"Nothing happened. The picture looks bad, I admit, but honestly, it was nothing." I snatch my phone back and see if there are any other pictures that show another angle. Madre only sent me this one. Of course. I'll ask for the others.

His scoff rips me from the train of thought. Shaun shoves his hands in his pockets. "Is that what does it for you, Jen?" He cocks his head and studies me. "An actor. A fictional character. A man who can dress up as either and play to your fantasies." Bitterness edges his voice.

The insinuation slaps me, and I step back, speechless. What the hell is going on? Before I can reply, Shaun continues.

"I get it. You get fixated. Hyper attached to something. It hypnotizes you to the point where it consumes you." He shrugs. "Hell, it happened to me when I was younger."

"Shaun," I manage to vocalize his name, but he holds his hand up.

"I've been patient. Supportive. Hell, I've even indulged your little fantasies, and yes, I enjoyed it." His eyes narrow. "But over the past month or so, I've seen you struggle. With work, at home, with friends, family." He gestures to my apartment cluttered with memorabilia. "Shit. Even your apartment has been overrun by your obsession."

"It's not an obsession." I protest, but deep inside, I know he's right. The words twist deeper into my already struggling psyche.

"Jen. You have a problem. Admit it." He brushes his fingertips along my cheek.

"I don't have a problem." I step away from his touch. "This isn't an addiction."

Disappointment etches his features. "Babe. Look around. Think about the last few months and tell me you haven't fallen down a rabbit hole."

I drop my gaze and study the peeling nail polish on my toes. I can't look at him. I can't admit he's right. Instead, I stuff it away and keep silent.

"You're all over the place. You're distant. You're not. You're happy. You're sad." He runs his hand through his hair. "You won't talk to me about any of it. Even Lily and Maggie are concerned about you."

"I'm fine," I growl desperate to defend myself but unable to find the words.

"You're not fine, Jen."

"Yes, I am." I glare at him when he tries to reach for me.

He drops his hands and steps back. "This obsession is close to ruining every relationship you have, babe. I'm trying to help. I love you."

"You're jealous," I snap. The words pour out of me before I can process them, but it's too late.

Shaun's expression darkens. "Jealous? Of what, Jen? Of a fictional character? Of an actor? Of some dude who dresses up on the weekends who so happens to have a passing resemblance to someone famous?" He scowls. "Who the fuck should I be jealous of?"

I purse my lips together and cross my arms.

His patience disappears completely. "If you'd rather spend your time drooling over another man, that's your choice. But I'm done playing second fiddle to a goddamn figment of your imagination." He crosses to the door and pauses, turning to face me once more. "When you want a real man, one who loves you and can give you what you need, you know where to find me."

Shaun slams the door behind him. I flinch at the vehemence of the action. He never reacts this way. I've seen him face down irate customers and furious coworkers with grace and diplomacy. But tonight, with me, he lost it.

I crumble to the floor and the realization of what just happened slams into me like the express train at rush hour. Shaun and I are done. Over. Kaput.

The one man who showed me unlimited support and affection. Gone. The slow trickle of reality seeps into my mind and tears fill my eyes.

All these months, I worried he would leave over stupid shit. But the one thing I thought he understood ended up being the tipping point. Fuck.

I crawl to the couch and curl up, pulling my Ransom blanket around my shoulders. The lingering scent of him and the pizza sitting on the counter surrounds me.

I pinch my eyes closed and wipe the tears on the blanket. When I open them, I see the figures and photos lining my shelves. *Space Vendetta* everywhere. Ransom. Hughes. Every surface tainted by him.

Obsession. The word filters through my mind on repeat growing larger and brighter, demanding I see it. Demanding I acknowledge the truth. My obsession ruined my relationship.

CHAPTER TWENTY-ONE

On Wednesday, I'm finally able to drag myself out of bed and get ready for work. I called in sick on Monday and Tuesday. I never call into work. Ever.

When I didn't show on Monday morning, Lily blew up my phone. Dozens of messages and several frenzied voicemails later, I reply with the standard I'm not feeling well response. She tells me to call her if I need anything and the phone is blissfully silent after that.

Tuesday's absence earned me another series of messages. I sent the same response. Then Maggie called me at lunch and left a long, drawn-out message about how they're worried about me. I sent her a similar reply.

There's been nothing out of Shaun since he stormed out of my apartment on Sunday night. I've debated texting him on and off for days. Hell, I even composed a whole letter, but when I went to send it, I deleted it on accident instead. I took it as a sign I should keep my mouth shut.

It's been two days, and I don't want to talk to anyone. I want to be alone in my own fucking misery. I did this to myself. But the rent still needs to be paid and there's a shit ton of work piled on my desk. I don't have time to nurse my own insecurities. I have to adult as much as I don't want to right now.

When I reach the building, I keep my head down and focus on getting to my desk without being sidelined. I avoid Lily in the lobby and take the elevator when she stops at the café. A few familiar faces surround me in the elevator. I grab my phone and pretend to type up a message during the ride up to avoid any small talk.

Safely seated at my desk, I power up my computer and start sorting the stack of files six inches deep. According to my calendar, there's a meeting with corporate on Friday. As the acting lead, I'm required to provide the mid-year report for my department. My two sick days cost me time, but fortunately, I had access to most of the materials. Today I can work on uploading them into the database and making a printout with the details for my presentation.

"Jen, there you are!" Lily appears beside me. Her typically relaxed demeanor frays with every word. "Didn't you get the notice?"

"What notice?" I stare at her in confusion.

"They bumped up the corporate meeting. It's in five minutes." Lily fidgets with the notebook in her hands. "You need to get over there."

"Shit," I swear under my breath while trying to keep from freaking out. I'm not ready. Shit. "When did they change the day?"

Lily shrugs. "I only got the email this morning. Who knows why they changed it?" She worries her lower lip between her teeth. "Please tell me you're ready."

"No, I'm not ready." I hiss and scramble to print whatever I have available. I snatch it from the printer and tuck it into a folder. "But there's not a damn thing I can do about it now."

"I'm sorry." Lily looks like she's about to break into tears.

I want to join her. I'm fucked and I know it. Steeling myself, I grab whatever I have prepared and head for the conference room.

It's full, but I find an open seat along the wall. Mr. Roberts catches my eye from the front of the room. Whatever confidence remained disintegrates into fine dust. There is no way I skate through this meeting. He will know, and I'll end up out on my ass.

Another gentleman stands beside Mr. Roberts. I assume he's the head of something at corporate. A woman stands to his left wearing a deep red skirt suit and white silk blouse. I don't recognize her. Off to the right seated along the wall, I spot Shaun.

His gaze remains fixed on Mr. Roberts who starts the meeting. My heart aches at the sight of him. A rush of emotion threatens to choke me. I shove it aside and drop my gaze to my lap in a piss poor attempt to recoup my balance.

As Mr. Roberts speaks, I organize the papers in the file and scrape together a few notes for when he inevitably calls on me to give my report.

"I have the pleasure to introduce Mr. Collins, Head of the Board, and Mrs. Bradshaw, the CEO of Valentina." Mr. Roberts gestures to the two individuals standing beside him.

My heart stops fucking beating. Holy. Fuck. The CEO! While Lily and I have spoken at length about Mrs. Bradshaw, neither of us has met her in person. She's stunning with her shoulder-length gray hair and flawless style. Being in the same room with her makes me feel like the fraud I so obviously am.

I hang my head in shame. There's no way in hell I can present what I have. Not without looking like an incompetent idiot. Acid burns the back of my throat. There are only two courses of action. One, I bite the bullet, present what I have, and make a fool out of myself in front of my coworkers. This option does not sit well with me. But surely, it's better than the alternative. Which is to admit I did not meet the objective in time for the meeting and am unable to present my report at this time.

Half ass and fail or openly admit I failed. Neither option is ideal. Both will probably get me fired. I pinch my eyes closed and take a deep breath.

"Miss Ashcroft," Mr. Roberts calls out from the opposite side of the room. "Would you care to start with your report?"

I may puke. Slowly, I rise to my feet, purposely avoiding the pull of Shaun's gaze. The folder weighs a ton where it leans against my chest.

"I would love to start; however, my report is not complete at this time." I push forward focusing only on the impassive expression on Mr. Robert's face. "I apologize for the inconvenience."

"Do you have anything you could report for your department at this time?" Mr. Roberts asks.

I steal a glance at Mrs. Bradshaw who's penetrating stare bores into me. If I had to guess, I would put disappointment at the top of the emotions flitting through her head. I refocus on Mr. Roberts.

"No, sir." This time I drop my head in shame.

"Very well." Mr. Roberts shifts his attention to Dottie from Menswear. "Mrs. Finch, are you prepared to give your report this morning?"

Dottie quickly rises to her feet. "Yes, sir."

I sink down into my chair and resist the urge to hide behind my folder. Dottie launches into her report, and I focus on her, taking deep breaths to keep from blacking out.

Her report is flawless. She uses the exact same information I planned on using for mine, the only difference being the department. Mr. Robert's praise for her concise efforts echoes in my head like an express train barreling straight toward me.

On and on the meeting drags, and with each passing report, I sink deeper into my own mind willing myself to drown in the shame of my failure.

When the meeting finally ends, I shoot to my feet and escape to the nearest restroom. I slam my finger in the stall door. "Goddamn it!" I lock it and collapse against the wall.

I squeeze my eyes closed and hit my head against the tile repeatedly. The door opens and I freeze, holding my breath.

"Jen, are you in here?" Lily's voice echoes through the restroom.

"Yeah." My voice cracks. "I'll be out in a minute." I wipe away the tears.

"Is everything okay?" She pauses, and I know what's coming before she even says it. "Mr. Roberts wants to see you in his office."

"Thanks, Lily. I'll be right out."

I wait until I hear the door close and leave the stall. My mascara is smudged making me look like I'm trying to impersonate a raccoon. Using a paper towel, I clean up what I can. There's no hiding the red tint highlighting my eyes. Mr. Roberts will know I've been crying. Damn.

The last thing I want right now is his concern. Maybe I should save myself the trouble and clean out my desk. I can email him my resignation from home while I drink myself into a stupor.

On my way to Mr. Robert's office, I pass Shaun's open door. Without looking, I know he's there. I can feel his presence.

I nearly stumble as I pass. I miss him so much. I fucked up. He was right, about all of it. No matter how much I want to reach out, I can't. I'm too embarrassed. Ashamed of my response. Shaun deserves better than me.

Mr. Robert's secretary looks up from her computer screen. Her hazel eyes soften when she recognizes me. "Go ahead in, hon. He's waiting for you."

"Thanks." I knock on the door.

"Come in." The command echoes through the wood.

I push the door open and find him seated behind his massive steel desk. "Miss Ashcroft."

"You wanted to see me, sir." I stand at attention, but my body trembles sensing the inevitable.

"Yes." He gestures to the chair beside me. "Please, sit down."

With a nod, I settle into the leather chair.

"I must admit, Miss Ashcroft, I'm disappointed in your performance this morning." He steeples his fingers together and leans back.

"I apologize, sir. I have no excuse. Even though the meeting was scheduled for Friday, I should have been more prepared by this point." I stare at the carpet. "Enough to give my presentation today without hesitation."

"I'm glad you recognize your error and take responsibility for it." He sighs. "But it does not change the fact you were ill-prepared and showed a distinct lack of responsibility in front of corporate."

My heart seizes, but I nod in acceptance.

"I am disappointed in the deterioration of your work over the past few months, Miss Ashcroft." With a stern, but caring tone, he addressed my failure with decorum. "Starting immediately, Miss Astor will be taking the lead position. Please take the rest of the day and assess your priorities."

My gaze snaps to his. "You're not firing me?"

"Should I?" He cocks his head. "Would you rather I fire you?"

"No, sir."

"This isn't a guarantee of anything, but I am giving you the rest of the day to get your priorities in order." He pins me with his deep blue gaze as if driving home a point. "When you return, I expect to see the same level of commitment I observed at the beginning of the year." He sighs. "I'm not sure what's happened between then and now, but you have an opportunity to figure things out. I suggest you seize it."

"I understand, sir." Despair and hope take their dueling positions inside my chest. "Thank you."

"You're an intelligent woman." He grins, but I see the seriousness in his expression. "Don't make me regret this."

I nod.

"Go home. Get your house in order." He pulls his chair in and grabs a document from a folder. I take the queue to leave without hesitation.

I block Shaun's office with my hand as I walk by. At my desk, I gather my things and grab my coat. The last place I want to be is here. I can't face Lily's questions and Shaun's disappointment.

The only thing I crave right now is solitude. I can't think about anything else right now. I don't want to. Nothing matters anymore. How the fuck can I get my house in order when the only thing I have left is an apartment full of memorabilia and an aching hole in my heart?

CHAPTER TWENTY-TWO

Two days passed before I lost all track of time. I turned off my phone. I disconnected the doorbell. My laptop lay closed on the dresser in my bedroom. Whatever food I had in the apartment lays untouched. Even the television sits quiet.

My reflection on the TV screen silently judges me from where I lay bundled on the couch. The Ransom blanket wraps around me while my cheek presses against his image on the pillow. Shelves of trinkets stand watch over the apartment. Captain Ransom stares down into the room from the posters hung from lofty positions along the far wall.

Beneath the blankets, my stomach growls its demands, but I'm not hungry. The thought of food does nothing even though my body seems convinced otherwise.

What day is it? Not that I care. But my mouth is dry, and I don't remember drinking anything today. A pounding in my head only reaffirms this realization.

It doesn't matter. I don't have anywhere to be. Mr. Roberts' words hover in my mind like a blazing red neon sign reminding me of my failure. It could be worse. He could have fired me, but he didn't. I frown. He punished me, but he didn't shame me in front of the company. He could have. Should have. I deserved it.

This only confirms my worst fears. I'm not good enough to even be considered for the promotion, which is most certainly off the table after my fuck up. My decisions aren't good enough for my friends and family to trust me. My lack of confidence and self-worth even drift into my intimate relationship.

Shaun. Even his name triggers a painful ache deep in my chest. He showed me infinite patience and treated me like a goddamn goddess. My subconscious somehow managed to fuck that up with spectacular style.

Why couldn't I admit the truth? I wasn't able to disconnect from my own head. The tethers of the fandom enabled me to dive deeper into this fantasy. Nicholas Hughes, Captain Ransom. They gave me an escape. But no one warned me this bastion of fantasy would never release me from its hold. It tainted everything and left me with nothing but regret and insecurity.

I drift off, barely aware of the sunlight shifting across the wall.

A repetitive banging cuts through the dreamlike haze of half-sleep. The noise continues joined by shouts.

"Jen! You open this goddamn door right now or I will break it down!"

I stumble from the couch, clutching the blanket around me for protection.

"Jen!" The shouts and banging persist. "Open the fucking door! Don't make me call the cops for a wellness check."

Maggie. I brace myself for the oncoming storm.

Once I unlock the door, it swings open barely missing my foot as I jump back. Maggie and Lily burst through the door.

"Jen. Thank God, you're alive." Lily launches herself at me and wraps her arms around my blanket shrouded form turning me into a human/Ransom burrito. "We were so worried about you."

"Now we know you're alive. You can tell us what the fuck is going on." Maggie crosses her arms and glares at me.

Lily releases me and joins Maggie. Light and dark, they stand side by side waiting for me to speak. My conscience twists with guilt and regret.

"I needed time." I shrug unable to offer a decent excuse. It sounds lame to my own ears.

"Time for what?" Maggie asks clearly not backing down. "Time to make us all think something bad happened to you. Fuck. We've been trying to get ahold of you since Wednesday night."

Lily's hair bobs with her fervent nods. "After you left on Wednesday, Mr. Roberts called me into his office and asked me to take your task load for Shirley. What the hell happened?"

Shame fills me. "I fucked up." Giving the quick and dirty version of events, I tell them the truth of what happened in the meeting Wednesday morning and why I chose not to return to work.

"Shit." Maggie rubs her hand over her face. "I'm sorry, Jen."

"It is what it is." I exhale in defeat. "I can't change the past."

"What happened this weekend?" Lily's soft voice eases the invasiveness of her question. "Did something happen at comic con?"

Tears slip free spilling over my cheeks and onto the blanket. I shake my head unable to vocalize beyond my emotions.

"Well, something happened." Maggie taps her foot.

"Shaun?" Lily prods gently. "Did you two fight?"

I nod and pressure builds in my chest suffocating me. The tears fall faster. "I fucked everything up," I whisper between hiccups as the sobs consume me.

"Oh, honey." Lily pulls me into another tight hug. Her warmth steals what remains of my reservations.

I launch into a broken, sob-punctuated explanation. Maggie nods and remains blissfully silent while I speak. Lily clutches my hand between hers, offering physical support.

"He told me to call him when I wanted a real man and walked out." I hang my head.

Lily squeezes my hand and offers me a tissue. "Why didn't you tell us?"

"I ruined my relationship with a wonderful man over an obsession with this fantasy of a man who doesn't exist." I scoff and wipe my face. "You wouldn't have understood."

"Well, technically the actor does exist, but that's beside the point." Maggie shelves her hand on her hip.

Lily glowers at Maggie. "You're not helping."

"Fine." She throws her hands up and rounds on me. "I get why you didn't think you could tell us, but you could have called us on Wednesday night instead of locking yourself in your apartment and ignoring us all week."

"It wasn't all week." I try to figure out what day it is in my head.

"Actually, it was," Lily adds. "Today is Sunday."

My eyes fly wide. "Sunday? Are you serious?"

"Yeah." Maggie crosses the room and disappears into my bedroom.

"When was the last time you ate?" Lily asks when my stomach growls.

"I don't know," I lie. The last meal I ate was Wednesday morning before work.

"Come on." She pulls me toward my bedroom. "Take a shower, clean up, get dressed."

"Why?" Panic overwhelms me. "Where are we going?"

"Out to get something to eat. You need some fresh air and a change of scenery too." She pushes past Maggie who's found my phone.

I try to grab it, but she jerks it out of reach.

"After your shower. Go."

"Bossy bitch." I stick my tongue out.

"And you love me anyway." Maggie waves me away with her hand.

Lily turns on the shower and snatches the blanket from my grasp. "You have twenty minutes. We'll wait in the living room."

I'm stunned by the sudden shift in power. Lily's never this demanding. She leaves the room, and I catch a glimpse of myself in the mirror. My hair is a tangled rat's nest. Whatever makeup I had on Wednesday streaks beneath my eyes. I look like I woke up beneath a bush after a long night of bar hopping.

Once I step under the spray, the water sinks into my skin. The warmth revitalizes a piece of my soul and slowly radiates heat to the rest of my body. I wash my hair and face. I scrub my skin until it's pink. The sweet smell of apple blossom fills the steam-laden bathroom.

I turn off the water and exit the shower. One step done. I can do this.

In my bedroom, I'm haunted by Ransom's presence on my nightstand. I remember the night Shaun flipped the photos over. Had he seen my addiction so clearly and still shown me support even though it made him uncomfortable? Shame washes over me again.

A knock on the door pulls me from my dark thoughts. "You ready yet?" Lily calls out.

I stare at my dresser. The door opens behind me.

"Jen?" Lily steps closer. "What's going on? Why aren't you dressed?"

"I...I can't." Tears spill free uninhibited this time. "I miss him."

"Come on, honey. You need to get out of the house. Too many memories here right now." She rifles through my dresser and pulls out some clothes for me.

I slowly pull them on and let her lead me from the room.

It's not until I set foot on the sidewalk I can breathe again. My gaze shifts over the traffic, the people walking past, and the fading sunlight over the horizon.

Lily slides her arm through mine, and we follow Maggie down the street. I have no idea where they're taking me, and honestly, I don't care. I'm floundering and right now they're the only thing keeping me from letting the dark deep drag me under.

CHAPTER TWENTY-THREE

STAGE FIVE: ACCEPTANCE

After a twenty-minute walk, I'm refreshed. The world expands with every breath. Maggie stops in front of DeLuca's, the Italian restaurant up the street from Lily's brownstone.

Inside, the hostess leads the three of us to the room at the back of the restaurant typically reserved for groups and private parties. I glance around at the empty space with the large rectangular table taking up the back wall.

"What's going on?" I ask, uncertainty filtering through my blood igniting my flight or fight response. Maybe I should have stayed home. They're up to something.

"Sit down, Jen." Lily gestures to the seat at the head of the table. Maggie and Lily take the seats on either side blocking any possibility of escape.

The waiter takes our drink order and leaves.

My hands fidget in my lap, pulling at the small tear in the tablecloth. "Are we going to sit here in silence?"

"No. We're waiting." Maggie flips through the messages on her phone.

"Waiting for what?" I glance between my friends. My irritation grows by the second. I'm about to snap when my parents appear in the doorway.

"Jenny!" Mom rushes forward and wraps her arms around me. Her eyes are bright with tears.

Dad pulls me into a hug when Mom relinquishes me. He doesn't say anything, but he kisses me on the cheek and smiles before stepping aside to reveal Grammy.

"It's like a goddamn funeral in here." Grammy jabs me in the ribs with her bony finger. "Lighten up. I'm not dead yet."

"Mom." My mother rolls her eyes. "Knock it off. It's not funny."

"It's a little funny." Grammy winks at me conspiratorially. "Life's too short. Don't take it so seriously or you'll never get out alive!" Her laughter has the whole room smothering their grins behind their hands.

Grammy, Mom, and Dad all sit down at the table. I resume my seat. My gaze drifts over everyone's face. My friends, my family, the ones who surround and support me every day. My heart swells with appreciation. There's one face missing. I shove his image away and pain stabs my heart. It's too late to hope I can even attempt to salvage our relationship.

"Is everyone here?" Mom asks once the waiter leaves to get their drinks.

"No." Maggie sets her phone aside.

I glance at her in question, then a familiar voice fills the room.

"Sorry, I'm late." Shaun meets my gaze.

The room fades into the background. I'm out of my seat and across the room before I can even think about my actions.

"What are you doing here?" I ask, my voice low.

"Maggie texted me." He smiles and tucks a strand of my hair behind my ear. "I've been trying to reach you all week." His brow furrows. "I wanted to give you time to figure out what you wanted, but in the meeting, I saw the defeat in your eyes. I wanted to hold you. Give you support. Tell you it would all work out."

Tears fill my eyes and his figure blurs. I wipe my eyes with my sleeve. "You did?"

"I texted. I called. Hell, I even came over and stood outside your building debating what to do." Shaun's expression softens. "I didn't want to push you, but I was worried. So, I called in the cavalry." His gaze drifts to Lily and Maggie.

I glance at the two women and mutter, "Traitors," in my most loving tone.

"We love you, Jen." Shaun's statement pulls me back to face him. "Don't push us away when you need us the most."

His words crack my already fractured heart wide open. "I'm sorry. I...I fucked everything up. My relationships with my family and friends, my job and any possibility of promotion, and you," I cup his face with my hand. "Especially you." I drop my gaze.

When his hand covers mine, my breath stops. "You got lost. Distracted. It happens. But you didn't fuck anything up." He smiles. "We're here with you. You're important to us. To me, especially."

His words give me a boost of confidence. He's right. Life didn't end. No one died. Even though my heart ached, it would heal. I have all the support I need right here.

When I turn and search each loving face in turn, my confidence grows like a sunflower turning its face towards the warm rays of the sun. Lily and Maggie beam with tears in their eyes. Mom is openly sobbing into her napkin. Dad's wearing the biggest grin I've ever seen.

Grammy slowly rises to her feet and jabs her arm in the air. "Kiss her now! This is better than HBO."

Laughter bubbles up and spills out. Shaun joins me. When he wraps his arms around my waist and pulls me against him, the laughter stops. His mouth covers mine and cheers erupt behind us. I cling to him, digging my fingers into his shoulders needing more.

He pulls away leaving us both breathless. "God, I missed you."

"Me too."

Ever the gentleman, he leads me to my seat and pulls out the chair. Once I'm seated, Maggie slides down to the other side of Grammy and gives Shaun the seat to my right. He takes my hand and squeezes.

"Shaun, it's so nice to finally meet you," Mom says reaching across the table to shake his hand. "Jen's told us so much about you."

"It's a pleasure, ma'am." He turns up his charm while maintaining his midwestern modesty.

I shake my head in awe. How does he do that? Charm everyone he meets?

"Sir. It's an honor." He takes Dad's hand with a firm grip and shakes it.

"Likewise," Dad replies. "So, you work at Valentina's? What do you do?"

"Marketing and finance." Shaun shifts his attention to Dad, answering his questions. I let them have their moment. This is the first time they've met, and I'm glad they're bonding so quickly.

Shaun's hand returns to mine. He interlaces our fingers on the table while his attention remains on his conversation with Dad.

Mom's dabbing her eyes again with the napkin. "I'm so glad the girls invited us. We were worried about you when you didn't call to check in this week."

"I'm sorry, Mom." I offer a poor apology.

"Grammy and I noticed how distant you have become lately, and well, it's not like you." She sniffles. "You're blessed to have such wonderful friends." Mom squeezes Lily's hand and nods down to Maggie.

"We're family," Lily observes with a confident nod.

"I'm sorry. It's been so hard to balance everything. Then this fandom stuff got out of hand." I shake my head at how stupid it sounds when I say it aloud. "I lost track of reality. I never meant to hurt anyone or make you worry."

"We got you." Maggie raises her glass. "You can always count on us to tell you when you're being a shithead."

"Amen!" Grammy lifts her glass. The two clink their beverages and drink.

"Mother!" My mom scolds Grammy and hides her face behind the napkin.

"Thanks for kicking my ass and not hating me for being a shithead." Warmth infuses me at their unconventional declaration of unwavering love and support. Only I would find Maggie's harsh assessment endearing.

"And here's to Jenny finding herself a sexy man to climb like a tree," Grammy adds making me choke on my drink.

Shaun and Lily burst into laughter. Mom and Dad stare at her with their mouths hanging open. I'm fairly certain my face is six shades of red. Maggie is face down on her arms against the table, her shoulders shaking violently.

"Maggie!" I shout down the table. "You told her to say that."

She slams her palm down on the table twice before revealing her beet-red face. I've never seen Maggie laugh so hard in all our years of friendship.

"I'm sorry, I had to do it." She holds up her hand to high-five Grammy. My grandmother indulges her.

"Do you even know what you said?" I ask, my face still flaming hot.

"I may be old, but I'm not stupid." She winks. "If I were fifty years younger, I'd climb him like a tree myself."

Shaun's face turns pink before he bursts into laughter again. I shake my head in disbelief. Only my family and friends would find this to be suitable conversation for the dinner table.

We barely recover when the waiter appears bearing two trays. Saved by our meal, conversation regains some semblance of sanity.

A sense of normalcy returns while we eat. The stress of the last few months slowly disappears into the background as muted white noise. I indulge in the moment savoring the time spent in the company of those who went out of their way to show me how much they care about me.

Me. The obsessed fangirl who lost her way. That part of me feels detached now. It will take some time to find my footing again, but I have support. I can find balance. I saw it in Madre.

Shit. I realize I completely ignored Madre after I bailed last week. I should send her a message to make sure she knows it wasn't something she did. It was me. All me.

After a delicious meal and delightful company, hope returns to the shadowed piece of my soul. My parents invite Shaun to our weekly family meal the following Sunday. Grammy grabs his ass when she hugs him goodbye. Lily and Maggie promise to call in the morning and leave me in Shaun's care.

Outside the restaurant, Shaun takes my hand. "You want to come home with me tonight?"

This man. "You're too good for me."

He kisses my forehead. "Nah. We're two crazy, little peas in a fucked-up pod."

I chuckle. "No. You're pretty damn near perfect."

"I told you before, Jen." He takes my hand. "No one's perfect. One day you'll see all my flaws and run for the hills."

"I doubt that." We walk down the street toward his apartment.

Shaun takes a deep breath after a few moments of silence. "Ten years ago, I was part of a cosplay club based in Chicago. We traveled to different comic cons and did special events."

I stare at him in disbelief. "You're joking?"

He shakes his head. "No, I told you. I was big into the books at one point. I found a couple of local people and they sucked me into the cosplay life."

"*Space Vendetta?*"

He nods.

I'm floored by this information, but does it really surprise me? No. Then it hits me. "You weren't Ransom were you?"

"No." He keeps walking, his gaze fixed on some far-off point.

I rack my brain going through the characters in the series. "Who?"

"John Colton."

My mind spins through the series until it pinpoints the name. I whirl on him when it slams into me. "The Commander of the Space Rangers?" I shove him playfully. "No way."

"Yes, way. They thought I resembled him. I think it was the square jaw." He smooths his hand over his face. "Anyway, we traveled to comic cons and did events. This was before the series hit the mainstream with the films."

"And this makes you less perfect?" I tease.

He scoffs. "Well, after a year or two of playing Colton, the group consumed nearly all my free time. It sucked me in. All my money, all my time off, everything went toward it." He stops walking and grabs my hand.

We're beneath a streetlight and it casts long shadows over his face making him look like a noir detective. I study his face for a moment and see the sadness in the depths of his eyes.

"I loved it. The cons. The costume. The character. The attention." He rakes his hand through his hair.

"What happened?" I ask softly.

"Salt Lake City Fandom Central. We booked our hotel room for the con months in advance." He shook his head with a laugh. "Our group even got booked for a special appearance, we were so popular. Then I got a call for an interview for a position at an up-and-coming corporation. The same weekend."

"What did you do?" My heart races.

"I skipped the interview and went to the con." He faces me. "The following year, I found out one of the guys from my class got the job. The company expanded to a Fortune 500. He's now on the board."

"But you followed your heart, right?" I tug on his hand. "Going to the con was worth it."

"In the moment, I thought it was, but later that month the group split. We had a huge blowout over artistic differences." Shaun laughs. "It's ridiculous now. But I didn't know how to indulge in my love for *Space Vendetta* without it affecting my real life. I mean, I had goals, but I forgot the most important thing."

"What?" His words hit home. I know where he's going with it, but I give him my undivided attention.

"Balance." Shaun holds out both hands level. "Between real life and fantasy."

"That is the key, isn't it?"

"I should have told you this months ago when I saw you following the same path." He hugs me. "You're much stronger than I was. I hoped you would be able to find balance. But I can see even the strongest can be seduced by the allure of fandom."

"Truth." We embrace bathed by the flickering streetlight.

"Come on." He pulls back and takes my hand. "Let's get home."

The rest of the walk to his apartment passes in a blur.

"Wait here." He leaves me in the living room, and I settle on the couch.

He returns and hands me a stack of photographs. I flick

through them slowly.

"Is this you?" I glance at a younger version of Shaun dressed as John Colton from Space Vendetta. "Wow, you really do pull it off."

"Ha. You've got jokes." He sits beside me telling me where the photos were taken and the stories behind them.

When we reach a photo of a group of cosplayers posing in front of a sign, I gasp. No. It can't be.

"Yeah." Shaun nods at my reaction. "That's IAmRansom. He went by Ransom's Twin back then."

I cover my mouth with my hand. "I had no idea."

"How could you?" Shaun takes the photos from my hand and sets them aside. "I never mentioned my past life as a cosplayer."

"Yes, but..." I hide my face. "The photo you found. Of the two of us in Philly. Oh, God."

"Honestly, I was pissed." Shaun pulls my hand away from my face and tips my chin up. "He's the reason I left the group. Overly obsessed and demanding. Critical of anything that wasn't canon. He made me realize there was more to life than fandom."

"I'm so sorry, Shaun."

"Don't be sorry. I overreacted." He rakes his hand through his hair. "I had an apology all lined up for you Monday morning, but you never showed up for work. Lily said you were sick. I didn't want to bother you. Then Wednesday..."

I hold my hand up. "Don't remind me. Wednesday was a fucking disaster."

"It may feel like that now but give it time."

"Well, according to Mr. Roberts, I have to get my shit together." I sigh. "I'm paraphrasing, of course. But me bailing for the rest of the week isn't going to earn me any brownie points."

"Mr. Roberts isn't typically so colorful even though he is direct. I'm sure if you discuss it with him, he'll understand. We all have moments like that." Shaun laughs. "I wouldn't worry about it. Take this time to find balance. He sees the potential in you like I do. Just take a week off and see how you feel."

"What did I do to deserve you?" I brush my thumb over the back of his hand.

"I ask myself the same question about you."

"Thank you," I whisper as he draws closer, my pulse skyrockets at the rise in heat between us.

"For what?" His breath teases my lips.

"Everything."

Shaun kisses me stealing any remaining hesitation from my mind. He pulls me into his lap and deepens his exploration. I'm starving for him, desperate for his touch.

"I love you," I murmur between kisses.

"Good." He nips at my lip. "Cause I love you." Then he proceeds to show me just how much in orgasms and whispered sweet nothings.

CHAPTER TWENTY-FOUR

When I return to my apartment Monday morning, I'm overwhelmed by how much clutter I've accumulated over the past few months. Every surface holds figurines, pictures, and trinkets all relating to *Space Vendetta* in some form or fashion. Two Ransom blankets lay draped over my couch surrounded by pillows with various images of the same man.

I cover my face with a groan. After talking with Shaun and the girls, I slowly realized how deep I fell into the seductive embrace of fandom life. Not that there's anything wrong with being a fangirl, or fanboy as Shaun pointed out last night. But there needs to be a balance.

Obviously, I missed the memo. My gaze skims over the rest of my apartment. The kitchen seems to be the least affected by my growing collection. But still, there isn't a lot of space to begin with, and my slow accumulation evolved into an avalanche of memorabilia.

I grab my laptop from my bedroom, pointedly ignoring how many Vendetta and Ransom-themed items made their way into that space as well. What I once viewed as an innocent collection took on a life of its own and grew tentacles infiltrating every aspect of my apartment and my life.

Pushing aside the Ransom fleece blanket, I settle on the couch and power up the laptop.

The unrelenting uncertainty threatening to drown me yesterday has taken on a new form thanks to the comforting support of my friends and family. But what struck me was their unconditional love regardless of how much I neglected my relationships.

Shaun's confession of his own experiences with fandom obsession tore down whatever hesitation remained. He recognized the struggle and did what he could to support me knowing at some point I would reach this precipice. Not only did I throw my old relationships over the edge, I sacrificed new friendships too. They didn't deserve my sullen silence with no explanation. Especially Madre.

On the walk home, I decided my first order of business today would be emailing Madre and the other fangirls I abandoned in Philly. They at least deserved to know it wasn't personal.

I pull up my inbox and type out responses to Vicky and Jessica, who both sent concerned messages full of love and support. I smile at their thoughtfulness and curse myself for abandoning them without at least reaching out to assure them of my safety.

Then I open Madre, Bonnie's messages. There is a dozen unread blinking in the queue. Three from the first day alone. The day I abandoned her in Philly. Guilt settles in my chest. My sister from another mister and I discarded her like a piece of wrapping paper on Christmas afternoon.

I open each one individually and read them. They range from frustrated and concerned to hopeful but sad. My emotions mirror hers with each word I read. The last message, dated on Friday, rips my heart open.

*It's me again. I'm sorry if I did something to chase you off last weekend. I want you to know I'm worried about you, and I want to know you're alive and well. After that, I'll leave you alone if you want me to. *Sad emoji face* I don't know what happened, but you should know I'm a better person for having met you both online and in person. Love ya, hon. Take care.*

Tears roll down my cheeks. Now I really feel like an asshole. I open a new reply and pour my heart into my response.

Madre. First of all, you did nothing wrong. It was me. All me. I hit a damn wall and faceplanted on the sidewalk. Seeing Nicholas Hughes in person broke me. To be so close and yet not have a connection. I couldn't take it. I had to go home and ground myself. Unfortunately, my boyfriend and I had a huge fight. He walked out on Sunday. Then Wednesday, I fucked up at work and ended up taking a leave of absence. So, yeah, Murphy's Law caught up with me this week.

But none of it excuses the way I ignored your emails and messages. It was wrong, and I'm sorry. You deserved a response. You also deserved a hug goodbye instead of a note on your hotel pillow. I fucked up royally last week. I don't expect you to forgive me for my shitty behavior, but I miss our chats, even the ones not centered around Vendetta, Ransom, and Nicholas Hughes.

You are my sister from another mister. I agree. We're both better people for having met. You've helped me realize there's a whole world beyond the five boroughs. And yes, you're still welcome to visit me any time you want. I'd love to show you around.

*Anyway, I've decided I'm going to be taking a break from all social media, especially Vendetta-related forms until I can learn how to balance fandom life with reality. You seem to do it so well, maybe you could share your secret with me. *Winking emoji face* For now, I'm going to spend some time channeling my time into getting my life back on track.*

Thanks for everything. Email me anytime. Love, Jen

Once I hit send, I turn off the computer and set it aside. The light from the window hits the Ransom figurine on the shelf beside the television. I stare at it for a few moments before taking inventory of the rest of the items along the wall.

The passion I once found in the fandom doesn't overwhelm me as it once did. I don't feel the desire to spend hours online searching for new tidbits or reading every fanfic I can find featuring Nicholas or Ransom. The thought of watching one of his movies would have excited me a few weeks ago, but now, there's no urgency pressing against me.

I take a deep breath and grab an empty box from the pantry closet. With care, I pull each Vendetta-related item off the shelf and dust it with a rag before tucking it into the box. I fold the blankets and set them on the edge of the couch, along with the pillows.

Slowly, I make progress around the apartment gathering most of my memorabilia and tucking it into the overflowing box. I gather the last few items from the bathroom and bedroom, adding them to the pile on the couch.

Now, what do I do with them? I spent a lot of money on all this stuff; I can't toss it in the trash. But I can't take it to Goodwill either. No, I want someone to get some joy out of these items.

I flick through my saved locations and find the pin I

dropped on JD's store when Lily took me there what feels like an eternity ago. I hit call and wait for an answer.

"JD's Comics, this is JD, how can I help you today?"

"Hey, JD, this is Jen. I was in your shop a few weeks back. My friend bought a choker from you for a photoshoot we did." I bite my lip hoping he remembers me.

"Oh yeah, the Ransom pin-up girl." He chuckles. "What's going on? How'd the shoot go?"

"It was great," I reply and dive into my reason for calling. "I wanted to ask if you do any consignments or anything at your shop."

"Not typically, why do you ask?"

"Well, I'm purging some of my collection of *Space Vendetta* merch and wanted to make sure it went to someone who would appreciate it."

"So you're looking to sell it?" he asks.

"Not necessarily." I study the pile on my couch. "I mean, it did cost me quite a bit, but honestly, at this point, I'd be willing to give it away to someone who really wanted it."

"Well, I run a special program for the local children's hospitals. The kids love all things Vendetta. I could take it off your hands and donate it to the kids getting treatment."

My heart warms at the idea. "I think that'd be perfect. Thanks, JD. I knew you were the man to call."

"Anytime, Jen." He pauses, and I hear him shuffling papers in the background. "What's your address? I'll swing by after work and pick it up."

"I'm in Brooklyn. That too far for you?"

He laughs. "Not at all. That's where my apartment is too. Easy trip for me."

I give him my address and my number. "Thanks, JD. You're a saint."

"Nah, I'm just doing my part to share the love. I'll see you at six."

"Sounds great." I hang up the phone feeling like the weight around my heart lifted. No regrets. No loss. Pure peace with my decision to let it all go.

I grab the framed photo of Nicholas from my bedside and trace my finger along the angled curve of his jaw. "Thanks for the memories." I tuck the frame into the box.

"All right," I announce to the empty space. "Time for a makeover."

The rest of the day passes in a blur. I clean the whole living room, top to bottom, then move to the kitchen. My phone blasts some nineties jams while I work. Everyone else is off at work, so I make the best of my time and deep clean the apartment.

When my phone rings, I finally realize the whole day has passed. It's ten after six.

"Hello?" I answer the call.

"It's JD, I'm out in front of Mario's pizzeria."

"Awesome, I'll be right down." I hang up and grab an armful of freshly laundered blankets. Thank goodness the landlord lets me use his washer and dryer in the basement.

JD glances up when I step out onto the sidewalk. "Hey." He opens the back of the van emblazoned with his company logo.

"Thanks again. I'm glad it's all going to a good cause." I stack them to the side.

"They'll love it." JD follows me upstairs and helps me bring down the rest of the donations.

"That's all of it." I set the last item in the van and dust my hands off.

"Oh, I forgot." He reaches in his back pocket and pulls out a card which he offers. "For you."

"What's this?" I turn it over. A business card with small writing on the back. "Voucher for one hundred dollars at JD's comic shop." My gaze snaps up to his and my words fail.

He shrugs. "It's not much, but you deserve something for being so generous. The little stuff means a lot to the kids."

I hug JD. "Thank you."

"You're welcome." He climbs into the van and drives off.

"What's that about?" A warm masculine voice startles me.

I jump and spin around. "Shaun. Geezers, don't sneak up on me."

"Sorry. It looked like you were moving out." He smiles.

"Nope, just got rid of some things I don't need anymore."

Shaun nods. "Have you eaten dinner yet?"

"Nope."

"Want to grab some pizza?"

"Sounds great. I'm starving."

Shaun links his arm with mine. Together we head into Mario's and grab a pie.

CHAPTER TWENTY-FIVE

When I got demoted, I never expected it to give me the break I didn't realize I needed. For months, I'd been juggling too many things. I dropped every last one of them and found myself lying in a useless heap wondering what the hell happened.

My self-imposed week off passed quickly. I spent most of the time cleaning and organizing my apartment, giving it the update it desperately needed. I got permission from my landlord to give it a fresh coat of paint. The place definitely needed a change, like me.

On Saturday morning, I head to the market and pick up the items I need for dinner with the girls tonight and family dinner tomorrow. It'll be Shaun's first official dinner with my family. He offered to help cook, which I know will leave a good impression on Mom and Grammy once they taste his lasagna.

Once I get home and put the groceries away, I check my email. I still haven't heard anything from Madre. Jessica and Vicky both sent messages sending love and support. They completely understood. We exchanged email and phone numbers to keep in touch outside of the fandom accounts we created. But I was worried when I didn't hear anything from Madre.

I hold my breath when I open my email. Nothing. Disappointment settles around my heart.

Scrolling down, I notice an email from the night before. My eyes widen at the name. Jackson Roberts. Holy shit, Mr. Roberts? I open the email and scan the contents.

Miss Ashcroft,

I trust you're doing well and have taken time to get your priorities organized. That being said, this email is to inform you I require your presence on Thursday morning, eight a.m., to discuss your performance and decide the necessary steps concerning your future with this company. I will have my secretary call you on Monday morning to confirm the appointment. Enjoy your weekend.

Respectfully,

Mr. Roberts

The message dances in front of my eyes. I anticipated a meeting, but not a personalized reminder from Mr. Roberts. Wow. I'm not sure if I should be terrified or flattered.

I push the computer aside and shake my head. Nothing I can do about it now. Honestly, I'm excited to get back to work and prove Mr. Roberts made a wise decision in keeping me with the company.

In the cabinet by the refrigerator, I find my cookbook with Grammy's chocolate chip cookie recipe. Soon the house fills with the scent of baking cookies. I make a few dozen, tucking some aside for dessert tomorrow night, and set the others aside for the movie tonight.

At four o'clock, I take a quick shower and pull on some comfy clothes. An hour later, the doorbell rings.

"Hiya, honey! How was your week?" Lily bounds into the room carrying bags of Chinese takeout.

"Hey. It was good." I take a bag from her hand. "Hi, Maggie."

"Hey, girl." Maggie comes inside and shuts the door with her foot. A large box takes up the space in her arms. She slides it onto the coffee table. Her gaze slides over the room. "Damn. The place looks different."

Lily's eyes widen and she spins around, taking in the whole apartment. "Oh, my! It looks amazing. Is this what you did all week?"

I set the food on the table. "Yeah. I needed a change."

"It looks so much bigger," Maggie says snatching a cookie from the table and admiring the new paint.

"Yeah, it does." I grab plates from the cabinet. "What do you want to drink?"

"Oh, I'll get it." Lily dashes to the refrigerator and pulls out a couple of Yuengling bottles.

"What happened to all the Vendetta stuff?" Maggie asks

between bites.

"Oh, I donated it to the children's hospital." I shrug and correct myself. "Well, JD donated it on my behalf. He used his van."

"Awww." Lily hugs me. "I'm so proud of you. I know it must have been hard."

"Shaun and I had a long talk on Sunday night after dinner at DeLuca's." I scoop some lo mein onto my plate. "I realized it was time to let it go. Find some balance."

Maggie's fingertips brush over the miniature replica of Captain Ransom's ship, the Mendax, sitting on the shelf next to a pot of English ivy. "I see."

"How are you and Shaun?" Lily fills her own plate. "Have you found balance there too?"

I take a seat at the table. "Yeah. I think we have. He stops by every day after work to check on me."

Lily slides into the seat beside me. "That's so sweet. I'm glad you two have worked everything out."

"Yeah, we were worried. They don't raise men like Shaun anymore." Maggie takes the seat across from me and loads up on the broccoli chicken and fried rice.

"That's not true." Lily frowns. "There are some great men out there. You only have to find them."

"You live with three men. Do you think they're great?" Maggie laughs.

"My roommates are like my brothers. I can't think of them that way." She twists the noodles around her fork. "Gavin's a great guy. He got a new position as manager of software development."

I watch the conversation unfold between Lily and Maggie. Somehow the topic shifted from my relationship with Shaun to Lily's roommate, Gavin. I happen to know for a fact Maggie and Gavin do not get along. Not since the night Maggie kicked his ass at *Vendetta: Space Armada.* Gavin did not take the defeat well. To this day, Maggie and Gavin give each other wide berth, but I can practically feel the sexual tension crackling between them.

"Gavin is a shitty loser." Maggie stabs at her chicken with

too much force and it shoots off the plate.

"You can't hold it against him." Lily sighs. "I can't imagine it's fun to get your ass kicked by a girl playing your favorite video game." She points her fork at Maggie. "Plus, your little victory dance at the end only added fuel to the fire."

"Not my problem. My dance was no different than the little macho display they put on when they win." Maggie stuffs a piece of chicken in her mouth.

"You two should fuck and get it over with," I add innocently stoking the fire.

Maggie chokes on her food. "What? Fuck Gavin? You're insane. I'd rather hump a cactus."

Lily doubles over with laughter.

"Oh please. You two hate eye fuck each other every time you're in the same room." I'm enjoying this way more than I should.

"You're delusional. Gavin hates me. I hate him. End of story." Maggie forcefully ends the topic with a huff.

"I met someone." Lily's declaration makes me drop my fork.

"What?" Maggie screeches. "When the hell did this happen? Where?"

"Online." Lily pushes the food around on her plate. "He lives on a ranch in Wyoming."

Maggie and I share stunned glances before rounding on Lily.

"Wait, back up. No, where the hell did you meet this creep online?" Maggie asks.

"Oh, my pin-up group."

"What is a guy from a ranch in Wyoming doing on a pin-up group?" I'm genuinely curious, nothing about her statement even remotely makes sense.

"He joined the group by accident." Lily smiles at the mention of this mysterious cowboy. Shit, she's smitten.

"Please tell me that's the only place you talk to him," Maggie presses.

"No." Lily tucks a curl behind her ear. "We chat on the

phone. He has a sexy voice. All gruff and gritty, like in those old western movies."

"Did it ever occur to you he could be some creepy old man who's getting his rocks off talking to you?" Maggie digs in.

"Oh, our conversations are nothing like that. He's sweet and considerate." Her face blooms a bright pink.

"I'm sure he's great, Lily." I cut in before Maggie explodes. "Just be careful, okay?"

"I'm always careful." Lily bristles, indignant at our inability to support her. "You made friends online and met them in Philly without any backup." She stabs her noodles and stuffs them in her mouth.

"You met your online friends in Philly at the con?" Maggie's ire turns on me. "And you didn't tell me? Goddamn it, Jen!"

"Calm down, Maggie. Nothing bad happened. They were amazing." I try to soothe the situation before it escalates further.

"Amazing? You came home a fucking wreck after the con."

"It wasn't because of the people. It was because of my own fucking issues with my fandom obsession." I force myself to calm down. "I couldn't tell you because I knew you'd freak out. I didn't want you all to worry."

"Too fucking late." Maggie crosses her arms and growls. "Anyone else have any secrets they'd like to share?"

Lily and I exchange glances and shake our heads in unison.

"Good. Then I suggest we watch a movie before my blood pressure goes through the roof." Maggie finishes off the last few bites on her plate and puts the dishes in the sink.

We finish eating and clean up the mess before moving to the living room. Silence stretches between us thanks to the tension unleashed at the table during dinner.

Lily puts the movie on, and I sit on the couch beside Maggie.

"Mags, I'm sorry. I should have told you." I nudge her thigh with mine.

Maggie inhales sharply and exhales with a dramatic groan. "You two are going to be the death of me, you know this." She wraps her arms around me. "I love you. I'm looking out for you."

Her gaze focuses on Lily. "Both of you."

"We know." I hug her tight. "Thanks, babe."

"What are we watching tonight, Lily?"

"Oh, it's an older action flick I found at the store. It has Nicholas Hughes in it." She bites her lip when I frown. "Is that okay, Jen? We can watch something else."

I haven't watched anything with Nicholas in it since Philly. I don't know. I haven't tried to face my addiction since I ran away from the comic con.

"No, it's fine. I haven't seen it, but it was on my list." I smile, and she immediately relaxes.

"Good. It looks like fun." She curls up on the couch on my other side.

As the movie starts, I glance at the women beside me. My friends. They came to my aid when I needed them the most. They helped me ground myself again. Just like my family. And Shaun. I'm fortunate to have such stability in my life.

When Nicholas appears on the screen, I brace myself for the overwhelming draw of his presence. But it doesn't sideline me like it has in the past. There's still an appreciation there, but it has transformed into a gentle pull instead of an unrelenting need. He's handsome and the film plays on his skills as an actor. I love it, but I don't lose myself in the enjoyment.

Finally, I see balance taking root, and hope radiates through me.

CHAPTER TWENTY-SIX

"The lasagna should be done," Shaun calls from across the room where he's setting the table. "Would you take it out of the oven?"

I grab a set of oven mitts from beside the stove and open the oven. The heat washes over me in a whoosh. I reach in and retrieve the glass pan of bubbling lasagna.

"Got it." I inhale deeply and set it on the stovetop. "Oh, it smells so good."

Shaun chuckles. "I taught you how to make it. No excuses now."

"It's never the same when I make anything." I grab the tray of garlic bread waiting to be toasted and adjust the setting before popping it in the oven. I set the egg timer for ten minutes.

"You forget the key ingredient." He wraps his arms around me from behind.

"And what would that be?" I sink into his warmth. "Don't say love. That's corny."

He nips at my neck before kissing the same spot. "Well, it may be corny, but it's true."

"Whatever you say." I spin in his embrace and wrap my arms around his neck. Those warm whiskey eyes flash with amusement and admiration.

"Actually, the trick is to sauté your aromatics with the onions before you add the wine to deglaze them and then add the tomato sauce. Unlocks the flavors, gives it more depth." His smile transforms his mouth into a sensual promise.

I shove my hand against his chest. "I told you it wasn't love."

"Okay, not really, but people can always tell if you put time and effort into making them something. That's what makes it special. So technically, love is the secret ingredient." He kisses the tip of my nose.

I pull him down so I can cover his mouth with mine. He tightens his hold and kisses me deeply, exploring me with his tongue and his hands. I moan and press against him. He breaks the kiss and holds me at an arm's length.

"Simmer down. Don't start something we can't finish." Shaun winks.

I pout and stomp down the arousal coursing through me. The doorbell rings and Shaun drops his hold on me.

"See, I told you." He smooths his hand over his hair. "It would've been awkward to be interrupted by your family."

Sticking out my tongue at Shaun, I mentally redirect my focus on the family dinner we're supposed to be having, not the need zinging through my body at lightning speed.

With a deep breath, I open the door. "Mom, Dad, Grammy. Come in."

After they smother both Shaun and me with greetings and hugs, my timer dings in the kitchen. I run to the oven and pull out the garlic bread and set it beside the lasagna before turning off the oven.

"Dinner smells delicious," Dad says, taking a seat at the head of the table.

"Thanks. Shaun taught me to make his famous lasagna." I grab Dad a beer from the fridge and pop the top on the bottle.

"Nabbed yourself a man who could cook." He winks. "Smart girl."

"Yes, she is." Shaun moves the lasagna to the prepared spot in the center of the table.

I spy Mom and Grammy milling around the living room. "Dinner's on the table."

They both spin around.

"The apartment looks different. Did you redecorate?" Mom asks. "I love the color."

"Yeah, I took advantage of being home this week and did some major cleaning, donated some stuff, and then repainted." I shelf my hands on my hips and reexamine my handiwork. Pride fills me.

"It's different." Grammy sniffs. "But it suits you. Very mature. I hope you saved that warm blanket with the sexy man on it."

"No, Grammy. I donated most of my stuff to the children's hospital." A move I still don't regret, although she's right. That blanket was warm as fuck. I should have saved it.

She wraps her arms around me. "I'm proud of you," she whispers so only I can hear her.

"Thanks." I hold her and feel the strength of her flowing into me.

"Now, let's eat. I'm starving." Grammy lets me go and pats my hand.

Mom, Grammy, and I take our seats. Shaun and Dad are already engrossed in conversation about fishing.

"I didn't know you liked to fish, Dad." I stare at him open-mouthed.

He chuckles. "I love to fish. Just never find the time to get out and do it."

"It's a lot easier to do it back home than it is here," Shaun agrees as he slices the lasagna and serves each of us.

My heart warms at the sight of him showering my family with attention. He treats them as if they were his own family. God, I love him. How the hell did I get so damn lucky?

Shaun catches my eye and winks. I feel the effect of it down to my core. A gentle reminder of what almost happened in the kitchen minutes ago.

"Where did you say you were from?" Dad asks, cutting his lasagna.

"I grew up in Davenport, Iowa originally. Attended a local college." Shaun answers without hesitation. This is what he needed, what I needed. A family connection. A balance to keep us grounded. "But I've also lived in Chicago and Denver."

"Where in Iowa?" Mom asks taking a bite of lasagna.

"Right on the Mississippi River. It's a couple of hour drive to Chicago from there."

"Are you still close to your family?" Grammy throws in her own question.

"I am." Longing fills Shaun's expression. I take his hand in mine and squeeze. "I haven't been home in a while, but I'm planning on visiting them for Thanksgiving this year."

"I'm sure your parents will love that." Mom grins and takes another bite. "Mmmm, this lasagna is amazing. Did you make this, Shaun?"

"It's my recipe. Jen helped me make it." His cheeks pinken. "I made it for her on our second date."

"He's definitely a keeper." Grammy stuffs another bite into her mouth.

I chuckle and listen to the conversation continue. My parents take turns asking Shaun about his childhood, his education, his hobbies, anything, and everything. And he takes it in stride. Every question was answered honestly. I learn more about him in two hours than I did in six months of dating.

After I serve dessert, Shaun slides his hand into mine. Why did I wait this long to bring these two pieces of my life together? They nestle together so perfectly, it's shocking but wonderful.

A few weeks ago, I would have panicked at the thought of introducing Shaun to my parents, not because I was embarrassed of one or the other, but because I didn't want to ruin anything. My fear of Shaun waking up and walking away without a backward glance held me captive for so long, I didn't consider his perspective.

When he finally did leave, it gutted me. The worst happened, and the world didn't end. Granted, I didn't handle it the best, thanks to my mishap at work, but with the support of my family and friends, I was able to face the world again. I was strong enough to get back on my feet and refocus. Shaun's return solidified my resolve.

No one rescued me. They lent me their strength and encouraged me. It made all the difference in the world. Am I still terrified of fucking up and losing all of this? Hell yes. But life isn't worth living without a little risk.

Once my family leaves, Shaun helps me clean the kitchen and put everything away. We move together as a team and the feeling of peace is indescribable but satisfying.

"I should probably leave." Shaun pulls me in for a kiss. "Six a.m. comes early."

"Yeah." I step back, breathless, knowing his kiss will only drag me under. "I have a meeting with Mr. Roberts on Thursday morning."

The haze of lust fades from his eyes. "You ready?"

"Yeah, I got this." I nod with confidence even though I'm petrified.

"You'll do great. Mr. Roberts knows what an asset you are to the company." He hugs me tight. "I have faith in you."

"I'm glad someone does."

"Don't start." He squeezes me until I squeal and wiggle in his arms.

I laugh hysterically when he tickles my sides. "Okay! Stop. I can't breathe."

Shaun's hands still and I double over, catching my breath. Finally, he takes my chin in his hand and tilts my face up until we're eye to eye.

"You're amazing, Jen. If they can't realize that, then it's their loss." He kisses me softly. "I love you."

"I love you too." My uncertainty fades at the confidence in his words. "You'd better go before I drag you into the bedroom and finish what we started in the kitchen."

Shaun glances at the clock and then grabs me by the waist, tossing me over his shoulder. "I can spare an hour." He smacks my ass with his palm.

Heat blooms throughout my body, ruining a perfectly respectable pair of panties. Shaun proves he can do a lot with an hour when he sets his mind to it.

CHAPTER TWENTY-SEVEN

The meeting with Mr. Roberts went well. I presented him with the truth in the hopes he would see my effort to move beyond my mistakes and grow as both an individual and a professional. He requested I return to work first thing Monday morning. I heard the high expectations in his tone when he relayed the instructions. Relief infuses me with a newfound sense of purpose. This weekend will be one for celebration. I leave the meeting feeling refreshed and energized ready to take on the world.

Shaun invites me to spend the weekend at his place. I jump at the opportunity. His apartment is only a block from my favorite park. I hope to get out and enjoy some of the gorgeous summer weather while we still have it.

Life seems to be back on track. I return home and pack a bag for my weekend with Shaun. I tuck away a few fun surprises for him in the bottom of the bag. I hope I'm not crossing a line by including them, but this new, improved Jen isn't intimidated by spicing up things in the bedroom. I know for a fact Shaun isn't either.

The next day, I clean the apartment and leave for Shaun's at four. He doesn't get home until five, but since he gave me a key to his apartment, I decide to head over early and prepare my surprise.

Inside his apartment, I put my bag in his bedroom and head into the kitchen with the cooler I brought. With the jams turned way up, I prep the chicken I had soaking in a spicy marinade and then cut the veggies for the stir fry.

My phone rings. "Hello." I fumble with the buttons trying to put it on speaker.

"Hey," Shaun's voice echoes through the other line. "I'm running late tonight. Doesn't look like I'll be home until closer to eight."

Disappointment settles over me. "No problem. I haven't started cooking yet."

"Are you already at my place?" he asks, apparently surprised.

"Yeah, I wanted dinner to be ready when you got home."

"I'll be home by eight. I promise. See you then."

"Okay."

When the line disconnects, I put the items in the fridge and clean the counters. With everything prepared, I can easily pop it in the skillet closer to eight.

I glance at the time. Five-thirty. Plenty of time. I stretch and grab my laptop from my bag. Settling on the couch, I turn on the television for background noise and boot up my machine, making sure to plug it in. Damn thing can't hold a charge anymore.

My email is overflowing with spam. I take time to clean out my inbox and find an email from Madre buried in the spam folder. It's dated from the week before. Shit.

Jen. I totally understand. Sorry, it took me so long to respond. My kid broke his arm and then the other had summer camp. Ugh. It's been a madhouse here.

You know you're always welcome to reach out whenever you want. I'll be here for you. We may have connected through fandom, but that doesn't define us. We're so much more. We'll always have Philly. A memory I'll treasure even if it didn't end on a high note.

I'm sorry to hear about your week from hell. I hope you're able to patch things up with your boyfriend and get your job back on track. As for finding balance, I'm not sure I'll be much help there. It's a constant struggle for me. My husband often yells at me to get off my damn phone/computer and give him attention. I guess the only piece of advice I can offer is communication is key. I know it sounds trite, but it's true.

My husband knows how much I love my fandoms. He thinks I'm crazy sometimes, but he supports me. And I support him. I've had to delete accounts before when they became too overwhelming. I've had to take breaks from social media and yes, even writing fanfics. Fandom life can drag you underwater, even if you know how to swim and have a life vest.

Do what you need to do. Follow your heart and be honest with your boyfriend. He'll respect you for it if your obsession hasn't chased him off completely by now. Some men can't cope with something they view as competition. I hope that helps. I'm sorry I can't be there to give you a huge hug. You're amazing and I love you tons.

Keep me posted. My inbox is open. And here's my number if you want to text me directly or call. 555-607-0991

Chat soon. Xoxo, Bonnie.

For the last week, I thought she hated me. Damn internet misdirected the email. I'm relieved the one person who truly understood my struggle aside from Shaun hadn't abandoned me. I smile and type out a reply assuring her both my relationship and my job were salvaged in the wreckage of my week from hell.

I haven't logged into my Tumblr or Twitter account since I left comic con. I didn't want to see him or read other people's joyful experiences at comic con. At first, it was because I didn't want to feel the sting of jealousy, but then it evolved into a deeper sense of bitter loss. Now, it just doesn't matter in the architecture of my life.

Somehow, I moved beyond it. I know part of the reason for it is my life's epic implosion following comic con, but such a moment was inevitable. It was building to that point whether or not I saw it.

I send the response to Madre and add her number to my phone. I shoot off a quick text to her number. *It's Jen. Thanks for the email. I replied.*

A response comes through a minute later. *I'm glad you're still here. Miss you.*

Nothing compares to the feeling I get at her message. Bolstered in my resolve, I log into Twitter and delete my fandom account. Then I log into Tumblr and delete my account there as well. Each step lifts me higher and higher out of any remaining hesitation.

When I open my FanArchive account, the comments catch my eye. Notes of encouragement and support. Requests for more. Most of them are words of love. I can't bring myself to delete the account. Not yet.

I glance at the clock and see it's seven-thirty. Shit. Shaun will be home soon. I set the open laptop on the coffee table and dart into the kitchen.

Fifteen minutes later, the apartment smells heavenly with the aroma of Thai chicken and veggies. I check the rice cooker and see it only has ten minutes left. Perfect timing.

"Damn, I could get used to this," Shaun says from the doorway.

"What?" I stir the meat and veggies before removing them from the heat and covering it.

"Coming home to a sexy woman in my kitchen making me dinner." He drops his bag on the floor by the door and comes up behind me. "I like it." He wraps his arms around my waist.

"Don't get used to it." I rock my hips back against him. His hard cock presses against my ass.

"What if we took turns cooking? You one week, me the next." His teeth pull my ear lobe making me moan. "I'll even wear an apron."

"Only an apron?" I grasp the counter to keep from falling over. "Nothing else?"

He hisses. "Burn risk, but if you want me naked in the kitchen, I'm sure we can work something out."

"Tease." I bite my lip when he kisses along my jaw, his hand wrapping around my throat.

He releases me and steps back. "Touché."

I glower at him and thrust the spoon into his hand. "I'm going to rinse off in the shower."

Shaun's laughter follows me into his bedroom. I close the door and head into the bathroom. After a quick rinse, I throw on my surprise and don a pair of yoga pants and my favorite T-shirt.

When I walk back into the living room, I stop short. Shaun's sitting on the couch with my computer open.

"What are you doing?" I ask sitting beside him.

"Reading your fanfic," he replies without looking up from the screen.

"Don't read that!" I try to grab the computer from his

hands.

He swats my hands away. "Why not?"

Heat infuses me and my cheeks are burning. "Because; it's pure smut."

"I noticed." He pulls at his collar. "It's good."

"Really?" Hope blossoms in my chest.

He glances up and meets my gaze. "Of course. It may be smut, but it's really well written. Better than most of the fanfics I've read over the years."

"You read smutty fan fiction?" My jaw drops.

"I've told you before, you don't know everything about me." Shaun winks. "Although, I've never written it myself."

"Only *Space Vendetta* fics?" I pry deeper peeling back layers to this complicated man I love so dearly.

"No. I've read other fandom fics too."

"Like what?" I push.

"I can't tell you or I'd have to kill you." He resumes reading.

I nudge him in the side. "Please. I promise I won't tell anyone."

"I'm more worried about the hysterical laughter and you never letting me live it down," he grumbles.

"Tell me." I rock against him back and forth until he groans.

"Fine." He inhales deeply and mumbles, "TMNT."

I freeze. Did he say TMNT? "Say what?"

"Teenage Mutant Ninja Turtles." He grits out the words between his teeth. "It was a phase."

"Was it smut?" I blink at him wondering at the logistics of such a scenario.

"Yes. Can we please move on now?" He gestures to the screen. "I want to finish this."

"No. Let's eat first. You can tell me all about your foray into TMNT smutty fan fiction."

He relents and sets the computer aside. "Fine. We can eat. But I'm not talking about anything related to what I just confessed."

I pout and follow him to the table. We eat in relative silence until I ask about his day. Slowly the conversation eases into a comfortable topic again. Once we finish the meal, Shaun cleans up the dishes while I put the leftovers away.

He changes into gray sweatpants and a t-shirt, and we curl up on the couch together. "Can I finish your fanfic now?" He reaches for the computer.

"Do you really want to read it?" I ask, genuinely surprised at his interest.

"Yes." He opens the laptop.

"Why?" I hook my leg over his.

His hand settles on my thigh, and those enchanting eyes ensnare mine. "Two reasons. One, it's good. Maybe you should start writing erotic romance and publish it."

I scoff. "No one would want to read my stories. Besides, I'm using a universe that already exists. I'd have to make one up if I want to publish it. Has to be original."

"Oh, I'm sure you can find some good ideas." He kisses my cheek. "I can help you brainstorm." His kiss trails down over my jaw until he captures my lips in a passionate exploration.

I press my hand against his chest and break the kiss before he muddles my mind completely. "Wait, you said there were two reasons you wanted to read my fic. What's the second?"

Shaun takes my hand and rests it on his cock standing at full attention straining against his sweatpants. "Because it turns me on, reading your words. Imagining you doing to me what the heroine is doing to Ransom in the story."

Well, fuck me, that was not what I was expecting. I nod a few times and blink, unable to form a coherent thought.

He sets the laptop back on the table and pulls me into his lap. "Does it turn you on to write it?" His hand slides over my hip and toys with the waistband of my yoga pants.

"Yes." I cling to him unprepared for the need coursing through me.

Shaun tugs my yoga pants down and stops. I whimper and then realize what he's staring at.

"What do we have here?" He snaps the red lace underwear before pushing my pants off completely.

I bite my lip and hide my face in his chest.

"Is this the crest of the Space Rangers?" He traces his fingers over the emblem centered above my mound. "I almost bought these for you."

"You did?" My gaze snaps to his. Lust sparks in his handsome eyes.

"Yes, I imagined peeling them off you with my teeth."

My gasp makes him grin.

He pushes the fabric of my t-shirt up revealing the matching red lace bra. His fingers brush the charm dangling between my breasts. "Lynnea's ship."

I lick my lips. "Do you like it?"

Shaun tugs the shirt off completely leaving me with nothing but the red lace. "I love it. Red lace suits you much better than green silk and black leather." His eyes flash with the implied meaning.

"Is that you talking or Commander Colton?" I thread my fingers through the hair at the base of his neck.

His wicked smirk fits Ransom more than Colton, but I don't care because this man is neither of them. He's mine. All mine. And the mere fact he's willing to indulge in my little fantasy makes me infinitely more turned on.

As if reading my mind, Shaun slips his fingers over my damp panties pressing into the wetness until he finds my clit. I arch against him and tighten my grip on his hair.

"That depends. Is this for Ransom? Colton?" He slides his fingers beneath my panties and parts my folds with two fingers.

"Neither." I gasp when he thrusts them into me, curling them to brush against my g-spot.

"Then who?" He moves with deliberate slow strokes, his thumb brushing my clit.

Sensations ricochet through me. "You." I gasp and rock my hips in rhythm with his hand. "Only you."

"Good girl." He kisses me as he quickens his pace. I'm caught up in the moment spiraling higher with every pleasurable stroke. "Are you going to come for me?"

I nod. He takes my mouth in a bruising kiss, doubling the pace of his hand as he fucks me with his fingers.

"Come for me, baby." He chuckles against my mouth when I moan. "I want to hear you scream my name." His thumb circles my clit pressing hard. Sparks shoot through me and my orgasm pulls tight in the pit of my stomach. "My name. Only mine."

"Shaun!" My eyes flutter closed and fireworks explode behind my lids when my climax rips through me. I grip Shaun hard, my nails digging into his shoulders. He milks every last drop of my orgasm from my body, slowing his ministrations to a featherlight stroke before sliding free.

"Holy shit," I mutter, stunned by the force of it. "That was amazing."

Shaun's studying me, passion blazing in his brown eyes. "I'm not done with you. Not by a long shot." My sated smile makes him raise a brow in question. "What are you plotting?"

"Well," I say, licking my lower lip seductively. His gaze darkens at the motion. "I brought some, uh, toys. If you're interested in playing?"

Without a word, Shaun sets me on my feet, stands, and then hefts me into his arms. He crosses to the bedroom and tosses me on the bed beside my bag.

"Show me."

I unzip my bag and shift through the contents. I remove a small leather paddle, silk scarves, a vibrator, and a small red plug. His mouth twitches with amusement.

"Feeling adventurous, are you?" He picks up the plug and twists it in his fingers.

I swallow hard. He didn't freak out; in fact, judging by the bulge in his gray sweatpants, I would say he's even more aroused than he was while reading my fic. At my nod, Shaun tosses the toy on the bed and sets the bag on the floor.

He prowls closer, pushing me back on the bed and covering my body with his. We both scramble to pull his shirt over his head in a flurry of movement. He frees my breasts and pushes off my ruined panties. I push his pants down over his hips, freeing his cock.

My hands wrap around it. He groans so loud it echoes off the walls.

Shaun grabs my wrists and pins my arms to the mattress. He slides between my slick thighs and straight into my sensitive pussy.

"Oh, fuck." I grind my hips against his.

"Is this what you wanted?" He pistons his hips, pounding into me.

I ride every thrust and the pressure of another orgasm builds inside me. He holds my hands fast restraining my movement.

"Yes." I pant meeting his movement with the same amount of frenzy. I chase my climax, needing to feel him deeper, faster. More. Higher and higher. "Please."

Shaun releases my hand and applies pressure to my clit. Another orgasm rips through me. I tighten around him, pulsing and riding the waves of pleasure down.

He pulls out and comes on my stomach. Only then do I realize even in the heat of passion, he was still aware of his actions. He traces the head of his cock against my thigh.

"You made me forget a step." He sighs.

"It's okay. I have an IUD."

He laughs. "Good. I hate condoms."

"Me too." I trace my fingers through the mess he left painted on my skin. "But they do make cleanup easier."

We both break into laughter.

"Wait here." Shaun climbs from the bed and gets a wet washcloth from the bathroom. He cleans me up and then lays down beside me.

I nestle closer, draping my leg over his, pressing my body to his. His heat surrounds me. I've never been more contented.

"Did you buy those toys recently?" he asks.

I prop myself up on my elbow and stare down at him. "Why?"

"Curiosity. But I do wonder if you've been holding out on me."

"Holding out on you?" I'm confused. "What do you mean?"

Shaun chuckles. "Well, do you have a lot of experience with

these things?" He picks up the rope and slides it between his fingers.

I shake my head and swallow. "No, why?"

"Let's just say, there are things about me I haven't told you."

My eyes widen at the possibilities. "Are you a serial killer?" I tease.

He laughs. "Not even close, sweetheart."

"Are you going to show me how to use this?" I hold up the plug.

Shaun takes it from my hand and pulls me in for a heated kiss. My body responds instantly like I haven't had two earth shattering orgasms already.

"Later," he growls against my mouth. "Right now, I want dessert." He flips me on my back and slides down my body, parting my thighs.

When his mouth covers me, I lose all coherent thought. Yes, a girl can definitely get used to this. I'll cook and clean and do whatever he wants if he pays me in orgasms. Forever.

CHAPTER TWENTY-EIGHT

Three months later and life is good. I take the F line from Manhattan to Brooklyn after work. The commuting crowd settles into the train around me. Shaun takes my hand and smiles. We slide into a corner and hold tight when it lurches into motion. I like this little routine we have; it soothes me. We've talked about moving in together but haven't quite figured out logistics yet.

I'm back at work, and while I didn't get the promotion I wanted, I got something even better. Mr. Roberts offered me the position as his assistant since his retired last month. I'm still not sure what he sees in me, but I'm grateful for the opportunity.

Shaun teases me relentlessly about how I got the position. Never at work, only when we're alone together. He thinks I have a thing for Mr. Roberts and his distinguished silver-fox good looks. I remind him daily there's only one man for me. And it's not him.

This often earns me a growl and him hauling me across his lap where he torments me with his fingers until I recant my statement multiple times. Only then will he allow me any release.

Finally, there's balance. A blissful and tenuous thing. I'm still petrified Shaun will wake up one morning and realize he's made a horrible mistake and no longer wants to be with me. Or Mr. Roberts will fire me because I mistakenly sent him one of my erotica manuscripts instead of the notes from the meeting he requested. Most of all, I worry I'll fall down the rabbit hole again over Nicholas Hughes or some other handsome actor playing a seductive villain.

But I know my friends and family will haul me out by my ankles and remind me exactly what's at stake without hesitation. They didn't rescue me, they reminded me. And everyone needs a gentle reminder once in a while, right?

The train reaches our station, and Shaun tugs on my hand leading me through the crowd. Once we reach the street level, the sun is already low on the horizon hiding behind the buildings.

"What do you want to do for dinner?" Shaun asks. We cross the street heading for his apartment.

"Whatever you're cooking." I spin around and walk backward, searching his face.

"Pick something or you can eat oatmeal for dinner."

"Rude." I spin around in time to barely miss colliding with a man swerving around us. My arm collides with his and the papers in his hands scatter over the ground.

"Oh my God. I'm so sorry." I drop to my knees and gather the papers before they float away on the late September breeze.

The man bends down and gathers the papers, his hat pulled low over his eyes. "It's okay. I wasn't paying attention to where I was going." The gruff voice tugs at my memory.

"Welcome to New York," I joke.

Shaun joins us and chases after an errant paper spiraling toward the street.

The stranger and I reach for the same paper, and our fingers brush. I jerk my hand back. "Sorry."

"Nothing to be sorry for." He tilts his head back. I recognize the vivid blue-green of his eyes and the lopsided smirk on his lips. My world spins on its axis, hits a speedbump, and ricochets off into space pinging around Mars and barely missing Jupiter on its journey through the galaxy.

Nicholas Hughes in the flesh. My heart stops beating for a moment then lurches into gear at two hundred miles per hour.

I offer him the papers in my hand.

"Thanks." He takes them and tucks them under one arm, extending his hand. "Nicholas."

"Jen." I shake his hand. "I loved your work in *Disruption of Desire*."

His eyes sparkle and he chuckles. "Ah, you recognized me."

"Of course. I'd be blind not to." I regain some semblance of speech at his humility. "Are you in town for a new project?"

"No. I'm visiting a friend." He glances at this watch. "And

I'm late. I must have gotten turned around trying to find the restaurant."

"Which restaurant?" I offer a reassuring smile. "I've lived here for fifteen years. I know this place like the back of my hand."

"Antonella Vinci's Bistro?" Nicholas pulls out his phone to verify the name. "Yes. That's it."

"One block over." I point toward the direction Shaun and I just came from. "You can't miss it. Their sign is visible from the corner."

"Ah, you're a lifesaver. Thank you." Nicholas sighs with visible relief.

Shaun appears with three papers in his hand. "They almost got away." He offers them to Nicholas who takes them with a grateful smile.

"Thank you. I appreciate the help." Nicholas adds the papers to the pile in his hand.

"Antonella makes the best carbonara. I highly recommend it," I add as an afterthought.

"Noted." Nicholas smiles and my heart flips. "Thanks again. Have a lovely evening. Both of you."

With a nod, he ventures off down the street and disappears around the corner.

Shaun and I exchange a stunned look.

"Was that..." he begins.

"Yup."

Shaun blinks in surprise. "What the hell is he doing in Brooklyn?"

"He said he was visiting a friend." I shrug my shoulder.

"You okay?" he asks.

"Of course, why wouldn't I be okay?" I scrunch my nose up at the silly question.

"You literally ran into Nicholas Hughes." He takes a breath. "I expected your inner fangirl to freak out."

I slap his arm and then grab it pulling him toward me before setting us off toward his apartment. "My inner fangirl is fine. I'm good. He's quite the gentleman."

"You're handling this well." Shaun shifts his hand to mine and interlaces our fingers. "I'm proud of you."

"He's human. I'm human. It's all good." I grin up at Shaun.

"Yes, a famous, rich, and extremely handsome human you wrote smutty fan fiction about."

My face heats. "Stop. We don't talk about it. Ugh. I hope he doesn't read my stuff. I should delete all of it."

Shaun laughs deep and loud. "No. Keep it up. People enjoy the little escape. I know I do." He winks. "Especially the one featuring the threesome with Lynnea, Ransom, and Colton."

"Everyone loves that one." The visual in my mind leaves me breathless. "I should probably update it. It's been a month since my last chapter."

"Yes, love. Your readers will kill you if you don't give them another chapter soon." He pulls me in for a kiss. "I'm dying to know what happens next."

"You're ridiculous." I love hearing him talk about my work like he can't get enough. It's good for my ego and our sex life. "Cheesesteaks."

Shaun glances at me in confusion. "What?"

"For dinner." I lick my lips at the thought of the tasty sandwiches. "I want a cheesesteak."

He opens the door to his building. "I was thinking the same thing. Good thing I picked up the stuff this week to make them."

Once we reach Shaun's apartment, I change into sweats and a hoodie before joining Shaun in the kitchen. By the time we head to bed, the encounter with Nicholas Hughes fades from my memory like a daydream.

CHAPTER TWENTY-NINE

~~STAGE SIX: REPEATING THE CYCLE~~

By mid-October, my life has finally reached a manageable balance. Work, family, friends, and Shaun in fluid motion from one day to the next. I still talk to Madre and write fan fiction when the mood strikes me, but I've unplugged from the rest. Some people can handle the overwhelming chaos of fandom, but I'm not one of them it seems. And I'm at peace with this realization.

"Babe?" I call out the moment I get home from work. Shaun was out today for an appointment uptown. "You home?"

Silence greets me. I frown. It's after six. He should be home. I set my purse on the table by the door and kick off my heels.

The scent of rosemary and thyme lingers in the air making my mouth water. I round the corner. The kitchen is empty and clean. My gaze skims the rest of the apartment. A flicker of candlelight catches my eye. I round the island and see the dining room table set for two with covered dishes in the center next to a tall candle and a bouquet of a variety of colorful daisies.

It's beautiful and romantic. I grasp the counter to steady myself. "Shaun?"

"Surprise." Shaun's voice echoes behind me.

I spin around and stifle my gasp. He's wearing his Colton cosplay bearing a large pink daisy between his outstretched fingers. A grin splits my lips wide. He looks absolutely perfect, albeit a tad ridiculous in the space commander's uniform. But the sight is magnificent nonetheless.

"Did you dig this out for me?" I run my fingers down his chest.

"Yes, I did." He tugs at the collar. "Although, I think I gained a few pounds since I wore it last."

I unbutton the top two buttons baring some skin. "Better?"

"Yes. Thank you." He breathes deep in relief.

"What is all this?" I gesture to the costume and the meal.

"I can't do something nice for the woman I love?" Shaun pulls an offended sneer.

"Of course, you can." I wrap my arms around his waist. "But I feel underdressed."

"You look perfect." He kisses me, slow and insistent. I melt against him letting my hands drift down to his leather-clad ass.

He moans when I grab both cheeks and squeeze. "Baby, if you keep it up, dinner will get cold."

"But I'm hungry."

"Then let's eat."

I smile against his mouth. "Not that kind of hungry."

"Damn, woman." He kisses me hard, stealing my breath this time.

I sway when he breaks away. His kisses scramble my brain. It takes me longer than it should to realize Shaun has dropped to his knee. My heart stops beating and my jaw drops. "What are you doing?"

He grins and reaches into his pocket. "I may not have traveled the universe or saved mankind from the brink of extinction, but I promise, I will do everything in my power to love and support you for the rest of our lives. I can't imagine spending another day without you in my life. Jen, will you marry me?"

My vision blurs with tears. I wipe my eyes and see the emerald solitaire ring between his fingers and the glow of love surrounding Shaun's face.

"Yes, I will."

He takes my hand and slides the ring on my finger. I pull him to his feet and kiss him through my joyful tears. He lifts me off my feet and spins me around.

"You went to all this trouble to propose?" I whisper in his ear.

"Of course, I did. You're worth it, baby." He kisses me again.

I bury my face in his chest.

He strokes my hair. "I love you, Jen."

"I can see that." I gaze up at him. "I love you too."

"Shall we eat or are you still hungry?" Shaun winks.

"I'd hate for this delicious meal to get cold." I turn and admire the table aware of the man behind me. My fiancé. I could die happy right now.

"Allow me." Shaun pulls out my chair. Once I'm seated, he takes his seat across from me.

We dive into the meal. Shaun is a world-class chef, whether he acknowledges it or not. I eat every bite and relish the delightful flavors. The conversation shifts to work.

"How are we going to tell everyone at the office?" I take a sip of wine. "It'll spread like wildfire through the building once we tell Mr. Roberts."

"Oh, I've already spoken with Mr. Roberts about it." Shaun wipes his mouth on a napkin.

"Wait, you what now?" I narrow my eyes.

"I spoke to Mr. Roberts earlier this week about my intention to propose to you."

"That confident, were you?"

"Yes and no." His warm whiskey gaze settles on me. "I wanted to be sure there would be no conflict of interest."

"What did he say?" I lean forward curious as to the conclusion of this conversation.

"He wished me good luck." Shaun's lips stretch into a knowing grin.

"Uh-huh." I shake my head. "I can't believe you talked to my boss about this. Does anyone else know?"

Shaun chuckles. "Yes. I pulled your Dad aside last week after dinner and told him I wanted to marry you."

I nearly spit wine down my blouse. "What? I thought you were talking about fishing?"

"Nope. He promised not to say anything to your mom and Grammy until I got my answer."

Stunned, I study his handsome face. "You sneaky little shit."

"Zero regrets." He shrugs his shoulder. "I wanted to make

sure it was a surprise."

"Well, you succeeded." I lean back in my chair and smile when a random thought hits me. "Did you tell them you were going to propose wearing your old cosplay?"

His head shakes vehemently. "No. That was only for you, baby. No one else gets to see me in this much leather."

"I like it." My laughter bubbles up at the thought of him wearing it on our wedding day. "Maybe we should do a *Space Vendetta-themed* wedding? You wear your Colton costume and I'll dress as Lynnea."

Shaun snorts. "Are you serious? You don't want a huge fancy, proper wedding?"

"Hell no. I've never been a stickler for tradition. If we're throwing a wedding, it should be a party. Let's make it fun."

"I knew you were a good catch." He rounds the table and pulls me out of my chair.

My arms wrap around his neck, and he rubs his cheek against mine. "You did?"

"Yeah, I did." He pulls me toward the couch and sits down, tugging me into his lap. "During our first date, I knew I couldn't let you get away."

I curl against him. "That was before my obsession spiraled out of control."

"We all have those moments, Jen." He brushes my hair away from my face. "You stumbled like I did. But we're both stronger now than we were before."

My body warms at his observation. "Thanks for sticking around."

"Always, babe." His kiss makes my toes curl. When he draws back, I see the sincerity reflected deep in his soul. "Are we really doing a Vendetta-themed wedding?"

"Yes. Let's do it. I want something fun and memorable."

He laughs. "It'll definitely be both of those."

"Can I invite Madre, I mean, Bonnie to the wedding?" I bite my lip.

"Of course. But if anyone dresses up as Ransom, I'm kicking them out of the ceremony." His brow furrows. "I won't have anyone distracting my woman on our wedding day."

I burst out laughing. His expression is dead serious. "Shaun. You're my Ransom and my Colton. No, you're better than both of them. You're real." I cup his face between my hands. "And you're mine."

Shaun growls and pulls me tight against him. "I like when you get all possessive."

Heat curls through my core. "I do too." I lick my lips. "I mean when you get all possessive with me."

His hand comes down on my hip and the crack echoes through the room. "Mine."

"All yours, commander." I purr and rub against him.

He inhales deep restraining himself, I can feel it. "Go change. I have something I want to show you."

I arch my brow in question and cup his cock through his pants.

"Later." He presses a kiss to my hand and releases me. "Hurry. I have plans for you."

Motivated, I race for the bedroom and change into a comfortable pair of sweatpants and my favorite sweatshirt with the Vendetta logo on it. When I return, Shaun's ditched his cosplay costume for gray sweats and a black T-shirt.

"How did you?" I glance at the bedroom. "Never mind."

"I have the movie ready." He pats his lap, inviting me to join him.

I sit beside him, and he grunts, pulling me into his lap like I was before. I lean against him angling myself to see the television.

"What are we watching?"

"One of my favorite shows."

"Oh, another science fiction series?"

He chuckles. "No. This one is a medieval fantasy."

"Ohhhh, that's different. I've never gotten into fantasy before."

"If you like Vendetta, you'll love this one." He presses play.

We watch the introduction in silence. The theme song is catchy and dramatic. I see an emblem of a dragon and gasp. "There are dragons?!"

"Shhhh. I'm not giving you any spoilers."

Thirty minutes into the show and I'm riveted. The story itself is slow, but the tension is building brick by solid brick. There are a hundred characters to choose from, I don't know who is who, or who's loyal to whom, but damn it, I'm here for this.

Then I see him, with his dark hair and winter blue eyes and a smolder sharp enough to kill. My insides twist when he talks, deep and gruff. There's little challenge for me to imagine all the wicked things I want to do to this man.

"Who is that?" I ask, hoping my voice sounds dispassionate and casual.

Shaun's grip on me tightens. "He's the Forgotten Knight. Pay attention."

We watch in silence. I'm invested in the Forgotten Knight and his dark intentions. When the first episode ends, I whip around to face Shaun.

"How many episodes are there in season one?"

Shaun laughs. "I take it you liked it?"

"I love it. Especially the Forgotten Knight. Who's the actor who plays him?" I try to stand so I can get my phone out of my purse, but Shaun's grip holds me fast.

"No." He growls. "Remember what happened the last time you asked that question."

I remember. Disappointment fills me. "I promise I won't chase the rabbit this time."

Shaun threads his hand through my hair and pulls me close. His mouth captures mine in a dizzying kiss. I cling to him, shifting myself in his lap to get closer. He teases my mouth open and steals every whimper and moan.

My head swims when he releases me. I grasp his shoulders to keep myself upright. Passion burns bright in his eyes and I grin.

"I'm the only man you need to worry about, sweetheart." He turns off the television and carries me into the bedroom.

I kick and squirm even though my body is aching for his possessive conquest. All thoughts of the Forbidden Knight and

Captain Ransom and Nicholas Hughes, hell every other man in the universe, fly right out of my head the moment Shaun tosses me on the bed.

He's right. Shaun is the only man I'll ever need. He's mine, and that's all that matters.

THE END

KIRSTEN S. BLACKETER
Confessions
of a
Gamer Girl

CHAPTER ONE

One year ago…

"You're gonna die! Don't do it!" The shout echoes through the immaculate brownstone, followed by a chorus of disgruntled groans and several colorful metaphors my mother would disapprove of. Those words, those groans of agony, are etched upon my soul, and they lure me down the hallway.

They're coming from a dark room where an eighty-inch television sits against the far wall, its glorious glow casting three men in flickering shadows. The two with controllers sit bickering like five-year-olds over the game flashing on the screen. The third lounges off to the side, his face hidden. Looks like the most recent *Space Vendetta* game. The one I haven't had a chance to play yet but have been dying to buy because it allows both in-person and online player-versus-player battles.

"You found it! I didn't hear you knock." Lily appears at the end of the hall wearing her signature pinup-red lipstick and a vintage cream blouse paired with a black and white houndstooth print skirt. The Betty Boop apron tied around her waist makes me grin. This girl was born in the wrong decade.

"Hey, Lily. Sorry, I just let myself in." My gaze drifts to the room where her three roommates sit in the semi-darkness glued to their video game. "No one answered when I knocked."

"I told them to listen for the door." Lily glares at the room before turning back to me. "I'm sorry. Jen and I had music playing in the kitchen. Come on. We'll leave the boys to their game."

"Aren't we watching a movie tonight?" I follow her down the hall, though there's part of me that wants to run back to the living room and watch them play. No. Fuck that. I want to take them on. I rarely get to challenge anyone in person. No one wants to play against me. Not face to face at least. Guys don't like when girls kick their asses in a video game.

"Yeah, but I told them I was commandeering the living room at seven. They've had time to play their silly games." She tosses her head back and her set curls bounce against her shoulder. I flinch at the way she says it. Her huge blue eyes fix on me and she bites her lip. "Sorry, I forgot."

"It's okay, Lily. I didn't take it personally," I lie. It stings to hear the condescending tone. Not that she meant to imply gaming was silly or a waste of time, but that's typically the response I get when people uncover my secret passion. It shouldn't have to be a secret, and I shouldn't have to apologize for liking video games. I grit my teeth and force a smile.

Jen pops in from the other side of the kitchen. "Hey, I'm glad you came." She smiles and hugs me. Her dark hair lays in a braid over her shoulder. The oversized sweater she's wearing looks warm and comfortable. Paired with jeans, she resembles one of those cute heroines from a Hallmark movie right before she meets the town hunk. I shake my head. We are such a trio of oddballs.

"Yeah, well. I have to admit, these girls' nights are becoming the highlight of my week." I take a seat beside Jen at the island in the center of the kitchen.

"Mine too." Lily pulls something steaming and delicious out of the oven. The scent makes my stomach growl like a rabid dog. I shouldn't have skipped lunch. She sets the casserole on the stovetop to cool and bustles to the fridge. "Want a beer?"

"Got anything stronger?" I joke, but I'm half-serious.

"Of course." She grins and pulls a bottle of vodka from the freezer. "Don't tell Gavin." She winks conspiratorially and pours me a double in a whiskey glass. "Want some, Jen?"

"I'll stick with the beer, thanks." Jen watches with wide eyes as I lift the glass to my lips and down it in one swallow.

The ice-cold vodka burns straight to my gut, ripping away the thoughts of the past week and my asinine bosses. I set the glass on the table and Lily gapes at me.

"Rough week?" Jen asks with a smile as she pops the top off her Yuengling.

"If your boss was anything like mine, you'd be drinking straight from the bottle as soon as you got home." A stifled laugh breaks from my throat. "Those two think I'm a fucking miracle worker."

"Mr. Roberts can be like that, right Jen?" Lily takes a sip of her beer. Her pale face pinkens at the mention of their boss, but before I can say anything, Jen cuts in.

"Yeah, though he's reasonable most of the time, from what I've noticed. But I don't know him all that well. He keeps to himself." Jen takes a drink.

"Well, Mr. Sunshine and Major Grump think I have nothing better to do with my personal time than chase their fucking mistakes." Lily and Jen chuckle at the nicknames I've bestowed upon my ungrateful bosses. "They're lucky I know my way around that office blindfolded."

"It has nothing to do with the fact you need that job and can't afford to get a poor character reference because you cursed out your employer and burned down the building, right?" Lily smirks behind her frosted mug.

I shove away from the counter, rip open the freezer, and pour another double. She's right. One hundred and fifty percent. I do need the job, and I can't afford to have my reputation ruined for all eternity because I couldn't hold my tongue.

"This is why I have friends." I toast them, raising my glass high. "You catch the brunt of my rage so I can keep my pristine reputation and my job. Thank you for your sacrifice." I pour the liquor down my throat and shiver at the intensity of it.

"Hear, hear." Lily and Jen both drink to my pathetic admission.

"Is it movie time? I need to eat something and vegetate for a while." I hedge around their concerned looks. They want to ask me what happened, I can tell, but I don't want to talk about it. I just want to escape for a while. Normally I'd lose myself in a game from Friday night to Sunday afternoon, but since girls' night became a weekly thing, it's thrown off my *me* time. My fingers itch for the plastic comfort of the PlayStation controller.

"Yeah." Lily sets her glass aside and prepares plates heaping with the gooey delicious casserole cooling on the stovetop. "Here." She hands one to both Jen and me before taking up her own and retrieving her beer. "Let's go kick the boys out. They can go find something else to do."

"How the hell do you put up with having three guys for roommates, Lily?" Jen asks.

"I don't know. They kinda grew on me I guess." Lily beams as though it explains everything.

"Don't they drive you crazy though?" I'm curious because I hate people and the thought of sharing my living space with another person, let alone three men, makes me want to rip the fabric of space and time apart with my bare hands. Although living in a vintage old brownstone like this might be worth the frustration.

"Sometimes. But they always help out when I ask and pay rent on time. Even though they *can* act like children, they're really sweet." Lily smirks. "Plus, they're a great deterrent if there's a guy who's interested in me, but I'm not into him."

"How do they feel about the ones you *do* like?" Jen's question mirrors my thoughts exactly.

"I haven't found one worth bringing home that I wanted to keep." Lily half-heartedly defends herself.

"You have a kinky side, woman, I can see it." I snatch a fork from the pile on the counter. "One of these days, you'll share your dark secrets."

Lily flounces from the room without a word, leading the way down the hall. She sets her glass down on the table beside the couch and flips on the light switch, flooding the living room with a brilliance that blinds her roommates.

Their loud groans melt into complaints as they shield their eyes behind their hands.

"Come on, Lils, ten more minutes." The one winning complains with a pout, shoving aside the blond hair hanging in his eyes.

My gaze shifts between her roommates. The two engaged in the battle when I first arrived were still at it. They look similar, in a distant cousin kind of way. Both have lanky builds with sharply defined jaws and handsome features, but one sports slick, jet-black hair while the other rocks shaggy dirty blond hair.

"Please, Lily. I've nearly got him. One more, please?" The black-haired roommate inclines his head and pouts, batting impossibly long lashes in Lily's direction.

"Tough. I said seven, and it's five after. Get out." No nonsense Lily shelves her hand on her hip. Pride wells up in my chest. She doesn't bend easily to their demands. Good for her.

"But Gavin hasn't had a chance to play yet." The blond pleads. "Can't you guys watch a movie upstairs?"

My attention shifts to the third roommate, the one who seems to favor the shadows, and my lady bits decide to take notice of absolutely everything and approve wholeheartedly. His soulful brown eyes, the scruff along his jaw, and the short, dark curls crowning his head. His gaze rests on Lily, and with his chiseled good looks, I can't help but catch the passing resemblance to a young Shemar Moore from *Criminal Minds*. Hot damn. I resist the urge to fan myself because I do not fan myself in the presence of delicious men. No, I do not. When he meets my gaze, I stiffen as a slow smile curves his sinful lips. Bastard knows exactly what he does to women.

"Tell you what, Lily." Gavin leans forward. "Let me play a round against your friend here, and we'll leave you alone for the rest of the night."

I swear he's Shemar's twin. That silken voice could seduce a whole convent of nuns into sinful abandon. I can almost hear him whisper the words *baby girl,* and I shiver. Then the implication of his words registers. Was he challenging *me*? I click my tongue about to form a response, but Lily interjects.

"One game?" Lily taps her chin, skepticism written all over her face. "With Maggie?" A satisfied smile curves her lips. "It's a deal."

"Wait, what?" I've never even played the game! I tend to stick with military-style first-person shooter games. This one looks similar to that, but I know nothing about it aside from the characters. I'm relatively confident the same tactics apply, but still—

"You got this." Lily pats my shoulder. "I have faith in you."

"Thanks." I turn to Gavin, who seems amused by this whole exchange. Confidence oozes off him in waves. He underestimates me. They all do. I grin and all my uncertainty scatters. He's going down. This cocky shit has no idea what he's in for.

Surfer boy hands his controller to Gavin while Maybelline gives me his. I don't actually know their names as they forgot all their manners and never introduced themselves. So nicknames it is. I scoff. *Men.* They both move from their seats, allowing Gavin and me to have the center stage. Our audience flanks us, Lily and Jen to the right, and the two guys on our left where Gavin had been sitting. I flex my hands as my challenger chooses the settings and battle mode.

We're not touching, but his heat surrounds me. God, he smells good. Like Gucci and wintergreen gum. There's something else lingering beneath it, a haunting scent I just can't place. I lick my lips and focus on the screen. I won't let him distract me. Damn him.

"Don't worry, baby girl. I'll take it easy on you." He mutters under his breath.

Lord, he really is channeling Shemar. It takes the restraint of a nun not to react to that tempting purr and the deluge it releases inside me. I bite my tongue instead of unleashing my uncensored thoughts. "Thanks."

The game starts. Immediately I jump into the zone. Everyone around us disappears into the background. I'm in the world on the screen. The controls are exactly like my favorite game, so I adapt quickly. Stumbling a few times, I miss a few obvious things, which makes my opponent chuckle. I curse under my breath and redouble my efforts.

Beside me, I feel Gavin's presence, his focus. But he's too relaxed. Too confident. Once I see my opening, I shift into action and steal into the position I need to ensure my victory. The moment I do, I feel the transition. He leans forward, his elbows resting on his knees. I hear him swear when I steal the health pack and weapons cache from under his nose.

A smirk plays on my lips as I sneak up behind him on the screen and put a bullet in his skull before he even realizes I've made it past his defenses. *Game Over* flashes on the screen in bright green lettering.

His jaw hangs open while the controller dangles between his hands. "What the actual fuck?"

I stand up and do a little victory dance. Drinking up the look of pure disbelief and rage on his face, I add a little more sizzle to my dance and drop it to the floor, ensuring he sees every twitch of my ass when I bring it back up.

"Thanks for taking it easy on me, sweet cheeks," I murmur in his ear before handing my controller to Lily. "To the victor go the spoils."

Surfer boy and Maybelline grumble as they gather their drinks and leave the room. Gavin slowly rises from his spot on the couch. He towers over me. The top of my head doesn't even reach his shoulders. It hurts my neck to look up at him, and I take a step back.

"Good game." I offer my hand in a truce.

With a dirty look, he pushes past me and leaves the room. I stand there with my hand hanging in midair. Disappointment crowds me. I shove it aside, rubbing my palms on my jeans.

"I knew you could do it, Mags." Lily hugs me before sitting on the couch.

"You were amazing!" Jen settles down beside Lily.

I sit in the spot Gavin just vacated. His scent lingers and I close my eyes. The image of his handsome face skewed in shock and disgust fills my mind. Damn it. This is why I don't challenge people in person. Losing is bad enough, but it's almost like losing to a girl brands you with shame. Losing to *me* is a surefire way to end any possibility of a friendship or more. I curse my competitive nature and my love of gaming. Not that it matters. I don't need a man. I've got a good thing going without one.

As for Gavin, he'll get over it. They always do.

CHAPTER TWO

Present Day

"Where in the hell…" I grumble under my breath while sorting through the nearest twelve-inch stack of files and loose papers on my desk. "I'm going to kill them." Praying for an ounce of serenity so I don't murder my bosses, I carefully leaf through each file until I find the one containing the contract they requested.

I warned them about fucking with my system, but no, they thought it would be a good idea to do some spring cleaning and order new file cabinets for my office. Unfortunately, that means all the files contained within the old cabinets are now cluttering up my desk and overflowing onto the floor beneath the window.

"Hey, Maggie, did you find…" Evan's voice dies on a strangled cough when he meets my gaze. The expression on his face teeters between shame and guilt before settling on innocence.

I glare harder and hold up a file.

"Sweet." He steps tentatively over the threshold into my domain, and I hug the file against my chest.

"When are the new cabinets arriving?" I demand, allowing myself a little, silent cheer of victory when he flinches at the seriousness in my tone. "I refuse to work like this, Evan."

"They should be here by the end of the week, I promise." A red hue creeps into his cheeks, and he drops his gaze to the mess scattered throughout my office. He runs his hand through his thick, dark blond hair. His broad shoulders deflate, making him seem shorter than the six-foot-something I know he is. Both my bosses tower over me, but they know who keeps this place running with the efficiency of a well-oiled machine. Hint: it's not them. "Ben thought they would be—"

"So this was Ben's idea?" I grip the file tight to my chest

and storm the five steps from my office to Ben's. When I said I wanted my own space as a stipulation of employment, I should have specified that I wanted it to be as far away from their offices as possible, not stuck between their insufferable asses.

Without knocking, I open the door. "Where the hell are my cabinets, Statler? I refuse to work in that chaos a moment longer."

Ben Statler glances up from the paper he's reading. Those whiskey eyes narrow on me as though assessing the best way to terminate my employment when he sets the paper aside. "I'll call you back, Walter."

Oh fuck. He was on the phone. I square my shoulders and hold his gaze, unwavering in my conviction. I'm not one to back down from confrontation. He knows me better than that.

Ben ends the call and folds his hands on the desk. "Is there something wrong, Margaret?"

My teeth grind. Only my mother and grandmother are allowed to call me by my given name. "Damn it, I told you before, don't call me that."

The distant strains of instrumental fight music echo in my head. I shouldn't feel like I'm taking on a mini-boss, but the urge to dragon punch my actual bosses intensifies with every passing moment.

A half-smile steals across his stern lips. Ben Statler is attractive in the most unconventional, complicated way. His tall, athletic build plays at odds with the dark emo thing he has going on with the longer-than-professional dark hair and his pale skin smattered with faded freckles. But it's the strange way his ears poke out from beneath his long hair and the awkwardly curved nose that throw me off. There are days I can't decide if he's handsome or if my eyes are playing tricks on me. He must be a sorcerer or some shit.

I fold my arms across my chest and wait for him to apologize before I continue.

"Maggie." Evan steps into the room with his hands extended as though trying to soothe a pissed bison before it charges and rips him a new one. The thought of doing just that elevates my mood a fraction. He turns to Ben. "She needs her space back to normal. The cabinets didn't arrive on time and her office is a disaster."

If Ben is the dark void of space, then Evan is a glowing star. He is sunshine personified. From his golden hair and bright blue eyes to his happy-go-lucky personality, nothing seems to damper his positive attitude. But he's not without fault. No, he's a button pusher of the first order. This man has the ability to find the one thing that will piss me off and slam that button like it's the golden buzzer. I don't know which I hate more, Ben's broody silence or Evan's perky positivity.

Ben holds my gaze for a long moment before turning to Evan. "Have Andrew call the company and make sure they have them delivered by the end of the day." He pauses as if pondering his next words carefully. "If they want to do business with Solus, then they are expected to keep the timeline they promised in the agreement."

Evan nods and slips from the room, leaving me and Ben to face off.

"Something else you'd like to say, Miss Dawson?" Ben leans back in his chair and strokes his jaw.

"Actually." I take two deep breaths and roll my shoulders. It takes all my effort to bring my voice to a polite, professional level. "I apologize for my outburst, but if you expect me to continue to run this company in the same manner I have for the past five years, you cannot upend my workspace and leave me to drown in the chaos."

Ben slowly rises to his feet. Even with the desk between us, he towers over me. I lift my gaze to hold his.

"I had hoped they would be restored before you returned from the long weekend." He rounds the desk and sits on the edge facing me. "It was an attempt to grant your request for a better filing system. I apologize for any inconvenience it may have caused."

I blink twice. Did he just apologize? Hell must have frozen over.

Evan reappears in the doorway. "Andrew called the

company. They're on their way now to install the new file cabinets." He grins and stuffs his hands in his pockets.

"Thanks." I turn back to Ben. "When I mentioned our shitty filing system, I was referring to the computer system, not the paper filing system."

Ben's eyes darken two shades before he shifts his attention to Evan.

"Don't look at me. This was your idea." Evan lifts his hands.

With a heavy sigh, Ben pinches the bridge of his nose and shakes his head.

I should excuse myself and retreat to my office, chaos and all. It would be better than getting caught in the storm brewing between Ben and Evan. When Ben looks up, his mood shifts.

"Well then, Miss Dawson, how do you propose we improve our system?" He folds his arms across his chest.

Evan beams at me and nods in support.

"The system we have is outdated and lagging. We need to update our servers and the security protocol. It should be streamlined and upgraded to handle the influx of orders and expansion of the company." I list off a few of the many reasons on my fingertips.

"The system was custom built for Solus. We would need to bring in a programming specialist to upgrade it from scratch." Ben scowls at the thought. "It will be time-consuming and expensive."

"If you don't, you run the risk of it crashing and losing all the accumulated data. But it's your company. If you want to see it crash and burn, that's on you."

"Can *you* do it?" Evan asks, hopeful.

"This project is way above my skill set and my paygrade." I laugh. "You're going to have to hire a damn good programmer to modernize this disaster."

"Do you have any recommendations?" Evan interjects, ignoring Ben's darkening countenance.

"I'll do some research first to vet the prospective companies, make some calls, and have a list to you by the end of the week."

"Whatever you have to do." Evan's smile blinds me. "Looks like that's settled."

"Whoever we choose, Miss Dawson, you will ensure they're doing what I'm paying them to do." Ben stands and straightens his sleeves with a tug on each cuff.

I'm not a babysitter for some outsider. They're professionals, and I shouldn't have to micromanage a project of this size or scope.

"What about my other projects?"

"Focus on the ones of immediate importance. The rest can wait." He returns to his position behind the desk and settles into the leather chair. "This project must be completed before the end of the third quarter."

"Why don't we see what the specialist has to say about it first, huh?" Evan steps in and my heart bursts at the support.

"Very well." Ben grunts. "Let's get it done as quickly as possible." He fixes his dark gaze on me. "And please knock next time, Miss Dawson."

"Yes, sir." I manage to curb my sarcasm and seize my dismissal with grace, sliding past Evan who's practically a door himself.

When I reach my office, there's a combination of triumph and shame twisting in my stomach. This was not how I envisioned my day going. I groan at the mess surrounding me and slump into my chair.

"Hey."

I glance up to see Evan studying me with concern. "Hey."

"I'm sorry. We should have consulted you first." He shrugged a shoulder. "We wanted to surprise you."

"Color me surprised."

"Want some help getting organized before they show up?" Evan shoves his hands in his pockets. "With two of us, we can get this place cleaned up in no time."

"Don't you have a meeting at eleven-thirty with Empire?"

"Shit." Evan glances at his watch. "I gotta go. Have Andrew and Luna help you. Sorry, Maggie."

"Don't worry about it." I wave. "I got this. But bring me back a large caramel macchiato with extra whipped cream."

"Will do." He dashes out of my office. I hear him shuffle around in his for a few moments, then silence descends when the door closes behind him.

On the other side, I can hear Ben's voice through the wall. He's pissed. The only time I can hear him through the wall is when he shouts, which isn't often. I wonder who the poor sap is on the other end of the line.

I sigh and shift piles out of the way. When the file cabinets finally arrive, I'm prepared. It takes me the rest of the day, the fortifying strength of a caramel macchiato, and the aid of two coworkers to get my office back in order. But I can breathe again. Thank God.

After work, I grab a hero from the corner market and a six-pack of Yuengling. Settled at home, I fire up the laptop and do a little recon. Honestly, I'd rather be playing *Space Armada* or break out old-school *Zelda*, but if I don't want to get stuck with their horrible choice, I must do this myself. I need the best software programmer in New York City, and that's exactly what I'll ensure Solus gets.

CHAPTER THREE

Three days pass, and I'm frustrated by the lack of suitable candidates available to reprogram our internal computer network. Few of the companies I called seemed up to the task, and the ones who were can't get us on the calendar until next year. I'm ready to tear my hair out.

Shutting the laptop, I decide to call it a day and head out. It's four-thirty, and I'm not going to get any more work done in the office. Although I must admit relief at having my workspace back to some semblance of organization.

This morning I found a potted plant with a teal bow sitting on my desk. A dark purple violet exactly the same shade as the highlights in my hair. Evan's way of apologizing, I'm sure. Ben would never think of giving me something in gratitude. He rarely gives compliments. I snort as I pass his office.

He's still in there. I can hear his voice through the door. Must be rough to be married to the business. That man needs to find a girl and get laid. Something to get him to loosen up. It would definitely be an upgrade to the brooding beast we deal with on a daily basis.

Evan's office is empty. He's probably flirting with one of the girls from the shop downstairs. I shake my head. How did I get stuck with these two?

Once I reach the street below, I breathe in the spring air. It's tainted by the city funk, but I don't care. It feels good to be outside. I check my phone. Lily should be home soon. I don't have any reason to rush home, except maybe to finish that gnarly level I couldn't quite get through on expert mode in *Space Armada.* Maybe she'll be up for a drink on the roof tonight? Girls' night is still two days off, and I need to decompress. I could swing by Jen's, but she's been busy with her promotion at work and her new boy toy, whom we still haven't met. If Lily didn't work with them both, I'd think he was a figment of Jen's imagination. She has an affinity for fictional men.

I take a detour away from my apartment and head toward the Heights where Lily lives in her gorgeous brownstone. That girl has the hook-up. Those places are ridiculously expensive and coveted like gold. If she ever needed a roommate, I'd move in. As long as she boots Gavin first.

The thought of him irritates me, and I clench my hands into fists. After I kicked his ass playing *Space Armada*, he refuses to be in the same room with me. If we happen to cross paths, he pretends I don't exist. Which is completely fine because I require nothing from Gavin. Not a damn thing.

By the time I reach her apartment, I'm dying for a cold beer. It's been too long since I've been to my jujitsu classes and I'm terribly out of shape. I should get back into it, but I've been so fucking busy with other things. If the state of my cardio is any indication, I should probably rearrange those priorities. Gaming does not supersede physical health. Well, it shouldn't, but unfortunately for me, it does.

I bang my fist on the door. "Lily!" I shout, knowing I'll probably piss off the neighbors.

It swings open under my hand and I sway forward. But it's not Lily. It's Gavin.

"Little early to be drinking, isn't it?" He folds his arms across his magnificent chest.

I gesture to the time on my phone. "It's five o'clock. Happy hour started an hour ago." I mimic his stance as we face off. It doesn't matter that he assumes I'm drunk. I'm not defending my life choices to this asshole.

"What do you want?"

"Well, I didn't come here for your charming hospitality." As if I need to say it, honestly. I step over the threshold and shove past him. "Lily. Where is she?"

He huffs in exasperation and closes the door. "She'll be home soon. Had a few errands to run after work."

"Oh." I stalk down the hall, uncaring of the fact I just barged into their home. "I'll wait for her then."

"Make yourself at home." The sarcasm drips from every word. Only then do I realize he's following me.

His scent teases me when he slips past to enter the kitchen first. I pause in the doorway and ignore the way it leaves me off-kilter, filling my head with sensual visions of chocolate cherry cordials, velvet, and *him* naked. I vehemently shake the image from my mind. No. No. Absofuckinglutely not. I will not go there. I don't care if he smells like temptation incarnate. I will not give him the satisfaction of knowing what he does to me. We are not lovers, and we are most certainly not friends. Full stop.

"You want a beer?" He reaches into the fridge, and all I can do is nod as the fabric pulls tight over his ass when he bends over. He straightens with two Killians in one hand and twists the caps off before handing one to me.

Grateful for something to do other than eye him while my face turns beet red, I take a long drink, downing half the contents. When I lower the bottle, Gavin's brows are nearly in his hairline.

"Rough day?"

I snort and take another quick sip. "Rough week."

"Ah." He takes a drink not bothering to push for details. I appreciate that more than he realizes.

My gaze skims down the length of him. White t-shirt, gray sweatpants, and a navy zip hoodie pulled over his broad shoulders. I narrow my eyes.

"Don't you have a job?" I blurt the question without thought, kicking myself for being so blunt. I mean, it's my nature, but I'm not normally so damn rude about it. Gavin brings out the worst in me I guess.

"Several, actually." He leans against the counter and grins.

Sweet fucking mercy. I swear he's Shemar's long-lost brother when he does that. I need to stop watching *Criminal Minds*. It's starting to warp my sense of reality. Yes, more gaming, less television. Pushing the distraction aside, I refocus my thoughts.

"You work from home then?"

"Yeah. I only go into the office on Mondays. The majority

of my work I can do from home, aside from site visits and on-location gigs."

Impressive. I nod, a smidge jealous of the freedom he has. "I wish I could work from home. I'd probably be more productive if I didn't have my bosses fucking with my system all the time."

"What do you do at Solus anyway?"

"How did you know I work at Solus?"

"Lily told me." He takes a drink. "They're one of the top fifty up-and-coming businesses in the city."

"Yeah. Well, it's not all sunshine and roses, let me tell ya." I sniff and shift my gaze to the cake sitting beneath a glass dome in the center of the island.

"Sounds like a sweet gig to me."

"I basically babysit the two adult men who own the company." I chew my lower lip and try not to detract from the enormity of the role I have at Solus. "I'm their office manager/personal assistant. I make sure everything runs smoothly at the executive level. Well, Andrew and I. He's my assistant personal assistant." Wow, that sounded smooth. I cringe.

"Assistant Personal Assistant, is that even a thing?" Gavin chuckles.

The sound alone sends a bolt of heat straight to my lady bits. Stop. It. No. Down girl. He's off-limits.

"It is." I pull out the stool beside my hip and sit. "What do you do?" I ask unable to tolerate the thought of the conversation remaining focused on me.

"I run an online gamer website. We sell guides, merch, host events, and forum chats."

"Wow, what's the site?" I make a mental note to check it out when I get home. Only because I want to see how bad it is. At least that's what I tell myself.

"Gamer Legacy."

I choke on my beer mid-sip. Sputtering and coughing, I meet his amused gaze. "No fucking way."

"Yeah. James and Mike help out with it. It started as

something for fun, but it's now a part-time gig for all three of us." Gavin sets aside his empty bottle and rests his hands on the counter by his hips. The hoodie pulls tight across his shoulders.

I swallow the drool pooling around my tongue. Get a grip, woman. "Who are James and Mike?"

He looks amused. "Our other two roommates. You've met them before."

"Oh, right." It takes me a second to realize he's referring to Surfer Boy and Maybelline. Still not sure who is who, but I'll figure that out later. "So, what's your day job then?"

My tone may sound disinterested, but I'm invested now. What the hell is wrong with me? I don't even like him. My hormones do, but he is absolutely, one hundred percent not my type. Not with that cocky attitude. No, sir. Definitely not a turn on.

"Programming." He glances at the fridge and pulls off a business card. "Here."

I take the card unable to believe my ears. Did he just say he was a computer programmer? I scan the card information. No fucking way.

"You work for MuseLab Networks?!" There's no containing my shock. I slump deeper onto the stool, wishing I could sink into the floor. MuseLab was the first company I contacted in regards to the contract for the Solus system upgrade. They have no availability until next March.

"Yeah. Got an internship right out of college. Guess they thought I was worth keeping around."

"Wow." I slide the card back across the table. "Too bad you don't freelance," I mutter under my breath more to myself than to him.

Gavin makes no move to take the card and runs his hand over his scruffy jaw. "Yeah, they keep me busy for sure."

"And they let you work exclusively from home?"

"Pretty much."

"Gavin!" Lily's voice echoes down the hallway. "You here?"

"In the kitchen." His deep voice reverberates through me.

"I stopped and got…" Lily appears in the doorway. "Oh,

Maggie! What are you doing here?" She slides the two grocery bags on the counter.

I stand up and hug her. "Figured I'd stop for a drink before I went home."

Her ruby lips pout. "Oh, darn. I wish I had known. I'd have come straight home." Sweet, caring Lily. This girl is too pure for this world.

"It's okay, Lily. No worries." I motion to her roommate. "Gavin offered me a beer. We were just chatting while I waited for you."

Lily's eyes widen and her lips round in an *o* as her gaze flickers between us. "You two are on speaking terms now?"

"A temporary truce, more like." Gavin chuckles. "I'll leave you two to chat. I have some work to finish." With a tilt of his head in my direction, he leaves the room. "See ya, short stuff."

"Thanks for the beer, dickhead," I call after him, and Lily laughs.

As Lily puts the groceries away, she asks about my week. I tell her about my asshole bosses and what they did to my office. We grab a beer and head to the roof. The pressure of the week eases, and I feel more like myself.

When I get home, I pull Gavin's card from my pocket and put it on the fridge. It has his cell number on it. I bite my lip. Is it a temporary truce, or have Gavin and I reached an understanding? Either way, it doesn't mean we're friends. Nope. Absolutely not.

He's still an asshole, and I hate him. But why does he have to be so hot and infuriating? I fire up the PlayStation. Maybe killing some alien warlords and evil empire lackeys will soothe the itch beneath my skin.

CHAPTER FOUR

After the shortest weekend of my life, I drag myself to work. Not even movie night with the girls on Saturday and a full day of gaming on Sunday did anything to bolster my mood. I'm deflated. Last week, I called every programming firm worth their clout to offer them the opportunity to upgrade our systems, but I have nothing to show for it but a stack of polite rejections. Damn.

"Hey, Maggie." Andrew waves from his desk. "I love the earrings."

"Thanks." I touch the Triforce emblems dangling from my earlobes. "Got 'em for Christmas." I make a beeline for my office to avoid getting sucked into a debate about which *Zelda* is better.

On Friday night, I sent Ben and Evan the list of companies I contacted with the responses from each company. I even ranked them according to reviews and their track record. That took some time, I'll admit. But it was worth it because I don't want someone half-assing this job. It needs a special touch. Solus might not be my company, but I have invested too much time and effort in it to see our success get flushed down the drain by some computer hack. I just hope they can find someone reliable for the job.

Tossing my bag in the drawer, I catch a glimpse of the violet on the edge of my desk. The leaves are wilting and the flowers look droopy. Maybe it needs more light and a drink. Kind of like me. I chuckle and move it to the window overlooking the park.

With my empty coffee mug in hand, I head for the break room to get some water. On the way back to my office, I collide with Ben who rounds the corner at the same time I do. The water splashes out of the mug and down his white dress shirt.

"Oh shit." I cradle the mug in my hands. "Sorry."

Ben lowers his raised arms and surveys the damage. He growls before turning and stalking back to his office. No shouting. No swearing. Nothing. Oh shit.

I pinch my eyes closed and swear before returning to the break room to refill the mug. This time I protect it like a coveted dragon's egg in the midst of a raider's den as I make my way back to my office. Once the violet is watered, I sit at my desk and groan. This is what comes from me trying to be nice.

"Maggie, there you are." Evan's perky smile fills me with intense loathing. It's Monday morning. Why the hell is he smiling like that? Sunshine. Ugh. I wish I could hate him solely for his positive, *life is good* attitude, but I can't. Deep in his soul, he's a good man, and those are hard to find. Even if he does push every fucking button just to get a response.

"Where else would I be, Evan?" I mumble and pull out my planner. "You need something?"

"Yeah, I wanted to tell you good work on sorting through those programmers." His megawatt smile enhances the sincerity of his words. I can't help but preen under his praise. Just a smidge. "You put a lot of work into that. We appreciate it."

"Thanks. But it doesn't matter. None of them have anyone available for six months at the earliest."

"See. That's the thing. I don't know what magic you worked, but one of the companies called me this morning. They're sending over their best programmer."

That's amazing. I lean forward, planner forgotten, curiosity burning through me. "Which company?"

He stuffs his hands in his pockets and puffs his chest out. "The one at the top of your wish list."

"No fucking way!" I slap my hand over my mouth, knowing that was way too loud for this professional space, but the whole office knows I have moments like this. "MuseLab Networks called you this morning?" I shake my head. "They told me they were booked out until next year."

"Well, I guess someone up there likes you." Evan points toward the sky.

I snort. "Yeah, sure. I'm no saint, and I think the Big Guy

has some reservations about me."

"He shouldn't." His smile never falters. "This is all you, Maggie. I told Ben as much."

Ben. Shit. I bite my lip and glance at the wall dividing our offices. I feel guilty as hell for spilling water all over him this morning. He keeps a spare set of clothes in his office, so there's that. But still. Smooth move, Maggie.

"So when are they starting?" I shove aside my guilt and focus on the one positive in my life.

Evan glances at his watch. "Five minutes."

I shoot to my feet and knock my planner to the ground. "What? *Five minutes?* Damn it. I don't have anything ready." I jerk open my desk drawer and pull my notes for improvements.

"Don't rush." Evan laughs. "Get your stuff together. We'll meet you in the conference room."

"Yeah, okay."

Evan leaves, and I shuffle through my papers. It doesn't take long to find what I need. I like keeping things orderly; it's the one thing I can control. I slip the notes into a folder, and after several deep breaths, a calm settles over me.

With a glance in the mirror, I fix my hair and touch up my lipstick. Ben and Evan couldn't care less, but I want to make a good impression on whoever they brought in to fix the system. Truthfully, I want to make sure they don't fuck it up, but if it's the company they claim, I shouldn't have anything to worry about. Their track record is pristine.

Tucking the folder under my arm, I step out of my office and pull the door closed behind me. When I spin around, I collide with a solid body and the file falls to the floor. My papers scatter across the carpet.

"Damn it, not again." I drop to my knees and pick up the papers. The faint, warm scent of Gucci cologne fills my senses.

"Are you always this clumsy?"

It can't be. Oh, God. Please, no. Tell me I'm conjuring him in some depraved fantasy. Gavin, with his infuriatingly charming grin, is kneeling beside me. He hands me the papers he gathered and his eyes sparkle with amusement.

"What the fuck are you doing here?" I hiss and snatch the papers away, tucking them back into the folder. When I try to stand, he offers a hand to help me. I ignore it completely and rise to my feet.

"Gavin Howell?" Evan interrupts, and I take a step back as he joins us. He extends his hand and they greet each other like old friends. Evan could make friends with anyone, no sweat. He makes it look effortless.

Gavin laughs at something Evan says and a familiar warmth engulfs my insides. Oh, no. *Don't you start now*, I warn my hormones.

"Come on, I'll introduce you to Ben." Evan turns to lead them down the hall.

Dipping his head, Gavin glances at me with a cocky grin before following Evan. I lag behind, cursing my luck and wishing I had something solid to throw at the back of Gavin's head. I should have known it was going to be him. I'm cursed. But I did offhandedly quip about him freelancing. Ugh. I take it back. Take him back. How the fuck am I supposed to work with him in the same office space? I can't. This is going to be torture.

The suit he's wearing fits him like a diver's wetsuit. Okay, maybe not *that* tight. But it's tailored and stylish. The worst part? It looks good on him. Fuck. Curse whoever made that suit with its dark blue fabric and tiny white pinstripes. It will forever remind me of Gavin now.

When we reach the conference room, Ben is already there, sitting at the head of the table. He slowly rises to his feet and extends his hand to Gavin. His white shirt has been changed out for powder blue. Guilt makes my face warm. He glances at me briefly before turning his attention to Gavin.

"Please, have a seat." Ben gestures to the chairs.

Evan rounds the table and sits, leaving Gavin and me on the same side. Ben resumes his seat.

As they launch into a discussion about the contract and negotiations, I watch the byplay silently. My hands remain fixed on the file laying on the table. It takes every ounce of effort not to stare at Gavin. I've never seen him in anything other than casual wear. Sweatpants, and maybe jeans once or twice, but never business attire.

His quick glance in my direction has my blood heating. The light streaming in the windows illuminates his pale-yellow dress shirt. Damn it. Why does he have to look so hot? I'm positive he knows exactly what he's doing. He probably has this effect on every woman who enters his presence.

I lean back and put some distance between us, half-listening to their conversation as the arousal and irritation battle inside me. Once this is over, I'm going to lock myself in my office until he finishes the upgrade.

"Maggie, you said you had notes about the project?" Evan's voice cuts through the haze of my thoughts.

I snap out of my bitter daydream and find three pairs of eyes fixed on me. Ben looks exasperated, but Evan is smothering a grin behind his hand. Gavin's eyes are smoldering and brimming with challenge. Damn him.

"Yeah, I have them here." I open the file and itemize the issues I've found in the current system. After a few minutes, Gavin interjects with some questions, and I clarify as best I can. When I outline my wish list for the new system, he nods and pulls my notes closer.

"So, you up for the challenge?" Evan asks, breaking the silence.

"It'll definitely be a lot of work." Gavin glances up and rubs his jaw. "I can make it happen, but I'm going to need some help."

"Whatever you need." Ben folds his hands together, looking one hundred percent like a mafia don about to make the deal of a lifetime.

Gavin turns to me, and I'm pissed at how easily he can catch me off guard with that charming grin. "You seem to know this system in and out. It would be great to have your input as I work to ensure you're getting exactly what you want."

It wasn't overtly sexual, but I heard the challenge in his tone. Is he teasing me? Can he tell how much he affects me? Before I can reply, Ben cuts in.

"Maggie, you're with Gavin until this project is completed."

He raps the table with his knuckles.

"What? No, I can't—"

"Andrew will fill in for you until it's done." His hand slides over his shirt and tie, right where I spilled the water earlier.

"Fine." It takes all the restraint I possess not to unleash on them. The ever-present hum of instrumental music rises in the back of my mind. I feel like a soldier going into battle. Gathering my papers, I stuff them into the folder and retreat from the room.

Gavin means nothing to me. This is temporary, it's for the company. I square my shoulders and head back to my office in a huff, my heels clicking on the laminate floors. Damn him.

Right now, all I want to do is get home and decompress with some virtual reality. I've nearly completed all the missions for *Space Armada.* Just in time, too, because the new one releases next week. I desperately need a distraction.

CHAPTER FIVE

I slept like shit, and I blame Gavin instead of the fact I was up late playing video games. When my alarm goes off at six a.m., I'm sorely tempted to toss the phone across the room and burrow beneath the blankets. My mind decided it needed to immerse itself in a fictional realm until three a.m. to process the reality in which I find myself. Then when I finally did fall asleep, I dreamt of chocolate covered cherries and a man who seems to bring out a warring duplicity within me. A lustful kind of hate, if I had to describe it.

Somehow I drag my ass out of bed and get ready for work. I could sleep for a week and then some, but I have work to do. It's five minutes to eight when I reach my office. If Andrew is taking care of my duties while I'm babysitting—I mean, helping Gavin with the update—then I need to make a list for him to ensure I don't have mountains of paperwork to catch up on.

I'm not being fair, and I know it. Andrew is more than capable of taking care of my workload for a few weeks. He's organized and thorough. It's not like I'm physically leaving the building. He can come to me any time. I'm taking my irritation out on Andrew when I really want to harness it into a laser beam and blast Gavin for making me a convoluted mess.

Dropping into the chair behind my desk, I take a deep breath and grab the notebook from the top drawer. I'm halfway through the checklist when a soft knock interrupts me.

"Morning, Maggie." Evan beams over his cup of coffee. I swear I hope he spills it all over that red silk tie. No one should be that chipper at this hour.

"I can't believe you intruded on my morning without bearing gifts." I finish my thought on the checklist and set the pen aside. A coffee cup appears before my eyes. The sweet scent of caramel drifts up from the cup sitting in the center of my desk.

"You're lucky." I grip the cup in one hand and peel the lid off, allowing the steam to curl up from the sweet concoction. Cradling it between my hands, I lean back in my chair and blow across the liquid's surface.

"Mind if we chat for a moment?" Evan grabs the seat by the door and pulls it closer to the desk.

"Sure." I narrow my gaze.

He shuts the door and sits down across from me. I shift uncomfortably and sip my macchiato. Is something wrong? Have I finally crossed the line and human resources decided it's time to eighty-six my ass?

When Evan's gaze meets mine, I straighten and clear my throat. "What's up?"

"Yesterday at the meeting with Gavin, you looked uncomfortable." He twists the cup in his hands. "Are you two acquainted? I mean, before yesterday, obviously."

"No, yeah. I'm fine. It's fine." I drop my gaze, following my fingertip as it traces the logo of the coffee company on the cardboard sleeve. "It's just…well, Gavin lives with my friend Lily. They're roommates. She lives with three guys." I scoff at the thought of being surrounded by that much testosterone on a daily basis. Then I remember who I work for. I refocus my thoughts to answer Evan's question. "Gavin and I have met a few times before, but we're not friends or anything."

"Uh huh." Evan presses his lips together. He's searching me, and I know that look. He's trying to assess the level of truth in my statement. "Will you be able to work alongside him? I don't want to hire someone to do this job and have you kill him the first week." He adds that last bit in a teasing way, but Evan knows me well. I know him too, and if I had a problem with Gavin, he would find someone else for the job without further questioning. He might be my boss, but he's also a decent guy.

"Yeah, I can handle this. It's only for one job." I chuckle. "I won't kill him. I promise."

A smile of relief breaks on his lips. "Good, because I don't have the funds to bail your ass out and retain a solid defense lawyer for your trial."

"You're worth at least three million dollars, Evan." I scoff. "Don't be modest. I'm sure you can cover part of the cost. Ben can take care of the rest."

Evan nearly chokes on his coffee, and a stray drop lands on his tie. "Damn." He sets the coffee aside and grabs a tissue to blot the stain. "You did that on purpose."

"Did what?" I grin. It's fun to see him off-kilter.

He groans at the futile battle with the stain and tosses the crumpled tissue into the garbage. "For the record, my *assets* are worth three million. It's not like I have that money sitting in the bank."

I pout, feigning disappointment, and sip my coffee. Evan is such a small town, country boy. Even mentioning his personal finances leaves him flustered.

"Don't even get me started on Ben." He scoffs. "I don't think he'd come to *anyone's* rescue if they got arrested."

"Even you?"

"Especially me." Evan slowly rises from his seat and grabs his coffee. "I'm going to go change my tie now." He glares at me, and I give it right back to him.

"Good thing you keep a spare in your office." I lift my coffee in salute. "Thanks for the pep talk, boss."

"Ah, Maggie. Never a dull moment with you here." A laugh escapes him, and he shakes his head. When he reaches for the door, he pauses and glances over his shoulder. "You sure you're okay with Gavin working on this project?"

"He's the best candidate for the job. I'm good. Trust me. I *can* be professional."

"I'll believe it when I see it." He opens the door. "He'll be here first thing Monday morning to get started."

"Can't wait."

Once Evan vacates my office, I collapse forward, resting my face against my desk. I want to repeatedly bash my head against the solid wood, but instead, I mutter beneath my breath and sit up. After opening the planner to the following week, I circle Monday in red marker.

It glares at me like a massive, flashing neon sign. I don't

know how the hell I'm going to manage to work alongside Gavin for prolonged periods of time. Every time we're in each other's company we butt heads. But worse than that, it's getting harder to ignore the chemistry percolating between us. Maybe I should tell Evan this is a bad idea.

No. I will be professional. I know we can ensure the company gets exactly what it needs to thrive and grow. I may not know everything about computer programming and software, but I'm no slouch either. I've tried for two years to make the current system work. It's hopeless.

Putting my raging hormones and personal dislike of Gavin aside, I focus on the positives. At least it's temporary. It's not like I haven't shelved my distaste during corporate meetings or group projects. This partnership may not be ideal, but for the sake of Solus, I have to make it work. Let's hope Gavin can too.

CHAPTER SIX

I really don't want to do this. Staring up at Lily's brownstone, I grip the bag in my hand tighter. Tonight the girls wanted something different than the typical movie night. Lily suggested game night.

Now, I'm all for games, especially when it involves inappropriate conversations and alcohol. But when Lily told Jen she could bring her boyfriend, I knew I was fucked. It wasn't going to be just the three of us. According to her text earlier, Gavin would also be joining in. Her other two roommates were out of town for a convention.

At first, I was stunned to hear it. Gavin wants to voluntarily spend time with Lily's friends? I mean, I don't know why I'm shocked. It's not like I know him all that well. Do I really *want* to know him better? My body whoops with excitement, but my brain is slamming the nope button hard and ominous music begins to swell in the background of my subconscious.

I take a deep breath and climb the stairs. After the first knock, the door swings open revealing Lily in a sleeveless peach swing dress. Her curls bounce with excitement.

"I'm so glad you made it." She glances up and down the street before frowning. "Have you seen Jen and Shaun?"

"Looks like they're running late." I give her a hug and step inside. "Probably had to get a quickie in before they came. You know, since they can't keep their hands off each other."

Lily's cheeks pinken, and she takes the bag from my hands. "Don't forget, you instigated the whole thing." She winks before heading toward the dining room.

"What?" I laugh. "She needed to get laid. I just provided friendly encouragement."

Lily drops the bag on the table with more force than necessary. "You told her to—and I quote— 'Climb him like a tree and ride him into the sunset.' Exact words, honey, don't deny it."

"I'm not denying anything," I trace my hand over the scrolling on the back of one of the dining room chairs. "Where's Gavin hiding?" I ask, changing the subject because all I can see is an image of me climbing Gavin and I do not need that mental picture right now.

"He'll be down once he gets out of the shower." Lily straightens the bowls of snacks on the buffet along the wall. "Come help me with the sangria."

I'm still fixed on the first part of her statement. A mental image of Gavin naked and dripping wet flashes inside my head, and I grip the chair tighter. Fuck. I need to get this under control. Lily disappears through the doorway and I lag behind, trying to banish these lustful thoughts.

We're supposed to be working together starting Monday morning. I cannot—*will* not—let whatever is or isn't between us interfere with my job. I've worked too damn hard to have a sexy piece of man meat fuck it up for me.

I give Lily a hand with the last preparations for our evening. She pulls a tray from the oven with tiny puff pastry hors d'oeuvres. A loud knock echoes through the hall.

"Shit, can you get that?" Lily juggles the tray between her gloved hands.

"Yeah, no problem." I jog down the hall and open the door. Jen and Shaun smile at me.

I lean against the frame and cross my arms. "Hey, lovebirds. We were taking bets when you two would show." I pause for emphasis. "If you came at all."

Shaun glances at Jen briefly before turning back to me. "Jen was busy with her new toys."

"Stop." Jen elbows him in the ribs.

Oh, this is juicy. These two are so cute together it's almost disgusting. I'm almost excited to hear what kind of kinky depravity these two unveil during our inappropriate game night. I step to the side and allow them entry.

"I don't want to know," Lily sing-songs as she walks past

with the tray of puff pastries.

"I do." I close the door behind them. "Are we talking floggers and nipple clamps here or a new vibe?"

Shaun's laughter makes me grin. He leans against the door frame and admires the blush creeping up Jen's neck.

"None of the above," Jen snaps with a groan and hides her face. "Seriously, Maggie, all you think about is sex."

"You've known this about me for ages and never made a stink about it before." I make no apologies for embracing my sexuality and my humor. Both intermingle quite frequently and I never shy away from either. The fact that I haven't gotten laid in over two years will be my little secret.

"Well, that's because you weren't talking about *my* sex life," Jen growls.

"Maggie's just bitter because she's not getting any." Gavin's voice slides against my skin, leaving gooseflesh in its wake. Did he read my fucking mind? I feel the heat seeping into my face and throw an elbow back, hoping it hits him in the groin. Unfortunately, it grazes his hip.

"Hi, Gav." Jen greets him with a smile.

"Hey, Jen." Gavin's attention shifts to Shaun. I watch as the two exchange pleasantries and shake hands.

I note the ease with which the two men interact, sealing their newfound friendship.

"Okay, game night. Hope you're ready for a little inappropriateness." Jen bounces on her toes.

"A little?" I snort, rubbing my hands together with evil glee. "Bring on *all* the inappropriateness."

"Oh, did you bring the expansion pack?" Lily calls from the dining room.

"Yes. And the nineties one too," Jen responds.

"Wicked." Gavin slides past me, brushing his arm against mine.

Sparks skitter down my spine at the brief contact. I beat down my libido and follow him, admiring his ass in those gray sweatpants. I glance over my shoulder. Jen and Shaun are whispering, their eyes locked. It's romantic. I want to tease them, but I don't. I won't kill their fun just because I'm a smidge jealous. I'm a better friend than that.

After snacking and copious amounts of sangria, the game gets interesting. Jen inadvertently reveals her online predilections for talking with other fangirls who fantasize about a man they've never met and a character who isn't real. Even though I'm worried she may find herself in an unsavory situation, I bite my tongue. Shaun doesn't seem particularly bothered by it, so why should I be.

When Jen tries to steer our attention back to the game, Lily blossoms in spectacular fashion, giggling and swaying in her chair. Shit.

"You're cut off." I remove the nearly empty wine glass from her reach. "Drink some water."

Lily pouts and then sticks out her tongue for good measure.

"Okay, children." Jen clears her throat and continues reading the card in her hand. "There's one *blank* in the *blank*. Make it count."

Oh, I've got a good one for this. Gavin and I lay down our cards at the same time. Jen gathers them in stacks in front of her and closes her eyes as Shaun rearranges them.

I stretch my legs as she reads the cards aloud, snickering at each pair. My gaze drifts to Gavin, who's sitting to her right. He's watching Jen with a smirk tugging at the corners of his mouth. He smothers it behind his hand as she searches our faces before choosing her favorite cards.

He licks his lips, and I'm mesmerized by the innocent movement. Jen reveals the winning cards, and Gavin snatches them from her hand. His triumphant grin makes my heart do somersaults inside my chest.

"I'll be right back." I excuse myself from the game and head down the hall to the restroom. Inside, I face myself in the mirror and groan, fingering my fading teal and purple highlights. I need to get them touched up. My hand falls away from my hair.

Why the hell am I hiding in the bathroom? Damn it. I don't know how the fuck I'm going to work with him on Monday if I can't stop lusting over him during a fun evening with friends. It's been too long since I've been with anyone. Maybe I'm just spun up over him for no other reason than he's the first man who's caught my attention in ages.

I slip from the bathroom and head into the kitchen to get water for both me and Lily. Laughter filters in from the dining room as one of the pocket doors slides open. Lily stumbles through, swaying against it as she slides it closed again.

"Everything okay?" she asks me, gripping the island for support.

"I should be asking you that question." I cock my head in amazement, wondering how she hasn't fallen over yet. "How many did you have, Lily?"

"A few." She flashes a drunken grin. "C'mon, Mags, it's not like I have to drive home."

"I'm just being a good friend." I slide the water across the counter. "Drink this before you go back in there."

Lily frowns, but picks up the glass and sips the water. "Is there something going on between you and Gavin?"

I nearly drop the glass in my hand. "No," I sputter. "We're—well, my bosses hired him to update our system at Solus. He starts on Monday."

"That's great!" Lily beams. "He's an amazing programmer."

"So I keep hearing." I take a drink.

"Why is that a bad thing?" Lily studies me, her blue eyes wide. Drunk Lily can be fun, but she can also be too empathetic.

"The boss duo from hell asked me to supervise the project and ensure we get exactly what the company needs." My hand rakes through my hair.

"Are you worried he won't follow through?" Lily's brows furrow and her little pout is adorable. "Because he's damn good at his job. He'll do it right, you don't have to worry about that." She nearly overturns her glass of water with her vehement declaration and flailing hands.

"No, it's not that." I twist the glass between my fingers, unable to meet her gaze. "I don't think he likes me very much. I don't want it to be awkward having to work together on this project."

"Gavin's reserved, but once you get to know him, he's a really sweet guy." She drops her gaze. "We went to school together. I've known him for years. Trust me, he's one of the good ones."

Her words do nothing to settle the uncertainty spinning in my gut like a hurricane. If anything they up the ante, turning a Category 3 into a Category 5. I pound the rest of my water and fill the glass again.

Lily comes up beside me and hands me her empty glass. She bumps my hip with hers. "I thought maybe you and Gavin had something *else* going on."

My hand freezes beneath the stream of the tap and the glass overflows. I turn off the water and dry my hands, avoiding eye contact. "Yeah, right. Like I'd be interested in his cocky ass."

She lifts her shoulders in a noncommittal shrug. "Deny it all you want, but every time you two look at each other, a heatwave hits the room. Seriously, any hotter and you two will start a fire."

I blow a raspberry and brush her off with a wave of my hand. "You've definitely been drinking too much. C'mon, let's go back to the game."

Thankfully when we return, Lily diverts any questions by telling everyone what a spoilsport I am making her drink water. They laugh but are in full agreement with me. We dive back into the game.

I catch Gavin watching me and hold his dark gaze. He gives nothing away. I wish I could read his thoughts, but he's a veritable sealed vault. Nothing in, nothing out. He turns to Shaun who's reading the next card.

Monday is going to be the Mondayest of all the Mondays, and I don't know how the hell I'm going to make this work without losing every ounce of sanity I have. Thankfully I can lose myself in the new *Space Armada* game until I'm required to adult.

CHAPTER SEVEN

Armed with an extra-large glass of iced tea and a bowl of chips, I settle onto the plush loveseat across from my sixty-inch television. The lights flicker and beep on the PlayStation console when I press a single button. The beast roars to life, waking from a deep and dreamless sleep. I lean back against the cushions and pull on my gaming headset.

It's been a hell of a week, and I just want to decompress. Even game night at Lily's yesterday left me agitated. I love my friends, but sometimes I just need *me* time. The main screen loads and peace surrounds me. Gaming is my release. Some people exercise, some read, some write, but not me. I shoot people. In a safe digital space, of course, I'm not a damn psychopath.

Although I'm pretty sure Gavin thinks I am at this point. Every time I'm around him, it's like I'm being torn in opposite directions. One side of me wants to jump him, and the other is firmly against even pretending we're something resembling friends.

The only thing we have in common is our love of gaming and the project for Solus. That's it, and it's not nearly enough to encourage this one-sided lust with hope of something more.

Once I log into my profile, I press play on the game in the system. The intro screen fills the television. *Vendetta: Space Armada,* the game I played with Gavin that first night. The one where I whooped his ass and did a little stripper victory dance. Not one of my proudest moments, but he deserved it. The cocky shit underestimated me, and I made him eat his challenge.

An invitation pops on the screen. *User PinballWizardOG would like to add you.* Who is this? I click on the invite and see a message in the inbox. *Hey, it's Gavin. Rematch?*

I blink twice and reread the message. Then I notice the

timestamp. Five minutes ago. This could be bad. Really bad. He didn't take it well the last time we went head-to-head, but that was over a year ago. Fuck it. I click accept and type in a new message.

I'm not even going to ask how you found me. Are you sure you want your ass kicked again? Send.

I fidget, waiting for a response, my leg bouncing up and down. Another message appears.

Bring it. Mic on, I want to hear you beg for mercy.

I scoff. Beg for mercy? I roll my eyes and open the game, allowing it to add him to my network this time. When the line connects, I'm in go mode. He has no idea what he's in for.

"You sure you want your ass handed to you again?" I skip the pleasantries and go straight for the jugular.

"You like to talk shit, huh?" His deep chuckle wakes that desperate part of me again. I shove it aside.

"Guess you're about to find out firsthand." I open the menu and add a second player. "New game?"

"That works. How long have you been playing this one?"

"I picked it up after I kicked your ass, but I typically only play on the weekends." The game loads and we lapse into silence when it starts.

We're playing against each other. He's chosen Commander Colton, and I'm his nemesis, Captain Ransom. The game is loosely based on the *Space Vendetta* books and films. It wasn't my game of choice before I met Gavin, but it grew on me. Tonight it seems appropriate considering our first battle took place in this world.

The mission is simple. Retrieve the disc with President Myron's directive. But to do that, we have to battle the clock and each other while rampaging across a space cruiser the size of Manhattan.

We start at separate points but quickly demolish the guards while making our way through to the main control center. It doesn't take long since we're both familiar with the game. The immersion sets in, and I'm lost in the game world.

I slip through a small corridor and appear in front of the

control center before he does.

"How the fuck did you do that?" The surprise and irritation in his voice make me grin.

"If I told you, I'd have to kill you." I chuckle and bypass the codes to access the control room.

"Not so fast, baby girl."

I shiver, and he seizes the momentary distraction with a shot from his blaster over my head. It ricochets off the control panel, leaving it smoldering and sparking. I slip into the room and take cover behind the console, but there's no way to stop him.

"You did that on purpose!" There's no way I can close the door. Shit. He has me trapped. I refuse to go out without a fight. I pull a slip grenade from the pocket on my hip.

"All's fair in love and video games." He peers around the corner, the blaster aimed and ready.

The moment he steps into view, I hold my breath and pull the pin. After tossing it over the console, I brace for the blast, my heart hammering in my chest.

"Son of a bitch!" He shouts into the mic a fraction of a second before the explosion fills the screen. A black hole appears and sucks him into the vortex before slamming shut.

I rise from behind the console and retrieve the disc. *Mission completed* flashes across my screen. *Player two defeated.*

"No fucking way." Gavin sounds stunned. "How the hell did you pull that off? Was that a slip grenade?"

"Yeah." I preen at his defeat. Victory is so sweet.

"Where the hell did you find that?" he asks, genuine curiosity in the question.

"You always pick Colton, don't you?"

"Yeah." He groans. "Mike keeps telling me to try the other characters, but I like Colton."

"It took me a while to figure it out, but each character has a special cache of weapons to match their role and story." I pop a chip in my mouth. "Ransom seems to have the best ones because he doesn't play by any rules. Slip grenades are illegal according to the Galactic Reformation Alliance, but Ransom doesn't care. He's a pirate and lives for chaos."

"That makes sense," he concedes. "Another round?"

"Sure." I fire up the next scene. We lapse into silence with the occasional exclamation and copious amounts of swearing.

Gavin manages to beat me in the second round. I have to give him credit. He's good. Really good. I wonder if he's ever done gaming competitions. We're sucked into another round, and then another. Before I realize it, four hours have passed and we're laughing when I beat him to the Lunar Outpost on Moes Blick.

"How long have you been playing?" His question catches me off guard.

"Since high school," I reply cautiously. Why's he asking this? No one has ever shown an interest in my gaming past before. "I had a Super Nintendo. Played that thing all the time."

"Classic. I had one too. Drove my mom crazy. She wasn't a fan of me spending time with games or on the computer. Told me it would rot my brain." He laughs.

"My parents were the same. They got me a computer, but when I started gaming online, they threatened to take it away if I didn't get my grades up." The memory rises in my mind. "It's hard to find a balance when it's something you love to do."

"Isn't that the truth." He clears his throat. "Do you prefer PC gaming to console?"

"They both have their benefits." I stand up to stretch my legs between battles. "I miss the simplicity of games like *Counterstrike* and *Doom*. But I definitely spend more time on the consoles now. Especially if I find a game that challenges me. Then I fall down the rabbit hole."

"That is easy to do." He moans, and my blood runs molten through my veins. "Had to get up and stretch after that. You're brutal."

An uncomfortable laugh escapes me. "Thanks, I think."

"That's a compliment." His soft laughter reverberates deep inside me, warming my cold heart. "Most of the players I take on aren't half as skilled as you."

Damn him for plying me with compliments. "Thanks."

"I've played female gamers in the past, but they don't hang

out long."

"Yeah, well that happens when guys act like assholes and refuse to play against a chick." Anger bubbles inside me. "I can't remember a moment where I wasn't verbally accosted during a game for the sole reason of being a woman."

"Well, they're assholes because I'd rather take you on than half of their lame asses any day of the week." I can hear the smile in his tone. "At least you make me work for it."

"Yeah, same. It's nice to have a challenger who doesn't act like a dick and berate my sex when I kick his ass." I refill my glass and catch myself grinning in the window's reflection.

"I will admit, I was sore as fuck when you beat me the first day we met." His deep voice turns husky. "I've been wanting a rematch ever since."

"Me too." I shake my head. No, I must be imagining the sexy inflection of his voice.

"Well, whenever you want to play, just let me know."

I don't miss the unintended double entendre. I stumble over my jumbled thoughts before I can form a coherent phrase. "Sounds good."

"I'm logging off to get some work done for tomorrow." His words make me pout. "I'll see you at the office."

"Yeah, sure. See you then." I brush off the disappointment. "Goodnight, Gavin, and thanks."

"Anytime. Sleep well, baby girl." The line disconnects before I can recover my wits.

I rip off the headset and throw it on the couch. How dare he tease me? How freaking dare he say such things to me and leave me in a pool of my own want? Truth is, he probably has no idea what his words did to me.

With a groan, I power off the game console and the television. Tomorrow we start work on the Solus network upgrades. I can't be a tinderbox sitting next to an open flame.

Retreating to my room, I take a shower and relieve some stress. But nothing can take the edge off. Gavin is under my skin, and I'm not happy about it. Not one, single iota.

CHAPTER EIGHT

I swear, if one more thing goes wrong today, I'm going to lose my shit. After a night spent tossing restlessly because my next-door neighbors decided to have a screaming match at midnight, I had to detour three blocks around the park because it was closed for renovations. Then, as if the universe wasn't done fucking with me, the shop on the corner where I grab my morning coffee was closed. I barely made it to work on time.

By the time I reach the building, my teeth are clenched so tight I might snap a crown. I can only pray this Monday shit has worn off by noon. I don't know if I can deal with anything else going wrong today.

"Good morning," Evan greets me with a smile. His eyes widen when he meets my glare and steps aside.

I grunt in acknowledgment, pushing past him. Once I reach my office, I throw my purse on the desk and collapse on my chair.

Any minute Gavin will appear in the doorway and my day will implode like a supernova. I take several deep breaths and try to gather what remains of my sanity. Yesterday's little online battle left me with conflicting emotions. I still don't consider Gavin a friend, but the olive branch he extended by sending an invite to game softened my strong opinion of his character. But it does nothing to explain my body's visceral reaction to his presence and his voice.

Why did Ben and Evan decide to hire him of all people? I mean, I know he's the best in the city, but goddamn, I can't trust my own body to cooperate with my mind. Shoving aside the negativity, I try to focus on the benefit his work will have on the company. Maybe I can even learn a thing or two from him during the process that will help me with my own personal pet projects. I've always been interested in software design, especially apps.

This is a learning experience, a partnership between colleagues. Yeah, I'll just ignore the fact I want to ride him into the sunset and let him whisper dirty words in my ear.

I groan and hang my head, cursing the man for getting me all spun up and turned on. "Fuck."

"Uhhh." The uncomfortable sound emanating from the door makes my head snap up. Evan offers a wobbly smile and steps into my office. "Am I intruding?"

"Always." I stand and straighten my suit jacket.

"Here." He hands me a steaming mug with the Millennium Falcon on it. It's his personal coffee mug. "It's not your usual, but I figured you needed a pick-me-up."

I sip the brew and savor the faint caramel flavor. He tries, bless his heart. I smile, feeling some of the stress melt away. "Thanks."

"No problem." Evan's lopsided grin appears. "Rough night?"

"Don't start with me, Waldorf. I'm not in the mood." My smile flips upside-down instantly.

He chuckles and turns to leave, pausing in the doorway. "Oh, Gavin is waiting for you in the conference room."

"Shit." I nearly spill my coffee in the mad scramble to gather the files I need as well as my notebook and Triforce planner. "Son of a bitch."

Evan's laughter follows him down the hall. He just can't help himself. Button pushing bastard.

I somehow manage to balance everything under one arm and make it down the hall without dumping my coffee down someone's shirt or falling flat on my face. I push open the conference room door with my hip.

Gavin glances up from the paper he's reading and smiles. A dimple appears on his left cheek. My hormones decide to make note of this and have a party. I quickly pull the plug on it and clear my throat.

"Morning." I join him, setting my pile of papers down and taking a sip of my coffee.

"Morning." He sets the paper aside. There's a spread of

documents before him on the table. "Don't you start work at eight?"

I nearly choke on the mouthful of coffee. Instead of defending my tardiness, I grin. "Yes, but I had to dispose of a body in the bay before work and traffic was a bitch."

His eyes widen a fraction before he bursts into laughter. The sound ignites a glitter bomb at the aforementioned hormone party, turning it into a rave. Goddamn him. I shut that shit down faster than John ruining Christmas for Hans at Nakatomi Plaza.

"What's going on here?" I wave my hand over the scattered papers.

"Just trying to get an idea of the company's paper trail and how we can incorporate it into the internal database." He glances up and grins. "You know, maybe save some trees in the process."

"Good plan, sunshine." I nod in appreciation and sit in the chair beside him. "What do you need from me?"

His amber eyes darken to mahogany, and he licks his lips before turning back to the papers. I hadn't meant it as a double entendre, but it seems he's as aware of the tension here as I am. Shit. This can't be good.

"How much do you know about software programming?" He pulls out a notepad and a pen.

I cradle my coffee mug tight between my palms and focus on the pen in his hand. "Not enough, obviously, if we needed to outsource this." I tamp down my snark and try to answer his question honestly. "But I am familiar with the basics and some coding. It's just not something I've spent a lot of time with. It evolves so quickly it's hard to keep up during my free time."

"So you're familiar with Python, HTML, CSS, and C++?" He scribbles a few notes down, but I can't read his handwriting from this angle.

"Yeah, I took a few classes, but I haven't sat down and applied the information." I raise my mug and salute in the general direction of my bosses. "They keep me busy enough here. Those kinds of services take a finesse I don't have at the moment."

"Maybe you should brush up on those skills instead of playing video games." His statement makes me pause, but the smile playing on his lips says not to take it personally. He's teasing me, but I can't seem to brush it off.

I press my lips together and hold his gaze with the intensity of a velociraptor fixed on her prey.

"Sorry." His smile disappears. "I didn't mean—"

"Didn't mean what?" I tap my fingers on the porcelain. "Listen, sunshine. I'm a successful forty-year-old woman who answers to no one but myself. What I do with my downtime is my prerogative." I inhale sharply. "You're right. I should do something to improve my skills, but I'm pretty fucking comfortable where I am right now. So sue me if I want to take some me time and play a fucking game to decompress."

"Maggie, I—"

"No." I hold my hand up and stop him. "I thought you of all people would understand. Playing video games isn't just for smart-mouth teens who want to piss off the establishment. They're the *one escape* I have that's just for me. I deal with a lot of shit in-game, but I keep going back because it's something I enjoy." By the time I finish, my chest is heaving.

"Wait," Gavin says almost hesitant to speak. "There's no way you're forty."

I pull back like he slapped me. Disoriented, I stare at him, turning over the words in my mind. "What?"

"I assumed you were the same age as me and Lily." He leans back in his chair and draws the pen between his teeth.

Typically, I'm a mental whiz, but it took me a moment to pull the shock from my brain and do some quick calculations. Lily's thirty-two this year. Gavin and Lily went to school together, same year. Fuck. Fuckity fuck fuck. Every lustful thought I had about Gavin slams into me at the speed of a bullet train. I'm a goddamn cougar. I close my eyes and take a deep breath. When I open them, Gavin waits patiently with that molten gaze.

"Don't like taking instructions from your elders, or just women in general?" The singsong tone of my voice doesn't stop the snark from tainting every word.

Gavin drops the pen and leans forward with graceful ease.

Our eyes lock and there's no way in hell I can pull my gaze away from his. I'm trapped. His lips curl into a sensual smile full of promise. I brace myself even though I know I should run like hell.

"I don't have a problem taking orders from my elders *or* women." He draws his lower lip between his teeth and lets it slide against those pearly whites as he releases it in slow motion. "I prefer a partner with a little more…experience."

My heart's racing and alarm bells ring at full volume in my ears. I can't look away. It's like he's drawing me out, baiting me. I refuse to give in. I won't submit to his teasing. There's no way for me to know if he's truly interested in me…in us. But we can't. I can't.

Before my restraint snaps, Gavin leans back and picks up his pen. All teasing vanishes in an instant. We're back in the office conference room working on the new system upgrade. Gavin seems unaffected by the tension pulsing around us.

"We should start with the invoice systems and then work our way through the other filing and data entry points." He glances at me. "What do you think?"

I clear my throat. "Sure, that sounds good."

We settle in and focus on the task at hand. The tension never fully abates, but I have to ignore it. This job needs to get done and I'm the only one with a full understanding of what the company needs to function properly.

While we're in this room working on this project, we're a team. There's one mission: fix the system. There is no room for erotic fantasies or teasing banter. This job needs to be done right. I just hope Gavin understands this.

"Listen," I interrupt when he pauses. "About earlier, I think we need to keep it focused while we're working on this project. No personal jabs. Purely professional." I emphasize my statement with a nod. "Agreed?"

Gavin holds my gaze for a moment and I think he's going to say something, but he pushes it aside. Finally, he nods. "Agreed."

"Good." I pull a paper out of my file and place it on the

table in front of him. "Now, what do you think of this idea for the invoice system?"

He scans the paper and I admire his profile briefly before cursing myself. Damn it. Truce or not, this is going to be a never-ending battle. But is it one I really want to win?

CHAPTER NINE

I hate to admit it, but I'm actually enjoying Gavin's company. That's been a bitter pill to swallow. My ego and my hormones are still taking the hit. I'm impressed at how amazingly productive we've been in such a short time. In one week, we were able to come up with a plan for a system specifically for Solus that will suit all the company's needs and leave room for expansion should it be required in the future.

I've picked up some tips and tricks for my own personal edification when it comes to computer programming and software design. When working with one of the most talented programmers in the city, it would be stupid not to take notes and absorb as much information as possible. Plus, it gives me an excuse to lean over his shoulder to read his notes. Damn it, he smells so good.

I glance at the clock. Shit. Four already? Typically I would be stoked to see this on a Friday afternoon. My gaze shifts to Gavin who's writing in his notebook. His lips move as he writes, mouthing the words silently. It's a cute little tic I've noticed over the past few days. I gather the papers on the table before stuffing them into the folder. Stop ogling the man for fuck's sake.

He closes the notebook and clicks his pen before tucking it into his messenger bag. "I think that's about it."

"What?" I set the files aside and face him.

"I have everything I need to get the system up and running." He grins, and part of me melts. "I should be able to do the rest remotely now that I have access to the network."

Confusion fills me for a brief second before it disintegrates into defeat. "So, you're not coming in next week?"

"Nope. Not unless there's a hardware issue." He gathers the rest of his stuff and tucks it into his bag. "If I have any questions or encounter any problems, I'll call you."

"Oh." I stiffen against the unwelcome disappointment. "Okay. That works."

After our truce on Monday, we found a companionable groove, teamwork with a mutual goal. I admire his dedication and efficiency. He's focused and driven with some strong work ethics. If I had to admit it aloud, I would. Gavin is damn good at his job. It's no wonder his schedule is completely booked. As if I need another reason to be attracted to him. This only solidifies my decision to keep our relationship strictly professional. I don't want to jeopardize it over some raging hormones and a misunderstanding.

I'm still not sure if he was teasing me that morning or if I misread the scenario by taking his words out of context. I have a warped mind, and sometimes it twists inane observations into something sexual or perverse. I normally have full control over it while at work, but Gavin brings out that darker side of me. I imagine it's the raging lust burning beneath my calm exterior.

When he stands, I join him. There's nothing more for us to do here, but I'm straining for an excuse for him to stay. For us to work together a little longer. I have nothing. Damn.

"Have any plans for the weekend?" He slings his messenger bag over his shoulder.

"Uh." His question jerks me from my internal misery. "Movie night with the girls, I think. But that's about it. You?"

"Lunch with my mom in the city tomorrow." He shifts his weight and leans against the wall as I gather up the files in my arms. "She loves those insanely expensive bistros near Central Park."

"That's nice of you, taking your mom out like that." I turn and head for the door acutely aware of his presence behind me.

He opens the door for me, and I catch a whiff of his intoxicating scent again. Curse him.

"Yeah, well, it's the least I can do. She's the reason I am where I am."

Gooseflesh prickles along my arms at his close proximity. I'm not sure how much more of this I can take without giving in to the dirty thoughts racing through my mind. I need to put distance between us.

"I'm sure you'll have a blast." I head down the hall in the opposite direction of the stairwell. "Let me know if you need anything for the update."

"Will do." His response echoes behind me.

At the end of the hall, I catch sight of him before I round the corner. He's standing with his hand in his pocket, watching me with a peculiar look on his face. I don't stop to ponder it. Instead, I dash out of sight and collapse against the wall. Fuck. Why is this so damn hard?

Ignoring the little voice in my mind, I head for my office and file the items we used. I can hear Evan and Ben in his office talking. Without saying goodbye, I gather my shit and leave.

I spend the evening cleaning and organizing my apartment. Anything to purge the wicked thoughts in my mind and give me a distraction. I can't even log into my game because I don't want to see Gavin, even though I really want to spend more time with him. And it pisses me off. I could play offline or hide my status, but it's not the same now. Because I know he's there and he's tainted the one escape I had. Not even my *me* time is sacred anymore.

On Saturday, I enjoy movie night with the girls at my place. But once they leave, I'm left alone with my thoughts. I glance at the clock. It's ten. Fuck it. I change into my pajamas and curl up beneath a blanket on the couch before flipping on my game console and putting on my headset.

When the main screen loads, I take a deep breath. The light beside Gavin's screen name is green. He's online. The cursor hovers over his name for a brief moment. No. This is my time. I select *Vendetta: Space Armada II*. It released a few weeks ago, so everything is still shiny and new. But it's still not enough to entice me fully. I want to play it with Gavin.

While it loads, I chew on my fingernail. Maybe I should ask him to play? It's no fun playing against the AI. Plus, if some other jackwagon asks me to battle, I might rip his head off. At least Gavin would laugh my rage off.

I grab the throw pillow beside me and scream into it. Why

does this man taint everything now? It's like he's infiltrated my life, a virus sent to destroy me from the inside slowly stripping away everything I love until only a husk remains.

A message pops on the screen. *Care for a little one on one?*

Relief fills me when I see Gavin's name beside it. I connect to the headset. "You'd rather take me on than your roommates?"

I hold my breath, waiting for his response.

"Yeah." His voice surrounds me like a warm hug. "You in?"

"As if you need to ask." I queue up the main screen and select a new game.

Once it starts, we slide into snarky banter and smack talk, but silence descends when the tension of the game ratchets up a notch. After two rounds, one to him and one to me, I manage to snare a second win by luring him into a sandpit filled with Bopet Vipers.

"Shit." Gavin groans at the appearance of *Player Two: Mission Failed* flashing on the screen.

I chuckle at his misery. "You almost had me."

"Yeah, I did." The disgust is evident in his tone. "Then you had to go and pull some sneaky shit with that viper pit. I don't even want to know how you found that."

"Have you played this one since it released?" I snicker, feeling better than I thought I would.

"I haven't had time." He snorts. "This is only my second opportunity."

I bite back my snarky comment. I should be nice. Gavin gives me the challenge I don't get with other gamers. He respects my talent even though he doesn't like that I can whoop his ass. All the other gamer groups I'm in push me away when they take me on. They don't like being bested by a woman. It hurts their delicate egos. I've learned to deal with it, but it still stings. Rejection is never easy.

I bite my lip. "Want me to let you go play someone who will let you win?"

"Tired of me already?"

"No, it's just—normally guys get bent out of shape when I kick their ass twice in a row. Just wanted to give you the chance to escape with your dignity."

"If I had any dignity, I would accept your offer." He pauses, for emphasis I assume. "But I don't. So, shall we continue?"

"Are you just humoring me? You don't have to. I have other people I can play against. You're not the only man in my universe."

"Well, after a few more rounds, I will be. Once you've played with me, there's no going back." The teasing tone I heard on Monday returns with a vengeance. I'm tempted to seize the opportunity, but there's too much at stake. I can't.

"Are you always so full of yourself?"

"Are you?"

"Touché." I throw my hands up. "Fine. Let's play."

"I have another question first."

It throws me off for a moment, but I recover quickly. "As long as it's not sexual in nature, then go for it."

"No, those questions can be saved for the third date." He laughs. "Earlier this week you said you were teaching yourself coding and programming. That's a lot of work. You don't need it for your job. Why waste your energy on it?"

He waited to ask this question, I realize with a start. At any point during the week, he could have asked me. Hell, we spent lunch breaks working side-by-side talking about random shit like the weather and our coworkers. But this question never came up. He chose this moment to ask. Why? Then it hits me. I'm where I'm most comfortable, and we're not face to face. Sneaky, Gavin. Sneaky as hell. I relent with a sigh.

"I want to design something for women who game. A space where we can connect and compete without the constant barrage of men telling us we're wrong, or lame, or stupid." I smooth my fingertips over the controller in my hand. "There's so much bias in the gaming world. I wanted to offer a space where we can let our hair down and enjoy doing what we love."

"Hmmm." His response doesn't offer any insight into his thoughts, so I continue.

"I've been researching and trying to teach myself how to code, but it's taking me forever." I clear my throat. "Might never happen, but it's worth a shot, right?"

"I think it's a great idea."

"You do?" I wasn't expecting him to like my idea. In fact, I was positive he would laugh it off like so many others have. I stopped telling people about it years ago because none of them took me seriously. His response fuels my determination to keep the dream alive.

"Of course. And if you need any help, just ask."

"Thanks, Gavin." My heart swells with joy at his offer.

"Now, let's play. I need a chance to redeem myself."

"You're on, but don't think I'm going to take it easy on you." I unleash an evil laugh.

"If you did, I'd be highly offended." He chuckles, and the sound wraps around my libido with a boa constrictor's strength.

I select the next level and start the game.

We play on until he calls it quits at midnight.

"Thanks for the challenge." I set the blanket aside and stretch. "You're merciless."

"Was that a compliment?"

"Take it how you want, sunshine. All I know is I haven't had this much fun in forever."

"You know I'm always around to show you a good time, baby girl."

My whole body transforms into molten lava. Seriously, must he keep teasing me? I feel like I'm going to combust from the sound of his voice alone. There's no need to kick up the heat. I choose to ignore it and suffer in silence.

"Goodnight, Gavin."

"Night."

I disconnect the headset and power off the game. Then I head straight for bed where I'm going to refrain from touching myself to alleviate this ache burning me alive. *Damn you, Gavin. You do this on purpose.*

CHAPTER TEN

Lily calls me in a fluster, demanding I come over for an emergency meeting. She's probably overreacting, but friends show up for each other regardless. At least that's what I tell myself when I climb the steps to her brownstone on Sunday afternoon.

I knock on the door. My stomach twists in knots. Gavin's probably home. I haven't seen him since we parted ways at Solus a few weeks ago, but we have spoken in-game on a regular basis. Friday nights have become a standing ritual. We meet at nine and play until midnight. Just the two of us.

Life has been moderately peaceful since Gavin and I found common ground. While his words knock me off balance, I can take it because I'm on the other end of the console, not standing face-to-face with the one person who makes me feel like I've swallowed a hive of bees. I'm not sure I could withstand the constant onslaught of hormones being in the same room with him. It's like his scent combined with his presence creates a whirlwind around me, blocking out any rational thought. I hate that it leaves me off-kilter.

The door swings open. Lily drags me into the house by the arm and kicks the door shut.

"Everything okay?" I ask as she pulls me down the hall into the kitchen.

"No." She releases me and wrenches open the freezer. Armed with the vodka bottle Gavin keeps in the back of the freezer, she spins around, her hair frazzled and pulled in a messy bun. She's not wearing makeup either.

I'm stunned for a second at seeing fresh-faced Lily. It's a good look on her, like everything else, but I can tell something's wrong. Lily is never *not* put together. She always looks immaculate. The picture of glamour and sophistication. I frown.

"What happened?" I grip her shoulder as she attempts to pour two drinks. "Did one of your roommates do something stupid? Are you hurt?"

"No, no. Nothing like that." She pours the two shots and downs hers before I even reach for my glass.

"Tell me already." I grab the vodka and toss it back. It burns, but I appreciate the top-shelf liquor nonetheless.

"I'm worried about Jen." Her luminous blue eyes meet mine. "This fandom stuff she's involved in. I think it's affecting her work." She bites her lip. "And her relationship with Shaun."

"What do you mean?" I slide onto the bench beside the island. She's not the only one who's noticed the shift in Jen's personality and her priorities. I have too. But something must have happened or Lily wouldn't be in panic mode.

"Remember her new online fandom friends she's been talking to?" I nod, and she continues. "Well, she's leaving next weekend to go to Philly for the comic convention."

"Shaun's going with her, right?" A nervous energy skitters along my spine. This can't be good.

Lily shakes her head and downs another shot, hissing at the alcohol's kick.

"She's going by herself?" I screech. My voice echoes through the entire downstairs. "We would have gone with her. Why didn't she tell us?"

The pout on Lily's lips tells me all I need to know. "She told you but asked you not to tell me." I bang my fist on the table. "Why?"

"Maybe she didn't tell you because she knew this was how you'd react," Gavin adds from the doorway.

I jump at the intrusion and glare at him, ignoring the way my body warms at his presence. "Uh, private conversation. You're not invited."

He ignores me and grabs the bottle from Lily's hand mid-pour. "Take it easy, Lil. You're not twenty anymore. Doing shots that fast is going to leave you with a wicked hangover and a shit ton of regrets."

Lily sticks her tongue out at him and folds her arms across

the NYU embroidered on the hoodie she's wearing. "Must you eavesdrop?"

"I can hear you upstairs in my room. It might as well be a broadcasted event." His gaze shifts to me and I straighten under his scrutiny. "What's the problem?"

"Jen is going to comic con in Philly. Alone," I clarify.

"Actually, she's meeting up with her online friends at the con. And crashing with that Madre character at her hotel!" Lily's eyes fly wide. "What if she's a serial killer? What if she sells Jen on the black market? That shit happens!"

Gavin shakes his head and wraps his arms around Lily's trembling body. Jealousy infuses me, but I shove it aside and focus on this new information. I grab my phone from my pocket and pull up Jen's number.

"What are you doing?" Lily shouts and lunges across the island. "She asked me not to tell you. You can't call her!"

I yank my phone out of her reach and lock the screen. "Fine. I won't call her. But what the hell am I supposed to do? Let her walk into her own abduction?"

Gavin's laughter fills the room. "Will you two calm down? Jen is an adult. She's capable of making her own decisions and dealing with the consequences. If she wants to go to the Philly comic convention by herself and meet up with some friends she met online, I say good for her."

Both Lily and I stare at Gavin as though he's gone completely insane.

"So we're supposed to sit back and do nothing?"

"Yes." Gavin returns the vodka to the freezer and closes the door, punctuating the word. He turns his gaze to me. "How would you feel if Jen and Lily came barging in telling you to not do something you're dead set on doing anyway? Something you've been looking forward to for weeks?" He arches a brow, waiting for my response.

I have none. He's right, damn it, and I won't give him the satisfaction by affirming the fact.

Lily nods and pushes aside the half-full shot glass. "If she wants our help, she'll ask for it. Right?"

"I would hope so." I groan. "But honestly, I'm not happy. Jen's been distracted lately, and I'm afraid this may push her over the edge."

"Distracted?" Gavin cocks his head. "How?"

"Like obsessed." I pick at the edge of the counter. "She's been bailing on girls' night and not answering texts. It's not like her."

"Well, regardless, she's an adult." He grabs two bottles of water from the fridge and hands one to me and the other to Lily. "If she wants your help, she'll ask for it."

"I'm just saying, nothing good will come from this." Twisting off the top, I imagine it's Gavin's neck.

"Well, all we can do is be here for her when she needs us." Lily takes a deep breath. "I'm going up to take a long, hot bath." She turns to me and pulls me into a fierce hug. "Sorry about the false alarm. I was freaking out over nothing."

"It's okay. I'm here for both you and Jen, whenever you need me." I squeeze her tight. "Go take a bath. You deserve some pampering time."

"Text me when you get home." Lily kisses my cheek and swans from the room with her usual grace, even in sweats and a hoodie.

"Well, I'm gonna head out." I snatch my phone off the counter.

"Come here." Gavin's command rips the breath from my lungs.

I spin around to find him walking out the door. My brain scrambles to catch up with the rest of me as I follow him. Where's he taking me?

He climbs the stairs and enters the first room at the top of the landing. His bedroom.

I bite my lip and whisper a little prayer for strength. I swear, it's so hard to keep my mind from wandering around him. *Hard.* Ugh, I slap myself mentally. Stop. Are you a fourteen-year-old boy? Seriously.

My eyes struggle to adjust to the dim lighting. The queen size bed dominates the right side of the room, neatly made with a dark blue comforter. A bookshelf stands tall beside it. I can't read the titles from here, but the shelves are uncluttered and organized. The photograph hanging on the wall catches my eye. Is that computer code? I step closer and gasp. It's the city etched out in code from the Matrix.

"It took me a while to get it right." Gavin's soft tone makes me jump and spin around.

I press my hand to my chest trying to calm my racing heart. "You made this?"

He nods with a faint smile.

"Huh." I turn back to admire it. "It's beautiful."

"Thanks." He takes my hand. "Let me show you something."

Sparks radiate from the simple touch of his fingers curved around mine. He pulls me across the room and I let him, sinking my hand deeper into his.

Two massive computer screens dominate the far wall on a desk bigger than the kitchen island downstairs. A gamer chair sits empty to the left, as though shoved aside in haste.

Gavin releases my hand and bends down, using the mouse to open a program on the computer.

My hand tingles from the residual warmth, and I cradle it to my chest. Don't fixate. It doesn't mean anything. It's an innocent touch. After several deep breaths, I'm able to focus on the screen instead of the strong bow of his shoulders flexing as he moves.

"Here." He steps aside and gestures to the screen.

I come alongside him and lean closer to the monitor. On the screen is a familiar application. The system we use at Solus, but different. I glance up at him.

"Is this the update?" I return my attention to the screen and click through the different files and applications.

"Yeah, but it's not finished. I have a few bugs to work out and some details to add." He leans against the desk, brushing his thigh against my arm.

"It's so fluid. Much easier interface than before." I lick my lips and focus on admiring the improvements he made to the antiquated system. When I return to the home screen, I step back from the computer in awe. "Evan and Ben are going to be thrilled."

"What about you?" Gavin's dark gaze searches my face.

"I think it's fantastic." I nudge the mouse with my fingertips. "You've done an amazing job. It'll make my life a whole lot easier, I can tell you that."

"I couldn't have done it without your guidance." He covers my hand with his where it rests against the desk surface. "You gave me all the ideas. I just brought them to life."

My breath lodges in my chest. His touch burns through me, igniting a riot inside my stomach and sending my brain into overdrive.

"I know I'm good, but—"

"Maggie." He leans closer, and his heat and heady scent wrap around me, drawing me deeper into madness. "Stop talking."

"But I—"

His mouth covers mine and I'm fucking lost. Fireworks explode somewhere in the back of my mind, raining sparks and igniting the long-denied desire curled deep inside me. Gavin threads his hands in my hair and pulls me against him. I come willingly, wrapping my arms around his neck and rising up on my toes.

He lifts me and sets me on the desk. Stepping between my thighs, he dominates me. His mouth claims mine once more. His lips taste like peppermint and pure fucking sin. I draw his lower lip between my teeth and bite gently. He chuckles against my mouth before delving deeper.

I gasp at his invasion. He steals my breath with his kiss as he explores my mouth. It's like he's making love to it, mimicking the act itself. I groan and arch my hips against his. His grip on my hair tightens as he pulls away.

"Tell me what you want, baby girl." His wicked voice sends a shiver through me with a burst of hot need.

"I…" My brain spins and I can't form a coherent thought. I want him. He wants me. This is…wrong. Shit. Not here. Not now. We're still working together. I can't separate the two in my mind.

"We can't." I press my hand against his chest, putting distance between us when he backs away a step. "We're still working on the project. It's…not professional."

Gavin's brow furrows, but he nods, stuffing his hands in his pockets. "You're right."

"I should go." I slide off the table and straighten my clothes.

He doesn't move as I head for the door. My conscience wilts under the weight of the guilt. I bite my lip. When I reach the door, I turn a fraction, unable to face him fully.

"Thanks for the sneak peek." I wince at my weak response and step out into the well-lit hallway.

Once I reach the street outside, the fresh afternoon air washes over me, purging the lust pulsing through me hot and demanding. I want nothing more than to race up those stairs and make a mess of those soft sheets on his bed. I stomp down my disappointment and chastise my raging libido before taking the long way home.

It does nothing to erase the feel of his lips against mine and the scent of his skin. My head buzzes with desire. That one kiss left me intoxicated. What the hell am I going to do now that I've had a taste? This makes it even harder to resist him.

I know one thing for certain. He wants me as much as I want him. This should be a good thing. So why am I running away?

Chapter Eleven

My whole body protests when I wake in the morning. Lingering memories of soft, warm lips and his heady kiss flit through my subconscious. I angrily swat them away. I don't need a reminder of Gavin's kiss first thing in the morning. Or ever. But I'm not that lucky. I get ready for work, plagued all the while by the man I swear didn't like me a few weeks ago.

I haven't had a good night's sleep in months thanks to him. But last night was by far the worst. The shittiest part was I couldn't even log onto the PlayStation without him barging into my thoughts with the grace of a Bantou Beast. He's tainted everything I love. All of it.

Even my dreams aren't free from his influence. He appears in the most random places like a haunting specter sent to torment me until I take my final breath. I refuse to admit that I'm not upset by this. In fact, I'm upset at the fact I'm not *more* disturbed by the shift in our acquaintance.

I could have pushed him away. Stopped the kiss from even happening. But I didn't, because I wanted it. I craved it like an ice-cold drink in the sweltering heat of summer. Shit. I can't believe I'm thirsting for Gavin. That steaming, smoldering kiss brought a match to the dry tinder surrounding me. I burn for him, and it makes me physically ill to even acknowledge it.

Somehow I manage to drag myself into work without incident. Both Evan and Ben's office doors are closed when I arrive. Safely enclosed in my personal space, I breathe a sigh of relief. Exhaustion settles around me as I sink into my chair. Maybe I'll be able to sneak in a power nap at lunch. I pray by then I'll have reached the point where my racing mind is tuned out by the desperation caused by lack of sleep.

My phone pings from deep inside my messenger bag. I ignore it and pull out my planner.

Evan and Ben have two meetings this morning. Ben has a lunch appointment with Empire at noon. There's a walk-through with one of the investors at three. Good, that will give me a chance to catch up on the paperwork I still haven't sorted from the week I took helping Gavin. Bless Andrew, but he's useless when it comes to organization. I have to hold his hand every time.

There's a soft knock at the door.

"Come in."

Evan pops his head in. "Hey, I come bearing gifts. Please don't shoot." He holds out a coffee cup from the corner shop in his hand like a shield.

I chuckle and lean back. "What's up, boss?"

He grins and comes inside the office, handing the coffee to me. "Not much. Andrew picked up coffee for us all."

My nose twitches at the sweet aroma and a sigh escapes me. "At least he's good at something."

"Be nice, Maggie." Evan mock scolds me and sits down in the chair beside the door. "How was your weekend?"

Thoughts of Jen's trip to comic con and Gavin's kiss twist in my mind. "I don't want to talk about it."

"You look tense. And there are bags under your eyes." Evan points out with no tact. "If I didn't know any better, I'd say you were having boy problems."

"Boy problems?" I scoff. "Are we in high school again?" I blow across the top of the steaming brew before taking a sip. He's not far off, and that doesn't bode well for me. Evan is far too observant.

"No, but whatever's going on, it's impacting your mood. I would say it's a lack of sleep, but I've seen you sleep on the floor in an airport with fire alarms wailing." He crosses his ankle over his knee and rests back against the chair, his blue eyes narrowing. "So, what's going on?"

I shift in my seat and set the cup aside. "Nothing's going on, Evan. I'm fine. Just leave it alone."

"It's Gavin, isn't it?" Evan's voice slides across my skin like cold steel.

I flinch at the mention of his name and swear when a slow smile spreads across Evan's lips.

"I knew it!" He leans forward, his coffee cup clutched in his hands looking like I'm about to reveal the secrets of the universe. "Has he been keeping you up way past your bedtime?"

"Evan." I pin him with a glare. "First of all, my sex life is none of your goddamn business. And second, this type of questioning isn't professional at all."

"Professional?" He snorts. "Mags, you swear like a trucker, have no qualms about calling both me and Ben on our bullshit, and crack jokes bordering on sexual harassment regularly. So don't give me this *professional* crap."

I fidget with the *Zelda* pendant around my neck and avoid his gaze. There's not a topic in the world I would readily avoid, except this one. I don't want to talk about it because if I put a voice to it…well, then I have to face the truth. And I don't want to do that. Why did Gavin have to butt his handsome self into my life?

"Mags." Evan's smile fades. "What happened?" He sets his coffee on my desk and folds his hands together. "Listen, if you need to talk about it, I'm here. Not as your boss, but as a friend. Please, tell me what's going on."

I groan and pinch my eyes closed. "I fucked up, Evan."

"I'm sure it's not that bad." His tone is soothing, and I can't help but take comfort in it. When I open my eyes, his blue eyes fix on mine, full of sympathy. Evan's such a nice guy it's painful. Damn his persistence.

"I told you before, Gavin's my friend Lily's roommate." I take a deep breath and it spills out. The story of the first time I met Gavin and beat his ass. The strain between us because of it.

"Why did you recommend him to work on the upgrade for Solus then?" Evan asks, invested in the conversation.

"I didn't recommend *him*. I recommended the company he works for." I clarify, wondering how fate seemed to work that whole thing out, but I shove those questions aside. "When you interviewed him, I couldn't demand you not hire him. He came highly qualified and we needed his help to get the database back up and running efficiently."

"At what point during the week of working together did you realize you wanted to 'climb him like a tree and ride him into the sunset' as you so eloquently like to phrase it."

I cover my face with both hands and groan. "Until yesterday, I thought he was tolerating me. Humoring me by challenging me to one-on-one battles online every Friday night and asking me why I love gaming so much. I thought it was innocent curiosity."

"Doesn't sound like he was humoring you. It sounds like you two overcame whatever animosity you had and found a common ground. I'm pretty sure that's friendship, Mags."

"I'm friends with lots of guys, Evan." I tap my finger on the desk. "This is different."

"Is it?"

"Yesterday, I was visiting with Lily and he invited me up to his room to show me his progress on the Solus update." I lick my lips. "He kissed me."

"And you got laid."

"No. I panicked and left."

"Wait, I'm confused. You don't think you're friends with him, but you kiss him and then freak out. Do you like him or not?"

My response digs into my throat refusing to come out. I nod, unable to say it aloud.

"So, what's the problem?"

"I crossed the line. This shouldn't have happened. He's contracted by Solus. Technically that makes us coworkers until he finishes the job. The last thing I want is to have some big misunderstanding cause a delay with the system upgrades." I groan in frustration.

"He's a contractor, Mags, not an employee of Solus." He regards me calmly, pressing his lips together in thought. "I'm pretty sure the fraternization rule Ben insisted HR put in the company contract doesn't stop you from pursuing something with a temporary contractor."

"But what if he hates me now?" I flick a piece of paper into the trash unable to meet Evan's gaze. It feels childish and stupid, but I still can't admit I'm scrambling for excuses not to take Gavin up on his unspoken offer.

"Mags." The gentle tone in which he says my name makes me look up. "He doesn't hate you. Trust me. It'll take a lot more than a case of blue balls for that man to hate you."

I chuckle at his poor attempt at humor. "How can you be sure though?"

"Guess there's only one way to find out." Evan slowly rises to his feet and picks up his coffee cup. "But judging from the way he was looking at you in the conference room, I'd say it's a sure bet he's willing to let you climb all over him like a spider monkey."

I throw my notebook at him. "Get out."

"Hateful." He puts his hand up to block any more incoming projectiles. "I'm just calling it like it is. It's not my fault you can't handle the truth."

"Forget I even said anything and leave me in peace."

"All right. I'm going." He pauses halfway out the door. "But remember spider monkey." He closes the door before I can whip something else at his head. His laughter echoes outside the door.

Collapsing against the desk, I surrender. Why did I even say anything? It's not like Evan could really understand. But he made a valid point. I can't use our professional connection as an excuse. Soon we would part ways in that capacity. A sense of loss settles around me.

We were enemies once upon a time, weren't we? Maybe that's a strong term. More like opponents battling for supremacy. But that's changed. It's evolved into something like friendship, but that doesn't quite fit either.

It's true. I want to climb him like a goddamn tree. I want to let him have his wicked way with me. Shit, am I rhyming now? A vision of Gavin setting me on his desk, pressing between my thighs and plundering my mouth leaves me breathless and aching. I pinch my eyes closed. Even though I can see something between us sexually, that's it. We have nothing in common but games and physical chemistry. I barely know him.

Hell, I barely know myself. What the hell do I even want out of life? I don't know, but I can't continue like this. Gavin woke something inside me, and I'm terrified to find out what that means for my future.

My text alert goes off again, pulling me from my thoughts. I grab the bag and fish out my phone.

"What is so damned important?"

Three missed messages from an unknown number. I open them out of pure curiosity.

Hey, it's Gavin. Lily gave me your number. My heart stops at the sight of his name. Shit. Why is he texting me? I read the second message.

Ran into a snag with the software update. Just wanted to let you know it'll be a week or two until I get it fixed because of my other jobs. I'm partially relieved by this news. He'll be working from home and busy. I bite my lip when I move on to the third message.

I can still taste you.

I suck in a breath at the tiny words printed on the screen. Heat floods me, leaving my heart pounding and my panties soaked. Holy shit. I lock the phone and set it aside.

There's no way I can respond to him. Not yet. I'll have Evan reach out to him later about the delay in the update, but I can't do it.

If I start something, I won't be satisfied until I finish it. That unknown ending hangs in the distance like a menacing cloud promising the storm of the century. On instinct, I take shelter. Maybe I can wait out Hurricane Gavin, but somehow I know I'll be swept up in his torrent and heaven help me, I don't want to be saved.

CHAPTER TWELVE

Two weeks. That's how long I manage to successfully avoid Gavin.

Unfortunately, part of the reason is Jen. The sweet, obsessed fangirl hit a wall. I knew her little trip to comic con would end in disaster. I saw it coming a mile away. She came home from the event in a funk, locked herself away, and then her world imploded. Lily's concerned texts blew up my phone for a week before we finally called an intervention. After dragging her back into the light and showing her how much we love and support her, Jen is ready to put the pieces of her life back together.

That's more than I can say about my own shitshow. Avoidance has worked wonders, but I know at some point I'm going to have to deal with my issues—and Gavin.

I cut through the park and grab coffee on the corner before I brave work. Evan's voice filters through the wall from Ben's office. They're here early. I set the coffee carrier on my desk and take off my suit jacket.

I glance at my calendar and see Friday's date marked in red. Gavin's expected completion date for the new upgrade. He's been working on the project diligently from home and sends intermittent updates via email.

Guilt twists inside me. I never responded to *the text.* I couldn't. What the hell am I supposed to say to that? Me too? I can't shake the memory of that kiss, or the all-consuming need it sparked within me. As much as I hated to see Jen suffering, I needed the distraction her meltdown provided. Otherwise, I would have ended up on his doorstep on my knees.

Okay, that may be a stretch, but still. I would have done something stupid. Like text him back and tell him I want more.

I grab the two cups marked for Ben and Evan. With a sturdy

kick to the door with my heel, I wait patiently as silence falls on the other side. It swings open and Evan greets me with a smile.

"Ahhh, you're a saint." He grabs the coffee from my hand.

I step over the threshold and hand Ben his cup.

"Thanks." He takes it without emotion and leans back in his chair.

"Am I interrupting something important?" I rest my hands on my hips. "I could hear you two arguing through the wall."

"No." Ben sips his coffee without elaborating.

"Did you check your email this morning?" Evan glances up as he peels the lid from the cup.

"Not yet, why?"

"Gavin finished the system upgrade. He'll be stopping by this week to finalize the installation and make sure everything works on location." Ben sets his cup aside and meets my gaze.

"Oh, well that's good." I force a smile, but inside, it's a five-alarm fire with full-on sirens wailing.

Evan smirks before sipping his drink. We haven't spoken about Gavin since that day in my office, but I can tell by the purse of his lips he's ready to ask all sorts of personal questions.

"Enjoy your coffee." I exit Ben's office and lock myself within the safety of my own.

"Shit." I turn on my computer and check my inbox. Sure enough, there's a note from Gavin. No specific time or day though. I bite my lip. There's no way I can escape this unless I call out sick all week. Damn it.

Ignoring the dread building in the pit of my stomach, I focus on getting as much done as I can in case I do decide to bail for the week. It'd be dumb of me to do that over something so stupid. We're both adults. I mean, we can have a rational conversation about this, right?

By one o'clock, my stomach growls, demanding sustenance. I push away from my desk and grab my purse.

Andrew passes me by the stairwell.

"I'm gonna pop over to the bistro quick and grab a bite. Be back in a few."

"Oh." He gestures to the conference room down the hall.

"Gavin just got here to finalize the update."

"Shit." I shake my head and cover my slip. "Well, I need to eat something or I'm going to get hangry. Tell them I'll be back in twenty."

"But..." He blows his hair from his eyes. "Fine. Hurry back before Ben has my head."

"Thanks." I head out into the sunny afternoon. Once the breeze hits my face, I'm able to breathe. I take my time walking to the corner, ordering lunch, and eating. By the time I get back to the office, forty-five minutes have passed. Gavin should be gone.

I step onto the floor and find the hall empty.

"Maggie, there you are," Evan calls from the conference room. "You should join us."

Gritting my teeth, I make my way down the hall and brace myself for the inevitable.

Ben and Gavin glance up from the computer when I walk into the room. Gavin's gaze bores into me as a smile twists his lips. Shit.

Commandeering a chair, I settle in as they lapse into conversation. Gavin explains the system to Ben and Evan, who seem impressed. If it's what he showed me at his place, then it's top-notch work. They should be hella impressed. Especially for the price they're paying for his services.

I'd like to utilize his services myself. My gaze lingers on his full lips as he speaks, making my mind wander. He could read a goddamned phone book and I'd get turned on. Heat lingers in my face, drifting lower and lower until it reaches my neglected nether regions. Oh God, this is a bad idea. I shift uncomfortably in my chair.

Evan raises a brow, and I shoot him a withering glare, warning him not to say a damned word. He chuckles and returns his attention to the computer screen.

Gavin reaches for the mouse and all I can see is his fingers wrapped around my throat with the gentlest pressure. I blink twice before I realize they're talking to me.

"Do you want to take a look at it?" Ben gestures to the

computer.

I shake my head to clear the fog and signal my answer since it's obvious I'm incapable of forming coherent words properly. "I'll check it later."

Gavin's dark eyes settle on me, and a single brow rises. Desire shoots through me like fireworks over the Hudson River. Why is it that when Evan does it, I want to strangle him, but when Gavin does it, my internal organs liquefy in a puddle of need? Witchcraft, that's all it can be.

Desperate for a reprieve, I pull the gloss from my purse and smear it over my lips.

"It looks great." Ben extends his hand to Gavin.

"I'll monitor the system for a few more weeks to ensure there aren't any other issues that pop up," Gavin replies.

"Thanks for all your hard work." Evan shakes Gavin's hand. "You two worked well together." Their gazes shift to me.

Fuck.

"Yeah, we do," Gavin adds with a smile.

I gather my wits and stand. "I'm gonna get back to work."

Ben and Evan exchange a look before I dart from the room. I'm halfway down the hall when I hear footsteps behind me. I quicken my pace when I see Andrew stepping from the elevator. He jumps out of the way as I brush past him and slam the close door button as hard as I can.

Gavin grabs the door right before it closes. He wedges it open and steps into the elevator. My heart pounds against my ribs. I pinch my eyes closed, unable to meet his gaze.

"I was worried about you," Gavin murmurs. "You haven't been online, and you won't respond to my texts."

The ding above us signals the doors closing once more.

My eyes fly open and I bite my lip before replying. "I was busy."

"Bullshit." The doors snap closed, punctuating his response. He reaches out and hits the emergency stop button, forcing the elevator to halt completely.

We're trapped in the small space, and I forget how to breathe. His scent fills my head with wicked thoughts. Shit.

Breathe. In. Out. In. Out.

He grabs my arms and backs me against the wall of the carriage. "You've been avoiding me."

I tip my chin up to meet his warm, brown eyes, challenge flashing in their depths. His lips thin as he awaits my reply. *Speak*, my mind screams. *Surrender*, my body demands.

"Yes." I try to pull from his grip, but he holds me firm. His body presses against me, pinning me against the wall. "Let me go."

"Not until you tell me what the fuck happened." The rumble of his voice sends shockwaves through me, making my knees wobble. "I thought we were friends."

"Friends don't kiss like that." I hold his gaze and slowly the fight seeps out of me. "What do you want from me, Gavin? Is it the challenge that turns you on? See if you can make me beg?"

His grin turns sinful with unspoken promises. "Oh, you're a challenge all right, and I would love to hear you beg. But I want so much more from you."

Before I can process his words, he kisses me. Hard.

The pent-up frustration unleashes a torrent of desperation and desire. I grip the lapels of his jacket and kiss him back. Our tongues dance as he snakes his hands into my hair, pulling the locks between his thick fingers. His thigh presses between my legs, and he delves deeper, claiming me.

I'm on fire. My face, my body, everything. I ache for him. I burn from the demanding need coursing through my veins. Gavin has poisoned me, branded me, and there's not a damned thing I can do about it except surrender.

He slides his hand down until it rests on my hip. His fingers drift beneath the hem of my blouse, caressing my bare side. I gasp against his mouth, and he smiles before removing his hand and releasing the emergency stop. He presses the softest kiss to my lips and pulls away.

I'm a surrealist clock sliding from the wall into a puddle on the floor. I manage to catch myself before I collapse and straighten my shirt. Gavin grins with kiss-swollen lips.

"What was that for?" I huff, trying to play it cool even

though I'm still aflame.

"A reminder." He leans close and whispers against my ear. "I want to taste all of you, baby girl."

He presses the button to open the elevator doors, winks, and steps back onto the second floor. I stumble out and beeline for my office. The last thing I need is for Evan to see me like this.

Safely inside, I collapse against the door and press my hand to my chest. What the hell am I going to do with him? Aside from the obvious of course.

One thing is certain, Gavin's persistence will be the death of me. Especially if it comes in the form of multiple orgasms. I welcome the challenge, but he's going to have to work a lot harder than that if he wants me in his bed.

CHAPTER THIRTEEN

Gavin. The elevator. That fucking kiss. It haunted me all week.

Five days of incessant obsession need to end. I cannot continue like this. He knew exactly what he was doing to me. Putting me in such a situation left me with no recourse. I couldn't berate him in front of the whole office, and I sure as hell couldn't let Evan know what happened.

So I buried the burning desire pulsing through my body and muscled through the week barely aware of anything my coworkers said. I couldn't have cared less if the building was on fire. After that nuclear kiss, survival mode activated. Now, I must kill something.

The moment I walk through my front door, I relinquish the façade. Within two minutes, I've stripped off my power suit and pulled on the most comfortable leggings in my drawer with the oversized *Zelda* hoodie Lily gave me for Christmas.

In the living room, I turn on the television and boot up the console. While it rumbles to life, I grab a beer from the fridge and the box of leftover pizza. My phone buzzes from the table by the door. I ignore the notification to update my phone and set the device next to the pizza box on the coffee table.

The cold beer quenches my thirst. I snag a slice of pizza and devour it while skimming the selections on the console. The cursor hovers over the connect to server button. I could always play invisible mode. Fuck it. The thought of chasing him down and putting him out of his misery sounds like the best cure for a shitty week. Especially since he fucking started it.

It connects in a blink of green. On cue, his message pops up on the screen.

I missed you.

I'm sure he fucking did. I connect the mic.

"Hey there, baby girl." He purrs.

The sound arouses me as much as it annoys me. "Save it, Gavin."

He chuckles in response. It only amplifies my agitation.

"I take it you didn't miss me this week."

"What makes you think that?" It's hard to keep the sarcasm in check. Gavin is the only man on the planet who can simultaneously make me horny as fuck and I'd still want to burn his house to the ground.

"You ignored all my messages." He selects something on the screen and the game loads. "I take it you didn't come here to chat?"

"Clever boy." I hiss between bites of pizza.

"Don't hold back. Tell me how you really feel." His teasing tone pushes me too far.

I toss the crust aside. "I have no intention of doing either."

The game starts in a flash of smoke across the screen. Mission: eliminate the enemy before they reach their ship. They mean the common enemy, but I fully intend to take Gavin out in the process.

Focused on my mission, I make my way through the space station on the Vega Moon. I've played this level before, so I know where to go and what I need to do. The trick will be locating Gavin without him knowing. That's why I chose Lynnea.

Playing as Ranger Lynnea Stark has perks too. Captain Ransom's character has the best ones because he's a damned space pirate and thinks the rules don't apply to him. Commander Colton is all rules and formality. I shake my head at Gavin's side of the split-screen. He always plays as Colton. How predictable.

Most players underestimate Lynnea. Sure, the boys have the upper hand on the ships, but in the space stations, Lynnea has the advantage. She can access levels the others can't without special clearance. It's obvious Gavin doesn't know this as he slips along the predicted route.

I slip through the control room, taking the shortcut to access the commanders' quarters on the upper level.

"Where the hell are you going?"

Ignoring him, I grab the extra boost pack hidden in one of the rooms and take the lift directly to the command deck. Inside, I scan for the weapons console. After entering a ten-digit code, I grin.

"Did you just arm the computer to fire on any ship leaving the port?" He sounds impressed.

"Worry about your own ass." I high tail it out of the command deck and race along the corridor toward the docking bay. With a quick glance at the split screen, I suppress an evil laugh. Right on schedule.

Gavin's on the other side of the doors in the docking bay.

I pull my blaster and step into the room, dropping behind a pallet of supplies to take a breath. Peering from behind cover, I spot him quickly. He's facing the computer screen near the bay doors.

I line up the shot and pull the trigger. He drops to the ground. Satisfaction fills me.

"Goddamn it." Gavin's screen flashes Mission Failed. "The mission was to eliminate the enemy, Maggie. Not take out the other player."

"I know." I preen, taking a sip of beer. "Want to go again?"

"Not if that's how you're going to play." Silence fills the line. "Are you pissed at me?"

"Clever boy." I snatch up another slice and bite into it.

Gavin sighs and disconnects the game, leaving the mic on.

"What the hell? I wasn't done kicking your ass."

"You're tense and violent. I think you need a healthier outlet."

"No." I throw down the half-eaten slice. "I came here to play video games, not talk about my fucking feelings."

"Don't make me come over there."

"You wouldn't." My breath catches in my throat. I realize he doesn't know my address and exhale in relief. "You don't even know where I live."

"I'm a computer genius, Mags. There isn't a piece of information on the planet I can't access if I want it bad enough and I'm willing to pay the price." A sultry promise resounds in every syllable.

"That's illegal, Gavin."

"Wouldn't be the first time," he murmurs so faintly I nearly miss it. "Are you afraid I'll show up on your doorstep and kiss you like I did in the elevator?"

"You wouldn't," I repeat, even though I don't believe it. My heart races. I can't admit I want it. That would be surrender. "We have nothing in common."

"That's a lie and you know it." He lists the items one by one. "Gaming, food, friends…chemistry."

"Chemistry doesn't mean anything when it's pure lust." I clear my throat. "Besides I'm nearly ten years older than you."

"You think I care about that?" He scoffs. "You're smart and sexy. You don't give a fuck what anyone thinks about you, and you live on your own terms. That's fucking hot."

"I'm too old for games, Gavin."

"And yet where are you now?"

"You know what I mean."

"Yeah, I do." He turns serious and inhales deeply. "Listen, if I overstepped, I apologize. I thought there was something there. But if you don't feel that way, I'll drop it."

I sit silently staring at the TV screen, my heartbeat pounding in my ears like a drum, adding to the tense theme music already playing in my mind. He's apologizing for kissing me. I chew on my lower lip, unable to respond, knowing I'll bare my heart if I open my mouth.

"I like you, Maggie." His words rumble through me, leaving a soothing warmth in their wake. "I like how I feel when I'm with you. But if you don't feel the same, then I'll respect your decision."

I bite my tongue, willing myself to stay quiet. My eyes water and I swipe my hands over them. Why does this have to be so fucking hard? Why can't I just give in? Isn't he worth the chance?

"If you change your mind, send me a text." The tension on the line crackles with electricity. "One word from you—and I don't care what time it is or where you are—I will find you, push you up against the wall, and make you come so hard you'll forget your name."

A delicious shiver wracks me at his promise. "I gotta go."

"Good night, baby girl." He purrs before disconnecting the line.

I toss aside the headset and stare at the flickering screen. What the fuck just happened?

It's not that I don't want Gavin. I'm not denying we make a great team. And he's smoking hot. Any woman would be lucky as hell to have him. But how long can it last?

Say I give in, and we hook up. Aside from the hot sex and smoldering chemistry, what do we have going for us? And what happens when that fades?

He has a promising future and unlimited career opportunities. I have my own career, and I'm content in my singleness. I have never needed a man to feel complete.

But…it feels nice to be wanted and cherished. I miss that. I miss sex.

I'm also not willing to throw away my principles for the most amazing orgasm of my life. Hell, I don't even know if that's guaranteed. Nothing is.

With a groan, I clean up my mess, turn off all the electronics, and take a shower. At midnight I'm staring at the ceiling when the million-dollar question slams into me with the force of a freight train.

What *do* I want?

CHAPTER FOURTEEN

Did I fuck up? It's been two weeks, and I haven't heard a peep from Gavin. He's never online when I log in, and I haven't gotten a single text since the night he apologized. I'm still pissed at myself for not being honest with him, but I don't want to admit my failure out loud. Who does that and feels better afterward? Not me.

The moment five o'clock hits on Friday, I'm out the door. I need to get home and relax. Ben and Evan have resumed their incessant harassment of my precious time since I returned to my original duties. The update should go live within the next two weeks. I should be overjoyed, but I'm miserable.

Between me and the violet sitting on my windowsill, I'll admit I miss working with Gavin. He listened to my ideas and helped me improve my vision before bringing it to life. He taught me tricks to improve my coding skills and shared his vast knowledge with me. It gave me the confidence to take the chance and start working on my side project.

The bustle of rush hour traffic swarms around me, but I'm lost in my thoughts while my feet take me home on autopilot. Fall's just around the corner, and I'm ready for the cold bite of winter so I have an excuse to stay home and play the new *Zelda* game releasing in October.

I pass by the restaurant where we sidelined Jen with an intervention for her fangirl obsession. Maybe I need one to help me get my head screwed on straight? Jen's already told me what she thinks I need. When Gavin's name came up in conversation during movie night, she took the opportunity to call me out. *You two should fuck and get it over with.*

Bullseye.

Not that I could admit that to either of them. No way in hell. It's not like the thought hasn't been chasing me around for the past few months. What if I relented and gave in? Would that really be so bad? I mean, I'm not looking for a long-term relationship, am I?

I scowl and the woman passing me sidesteps, giving me a wide berth. Resting Bitch Face Achievement: Unlocked. It works wonders to keep people out of my bubble.

I've thought about it for two weeks, and I still have no idea what I want. Strike that. I know exactly what I want, but what would be the long-term gain? Do I really want what Jen and Shaun have?

By the time I reach my apartment, I want to tear my hair out. I shove the key in the mailbox lock and nearly snap it off. I grab the handful of letters and head up the stairs. I'm more delicate with the apartment key and bump the door closed with my hip.

My gaze falls on the console beside the television. Is he going to be online tonight? No. I refuse to torment myself any further. Instead of gaming, I'm going to crack open a bottle of wine and binge watch the latest episodes of *Monster Slayer*. But first, a warm shower and comfy sweats.

After the steaming shower, I'm more relaxed. I pull on clean purple sweatpants and my trusty *Zelda* hoodie—no underwear required. With a chuckle, I grab my phone, put in an order for delivery from the deli down the street, and open that bottle of red sitting in the cabinet from Valentine's Day.

Three hours later, I've demolished my sandwich. I pour the remainder of the wine into my glass and press continue on the *Are you still watching?* prompt. I am comfortably numb, if not a little tipsy.

As the intro plays, my gaze drifts to my phone sitting on the couch beside me. Gavin would like this show. What's he up to tonight? He's probably busy. Maybe out with the guys, or playing a tournament. What if he's on a date? The thought of him out with another woman leaves me spiraling down a dark hole. There's only one way to solve this.

I open the app and type with one hand. *Hey.* I hit send before I can allow myself to overthink.

Hey. His response pops through immediately.

My intoxicated brain commandeers any remaining sense. I'm too far gone to care. *What are you doing right now?* I watch the three dots play across the screen as he types out his reply.

Finishing a project.

I bite my lip wondering if he's politely telling me to fuck off and leave him alone. *What are you wearing?* I chortle when I send it, wanting to get a rise out of him.

Don't tease me, baby girl.

I can almost hear him say it when I read the words. My restraint flies out the window, and I set my wine aside, taking the phone in both hands.

Who says I'm teasing?

Five minutes pass, and still no response. Shit. Maybe I pushed him too hard. I take a deep breath and focus on the screen.

Come over. I need you. If I send this, there's no going back. I press the button and off it goes into the universe. Oh, shit, what have I done?

He's read the message, but he's not responding. Five minutes pass. Nothing. I jump up from the couch and pace the room, clutching the phone in my hand. Another five minutes, nothing. Oh, fuck. I screwed up.

Twenty minutes pass, and still no response. He's probably pissed at me.

The knock at the door makes my heart stop. I glance through the peephole.

Gavin.

All the breath is sucked from my lungs at the sight of him standing on the other side of my door. I slide the chain free and unlock the deadbolt. The door swings open, and I swear he's the most devastatingly handsome man I've ever seen.

"Gavin, I—"

He crosses the threshold and catches me up in those strong arms. His mouth crashes against mine with a hunger I feel deep in my soul. We stumble back and he kicks the door closed.

My arms loop around his neck as he devours my mouth. I

cling tight, not wanting to be washed away by the unexpected tsunami of desire. The kiss deepens and I'm floundering at the overwhelming sensations. His scent and heat surround me. Even amid the overload, he holds me firmly against him, grounding me. I won't float away, I won't drown. He's got me.

"Maggie," he murmurs against my lips. Those dexterous fingers of his tease the hem of my sweatshirt, slipping beneath the fabric. My skin burns beneath the featherlight brush of his fingertips against my lower back. "Tell me what you want."

I meet his gaze and my reservations combust like fireworks against the night sky. "I want you to fuck me, Gavin."

His growl reverberates through me as he lifts me into his arms. I wrap my legs around his hips, grinding myself against the ridge of his cock through his sweatpants.

"Such a tease." He kisses me again, hard and fast.

I open my mouth to tell him the bedroom is on his left, but he's already halfway to the couch. Gavin collapses against the cushions, pulling me down across his lap. I straddle his thighs and brush my hair from my eyes. The movement brushes my pelvis against his erection.

His grip on my hips tightens, pinning me in place. "Keep moving, and this will be over before it starts."

I arch my brow. "Been a while, huh?"

"Longer than I'm willing to admit." Gavin's eyes narrow, and hunger flashes in those amber depths.

Resting my hands against his chest, I smile. "Couldn't find someone to give you what you need?"

"Finding her wasn't the problem." The corner of his mouth quirks into a lopsided grin. "Waiting for her to get over herself took some time."

My hands slide up to his shoulders and around his neck. The movement brings me closer, ghosting my breath over his full lips. Fire flashes in his eyes.

"A couple weeks?" I run my lips across his jaw, trailing from his ear to his mouth.

He shakes his head.

"Months?" I continue my teasing exploration of his

magnificent jawline.

Gavin shifts his weight and captures my chin in his hand. When our eyes lock, I gasp at the intensity of his expression.

"I've wanted you since the first moment I saw you."

"But you hated me." I'm stunned by his admission. "When I kicked your ass, you ignored me for months."

"I ignored you because I didn't know what the fuck to say to you." His grip loosens, fingertips sliding along my throat until they tangle in my hair at the base of my neck. The soft pressure of his touch sends heat straight to my core. "I never met a woman who challenged me like you do."

"Wait." It's getting harder and harder to ignore the desire building inside me, but I need answers. "So you're telling me you haven't had sex since the day we met?"

"I haven't even looked at another woman." Gavin cocks his head. "You've ruined me for all others. I crave only you."

"Why didn't you tell me?"

"I tried." His hand on my hip slides beneath my hoodie. "But nothing I said—or did—seemed to entice you."

I curse and draw his lips to mine. The kiss ignites the flame once more and I want to lose myself in him. Why did I waste so much time? He deepens the kiss, and I melt against him.

A moan rips from my throat when his roaming hand travels lower, dipping beneath the waistband of my sweatpants. He hooks his thumb around the elastic and tugs. We break apart long enough for him to remove my sweatpants and his.

His hand cups my aching pussy and he chuckles when I arch my hips into his touch. "You're so wet for me."

"Now who's the tease." I slide the hoodie over my head and pull at his shirt. He tugs it off in one fluid motion.

"Damn, baby." His gaze drifts over my breasts, down to where his fingers tease my folds, and back up, licking his lips. "You're even hotter than I imagined."

I grip his jaw in my hand. "If you don't fuck me, I may spontaneously combust."

With one slow slide of his finger over my slickened clit, he removes his hand. I shiver as he fits his cock to me.

"Ask me nicely." The head is poised at my entrance. One rock of my hips and I could claim him.

"Gavin, fuck me," I beg. "Please."

In one thrust, he fills me completely. Fuck, he's deep. So deep. And it feels *so* good. I clutch at his shoulders and let myself adjust to the sweet invasion. We're both breathing hard, struggling to maintain control.

His thumb makes slow circles over my clit. My head drops against his shoulder as the pressure spirals higher with every stroke. When I buck my hips against him, he growls.

"Fuck it." Gavin pushes me back against the couch and drives into me hard.

I cling to him, clawing at his back, his ass, anything to pull him closer. He drives his hips hard, grinding against my aching center until the sensations hover at the pinnacle. My climax lingers out of reach.

He kisses me, bruising my lips with the force and stealing my breath.

"Come for me," he murmurs against my mouth.

Those words unleash a hurricane inside me. I surrender to it willingly. My orgasm pulses through my body, and all I can do is ride out the waves nestled in Gavin's arms.

When his climax hits, he closes his eyes and groans at the release. I commit the image to memory.

He catches me and a sated grin steals across his lips. "What?"

"Looks like Jen was right."

"Jen?" he asks, confusion furrowing his brows.

"Yeah, she said we should fuck and get it out of our systems." I chuckle when he shakes his head. I press my hand against his chest, but he remains immovable.

"You think I'm done with you?" He slowly rises and pulls me up.

"What are you—? Gavin!" He sweeps me into a bridal carry.

"Where's the bedroom?" He strides for the only door in the apartment and kicks it open.

"Gavin!" I scream when he tosses me on the bed. Before I

can scramble out of reach, he climbs on top of me, pinning my wrists to the mattress.

"I'm sorry. Did you think we were done?" He shakes his head slowly as a sinful smile curves those wicked lips. "Baby, I'm just getting started."

"Do you hear me complaining?" My pussy clenches at the promise.

"I'm going to have you screaming my name." He leans down and takes a nipple between his teeth.

I hiss at the sweet sting of his bite. "Is that a challenge?"

"Always." He takes the other in his mouth, suckling hard.

"Bring it on."

He trails his mouth over my stomach, descending until his breath feathers over my swollen lips. When his tongue touches my clit, I bite back the cry strangled in my throat. Damn him, he's going to make me work for it. So I give him the same courtesy.

It's not until hours later when we're both sated and half-asleep I realize he won. I snuggle closer and drape my thigh over his. He holds me tight and kisses my forehead. Why the hell did I fight this?

He's right where I want to be.

CHAPTER FIFTEEN

The comforting scent of coffee pulls me from my dreams. I stretch my arms over my head and the events from the night before slam into me. My face warms at the memory. I glance at the empty spot beside me on the bed. *Gavin.*

I slide from bed and grab a pair of underwear from my dresser as well as a tank top. Passing the mirror on the wall, I cringe at the state of my hair. The tangled mess of black, purple, and teal swirl like a psychedelic kaleidoscope on top of my head. I manage to wrangle it into a messy bun and follow the tantalizing scent emanating from my kitchen.

I stop, speechless, at the sight. Gavin—wearing nothing but a pair of boxers—is standing in front of the stove. The air is sizzling. And it's not just the eggs cooking in the skillet. I lean against the wall and admire the view.

It's wrong, I know. But I can't help myself. I drink in his broad, muscular shoulders, following the curve down to his narrow hips. He's tall and lean, but every muscle is defined. I want to lick him.

"Mmmm smells delicious."

"Morning." Is it my hormones, or is his voice sexier this morning? "I didn't mean to wake you. I was going to bring you breakfast in bed."

"That's sweet."

He shrugs and I'm distracted by those shoulders again. "Just wanted to spoil you."

"You want some?" I hold the pot aloft to redirect the conversation.

Gavin nudges his empty mug closer. "Top me off."

"You need to be more aware of how you say things."

"Oh, I'm completely aware. I just wanted to see if you'd take the bait."

"Rude."

"It's not my fault you have a dirty fucking mind, baby girl."

"Why do you call me that?" I pour some caramel-flavored creamer into my coffee. "Are you channeling your inner Derek Morgan?"

"First of all, I love *Criminal Minds*. And secondly, I have been told I look like Shemar Moore, which is the highest compliment I could ever ask for."

"You'll get no argument from me there, but that doesn't answer my question." I carry the plates to the small dining table. "I bet you use that line on all the girls."

"Nope. Just you."

"Why?"

"At first, I did it to get a rise out of you." He sips his coffee. "I kept doing it because it fits."

"It fit?"

"Yeah."

"Gavin, I'm nearly a decade older than you. It most certainly does not fit." His eggs are fluffy and melt on my tongue. God, he really is a wizard, isn't he?

"Still stuck on that age difference, huh?" He picks up his fork and twists it between his fingers. The fingers that worked magic on me last night.

I chase the thought from my mind. "I'm not *stuck* on it. But there's no sugar-coating the truth. I'm older than you. That's a fact."

"Eight years, Maggie. That's hardly an age gap."

"When I was sixteen, you were eight. When you were sixteen, I was twenty-four."

"That was then. Now, it doesn't matter." He's unbothered by my statement. "We're both consenting adults. Age is just a number at this stage."

"Fine."

We eat in silence until the last bits of egg vanish from our plates.

"That hit the spot." He leans back and sighs, eyeing me over the rim of his mug. "Do you have plans today?"

This is hauntingly domestic. Reservations rear their ugly heads in the back of my conscience. I shift uncomfortably in my seat. "What the fuck are we doing, Gavin?"

"Having breakfast. Enjoying each other's company." He winks. "Hopefully fucking again."

Heat curls in my belly at the words, but I can't continue without knowing where we both stand on this. Whatever this is between us.

"I mean, us. What do you want from this?" I drum my fingers on the table before dropping them into my lap. "I just want to be on the same page before we get in over our heads."

"I think it may be too late for that." Gavin chuckles, but his expression sobers when he meets my gaze. "What do you want?"

"I don't know. That's why I've been so damn resistant. I don't know what I want, but I feel like if we start something here, there will inevitably be expectations."

"And you want to be mentally prepared for that." He nods with understanding. "I get it. But I also know it's best to have a goal and aim for that instead of worrying about what you can't control."

His response lodges in my brain and takes root. "Yeah, but what if this all goes to shit?"

"Such a pessimist." Gavin shakes his head. "When I was a kid, I wanted to work for NASA."

The abrupt shift in conversation leaves me stunned, but I manage to keep up. "Didn't we all?"

"I didn't want to be an astronaut." He leaned forward and clarified. "I wanted to work in the control center."

"Not seeing how this fits our conversation, but continue." I sip my lukewarm coffee.

"My mom dismissed it as being one of those childhood fantasies." He smiles at the memory. "Until I ripped apart the family computer to see how it worked."

"You didn't?" My mouth falls open. "She whooped your ass for it too, I'm sure."

"She wasn't happy. Neither was my dad. But the following week, they enrolled me in a computer science program at the local youth center."

I imagine Gavin as a kid surrounded by computer parts learning the intricacies of coding.

"The volunteer who taught the course was a full-time teacher at the prestigious Park Academy. He saw my potential and passion, encouraging it even though it could only advance so far in my limited sphere." Gavin takes a drink, leaving me poised on the edge of my seat for the rest of his story. "He convinced my parents to apply for a scholarship at the Academy. With his recommendation, I was accepted."

"You went to school with Lily. I remember her telling me that."

"Yeah." He runs his hand over his short curls. "She saved my ass. A couple of rich brats decided to fuck with the new kid and she stepped in." Gavin's eyes widen. "No one messed with Lily."

"Why not?" This was the first time I heard anything about Lily's past or her childhood. She doesn't talk about it, and I don't ask. But I am beyond curious now.

"You know who her dad is, right?"

"I know he's some rich banker who lives on Park Avenue."

Gavin scoffs. "He's not just some rich banker. He's the CEO and founder of Madison Financial."

"Holy fuck." I nearly choke on my spit. "He's worth billions! Shit, he owns half of Manhattan!"

"No one fucked with Lily because if she so much as complained to her father he could ruin their families. It earned her the nickname Daddy's Girl—but don't ever call her that. Not unless you want to end up in the ER."

"Why not? Lily's not prone to violence." I smirk at the thought of my best friend committing murder over a silly childhood nickname.

"She doesn't look the type, does she?" He snickers. "But in ninth grade, a boy asked her to the homecoming dance and when she turned him down, he clapped back with a snide remark and used her nickname. Poor bastard ended up winning an ambulance trip to the ER with his balls on ice."

I gasp and cover my mouth when a laugh escapes me. "I'm sure he deserved it. Kids are assholes."

"Yeah, they are. Anyway, I guess the point of my story is this. You can't be afraid of missing out or failing. If you let uncertainty hold you back because you're comfortable where you are, then you'll never know what amazing things are possible. You have to take a chance. Having a goal helps, but sometimes all you need is someone to help you step out of your comfort zone."

"You missed your calling as a motivational speaker." I laugh, but inside, my heart aches. He's right. I'm comfortable where I am, and I don't want to change for fear it'll fall apart and I'll be stranded.

"I actually do that too." He sets his cup aside. "Schools have me come in and give the whole 'You can do it, follow your dreams' speech."

"You're a computer genius, a motivational speaker, a phenomenal cook, and amazing in bed. Is there anything you suck at?" I level a teasing glare in his direction. "You're making me feel woefully inadequate."

Gavin stands and takes my hand, pulling me to my feet. He sweeps me up and carries me to the couch. Settling on the sofa, he cradles me against his chest.

"You're fucking amazing." He strokes my thigh. "You run a million-dollar company and have brilliant ideas. I couldn't have done the upgrade to the Solus system as effectively without your input. You can do anything you put your mind to, Maggie."

"You think so?"

"One hundred percent certain." He circles his fingers over my bare skin, distracting me. His voice drops an octave. "What do *you* want?"

My heart pounds. "I want to build my app. The one I told you about. And—" I draw my lip between my teeth, letting it slide free savoring the way his eyes darken at the gesture. "I want you."

"For how long?" he asks, his hand drifting higher until his wicked fingers slide beneath the hem of my panties.

"Fuck," I gasp when he brushes his fingers over my pussy. "For as long as you want me."

"Baby girl, I'm not sure if you're ready for that kind of commitment." He chuckles as he brushes my clit with his thumb. I arch off his lap and moan. "How about the weekend to start?"

"Yeah," I nod fervently, oblivious to everything around me but him and his talented fingers. I lick my lips and moan when he slides two fingers inside me. "That's perfect."

When my orgasm hits, I collapse against him in a heap unable to form coherent words. Gavin carries me to the bathroom and flips on the shower.

I make a mental note to text the girls. I won't be making it to movie night if I can judge anything by the sensual promise in Gavin's eyes.

I've never been one to choose a man over my friends, but I'm pretty sure the girls will forgive me this one time. Should I even tell them?

Gavin pulls me into the shower, and I forget all about movie night. His hot mouth against my skin and his thick cock pressed against my ass have me thoroughly distracted.

I'm sure I'll regret something on Monday, but I can't bring myself to care right now. Surrender never felt so fucking good.

CHAPTER SIXTEEN

After a weekend of mind-blowing orgasms, I feel like I can take on the world. Granted, this may be the surplus overload of orgasmic bliss talking, but I'm not discounting its ability to supercharge my mood.

"Morning, Andrew." I raise my coffee cup in salute as I walk past his desk. "How was your weekend?"

Andrew drops the file in his hand and stares at me with his mouth hanging open. He scrambles to pick up the papers littered around the base of his chair. "It was good."

"Fantastic." I stride past him with a bounce in my step and unlock my office door.

Evan peeks out of his office.

"Mornin', boss." I wink and push open the door.

Both his brows rise in shock before I disappear into my office. As I settle behind my desk, Evan appears in the doorway, staring me down. I ignore him and pull out my planner.

"Holy shit. You got laid!" His voice echoes a bit too loud, and he winces before coming inside and closing the door behind him. Evan slides into the chair next to the door. "Spill. Now. Was it Gavin? It was Gavin, wasn't it?"

"A lady doesn't kiss and tell."

"Bullshit, I've heard you discuss the nitty-gritty details of your sexual exploits over coffee in the breakroom."

"That was the old me." I open the planner with disinterest in continuing the conversation.

"Well, I'll be damned." He rubs his jaw. "What the hell happened? I thought you were hell-bent on avoiding him."

"Can't I have a change of heart?"

"Maggie, in all the years I have known you, you have never once had a change of heart. At least not of your own free will." He snorts. "We always have to drag you kicking and screaming."

"I don't know what to tell you."

A knock at the door interrupts us. Evan opens it and Ben fills the doorway, a scowl imprinted on his face. Not his typical scowl, this one is more defined.

"What the hell is going on in here?" Ben kicks the door closed behind him when several of the employees take notice of the commotion.

Evan turns to Ben with a grin. "Mags got laid this weekend."

"And that's worth distracting the whole office?" Ben glowers.

"She hooked up with Gavin," Evan adds with a smirk.

The scowl vanishes from Ben's face instantly. He whips his head in my direction. "What the hell, Maggie? He's still under contract with Solus. You can't fuck around like that."

"Technically, she can fuck Gavin all she wants." Evan chuckles. "There's no rule against fraternization between employees and contractors. Besides, he's finishing up the final details this week, so there's no issue with her getting a little action. Especially if it keeps her in this mood."

"Both of you can fuck right the hell off." I shoot to my feet and lean both hands on the desk, glaring at both my bosses. "Who I fuck and when is none of your goddamn business, am I clear?"

"Yeah." Evan pouts.

Ben broods. "Just keep it out of the office, got it?"

"Yes, Dad."

Ben harumphs and leaves the room, slamming the door in his wake.

"I think someone else needs to get a little action." Evan gestures to the wall I share with Ben's office. His laughter turns to a grimace. "On second thought, I don't need that visual in my head. Damn it."

"Has he always been this fucking broody?" My curiosity gets the best of me. I know Ben and Evan were childhood friends, but they don't talk about their lives outside of work.

"Always." Evan slowly stands and stuffs his hands in his

pockets. "Anyway, I'm just busting on you. I'm glad you're happy. Gavin's a great guy. Just don't wear him out, okay?"

X-rated memories of our steamy weekend spent naked in my apartment fucking on every conceivable surface fill my mind. My cheeks heat, but I manage to keep my composure. "No problem, boss. Can I get to work now?"

"Yeah." Evan opens the door to leave but pauses halfway through his exit. "Oh, by the way, Gavin will be over at nine to install the final hardware for the new system. Remember to keep your hands to yourself, ya sex fiend." His laughter follows him out of my office.

My heart pounds. Gavin hadn't mentioned he was stopping by the office today. I pound the rest of my coffee and check my planner. Nothing until noon. Shit. Did I miss the email?

I boot up my computer, and sure enough, there's an email sent last night from Gavin's work account letting us know he'd be by at nine on Monday to finish the installation. I glance at my phone. It's eight-thirty.

Gavin stayed until seven last night. I asked him to spend one more night, but he feigned exhaustion and claimed he needed to get a decent night sleep. Sleeping in my bed proved too much of a distraction for him. He's not wrong. My body still aches.

Lily and Jen nailed it. Gavin and I did need to fuck and get it out of our systems. But this goes further than one steamy weekend. He already invited me out on a date Friday night. When I begged him to tell me where we were going, he smirked and told me it was a surprise. Bastard. Now I'll be in suspense all week.

Thirty minutes later, I've accomplished next to nothing. A knock at the door startles me from my smutty musings about Gavin and his wickedly talented mouth. As if summoned from my thoughts, he appears in my doorway.

"Hey."

"Hey." I stand and smooth my hands over my black pencil skirt. His charming smile distracts me, and I'm transported to my small apartment and our weekend of never-ending sex.

"I hope you got some sleep last night."

"I did." My throat tightens and I cough to clear it. "You?"

"Sleep isn't fun when you're not next to me."

"Gavin." My admonishment dies on my tongue when Evan appears beside Gavin.

"Morning, Mr. Waldorf." Gavin shakes Evan's hand.

"Please, call me Evan." He claps his hand on Gavin's shoulder. "Shall we get to work?"

"Of course." Gavin glances at me. "Would you mind giving me a hand with the final installation, Maggie?"

"Sure."

"You know, if you ever need a job, Gavin, we'd be honored to have you on the team here at Solus." Evan ignores my pointed stare.

"Thank you. I'll keep that in mind should the need arise." He shakes Evan's hand once more before retreating toward the conference room.

"Cock block." I hiss at Evan. He knows full well that if Gavin works at Solus any relationship between us becomes a tricky negotiation with HR, as well as fodder for the office gossips.

Evan returns to his office, and I follow Gavin down the hall.

Beside the conference room is a small closet we converted into the server room where all the network computers and hardware are located for the whole floor. It's about thirty degrees cooler in here than the rest of the building. Gavin's sitting at the console already typing on the keyboard. He grins when I join him.

"Pull up a chair." He pats the rolling desk chair beside him.

I nudge the door until it's barely cracked so there's plenty of room for us in the cramped room. He grins when I slide into the chair beside him.

"So, what are you working on here?" I watch as he types some commands into the computer.

The code blurs before my eyes. His scent surrounds me. I lick my lips and try to focus on his explanation, but all I can hear is the sexy cadence of his voice as he coaxes me into another orgasm.

Gavin nudges me with his elbow. "You okay?"

"Yeah, I'm fine." I turn to face him. Shit, that was a bad idea. All I can think of now is how much I want to kiss him.

Gavin's gaze drifts over my shoulder to the cracked door. "You don't look fine." He drops his voice. "You look like you want me to bend you over this desk and fuck you."

I suppress a whimper and close my eyes. Ben's voice echoes in the back of my mind. *Keep it out of the office.* I'm trying, damn it.

Gavin leans close, his breath brushing my ear. "If that's what you want, all you have to do is ask, baby girl." He nips my earlobe.

I open my eyes. He's watching me intently. When he draws his lower lip between his teeth, my hesitation snaps. I nod, unable to voice what I want. All I know is I want him to make me come.

Gavin captures my lips fast and hard. The kiss leaves me breathless. He snakes his arm around me, and without breaking contact, he lifts me from the chair to my feet. We shuffle around the chairs until he backs me against the door. It clicks shut.

He pulls away and holds my gaze for a heartbeat as he slides the lock into place. My heart pounds, and I can't seem to catch my breath. I can feel the slick between my thighs. He has me in a perpetual state of arousal. Damn him.

He grabs my skirt in two handfuls and drags it up my thighs until the fabric is bunched around my waist. He tugs my panties down to my ankles and wedges his knee between my legs. His fingers glide over my pussy lips.

"You didn't get enough this weekend, huh?" He slides two fingers into me. "My greedy, insatiable girl."

I cling to his shoulders, my fingernails clawing into the fabric of his shirt and the skin beneath. I gasp and bite my lip to keep from crying out when he slowly moves in purposeful strokes. My panting breaths echo off the walls. I don't want to get caught, but the thought of Evan or Ben catching us like this only increases my pleasure. A moan rips from my throat when he brushes my clit. Let them catch us, I don't care.

Gavin's hand disappears and he replaces his fingers with the head of his cock. He slides in and I'm lost in the sensations.

"Is that what you wanted?" he growls against my ear as he thrusts deeper.

"Yes." I cling tight to him and grind my hips against his. "More. Please."

Gavin acquiesces and grips my hips, pistoning in and out until the motion shakes the door. My orgasm builds quickly, and I clench around his cock.

"Come for me, baby." He whispers in my ear, redoubling his efforts.

My climax knocks me off balance, and Gavin kisses me, swallowing my cry as I fall apart in his arms. He follows close behind with a groan, and I grin at the mess he's made of me. He leans his forehead against mine.

"Good girl." He kisses me softly and slides free.

We disentangle ourselves and fix our clothes. I catch him grinning.

"What's funny?" I ask, sliding my skirt into place. His warmth leaves me a sticky mess.

"Nothing." He tucks his shirt in and buckles his belt. "Do you want to finish this installation with me?"

"Yeah." I shake my hair back into some semblance of order. "Let me run to the bathroom quick."

I unlock the door and step into the hallway. Evan's leaning against the wall across from me, wearing a shit-eating grin.

"Don't say a word," I mutter as I close the door behind me. "Not a word."

Evan lifts his hands in surrender. "I wasn't going to say anything." He shoves them in his pockets and pushes away from the wall, heading back toward his office.

My face burns hot as I head for the bathroom at the end of the hall. Inside, I stare at my reflection. Shit. Messy hair, flushed cheeks, kiss swollen lips. Oh, God. No wonder Evan seemed so smug. I look thoroughly fucked.

I just hope he doesn't tell Ben.

A smile creeps across my lips. It was worth it.

CHAPTER SEVENTEEN

Friday night rolls around, and Gavin shows up at my doorstep exactly at six wearing jeans and an AC/DC t-shirt. I got home five minutes ago and haven't even changed out of my work clothes yet.

"Sorry, I'm running late. Ben wanted to make my life miserable." I motion for him to come inside. "I'll change quick."

"I think you look gorgeous as you are, but yeah, you're going to want something more comfortable." He pulls me close and kisses my cheek.

"Give me five minutes."

"No rush." He shoves his hands in his pockets and leans against the back of the couch.

I strip off my suit and throw on a pair of teal capris and a vintage Led Zeppelin t-shirt with the sleeves cut off. I grab my purple converse sneakers and head back into the living room where he's waiting for me.

I slip my shoes on and lace them up. "Are you ready?"

"Whenever you are." He slaps my ass when I exit the apartment first. The door slams behind us, and I lock it before we head out into the late July air.

"So." I nudge him when we reach the street corner. "Where are you taking me?"

Gavin smirks and focuses on the crosswalk signal. "It's a surprise. You'll have to wait and see."

"I don't like surprises, Gavin. It's the one thing Ben and I share in common."

"Ben Statler doesn't like surprises?" He glances at me with a chuckle. "Shocking."

"You act like you know him." We cross the street, heading for the subway.

"Personally, no, I don't know him, but I do know his type.

Anyone in a position like that must hate surprises." He takes my hand and veers left, down into the station.

We shuffle through the after-work crowd and reach the platform.

"Are we going into the city?"

"Yup." Gavin offers no hint as to where he's taking me.

When we get off on the lower east side, I'm completely stumped. Gavin holds my hand tight as we make our way up to the street and the sounds of the city surround us.

He takes a left, then a right, leading me down the sidewalk until we take a sharp turn and spill out on a narrow side street.

"Why do I feel like this is one of those thriller films where the serial killer leads his victim to a vacant building in order to chop them up and sell their body parts on the black market?" I arch my brow at him.

"Damn, you figured it out." He pulls me closer. "You forgot the part where I fuck you into submission before I kill you."

"Seriously, where the hell are you taking me?"

"There." He points to a glowing sign hanging from a brick building in the distance.

I squint to make out what it says. "Level Up?"

"Yup." He leads me further down the street. We stop under the lime green and pink neon sign.

"What is this?"

"You'll see." He opens the door and ushers me through.

The sounds hit me first. Pinging, coins dropping, the unmistakable cacophony of multiple video game theme songs warring for dominance. My jaw drops when I see the vintage games and retro décor. I spin around and grab Gavin's shirt in both hands.

"You brought me to an *arcade*?" I squeal, unable to contain my excitement.

Gavin looks worried for a half-second before I throw my arms around his neck and kiss him full on the mouth. When we break apart, he chuckles. "You like it?"

"I fucking *love* it!" I grab his hand and pull him toward the counter.

I'm bouncing on my toes like a damn teenager as he buys the token cards and two beers.

"You want food?" he asks, gesturing to the menu.

"Later." I snatch the cards from his hand and cradle them against my chest.

Gavin finishes paying and I practically drag him down the rows of games flashing their bright colors and catchy jingles. I spy an early-nineties classic along the wall and stop right in front of the large console.

"*Mortal Kombat II*?" Gavin asks with a laugh. "Of all the games in this room, this is your first choice?"

"Put up or shut up, hot stuff." I pass the card over the reader and the fever takes hold. "I'm about to show you how we settled shit old school." I choose my avatar. Kitana.

"Okay." Gavin's shoulders shake with laughter. "Maybe this wasn't the best idea for a date if you're just going to talk shit and try to kill me." Gavin chooses Scorpion.

I snort, but the snarky response dies the moment the game starts. The battle is intense. I'm transported to my childhood, taking on anyone willing to challenge me at the local arcade. When it closed years ago, I was crushed. So many good memories there.

Gavin delivers a wicked blow and it knocks me on my ass. I barely survive his assault, but after a swift comeback, I manage to eke out a win. We play three more rounds before he reaches for his beer. I didn't even see the waitress deliver them. He offers me mine.

I take it and drink half the glass in one swallow. Damn, that's good. My gaze drifts over the other games, and unbridled delight infuses me. Of all the places in the city, he brings me to an arcade for our first official date. How the fuck did he know I would like this over a movie or a fancy dinner?

"Which one do you want to play next?" Gavin leans against the machine.

"Let me look around." I wander along the rows, scanning the games as I go. There's only a handful of people here. I'm not sure how busy this place gets, but if it were up to me, I'd be here all the time.

"This one." I point at the familiar logo.

"*Mario Kart.*" Gavin sets aside the beer. "Finally."

I down the rest of my drink and grab the card from his hand. "Let's race."

We settle into the seats, and five minutes later, we're both cursing at each other when we're neck-and-neck for first place. Gavin throws a banana peel in my path and I spiral out of control. He barely squeaks past the finish line ahead of me.

"You little shit. Ya got lucky." I stand up. "Pick the next game."

Gavin rubs his jaw and glances around the arcade. He spots one he wants and grabs my hand. "Come on. When was the last time you played *Contra*?"

"Shit. Years." I think hard. "Do you remember the Konami Code?"

"Do I remember the code?" He scoffs. "Did you forget you're dating a genius?"

"Careful, your head can't swell any more or it'll burst." Lord, his ego. I grin when he swipes the token card.

We play two rounds of *Contra* before moving on to *Ms. Packman.* After *Street Fighter* and *Simpsons*, we decide to take a break for beer and pizza.

On our way to find a table, I spot *DDR* and tug Gavin's shirt. He stops and whips around.

"What?" His gaze follows my finger. "No. C'mon, Maggie. Not that one."

I rub my hands together with evil glee. "Are you worried I'll kick your ass at a dance game?"

"*Dance Dance Revolution* is for kids. You're practically an old lady." He smirks as I step up onto the mat. "I wouldn't want you to pull a muscle or something."

"Fuck you, Gavin." I point to the vacant opponent's side. "Get up here."

He grumbles but climbs onto the dance floor. I swipe the card and select a song. Adrenaline courses through me at the first strains of music. It's go time. Shit, I forgot how much of a workout this was. Sweat drips down my face, snaking over my chest. I glimpse Gavin out of the corner of my eye and stumble. Shit. Focus. He's hitting everything I'm not. How?

I slow my pace and turn to watch him. His feet fly across the pads, hitting every single beat. Damn, he's good. Either that, or he's right and I'm too old for this shit. Am I having a heart attack?

The song comes to an end, and I lean against the bar, struggling to catch my breath. "Why didn't you want to play this? You're fucking amazing at it."

Gavin shrugs and uses the bottom of his t-shirt to wipe his face, baring his abs to the whole arcade. I warm at the sight of the hair dipping into the waistband of his jeans. He steps close and leans down. His breath brushes my ear.

"Keep looking at me like that, and I'll have to find a quiet spot to show you what else I'm good at." I'm not going to pursue this conversation, knowing he will do exactly as he threatens.

Ever the gentleman, he helps me down and leads me to a table tucked against the wall at the front of the arcade. After he gives the waitress our order, he slides into the booth across from me.

My gaze drifts over the room, taking in the flashing lights and sounds. It's like coming home. When I return my attention to Gavin, he's watching me.

"How did you know I'd like this place?"

"A guess." He smiles and ducks his head. "I figured since we're both avid gamers, you'd appreciate the nostalgia of a place like this. Was I right?"

"Lucky guess." I chuckle. "This is fun. Thanks for showing me this little gem. It's amazing. I didn't even know it was here."

"Well." He smooths his hand over his hair. "We don't really advertise. It's more of a gamer's escape. Most of the time people rent it for big events and fundraisers. That kind of stuff."

"We?"

"Yeah, Mike and James found out the owner was selling it a few years ago, and we went together to buy out the business and the lease."

"You guys *own* this place?"

"Well, we're more like silent investors. The manager takes care of the day-to-day business stuff." He brushes it off like it's no big deal, but I'm impressed.

"Wow." I can't even form the words. "That's awesome. I'm surprised you never mentioned it before."

"Contrary to what you may think of me, I don't like to brag." He thanks the waitress when she places the pizza pie and two beers on the table.

My face heats and I reach for a slice. "Well, bringing me here was kind of bragging."

Gavin leans across the table and beckons me closer with a finger. I lean forward and grin, proud of myself for calling him out.

"When we get back to your place, I'm going to put that smart mouth to good use." His words make me shiver. "As much as I wanted to keep you inside all weekend and fuck you senseless, I think your bosses want you coherent on Monday morning."

I stuff the pizza in my mouth, unable to find a suitable response to his teasing. We finish our pizza and drinks before heading back to my place, where he follows through with his promise. It's well after midnight when we finally curl up on my bed, exhausted and well satisfied.

Whatever this is, it's growing on me.

CHAPTER EIGHTEEN

A month of blissful happiness consumes me. Every weekend, Gavin comes over. We eat, we game, we fuck. It's heaven. I couldn't ask for anything better. I'm actually getting into the groove of our routine and the anxiety that once haunted me sounds like a squeaky door in the background of my mind. I think I'm in love with Gavin.

Strike that. I *know* I'm in love with Gavin. He's sweet, sexy, and considerate. He might be a goddamn unicorn. We have a lot more in common than I thought. Even the age gap thing doesn't bother me like it once did. Best of all, he's supportive. Damn, that's sexy as hell.

"I think we should tell them." Gavin hands me the bottle of wine from the cabinet to set on the counter next to the snacks.

"No!" I stare at him in horror. Tonight is the first game night we've had in a while, and I've invited not only Jen, Lily, and Shaun but Gavin's two roommates as well. My apartment is going to look like a sardine can bursting with overpriced minnows, but hell, I'm up for the adventure. What I'm not up for is hosting a grand reveal for all our friends.

"Why not?" He arches a brow. "Are you embarrassed to tell them we're dating?"

"No." I fidget with the chip bag before opening it and pouring the contents into an oversized bowl. "Why would you think that?"

"Because you haven't told anyone that we're together." Gavin leans his hip against the countertop. His gaze burns, so I avoid it.

"That's not true." I scoff. "Evan and Ben know."

"Your bosses don't count, babe." A wicked grin crosses his lips. "They heard us fucking in the server room."

My face warms. "Remind me to kill Evan. He should've

kept his mouth shut."

"He didn't seem too upset by it. More amused than anything." Gavin pops a chip in his mouth. "Got a high five out of the conversation at least."

"You did not." I wonder if I could slip cyanide into Evan's coffee on Monday morning without him knowing.

Gavin shrugs noncommittally, and I'm left wondering if he's full of shit or being one hundred percent honest. It's hard to tell with him sometimes. "Twenty bucks says they already know."

"How could they know unless you told them?"

"I haven't told a soul." He crosses his heart. "But I spend most of my weekends here, and you've been avoiding Lily and Jen for weeks." He leans closer. "They know."

"I'm not confessing anything. We'll just play it off and see if they notice." I pull some glasses from the cabinet and line them up on the counter.

"Oh, they'll notice when I can't keep my hands off of you." Gavin wraps his arms around me and pulls me against his chest. His lips burn a path along my neck, leaving my knees weak. I moan when he nips my earlobe. I'm about to concede defeat and let him fuck me in the kitchen when the doorbell rings.

I disentangle myself from his embrace and try to scrape some semblance of sanity together as I stumble into the living room. Resting my hand on the door, I turn and glare at Gavin.

"Behave," I hiss, but it comes out more like a purr. I curse the fact my body has such a visceral reaction to his presence. With a deep breath, I open the door.

"Maggie! I've missed you." Lily launches herself into my arms as her two roommates wave.

"I missed you too." I step aside with Lily still clinging to me and motion for them to enter. "Come in, guys. Make yourself at home."

Maybelline and Surfer Boy. I know their names are actually Mike and James, but in my mind, this is who they are. The trio comes inside and greets their long-lost roommate.

"Hey, man." Maybelline fist bumps Gavin. "Where the hell

have you been hiding?"

Gavin hands him a beer and shoots me a glance. Good thing Maybelline and Surfer Boy are distracted by the alcohol or they would have caught the heated look.

Lily finally pulls away and grins at me. "I feel like I haven't seen you in ages!"

"Yeah, I've been…busy." I drop my gaze unable to meet hers or dare to look in Gavin's direction.

The doorbell rings again. Lily joins the boys, and I open the door to find Jen and Shaun bearing gifts. Shaun hands me a bouquet of tiger lilies while Jen holds a bottle of wine aloft.

"Come in, guys." I usher them inside and hug them both. They mingle with the rest of the gathering, and my heart warms to see them all together again. Like old times. Only now it's different. I swallow my uncertainty and sweep into my role as hostess.

Shaun pops open the wine and pours a glass for Jen and Lily. I grab a beer and twist off the top. Gavin is chatting with Maybelline and Surfer Boy when Shaun joins them. Lily drags her arm through mine and pulls me toward Jen.

"All right, where the hell have you been the past few weeks?" She eyes me over her glass.

"Yeah, we've missed having movie nights." Jen pouts and takes a sip of her wine.

"I've been busy."

"You're glowing." Jen snorts. "Do you see it, Lily?"

"Oh yeah, definitely that post-coital glow." Lily sidles up to me, her blue eyes narrowing. "Who's giving you the D?"

I nearly choke on my spit. "Lily!"

"Are we ready to play?" Gavin asks, bringing the group of men closer to the table.

"Yeah, should be." I gesture to the folding chairs. "Sit anywhere."

Everyone picks a chair, but I'm left standing. There are only six folding chairs and seven guests. I curse my inability to count. Gavin wraps his arm around my waist and pulls me into his lap.

"I fucking knew it!" Lily jumps up and punches her fist in

the air. She holds out her hand to Shaun. "Pay up, honey."

Shaun mutters under his breath and pulls a twenty from his wallet. Jen's laughing. Maybelline and Surfer Boy smother their grins behind their hands, but their shoulders are shaking with stifled laughter.

"I told you they already knew," Gavin mutters against my ear.

"That's no reason to put on a show for them to confirm it." I cross my arms and lean back against him. My gaze skims over my friends who stare at us in amusement. "What?"

"I've never seen you glow like that, Mags." Lily raises her glass in salute. "To Maggie and Gavin. I'm so glad you finally got the hell over your egos."

"To getting laid," Jen adds with a smirk.

"To getting laid." The rest chant in return before drinking to our sex life.

"Lord help me, I'm going to murder all of you," I grumble as I reach for the cards.

"You love us." Lily blows a kiss and steals the cards from my reach. "I'll take care of these since you're…occupied."

"That's it." I try to stand, but Gavin holds me firmly against him. His hardening cock presses against my ass. I squirm on purpose just to irritate him.

His breath brushes over my neck. "Keep that up, and I'll toss you over my shoulder, haul your naughty ass into that bedroom, and fuck you senseless. I don't care if they hear every single whimper and moan. Behave."

I still instantly, knowing he will absolutely follow through with that threat. Lily deals the cards and we start the game.

Three hours later, we've demolished three large pizzas and emptied all the snacks. My sides hurt from laughing. This game is the most irreverent, non-politically correct trash, but it's so much fun with the right group of friends.

Gavin relinquished me an hour ago when Jen offered me her seat. She's now settled in Shaun's lap, and I'm pretty sure they're up to no good if the red blush staining Jen's neck and cheeks is any indication. I bite my lip to keep from telling them to get a room.

Maybelline and Surfer Boy bail out around nine, practically dragging Lily with them since they refuse to allow her to walk home alone. She's slightly intoxicated. I hold her upright while the boys say goodbye to Gavin.

"I'm so glad you two fucked." Lily boops my nose. "Gavin's a great guy."

"Yeah, he is." I warm at her words. "Get some rest, honey."

Maybelline lifts Lily into his arms and cradles her against his chest as Surfer Boy opens the door. "Cab is waiting outside." He turns to me. "Thanks for the invite. We had fun."

"Yeah, thanks, Maggie." Surfer Boy smiles and ducks out of the apartment behind Maybelline and sleepy Lily.

"Bye," Lily's drunk voice echoes through the hallway.

I close the door and shake my head.

"We're gonna head out too." Jen gives me a huge hug. "Thanks for the awesome night. I'm so glad you took my advice."

"You guys are never going to let me live this down."

"We only tease you because we love you." Jen pulls back and grins. "Movie night next week?"

"Sure. Your place?"

"Of course."

"Sounds like a plan." I hug her again. "Now get out of here before you two start dry humping on my couch."

Jen chuckles as Shaun joins us, empty pizza boxes gathered under one arm.

"What did I miss?" He smirks. "Never mind. I don't want to know."

"Take it easy, Shaun." Gavin comes up alongside me and wraps his arm around my waist.

"You too, Gavin."

They wave and head out into the night, leaving Gavin and me alone. Now that everyone has left, the apartment feels huge.

"You okay?" Gavin nuzzles my neck.

"I'm good." I spin in his arms and meet his gaze. "I can't believe you did that."

"Did what?" He feigns ignorance, but I know better.

"Pull me into your lap and go all caveman on me."

"I had to assert my dominance." He grabs my hips and jerks me against him. I grasp his arms to keep from stumbling even though he's holding me tight. "You're mine."

"Yeah, and now the whole world knows it."

"Is that a bad thing?" He tips my chin up, and I can count the lashes framing his soulful eyes.

"No."

He presses a kiss to my forehead. "Want to play *Space Armada*?"

"Winner gets to be on top."

"Ohhh, that's a rough bet. You're on. But I'm going fuck you at least twice tonight. Top, bottom, sideways. You're all mine."

Heat floods me. I wiggle out of his grip and turn on the PlayStation. Gavin sits on the couch and I settle down beside him.

As he selects the game settings, I study his profile. Shit. Why is my heart pounding like this? But I know why. Because I love him.

But I'm too scared to say it.

CHAPTER NINETEEN

When Gavin sent me a text on Wednesday inviting me over to play *Space Armada II*, I didn't even have to think about my response. Of course I want to spend my Friday night playing my favorite game with my favorite person.

As much as I don't want to admit it, Gavin has become an intricate part of my life and my weekly routine. We text throughout the day. He sends highly inappropriate gamer memes and I often catch Evan and Ben glancing at me in curiosity. Evan chuckles, knowing exactly why I'm laughing. Ben just glares. Fuck 'em. For once in my life, I'm content, happy, and excited to see what the future holds.

After revealing our relationship to our friends, I'm much more relaxed about the whole situation. Still not quite sure what I'm going to do about the whole *I love him* revelation yet. If the right moment strikes, I may let it slip. But what if it all falls apart? I'm killing myself with worry over the unknown, but I can't change my core nature.

At six o'clock on Friday night, I head over to Gavin's armed with a bag of snacks and a six-pack of Yuengling from the corner market.

"Hey," he says as he grabs the six-pack from my hands.

"Hey." My gaze rakes over him when I follow him into the kitchen. Shirtless and coated in sweat, his muscles ripple beneath his skin and I'm left wiping drool off my chin. He must have just gotten done working out. I shift my attention to the silent house. "Where is everyone?"

"Lily went out. Not sure where." He stashes the beer in the fridge and skews up his face in thought. "Which is odd. She normally lets me know where she'll be and when she'll be home. Weird." He shrugs. "And James and Mike are at the arcade for a special event tonight."

"Why didn't you go?" I set the snacks on the counter.

He shrugs his shoulder. "I'd rather have you all to myself while everyone is out." He wraps his arms around me and pulls me close for a kiss. "That way we can mess around on the couch without fear of getting caught."

I lean into the kiss but jerk back when my hands graze his sweat-slickened skin.

"Ooops, sorry." He steps out of reach. "I meant to shower before you showed up. Took a run around the park while we still had nice weather."

"It's okay." I grab the back of his head and drag him down for another lingering kiss full of promise. "I like when you're all sweaty."

"Mmmm...does that mean I'll be getting sweaty again later?"

"Maybe, if you play your cards right." I gently shove him back. His pecs tighten under my hand, and his eyes darken with hunger. "Go shower."

"Okay." He's halfway out the door before he turns around. "Make yourself at home. I'll be out in a few."

"Don't worry about me. Just hurry up. I wanna kick your ass." I blow him a kiss.

"Tease," he mutters as he turns away and disappears down the hall. His footsteps echo up the stairs and down the corridor above me.

I grab a beer from the fridge and pop it open. Gavin's words echo in my mind. *Make yourself at home.* I wander upstairs. Gavin's bedroom door is cracked open. I nudge it with my foot, hoping to catch him with his pants down. Literally.

The sound of running water comes through the wall to my right. Damn, he's in the shower already. I imagine him slick and soapy under the spray of the water. Shit. I'm half-tempted to burst into the bathroom and join him, but I refrain, knowing there will be plenty of hanky-panky later.

With a sigh, I step into his room and admire how fucking neat it is. Everything is in its place. Dust free too. His bed is rumpled and a pile of laundry sits in a basket in the corner. I shake my head. He's such a guy. Even though he's organized, he still has his little messes. So, he's normal, I guess.

The computer screensavers flicker along the far wall drawing me closer like a moth to a flame. I pull out the chair and sit down. Curiosity burns through me. I know I shouldn't look because it's probably a project he's been contracted for with a multi-million-dollar company. But I can't stop myself. I admire Gavin's work and his dedication. Watching him in action is quite an aphrodisiac.

My gaze skims through the text. One phrase catches my eye. *Gamer Girl Inc.* What is this? I scroll down, reading as I go. My breath catches in my chest, choking me, and my heart constricts.

The more I read, the angrier I get. It's my game. My idea for a gamer girl safe haven turned into an application both for desktop and smartphone. What the fuck? Disappointment settles in the pit of my stomach, and I feel like I'm going to puke.

I scroll down further and see the manufacturer's name. Rebel Tech. The name sounds familiar, but I can't place it. A quick search on my phone brings up no results and my gaze drops to the papers on Gavin's desk. A business card sticks out from the corner of the pile. I pluck it out and skim the lines.

Rebel Tech. Gavin Howell, Co-Founder. What the ever-loving fuck is this shit?

I shoot to my feet and glare at the screen. Did he steal my fucking idea? Fury pulses red hot through me.

"Well, hello there." Gavin's voice breaks through the haze surrounding me.

I spin around to find him leaning against the doorframe, wearing a towel low on his hips. My body reacts, but my mind is hyper-focused on the betrayal I've uncovered.

"What the fuck is this?" I hold up the card between my fingers.

"My new business card." He looks confused, but smiles. "Why?"

"Don't you dare try to charm me right now, fucker. How could you do this?" I'm crushed by the weight of my disappointment and rage. I struggle to breathe, but still, I round on him, flicking the card onto the floor.

"What did I do? I don't understand." His look of genuine shock leaves me even angrier.

"You stole my idea. My dream. You fucking stole it and turned it into an app. Without my goddamned permission!" I scream, unleashing the fury within me. "You sweet-talked me, seduced me, made me believe you wanted to be with me…then you ganked the one dream I had and slapped your name on it."

"Babe, I—"

"Don't call me that. I don't want to hear your fucking excuses." I storm toward the door, ducking away from his grasp when he reaches for me. "Don't fucking touch me."

He lifts his hands in supplication. "Maggie, please, let me explain."

I shake my head and stomp down the stairs, making a beeline for the door. I can't stay here. I can't be with him. He took the one thing I had for me and slapped his goddamn name on it. Fuck him. Fuck this.

"Maggie! Wait," he shouts down the stairs, cursing when he realizes he's still naked and can't chase after me. Good. It'll make this break nice and clean.

"Fuck you, Gavin." I storm out the front door without a backward glance.

By the time I reach the subway station, my heartbeat has slowed, but I feel the pressure welling up inside me. I manage to hold it together until I reach my apartment. The moment I close the door behind me, I burst into tears and collapse against the door.

It comes in waves, washing over me, pulling me under. The betrayal, the anger, the grief. I'm being pulled in a hundred directions and there is no one to save me. No one would understand.

Gamer Girl was my dream. The one fucking thing in the whole damn world that belonged to me alone. How could Gavin steal it from me?

Wasn't it enough to take my heart? He had to take my dream

too. Fucking bastard. I sob harder and curl up into a ball, burying my face in my knees.

I should have known better than to trust him. I can't trust anyone. Not even my own heart. I thought I loved him. I gave everything to him. I welcomed him into my life, albeit begrudgingly at first. But he managed to weasel himself into my good graces and see where the fuck that got me? Shattered and broken.

After what feels like hours, I manage to drag myself to my feet and collapse on the couch. I curse my heart. I curse the world. And I most certainly curse Gavin.

I drag a blanket over my head and sob. My gaze lingers on the console and the allure of getting lost in another world sounds like heaven.

My phone pings as a message pops through. It continues. Two, three, four messages. Irritated, I snatch the phone from my pocket and turn it off without looking at the screen.

I don't want to talk to anyone, especially him. He fucked up, and I'm done.

Surrendering to my obsession is the only logical solution. Fuck my life. I turn on the console, making sure I'm invisible to all the other players. Reality sucks, so I'll lose myself in virtual reality until the pain eases.

CHAPTER TWENTY

The weekend passes in a blur of repressed rage and never-ending video games. I still haven't turned on my phone by the time I walk into the office on Monday morning.

Ben casts a sidelong glance as I pass him standing outside his office. Evan's mouth snaps shut the moment he sees my no-bullshit expression. Once I'm safely inside my office, I release the breath I've been holding. I don't want to talk about it. I really don't want to think about it, but it's not like I can switch off my subconscious. All I can do is hope I can drown myself in menial tasks and numb the pain until I get home and lose myself in another galaxy.

After organizing my desk, I skim through my planner. Good. There's shit to keep me occupied. I fire up the computer and log in to the network. Guilt pierces me when I see the culmination of all Gavin's hard work sitting on my desktop, but it quickly disintegrates into renewed fury.

How fucking dare he steal my idea and bring it to life? That was *my* goddamn dream. *My* project. How could he take something so sacred and make it his own?

This is why I never told anyone my idea. I knew they would steal it and slap their name on it, leaving me with nothing. I should never have trusted him. Ever. I knew better. Fuck.

Gavin stole not only my dream but the one thing I had for myself. He tainted my escape. I couldn't even enjoy a weekend of gaming because of the memories it triggered. Gaming typically pulls me from whatever funk I'm in, but this time, it only pulled me deeper. I want to drown in cyberspace and never surface. Greasy pizza and beer didn't help either. They only amplified the frustration and pain.

I shove the thoughts aside and open my email folder. After a few minutes, I find a rhythm and lose myself in work.

Evan pops his head in my door around noon. "Hey."

I glance up from my screen. "What's up?"

"You okay?" He postures himself behind the door, utilizing it as a shield. Smart man.

"I'm fine." I snap, wincing at my tone. "Did you need something?"

"No. We're just worried about you."

"We?"

"Yeah, me, Andrew, Ben."

I scoff at the thought of Ben being worried about anyone or anything other than his precious Solus. "Well, don't worry. I'm fine. I need to finish this."

"No problem. Just let me know if you need anything." Evan's brow furrows. "I'm here if you want to talk about it."

"I'm good. Thanks."

Evan disappears and closes the door behind him, leaving me in blissful silence once more.

I glance at the clock. It's two-thirty. Fuck it, I'm leaving early. The last thing I want is everyone in the office worried about my relationship problems. I wrap up what I'm doing and power down my computer.

Without a word, I grab my stuff and head for the door. Andrew watches me leave but doesn't say anything. I take the stairs down to the first floor and step outside. There's a gray cast over the city and rain threatens to pour down any second. I wrap my arms around my torso and head toward home. Halfway through the park, the storm cuts loose.

By the time I reach my apartment, I'm drenched and trembling from unbridled anger. Can't one thing go right? It's like the whole fucking world is out to get me. What the hell did I do to deserve this?

I shake off the excess water and step into the hallway. Thunder shakes the building. What should have been an enjoyable walk home turned into the storm of the century.

I step inside my apartment and heave a sigh. I kick the door shut and lock it before tossing my purse on the couch. A hot shower brings me a small measure of comfort.

After donning sweatpants and an oversized hoodie, I grab a snack from the cabinet and collapse on the couch. I don't feel like playing a game, so I turn on Netflix and scan through the new release section for ten minutes before selecting *The Hobbit*. I've watched it sixteen times before. It's a comfort thing, I guess.

Two hours and a bag of Doritos later, a knock at the door disturbs my brooding session. With a groan, I drag my ass off the couch and unlock the door, half expecting Gavin to be standing on the other side.

But it's not Gavin, it's Lily.

"What the hell, Mags?" Crimson rises in her cheeks at the sight of me. "I thought you were dead!" She huffs and pushes past me, peeling off her raincoat and hanging it on the rack near the door.

"Come on in." I close the door and lean against it, bracing myself for the inevitable lecture I know is coming.

Lily rounds on me with wide blue eyes filled with concern. Her ruby lips press into a thin line as she shakes her head. She bursts into tears and wraps her arms around my neck.

"I was so worried about you when you didn't show up for girls' night on Saturday. I tried calling you all weekend, but all I got was your voicemail. I thought your phone was broken." She squeezes me tight before relinquishing her hold. "I asked Gavin what happened—"

"Stop, right there." I hold my hand up and march around her, heading for the fridge. "I don't want to talk about Gavin."

"He said there was a—"

"I'm serious, Lily. I don't want to talk about Gavin. That fucker crossed the line and I'm not interested in his excuses." I pop the top on the beer and lift the bottle in salute. "We're done."

Lily snatches the bottle from my hand and takes a long drink. With a gasp, she hands the bottle back to me and straightens the cream-colored cardigan over her dark green wiggle dress. An unladylike burp escapes behind her hand as she covers her mouth.

A smile tugs at my lips. It's not typical for Lily to be so

brash. I lean against the counter and take a drink.

"Fine." She straightens her shoulders and meets my gaze. "I've heard his side of it. Let's hear yours."

"What part of 'I don't want to talk about Gavin' did you not understand, Lily?"

"You two were all over each other. You were glowing, for fuck's sake." Lily pouts. "I just don't understand what happened. You guys are perfect for each other."

I scoff at her assessment of our relationship. "I trusted him, and he betrayed me. Simple as that."

"What did he do, Mags?" Lily rests her hand on my shoulder, and a stone in my well-fortified wall breaks loose. I meet her gaze and the wall surrounding my heart crumbles to pebbles and dust.

"I told him about my dream project. An application designed specifically for gamer girls. A support network for those of us who were always pushed outside the gamer community." My hand tightens around the bottle as I explain it. "I've had the idea for years, but I've never had the coding skills to bring it to life. I was learning the ins and outs of the programming, but it was a slow process."

Lily nods with understanding. "You told Gavin about it?"

"I did, and then he fucked me over." The seeping wound on my heart bursts open once more. "He stole my idea, created the app, then slapped his name on it. Bastard!" I nearly throw the bottle in my hand.

"That doesn't sound like Gavin." She shakes her head and a blonde curl tugs free from the net holding her hair in place at the base of her neck. "Mags, I've known him for years. He would never do something like that."

"Believe it or not, I saw the proof of it myself. *My* app is sitting on *his* computer with *his* business name on it in bright bold letters." I finish the beer and toss it into the trash.

Lily grasps her chin in her hand and skews her nose up. After a few long moments, she sighs and shrugs her shoulders. "I don't know, hon. This doesn't sound like something he would do. We've been friends for a long time. He would never plagiarize someone's intellectual property. It goes against everything he stands for."

"Yeah, well, people change when there's money involved." I glower and push past her.

"You should call Gavin and talk this out. I'm sure it's a huge misunderstanding." Lily's voice digs into my heart and clenches like talons into the tender flesh. I don't want to talk to him. Because if I do, then I'll have to face the torment of his betrayal once more.

"I can't." A tear slips free and I brush it away before she can see it.

Lily rests her hand on my shoulder. "He's worried about you. I swear he's a wreck. He's tried calling a hundred times, but you don't answer."

"I turned my phone off." I sniff and face her. "It's over, Lily. I won't let him drag me back in with his sweet words and sexy voice. It hurts too much knowing he took this from me."

Concern mars her delicate features as she searches my face. Finally, she nods. "I understand. Can I at least tell him you're alive?"

"I don't care what you tell him."

Lily flinches at my tone and draws her lower lip between her teeth. She drops her hand and twists her fingers together.

"I didn't mean to bite your head off, Lily." I kick myself for being an asshole. "You're sweet to come all the way over here to check on me. But I'll be fine. Really. I'll get over Gavin."

Even as I say the words, my heart constricts with the pressure of the statement. I'll never get over him. He completed me in ways no one else even came close to doing. Losing him is one of the most painful things I've ever experienced. But I can't be with someone who betrayed me and lied to my face.

"I forgive you." She smiles, but it doesn't reach her eyes. She retreats to the door and retrieves her raincoat. Pulling it on, she meets my gaze. "If you need anything, you know where to find me."

"Thanks." I swallow the lump in my throat, knowing I won't be able to go to her house again without having every memory of Gavin sweep me up like a hurricane leaving me in tatters.

"I love you." She opens the door, and with a sad, parting smile, she steps out into the hallway.

"Love you too," I call after her.

I lean against the closed door and beat my head against the wood. Why, Gavin? Why did you have to ruin the best thing in my life, you greedy shit? I was happy, and now I'm a goddamn wreck.

Cursing a blue streak, I return to the couch and bury myself beneath the blanket. Maybe I should move. I hear Arizona is nice in the winter.

Truth is, there's no way to escape the memories or the hope I invested in my relationship with Gavin. We were too similar, too perfect together.

I knew it wouldn't last.

CHAPTER TWENTY-ONE

When I'm not at work, I'm lost in the games. I haven't spoken to Lily since Monday, and I'm still avoiding both her and Jen's frantic messages. I worry they might try plotting an intervention like we did with Jen a while back. But honestly, I don't care anymore. I've slowly and painstakingly recreated the wall I tore down for Gavin because I thought what we had was special. Different. I thought *he* was different. I was wrong.

I'm halfway through writing up the quarterly report due at the planning meeting next week when my intercom buzzes. I hit the button on the ancient device Ben insists we keep to remain connected.

"Yes." I finish my thought on the screen.

"Please come to my office. Now." Ben's deep voice resonates through the speaker, making him sound like Darth Vader.

With a sigh, I save my document and close the file. Whatever he has to say, it must be important. Both Ben and Evan have avoided any and all interactions with me this week. It's as if they can sense the tension streaming through me. I'm not sure if it's better or worse than lingering pity. But they don't know. They don't have to know. My personal life is none of their business.

Taking a deep breath, I step from my office and cross the five feet to Ben's door. This time I knock and wait for his response before barging into his space.

"You wanted to see me?"

"Come in." He gestures to a chair opposite him. "Sit down."

Maybe he's finally come to his senses and decided to fire me. Or reprimand me. I've been a bitch lately, and my mood impacts everyone, I've noticed.

Ben leans his forearms on the desk and studies me for a

long moment. The tension draws tight like a rubber band ready to snap against my tender skin.

"Do you own a formal gown?"

The question sails over my head for a moment as I exhale in relief. I mentally rummage through my closet at home. There's that one dress. But it's still in the original plastic. Does it even fit?

"I think so." My curiosity turns to skepticism at the curve of a smile pulling at the corners of his mouth. It vanishes as quickly as it appeared, masked with a pleasant but blank expression. "Why?"

"Perfect." He leans back in his chair. "Brooklyn's Bureau of Business is hosting a gala on Saturday night. Both Evan and I have plans for the evening and are unable to attend. I need you to go as a representative of Solus."

"You can't be serious." I shoot to my feet, indignant at his presumption I'd even be willing to attend some stuffy gala in the first place. "This isn't part of my job description."

His gaze remains steady, his voice calm. "You are a valued employee and the only person Evan and I can rely on to represent the company in our stead. I wouldn't ask if it weren't necessary to have a representative present at this event."

"I don't do black tie events. I don't do the ass-kissing, schmoozing, boot licking stuff." My hands ball into fists. This is the last thing I want to do with my time. But I can't tell him I have plans, because that would be a bald-faced lie. I have no life. No plans. Nothing but my games.

"No one is asking you to do any of those things, Maggie." He straightens, and I get the distinct impression he's not going to back down. It's not a request, it's a requirement.

"Please don't make me do this," I beg, hating myself for sounding this weak. "Ask Andrew. Anyone. Please, I'm the worst possible candidate for this."

Ben rises to his feet and rounds the desk. He rests against the surface and our eyes lock. I'm two seconds from breaking into tears, but I'll be damned if he sees me cry. He cocks his head and studies me carefully.

"You're the perfect candidate." He smiles, and it's genuine. Shit, he's a lot more handsome when he smiles. "You are the only person I can trust. Andrew is great, but he's not ready to step into that arena. You are the backbone of this company. Of all the employees, you treat it with a personal dedication that denotes your investment into the success of the company as a whole." He takes a breath. "Solus would not be the strong competitor it is without you, Maggie."

His admission knocks the wind out of me. I drop my gaze to the carpet and choke back the emotion threatening to tip the bucket of tears building inside me. The fact that he recognizes the amount of dedication I have poured into Solus is heartwarming, but it does nothing to quell the fears raging inside my mind.

"What if I fuck it up?" I mutter beneath my breath, half praying he didn't hear me.

"You won't." He extends his hand. There's an American Express card between his fingers. "Use this to take care of any expenses for the evening. Hair, makeup, clothes, transportation. Whatever you need."

"Are you serious?"

"You're worth the investment." He smiles again, and I swear it's a world record. Twice in one day. Should I feel honored or concerned at his sudden generosity? Guilt creeps in at my hesitation.

"Fine. I'll go." I tuck the card into my pocket and clear my throat before reaching for the door. "But this better not become a habit."

Ben waves his hand. A clear dismissal for me to return to work.

Once I'm back in the safe confines of my office, I collapse against the door and let the tears fall. What the hell am I doing? Why didn't I tell him to shove it and find someone else?

Because I don't want to be alone in my apartment all weekend, glued to my games and cutting myself off from all human contact. I pinch my eyes closed and wish I had my virtual wasteland in which to rage. After several deep breaths, the constant background music in my mind dims and I'm able to stem the waterworks. I wipe away the evidence of my meltdown with a tissue and toss it into the trash.

My phone sits on the charger beside my desk. I grab it and jam out a text to Lily.

Hey, are you free on Saturday?

Several minutes later, her response comes through. *Yeah, what's up?*

I have a gala to attend on Saturday night. I need you to work your magic. Boss gave me the AmEx, so money is no issue. Hook me up, girl.

Her response comes back immediately. *I got you. Let me make some calls.*

I sigh in relief. Lily has me covered. She's a fashionista at heart, but it's her love of all things vintage that really distinguishes her. Her connections run deep through the city. If anyone can turn this frumpy pumpkin into a glamour goddess, it's Lily.

Hair, makeup, dress, mani/pedi? She adds the cute little heart eyes emoji at the end, making me laugh.

The works, I respond, and then add, *Oh, and I'll need a ride to the gala. Limo?*

Oh, that one's easy. I've already called Cyril's Car Service, and they've got one reserved just for you. Event address?

I look up the gala information and send the location to her phone.

Brooklyn Waterfront Hotel? Swanky. That's doable. I'll send you the schedule for Saturday in a few. Want to go dress shopping tomorrow?

Biting my lip, I pull up my schedule for the following day. Do I want to go dress shopping? No. But if it means I get to spend the day with my best friend and not work? Hell yes. My gaze skims over the calendar. Doesn't look like there's anything I can't miss.

I type out a quick message to Ben and Evan. *Taking tomorrow off. Gala stuff.*

Tomorrow would be great. Let's do it. I send a reply to Lily and set my phone aside.

A few minutes later my phone pings. *I'll be at your place at 9, then we can go into the city.* There's a flurry of heart emojis and smiley faces across my screen. I laugh. At least someone is super excited about this last-minute adventure.

My stomach twists into knots at the thought of attending some fancy dinner party and schmoozing with the top business owners in Brooklyn. I straighten my posture and square my shoulders. Maybe this is exactly what I need. A chance to get out and show people exactly how capable I am. Ben trusts me. That says a lot right there.

He's right. I can do this. With the right armor, I can walk into any battle. Or gala as the case may be. This will be the perfect opportunity to mingle with the other professionals and show them the strong presence Solus has in the community.

Evan's response comes through on my screen. *Wear something that accentuates your personality.* He tacks on a little winking emoji at the end and I roll my eyes. But it makes me chuckle. The darkness I felt this morning has lifted, replaced by something else. Hope? Maybe it's just a distraction, but it does the trick.

I bury myself in my work, thinking about all the fun Lily and I are going to have in the city tomorrow searching for gowns. The last time I wore one was probably prom, which I never made it to, thanks to a family emergency. Hence the bag still sitting in the back of my closet. I don't even want to think of how out-of-date that dress is. Ugh. It's vintage now. Just like me.

By the end of the day, I've managed to catch up on all my correspondence and time-sensitive items. The rest can wait until Monday. At least I have a head start on the quarterly report. After I jot down a few notes in my planner, I add them to my phone calendar and power off the computer.

When I get home, I whip up a sandwich and settle down on the couch to do some recon work on my laptop. Who is going to be at this event and will there be booze?

CHAPTER TWENTY-TWO

"Oh, look at this one!" Lily rushes across the shop and stops in front of a mannequin wearing a long flowing gown. The bright red fabric and sequined bodice blind me.

"Not red." I point to my hair. "Purple or teal." I fold my arms across my chest and refuse to relent. "It has to match my hair, Lily."

She pouts and drops her hand, letting the fabric slide through her fingertips. "Fine. But Antonio is going to lose his mind when he sees how faded your hair is."

"Well, he can deal with that tomorrow, but if either of you think I'm changing the color, you're out of your fucking minds." I tuck a teal strand behind my ear when Lily pouts harder.

"Fine. You don't have to change the color, but it does need a touch-up." Lily shimmies between the racks in search of another gown. We already have a half dozen waiting at the changing room at the back of the store, but she's not convinced we've found the one yet.

I snort when I think about the selections she chose. I don't think we've found it either. Most of them look like teenybopper prom dresses. While I'm not a fan of current fashion, I don't think I'd be able to rock the pin-up vintage like Lily.

"Aren't there any vintage gowns from the eighties or nineties lying around in one of these shops?"

Lily scrunches up her nose. "You can't be serious. Those poufy sleeves and ruched torsos." She shivers with distaste. "Those gowns should never again see the light of day."

An image of my mom's yearbook prom photos and scenes from *The Wedding Singer* flash through my mind. "Okay, yeah. I mean, maybe not those gowns exactly. But the colors are much more my style. The neon and jewel tones."

This makes Lily pause. She taps her jaw with her fingertip.

Her gaze rakes over me. "You have a point." She shoves me toward the changing room at the back of the store. "Try those on first. I'll see if I can find something else."

Lily lives for fashion. Vintage pin-up may be her forte, but she's got an eye for color and fitting for body type. She should start her own design label.

But trying on the first dress, I begin to wonder if I can trust her judgment. The gown clings beneath my boobs. I look like I stepped out of a high school gymnasium. The maroon color enhances the bags beneath my eyes. I quickly strip it off. No. Just no.

The next two gowns join the first in the discard pile. Forest green and navy might be better suited to a boardroom, but they're not eye-catching enough for the gala. I want to make a statement, show my personality. I'm not pretending to be something I'm not. I may be representing Solus, but I'm also showcasing myself. Ben said I could. That's as good as gold in my book. I can't do that wearing something that makes me look like a frigid matron or a teenage beauty queen.

After three more dresses, I'm discouraged. Is there nothing to wear in this damn place? Maybe I can still fit in that prom dress I have squirreled away in the back of my closet.

"Hey. I think I found something." Lily is beaming when I open the door, and she hands me a hanger with a shimmery, deep teal gown.

Holding it up to the light, I turn it and the teal transforms into royal purple. I gasp at the mirage quality of the fabric as it alternates back and forth in the light.

"Holy shit…"

Lily squeals and claps her hands together. "Try it on."

The smooth fabric glides across my skin as I pull it over my head. It settles around me like a second skin, lighter than air. I slide the zipper up and turn to face the mirror.

Sweet mother of Abraham Lincoln.

It's like this gown was made for me. The alternating colors in the gown amplify the highlights in my hair. The Grecian style wraps around my waist, accentuating my torso and bust. I step forward and grin when my thigh appears in the high slit along the side. It vanishes beneath the waterfall of shimmering fabric when I stand still. The sloping neckline accentuates my neck, granting enough cleavage to be enticing without being gratuitous.

"Let me see!" Lily calls from the other side of the door.

I open the door, and she gasps.

"Oh, my God. It's perfect." She presses her fingers over her mouth and giggles. "Turn around. Let me see the back."

I spin around in my best impression of a runway model, flashing my thigh through the slit.

"Yes! This is the dress." Lily nods with certainty.

"Yeah, it is."

"Great! Now, hurry and get changed." Lily closes the door. "I want to get lunch at MacAvoy's before we hit Fifth Avenue. You still need a matching clutch, shoes, and appropriate undergarments."

"It's only one night, Lily."

"True, but I want you to knock them dead. You'll be the belle of the ball."

I dress quickly and shake my head at her romantic notion. "This is a work event. I'm not looking for Prince Charming."

"You never know. Best to be prepared for all eventualities."

When I open the door, I fix her with a shrewd look. "I'll never wear this again. Why go to all this trouble and expense?"

"Your boss gave you carte blanche with the company card." Lily shelves her hand on her hip. "Don't be such a prude."

I laugh. "Me? Prude?"

"When it comes to money, yes, Mags, you're a prude." She nudges me with her elbow. "Live a little. You need to pamper yourself."

With a sigh, I grab the gown from the hook. "You're right about the live-a-little part. Not the prude bit."

Lily rolls her eyes. "Come on. Let's pay for this and head uptown."

We manage to beat the lunch rush to MacAvoy's. It's a swanky little bistro near Rockefeller Center. Lily snags us a table near the window.

The city is bustling for a Friday afternoon. It's refreshing to be out with my friend enjoying the delights of city life for a change. I can't remember the last time I took a day off for such an indulgence.

We order club sandwiches and lobster bisque soup. She sips her iced tea and watches me pluck the lemon from my water.

"Gavin asked about you."

I choke on a piece of ice but manage to dislodge it before I cause a scene requiring the Heimlich maneuver. Swallowing, I take a moment to catch my breath.

"You promised you wouldn't bring him up." I sip the drink and a dark cloud settles over me.

"I'm sorry, it's just…" She fidgets with the napkin and sighs. "He's miserable, Mags. He hasn't left the house in days. James and Mike can't even get him to game."

"Not my problem." I fold my arms across my chest. "He did this to himself, stealing my idea like that."

"I really think you should call him."

"No."

"A text. An email." She leans forward practically begging me. "Please. Something. Anything. My heart can't take seeing him like this any longer."

"The phone goes both ways." I snap, irritated by my sudden sour mood.

Lily snorts. "Yeah, well, you've been ignoring all of us for a week. I'm pretty sure he's tried reaching out. You just haven't noticed."

Fuck. She has a point. "Okay, you can paint me as the bad guy here, but remember, he's the one who seduced me and stole my idea."

"Seduced you?" Lily's incredulous look catches me off guard. "You make it sound like he slept with you to get state secrets and betray his country for a shit ton of money."

"When you say it like that, it sounds stupid." I twist the glass between my fingers. "But it was my dream he stole, Lily. That's like someone coming in and stealing all the sketches and ideas you have for a clothing line then selling it to Versace or Gucci or some shit."

Lily frowns and a deep furrow forms between her brows. "I'd fucking murder them."

"See." Vindication washes over me when she finally realizes the scope of this betrayal. "Now tell me I'm crazy for cutting him off."

"I never said you were crazy, hon." Lily's expression softens. "I love both you and Gavin. It tears me apart to see you two at odds like this. Especially since you were getting along so well."

The memories threaten to overwhelm me. Gavin and I laughing while we battled at the arcade. His determination when he fucked me in the server room at Solus. The way he held me as we drifted to sleep in my bed.

"I can't do it, Lily. Not yet." I glance out the window, unable to meet her gaze.

"I understand." Her voice is gentle, understanding even. "Will you at least think about it? You don't have to do anything yet. But at least consider talking to him when you're ready."

"Fine," I concede. "Now, can we change the subject?"

The food arrives, and I'm grateful for the interruption. The soup is creamy and smells like heaven. I dive in.

We eat in silence for a few moments before her phone pings. She checks the message, and a blush creeps up her neck into her cheeks.

"Who was that?"

"Oh, uh, no one important." She says, shoving her phone into her purse.

"Uh huh." I jab my spoon in her direction. "Is that the guy from that Discord fashion group you've been chatting with?"

"Maybe."

"Look, you can't poke around in my love life and not expect the same treatment." I can't help it. She did this to herself. "Now, spill the tea, sister. Who is he?"

"His name is Sam."

"Where is Sam from?"

She blushes again and I'm enjoying this way more than I should. "Wyoming."

"A cowboy?" My brows shoot up. "Seriously?"

Lily nods. "He sent me a picture of his ranch north of Cheyenne."

"Holy shit." I drop my spoon and fumble to pick it up. "How do you know he's not a serial killer?"

"He doesn't sound like a serial killer."

"You say that like you have firsthand experience with murderers." I tease her, enjoying the way her face turns crimson. "Wait, you've spoken to him on the phone?"

"Yeah. A few times. He's really sweet and has a little bit of an accent."

Holy shit. Lily's got it bad for this cowboy. "Are you sure about this guy?"

Lily stiffens at my comment. "Look, if I can't butt into your love life, then you have no right to butt into mine."

I lift my hands in surrender. "Touché."

We return to our meal and finish in tense silence. Once we pay, Lily leads the way toward the next shop. I fall into step beside her.

"How's work by the way?" I ask, knowing she's been working alongside the vice president on a special project.

"It's fine." She tosses her hair when the breeze catches it across her face.

"Do you like working with the big boss?"

"It's fine. He's stern but professional."

I nudge her with my elbow. "You guys told me he's a stone-cold silver fox. I'm sure he's easy on the eyes if nothing else."

She meets my gaze and smiles. "He's definitely hot. But one hundred percent off-limits."

"You don't have to tell me. Ben and Evan are two of the finest men I've ever met. But they're definitely not on my list of eligible bachelors. That HR department can be such a bitch." I laugh and she joins in. The tension eases between us.

We wander a block or two before she gestures to a shop with scantily clad mannequins in the window.

"Do we really need to buy underwear?" I whine.

"Foundational garments are key. Trust me." She opens the door and gestures for me to enter.

"Fine," I grumble and step inside. "But I don't have to like it."

The rest of the afternoon passes in a pleasurable haze. I buy a matching set, panties and a bra, along with a garter belt and thigh-high stockings. We find shoes at Jimmy Choo that match my dress perfectly, and a clutch at Gucci. I don't even want to look at the receipts.

I'm pretty sure Ben will pass out at the bill when it arrives. But I don't care. He told me to have fun, and that's exactly what I'm doing.

I just hope I don't ruin it all by puking all over my gown when I walk into the gala tomorrow night.

Lily drops me off at my place with instructions for the following day. Hair, nails, and makeup. I'm pretty sure she's enjoying this whole process, and I'll admit, I am too.

I finish memorizing the prominent guests attending the gala and admire the gown hanging on the door of my closet. It glistens in the dim light.

The only thing that could make this better is if I had someone by my side to bolster my courage. But there's no one. I'm on my own. I square my shoulders and set my jaw. I can do this. I'm used to playing with the big boys in cyberspace. This is no different.

I'll hold my head high. That's the way I roll, and nothing can stop me. Boss level reached. Now to kick some ass.

CHAPTER TWENTY-THREE

The black town car pulls up to the Brooklyn Waterfront Hotel and it takes all my effort not to wipe my sweaty palms on the delicate fabric covering my thighs. I take several deep breaths as the driver exits the car and comes around to open my door.

The September breeze drifts off the bay and caresses my overheated skin. It's unusually warm and sweat beads on my forehead. The air cools me, but it does nothing to quell the chaos swarming like bees in the pit of my stomach.

Nick, the driver, offers his hand to help me from the car. I take it and step onto the curb. He hands me a card. "Call this number when you're ready to leave."

"Thanks." I tuck the card into my clutch.

"You look lovely by the way." He flashes a charming smile and my face heats.

"Thank you."

He returns to the driver's seat and pulls away from the entrance. I shift my gaze to the hotel towering before me. There's no going back. Not after all this effort. Shopping with Lily was a wonderful reprieve, but the pampering in preparation for tonight left my head spinning. I don't think I've ever done that much preening for one evening.

The results are undeniable. Antonio refreshed my highlights and styled my hair into a wrapped braid, complimenting the gown's style. My nails flash teal under the fading sunlight. Even my toes match, hidden beneath the most expensive pair of heels I've ever seen in person.

I press my hand to my chest and clutch the strand of pearls Lily loaned me, with matching earrings to complete the ensemble. There's no denying it. I feel powerful. A goddess sent to crush mortals with a withering glare.

As I take the first steps toward the hotel's entrance, my

heartbeat flutters. What if I fuck this up? I shake my head, banishing the thoughts to the abyss. I won't fuck this up. I am a goddess tonight and nothing can change my mind.

Inside the hotel, I'm stunned by the opulence around me. This is way out of my comfort zone. I'd much rather be home in sweatpants playing *Zelda* or *Space Armada.* But I promised Ben and Evan I'd represent Solus, and damn it, I'm going to make them proud.

When I enter the ballroom, my gaze sweeps the vaulted ceiling and gilded decorations. There are quite a few guests already, and I recognize some faces from the research I did Thursday night. Relief floods me. I thought I was overdoing it, but being able to put names to the faces surrounding me is empowering and boosts my confidence.

A waiter passes bearing a tray of champagne. He pauses and offers a drink. I take one with gratitude and sip the sparkling beverage. My gaze skims the crowd until I see Mr. Kennedy, the president of Empire Enterprises. He's worked with Solus on many projects in the past.

I cross the floor to where he's speaking with a small cluster of people. He sees me approach and his grey brows rise.

"Miss Dawson. What a delightful surprise." Mr. Kennedy takes my hand firmly. "You look stunning."

"Mr. Kennedy." I smile as the confidence reaches maximum power. "It's always a pleasure to see you."

His eyes scan the room before returning to me. "Mr. Statler and Mr. Waldorf are not here this evening?"

"No, unfortunately, they had prior engagements. I have come in their stead."

His gray eyes soften with understanding. "Allow me to introduce you." He turns and proceeds to introduce me to his companions.

I shake hands and commit their names to memory. On Monday morning, Ben will want a full rundown of everyone I interacted with, I know it. We enter into some friendly conversation, and I listen with interest while nursing my champagne.

This isn't too bad. I'm settling in quite comfortably when the tinkle of feminine laughter draws my attention to the right.

The air sucks from my lungs. Fuck. My. Life. It's Gavin.

He's standing with a tall blonde woman wearing a cherry red gown. Smiling. Laughing. He reaches out and touches her arm to steady her when she wobbles on her heels. Fury fills my vision with shades of black.

Lily's admission filters into my mind. *He misses you.* Like hell he does. From the looks of it, he's found an adequate distraction from his grief. I scoff.

The noise must have triggered a hidden sixth sense because his head pivots and our gazes lock. His eyes widen and their slow perusal down my body and back leaves me overheated and flustered.

I turn back to Mr. Kennedy's small group and excuse myself. Halfway across the room, I know it's pointless to try and escape. When I reach the bar, I set the champagne flute down and flag down the bartender.

"Double bourbon, neat."

He nods and grabs the non-descript bottle of whiskey off the bottom shelf. I shake my head. "Top shelf, honey."

The bartender smirks and grabs the Buffalo Trace from the glass shelf. He slides the drink in front of me and winks. I smile, but his amusement fades when his gaze drifts to something…some*one* behind me. He turns and leaves. I sigh when the familiar scent surrounds me.

I pause with the glass halfway to my lips. "Go away, Gavin."

His arm brushes mine as he comes alongside me. Those dark, intoxicating eyes roam over my body. "You look gorgeous." Appreciation sparks in his gaze as he licks his lips. Hunger replaces it.

I shoot the bourbon, savoring the burn as it slides down my throat and warms me. It's meant to be sipped, and I know better but I'm desperate to calm the nerves twisting inside me. His brow arches, but he says nothing. I set the glass aside and face him.

"If I had known you'd be here, I would have told my bosses

to shove it." I turn to leave, but he grabs my wrist, holding me in place. His touch ignites a desire I had been able to repress all week. But being here with him, surrounded by his heat and his scent, I'm drowning, and I don't want to be saved. Fuck.

"Dance with me." His breath ghosts across my neck. It's not a request.

I shiver. Swallowing the mewl of need lodged in my throat, I meet his gaze. "Are you a masochist?"

"When it comes to you, yes." He gently leads me toward the empty dance floor. The soft strains of an instrumental ballad filter through the speakers surrounding us. His hand snakes around my waist while the other intertwines our fingers together. As we sway to the music, he tugs me against him. Heat consumes me at the innocent contact.

He looks amazing. Like James Bond. Or better yet, the handsome duke from that Netflix series Lily introduced me to over the summer. There's something about a man in a suit that sets my hormones ablaze. What lingerie is to a man, a well-tailored suit is to a woman. Gavin is no exception to this rule. He's positively swoon-worthy. Which only darkens my mood further.

"You don't like my suit?"

"What?"

Amusement dances in his eyes. "You're scowling at my suit so hard it might catch on fire."

"As long as it takes you with it."

"You have every right to be angry with me."

"Damn skippy." My anger bubbles beneath the surface calm, but desire slowly infiltrates it. The combination is dangerous and heady. Or is that the whiskey kicking in? It's a toss-up.

"If you'll allow me to explain—"

"I'm not interested in your excuses, Gavin." I pin him with a fierce look. "You stole my idea and slapped your name on it. It would have been easier to forgive you if you had stabbed me in the back or blown me up with a slip grenade."

Gavin's resigned sigh fills the gap between us. He looks

over the crowd before returning to me. "I don't expect you to forgive me, but you need to know, I never meant to hurt you."

"Well, you fucking did." I snap and try to pull away. He lets me go. Free from his grip, I feel like I'm falling backward.

He grasps my hand and suddenly I'm grounded again. I hate the fact that he can do it without effort. I hate him.

"Come with me," he murmurs, his voice low.

"I'm not going anywhere with you." I unsheathe my claws. If he wants me to put on a show, I will. But I did promise Ben and Evan I would represent Solus. It would be a piss-poor way to show my professionalism by unleashing hell upon the man who gutted my soul.

"There are some people you should meet." He cradles my elbow and leads me from the floor. I follow only to keep from making a scene.

He comes to a stop beside two well-dressed women. One of whom is the blonde in the red dress. I scowl hard at him before turning to face the women.

"Ladies, allow me to introduce Maggie Dawson, the founder and brains behind Gamer Girl and Rebel Tech." He turns to face me with a smile.

My. Heart. Shatters. What did he say?

"It's so lovely to meet you." The woman in red offers her hand. "I'm Julia Garmond, and this is my partner, Vivien Link."

I take it without thought and smile. Confusion washes over me. "Nice to meet you."

"Julia and Vivien are investors—scouts—for FreeWheel Games. I sent them the beta version of your game, and they're interested in investing in your Gamer Girl app."

My gaze snaps back to the two women. "Oh. Wow. Really?"

"Absolutely," Julia says, her eyes sparkling. "We're both avid gamers and the concept is exactly what the industry needs to fill the gaps from other leading providers."

Vivien nods. "Women make up a large percentage of the gamer community, and yet they're often left feeling forgotten and ostracized by male players and game manufacturers alike." Her smile is sincere. "It's about time someone provides a safe, welcoming haven for female gamers to build connections and support."

"Wow. I'm flattered. Being a gamer girl through the nineties made me tough, but women shouldn't have to hide their passion for gaming because they don't fit the norm."

"We agree completely," Julia says.

"We would love to have you come into our office next week and share your ideas and goals for the app. There are so many possibilities for expansion. We would love to come alongside you and make those a reality." Vivien cuts straight to the heart of the conversation, leaving me stunned.

My heart explodes in my chest. I glance at Gavin, who's standing silently beside me, pride emblazoned on his face. I turn back to Julia and Vivien.

"I would love that. Thank you." I manage to choke out the words without bursting into tears.

"Great." Vivien hands me a card. "Call us on Monday, and we'll schedule a meeting."

"I'm so excited. Thank you for sharing your idea with us." Julia shakes my hand again.

"Of course."

The ladies venture off toward the bar, leaving me with Gavin.

I can't bring myself to look at him. I didn't do anything. He did it all. He saw the potential in my idea and brought it to life. He sent it to the people he knew would appreciate my effort and help bring my goals to fruition. Shame ignites the heat in my cheeks.

"Gavin." I turn, and when our gaze meets, all the words fly out of my head.

He cups my chin in his hand. "I told you I would never do anything to hurt you."

Tears threaten to ruin the winged liner and thick mascara. "I was an asshole."

"You were. But I was too. I should have told you."

My heart softens. "Why didn't you?"

"I wanted to surprise you." He reaches into his pocket and

pulls out a card.

I glance at it. There's my name in bold letters. Beneath it reads, *Founder of Rebel Tech.*

"What is this?" I study the card.

"Rebel Tech is yours." He chuckles. "A place for you to bring all your ideas to life."

"Gavin, I…" Words fail me. I'm touched by the gesture. I wrap my arms around him and he embraces me tightly.

"You like it?"

"I fucking love it."

"I'm glad."

"But what about you? This never would have even seen the light of day without your programming skills."

"I was hoping it could be a partnership, but I don't want you to feel like you have to keep me around if you hate me so much."

"I don't hate you." I give him a gentle nudge with my hip.

"Could've fooled me." He smirks, but it shifts to something vulnerable and genuine. "I love you, Maggie."

"I love you too." This time a tear slips free. I hug him tight. "Thank you."

He leans down and whispers in my ear. "Now, let's go somewhere a little more private. I have plans for you, baby girl."

"I hope you got a room."

Gavin holds up two fingers with a hotel card between them.

"So confident." I take him by the hand and drag him from the ballroom toward the elevator.

On the way up, I text my driver and let him know his services won't be needed. There's no way in hell I'm leaving before morning. Make-up sex awaits, and I have a lot of making up to do.

CHAPTER TWENTY-FOUR

This is more like it.

I stretch out on the couch, draping my legs across Gavin's lap and leaning back against the armrest. After a sleepless night spent at the Waterfront Hotel making up in every imaginable way, we returned to my apartment to spend our Sunday afternoon together. As a couple.

Never in my wildest dreams did I think Gavin would be at the gala, or that we would end up back together. Not that I'm complaining. Far from it. I'm content, like a lazy cat languishing in the afternoon sun. Life is fanfrickentastic.

Gavin hands me the controller and turns on the television. "*Space Armada II*?"

"Yeah." I snuggle closer and power up the PlayStation. "You ready to get your ass kicked again?"

"For such a petite woman you talk a big game." Gavin's hand rests on my ankle slowly massaging the joint.

"Ah, but I deliver the goods, don't I?" I jab him in the side. "It made you fall in love with me."

Gavin shakes his head. "The clincher was your sexy little victory dance when you beat me."

"You're weird."

"Two peas in a pod, I guess." He trails his fingertips over my shin. "I couldn't believe you trounced me like that. Made me hard as a rock too."

I laugh-snort. "And here I thought you were so butt-hurt about getting beaten by a woman that you couldn't stand to be in my glorious presence a moment longer."

"Actually, I had to go relieve some pressure after that." He winks. "Thinking about that sexy dance has me hard all over again."

"Oh my God, Gavin." I cover my face with my hand. "Did

you seriously get off thinking about that?"

"Yup. On multiple occasions." He waggles his brows and blows me a kiss.

"And here I thought you hated my guts." I skim through the menu and select the game.

"Quite the opposite, actually," Gavin replies. "I thought you hated *me*."

"I did." I meet his gaze steadily. "You were an arrogant shit." With a shrug, I turn back to the screen. "That doesn't negate the fact that I wanted to jump your sexy ass."

"I get it." He drops his hand from my leg and grips the controller. "I'm glad you finally saw reason."

"Lily vouched for you." I press start and allow him to select his player.

"She did, huh?" A soft smile crosses his lips. "She's a good woman. I hope she finds someone to treat her like the queen she is."

"Maybe her new cowboy daddy will."

Gavin's head whips around. "Cowboy daddy?" He raises a brow. "Who the fuck is that?"

I pinch my lips closed, wondering if I've crossed a line by telling Gavin. It seems Lily forgot to mention her cowboy friend to her roommates. "If she didn't tell you, then I'm not saying another word. You need to ask her about that."

Gavin shifts uncomfortably and frowns. "She's always been too nice. Too trusting. Lily doesn't like to break the rules. She doesn't like secrets. But if she's hiding this, then something's up."

"Don't be too hard on her." I rest my hand on his shoulder. "She's in a strange place right now. With Jen dating Shaun, and now you and me, I'm sure she feels like the odd woman out."

He scoffs. "Lily could have any man she wants eating from the palm of her hand. I just want to be sure they're not taking advantage of her." His scowl deepens. "We've been friends for so long. I can't *not* look out for her. She's like the sister I never had."

"The fact that her dad is one of the wealthiest men in the

country has nothing to do with that, huh?" After looking up her father's name, I understood the full impact of her desire to cut free from his influence.

"It makes it ten times worse. They always want to get to her dad," Gavin grumbles. "Lily deserves a man who loves her as she is, not for who she's related to or what they can get from her."

"You're right." I select my character and hit load. "We'll talk to her about it later."

He shifts his attention to the TV and sits up, pushing my feet off his lap. "Good. Cause right now I'm about to crush you in battle."

I slide up to sit beside him with an elbow jab to his side. "Don't get cocky."

Gavin's eyes glint. "Oh baby girl, you need to choose your words more carefully."

"I did." My tongue slips out to wet my dry lips. His gaze darkens. The controller vibrates in my hand as a droid shoots at me on the screen. "Shit."

Gavin laughs when I retaliate, knocking the droid's head off with Ransom's blaster. We fall into a rhythm and follow the instructions leading to our objective.

As I follow the corridors and decommission the enemy soldiers, I'm keenly aware of the man beside me. His thigh presses against mine. His arm brushing mine with every negotiation of the character on the screen.

He mutters and swears when I send a slip grenade in his direction.

"Sorry." I chuckle when a dark hole opens and sucks the surrounding items into the void.

Gavin barely manages to escape and pockets a health booster pack hiding in the corner. "You enjoy torturing me."

"Always." I smirk as I climb the access ladder into the main console room. With a few well-placed charges, I blow it to hell, narrowly escaping through the hatch.

"We should do this more often." He unlocks the panel, allowing him to hotwire the fighter bay doors.

"What? Infiltrate an enemy base and blow it up?" I skirt

around two M-class guards and slide between the doors before they snap closed.

"No." He whoops in triumph when the bay doors open.

I slip past him and drop a grenade at his feet. "Play one-on-one?"

"Fuck." He bolts into the fighter bay and stumbles when the explosion rocks the wall behind him. "Will you stop it with those fucking things?"

"Okay, fine. I'll stop trying to kill you. It's not my objective anyway."

"Could've fooled me." He chases me deeper into enemy territory.

"Oh, admit it. You love the challenge." Blaster fire punctuates my words.

I'm holding back the enemy's advance, and Gavin reaches the ship before I do. He closes the doors to the cruiser.

"Damn it, Gavin! Don't you dare leave me behind." I race toward the ship and barely reach the ramp before the door shuts with a thud.

Blaster fire ricochets off the hull beside my head. I spin around, opening fire on the low-level scum sent to stop me from stealing their ship. After taking them out, I decide to search for another ship, even though I know this is the only one.

The doors slide open behind me, and I slip inside. "You're lucky."

We manage to break free from the port and get the stolen ship with its valuable cargo into orbit above the small rogue planet. The cut scene takes over, filling in the story.

I glance at Gavin who's wearing a smirk on those sinful lips. I shove my weight into him. "Why did you do that?"

"Why do you keep throwing those damn slip grenades at me?"

"Because it's fun, and you jump every time." A smile breaks through. "But you didn't have to leave me there to die."

"I didn't." He clears his throat. "I let you tag along."

"After you locked me out." I pout. "I'm not sure I like playing with you, cheater."

"I didn't cheat. I made you work for passage on my ship."

"*Your* ship?" I laugh. "Get over yourself. If you want to work as a team, then fine. I can handle that. But you can't throw me into enemy fire while you make a getaway."

"Mags." His voice shifts deeper.

"What?" Damn it, he steals my breath and my sanity with those soulful eyes and that heartbreaker smile. They'll be the death of me, I swear.

"Do you want to?"

"Want to what?"

"Be a team." He brushes his thumb along my jaw and cups my face in his hand.

"Are we talking gaming, or something else?" My heart pounds at his touch.

"Everything." He licks his lips. "Games, work, life. I want it all, but only if I can have you beside me."

I can't breathe. Is he serious? "What are you asking me, Gavin?"

"I'm asking you to be mine, Maggie. For as long as I live—or until you kill me." He smirks at the poorly timed joke but sobers instantly. "Nothing matters without someone to share it with. And I want to share it with you. All of it. The good, the bad, and the ugly."

I'm lost in his eyes. His touch. His scent. All of him. The controller slips from my hands as I wrap my arms around his neck and climb into his lap, straddling him. His hands slide to my hips and hold me steady.

"Are you asking me to marry you, Gavin?"

"I am." He grins. "Are you interested?"

"I'm interested." I press my hand to his chest, stopping him before he can lean in for a kiss. "But I have one condition."

"Of course you do." Gavin leans back, all business. "Go ahead."

"No wedding."

He blinks twice and chuckles. "Are you serious?"

"As a heart attack." I maintain eye contact, and he nods in understanding.

"Can I ask why?"

"Because I'm not traditional. We can get married at the courthouse and then have a party with our friends if you want to include them in the celebration."

"I'm fine with that." He wraps his arms around my waist. "Any restrictions on the party?"

"Nothing formal or stuffy. I want it to be a reflection of us. Something fun. Surprise me."

"I thought you hated surprises?"

"I do, but I trust you."

"Good to know." Gavin's smile makes my heart clench. "You like *my* surprises."

"Yeah, I do." I kiss him and everything falls away. There's only me and him and this perfect moment. "I love you."

"I love you too, baby girl." He kisses me again.

When I pull away, breathless and overheated, I see the hunger in his eyes. Before he can act on it, I rest my hand on his shoulder.

"When should we tell our friends?" I toy with the collar of his t-shirt.

"Let's wait until game night."

"Sounds like a plan." I grip the back of his neck. "Now, shall we continue our game or take it to the bedroom?"

"Both."

My eyes widen at the thought of combining both activities. "Challenge accepted."

A ton of giggling and a few orgasms later, we manage to finish the game and each other before calling it a night.

CHAPTER TWENTY-FIVE

I lasted a whole week without spilling the big secret. A. Whole. Week. It definitely helped that I was distracted with work and setting up a meeting with Vivien and Julia to discuss my Gamer Girl app. By the time we reach Lily's brownstone, I'm practically lightheaded from the excitement.

Gavin takes my hand and gives it a squeeze. "You okay?"

"Never better."

When the door opens, I launch myself into Lily's arms and hug her tight. She reciprocates without hesitation.

"Hey, Maggie. Gavin." Her smile widens at the sight of us together. "Come in."

We follow her into the entryway. "Jen and Shaun here already?"

"Yeah, they got here about ten minutes ago." Lily sashays into the dining room.

"Where are James and Mike?" Gavin asks.

"Oh, they're at the arcade tonight. Some kind of contest or something." Lily rolls her eyes and waves her hand in dismissal. "They're so unpredictable since you left them unattended."

Gavin chuckles but says nothing in response. He glances in my direction and winks.

Shaun and Jen are laying out snacks on the buffet. A stack of board games sits in the center of the dining room table. Jen sweeps me up in a hug.

"I missed you. How did the gala go?" Her question blindsides me.

"It went well. Lily worked her magic to get me red carpet ready." I blow a kiss at her across the room. She curtseys with a blush.

"Everything went according to plan." Lily sets a pitcher of sangria next to the snacks.

"Wait, what?" I spin around in confusion and pause when I catch sight of Gavin's guilty expression. "Hold on. The gala was a setup?"

Jen and Shaun cover their mouths trying to smother their smiles. Lily whistles low and escapes into the kitchen. My gaze narrows on Gavin and I fold my arms across my chest.

"It wasn't a set up as much as a prime opportunity." Gavin holds his hands up as he explains. "You weren't answering my calls, texts, or emails. So I had to call in a favor or two."

"You convinced Ben and Evan to play along with this?"

"I couldn't think of another way to get you to listen to me." Gavin stuffs his hands in his pockets. "It was my last chance to clear up the misunderstanding and convince you to give me another shot."

Lily appears in the doorway carrying a tray of glasses. She slides them beside the sangria. I turn toward her.

"You knew. When I texted you about a dress and makeup and all that shit, you knew."

A deep crimson stains her cheeks. "Gavin has been one of my closest friends since middle school. You two are crazy about each other. I couldn't say no. Not when I wanted you together so desperately."

"OTP," Jen adds sagely. Shaun nods in agreement.

"I'm scared to ask what that means."

"One True Pairing," Shaun clarifies. "It means you two were meant to be together."

"So you all went behind my back and set this up?" I shake my head in disbelief. "I can't believe you guys."

"We only did it because we love you and we want you to be happy. Together." Lily clasps her hands.

Gavin grabs me by the waist and pulls me against him. "There was nothing malicious about it. I had to at least try. You mean that much to me."

I sigh and close my eyes. He's right. "I know. I'm glad you did it, but damn if it doesn't hurt my pride."

"I'm glad it worked out." Lily grins, but there's a tinge of sadness in her blue eyes.

"Oh, it worked out." Gavin gives me a conspiratorial look. "Shall we tell them?"

I nod.

"Lily, you're going to have to find a new roommate." His arms tighten around me. "Maggie and I are getting married next month."

Both Jen and Lily squeal and rush toward me. They pull me from Gavin's hold and squish me between them. Their chatter overlaps, and I'm too swept up in the moment to react or even understand them.

Shaun shakes Gavin's hand in congratulations. Lily abandons me and hugs Gavin.

"I'm so happy for you guys." Lily's eyes well up with tears.

Gavin holds her close and my heart melts at the sight. Their friendship led us to this moment. It must be hard for Lily, not only because of Gavin moving on with his life, but being single while everyone around her is falling in love. I hug them both.

"We're not going anywhere, Lily." I pull back and smile.

"I know." She wipes the tears away. "But now I have a wedding to plan for, and I'm not ready."

"We're keeping it small and simple." Gavin and I share a look of solidarity. "Nothing fancy."

"Okay, we'll save the wedding talk. There will be plenty of time for that later." Lily gestures to the table. "Let's play some games."

The five of us grab snacks and beverages before settling into our chairs. Lily's already taken out the most irreverent game she owns and starts shuffling the cards.

"I have to know." Jen leans toward me conspiratorially. "How did he propose?"

I choke on a mouthful of sangria, nearly snorting it into my lungs. Clearing my throat, I tap my chest. "Well, we were playing *Space Armada II*, and it just kind of happened."

Gavin shakes his head. "I fully intended to ask you mid-game, but the program doesn't allow my character to kneel. So I improvised." He winks at me. "It's hard to propose when your woman is throwing slip grenades in your direction."

"I wasn't trying to kill you, just slow you down."

Gavin takes my hand and gives it a squeeze.

"Okay, my nerd crew, let's focus on the game." Lily deals the cards and sets the pile in the center of the table.

We pick up our cards, and I skim over the phrases on them. There are some good ones here.

I sneak a peek at Lily over my cards noting the nervous way she glances at her phone and then bites her lip. She shakes her head and focuses on the cards in her hand. A telltale blush stains her neck.

Who is she talking to? Her cowboy? At first, I worry her discomfort is about her being the only single person at a table of couples, but it could be possible there's something going on with her and this mysterious stranger that we don't know about. I make a mental note to ask her when we're alone. There's no reason to make a show of it right now. Not when we're all content to be in each other's company and joking around.

Game night proceeds without incident. My sides hurt from laughing. It feels good to spend time with the people I love. After Jen and Shaun head home, Gavin and I send Lily upstairs, assuring her we can clean up. Reluctantly, she retreats to her room.

"Something's going on with Lily," I whisper, rounding on Gavin.

"Yeah. I noticed she's a little off." He kisses my forehead. "We'll talk to her tomorrow."

"Are we staying here tonight?" I ask, biting my lip. "We haven't broken in your bed yet."

Gavin arches his brow. "These walls are thin, baby girl." He leans close and nips at my ear lobe. "You're awfully loud when you come. Not that I'm complaining, but I don't want to be rude to my roommate."

"She's on the other side of the house. Her room doesn't even connect to yours." I moan when he kisses my neck. "Will you let me finish the dishes?"

He pulls away and drops his hands. Regret fills me. I want his hands and mouth on me. Damn him for being so addicting.

Within ten minutes, we're climbing the stairs. In the distance, I hear the shower running. Lily's in the bathroom. Good. Then I can have my wicked way with Gavin without her being able to hear us.

The moment we cross into his room, he kicks the door closed and locks it. His mouth is on mine before I can form a coherent word. I'm drowning in his heat, his kiss. We stumble back and collapse onto his bed.

Panting, we tear at each other's clothes until I uncover every delicious inch of him. He latches his mouth onto my nipple and a cry of need rips from my throat. He claps his hand over my mouth and laughs.

"I knew you couldn't keep quiet." Gavin removes his hand, and I groan as he fits his cock to my aching pussy.

"Inside me. Now." I wiggle until he slips in. It's not enough. I claw at his shoulders.

"So impatient." He rolls to the side, placing me on top. "Take what you want."

He slides deep, and my moan echoes off the bedroom walls. Gavin's hands rest on my hips as I grind against him, taking my pleasure. He caresses my sides, gliding up to pinch my nipples. I buck against him as my climax builds. When he slides his fingertips between my folds and makes insistent circles, his name breaks from my throat in a hoarse cry.

Gavin thrusts up hard with every stroke until my orgasm bursts free. It lifts me high and explodes in a riot of color and sensation. I ride him as I come down from the blissful peak. He rolls me onto the bed and drives into me until he claims his own release and collapses.

The orgasmic haze slowly subsides. A creak outside the door pulls me from the fog.

"Did you hear that?" I murmur against his shoulder.

He lifts himself enough to stare down at me. His eyes sparkle with amusement. "I told you. These walls are thin, and you're loud when you come."

I hide my face against his chest. Lily heard us. Even worse, she stood outside the door when—when we—ugh, I don't want to think about it.

Gavin kisses my forehead. "Don't worry about it."

"I'm not worried that she heard us fucking." I bite my lip. "I don't want her to be upset that she's alone while we're—"

"Enjoying each other's company? Fucking? Engaged?" He offers a plethora of reasons.

I nod. "Yeah."

"I'm worried about her too," he assures me. "We'll talk to her in the morning, okay?" His kiss draws me deeper into his embrace and soothes my concerns. I feel his cock harden inside me.

"So much for being quiet." I stoke the flame of desire. After another intense orgasm, we snuggle beneath the blankets.

"How did I get so lucky?" he murmurs against my hair.

"It can't be because you're a sore loser."

"Am I a sore loser though?" He inhales deeply. "Technically, I won in the end. I got the girl."

"You didn't just get any girl. You got a Gamer Girl." I smile when he chuckles.

"Those are the best kind." He kisses my cheek. "I love you, Maggie."

"That's good, 'cause I love you too."

CHAPTER TWENTY-SIX

Sipping my coffee, I watch Gavin take on a horde of salivating, rampaging Bantou Beasts on Luna Six. As much as I love battling against him one-on-one, sometimes it's nice to sit back and watch him work his magic. I bite my tongue when he crosses to the far side of the herd. That's a sure-fire way to get stomped, but I keep quiet and watch him navigate the horde with little effort.

He glances at me when he defeats the last beast. "You thought I was going to die, didn't you?"

I shrug. "Maybe."

"I could hear you screaming at me in my mind." Gavin picks up his coffee and takes a drink.

"Oh, so you're a mind reader now?" I shove him with my foot. He sets his coffee aside and grasps my ankle in his warm hand. His fingers massage the arch and I groan.

"Yes, and if you don't wipe those dirty thoughts from your deviant brain, I'll have to carry you to the shower and wash you off." The sensual promise of those words makes me whimper.

"Am I interrupting?" Lily asks from the doorway.

"Not at all." I slide closer to Gavin and pat the couch beside me. My face heats as she rounds the coffee table. I'm one hundred percent sure she heard us just now, and I know for a fact she heard us fucking last night.

Lily curls up against the corner of the couch and cradles her coffee mug. Her hair is messy in a lopsided bun. Even fresh-faced without her trademark winged liner and red pout, she's stunning. She's wearing an oversized sweatshirt and yoga pants paired with fuzzy socks. The dark smudges beneath her eyes betray the lingering exhaustion.

"Sorry about last night." I nudge her knee with my elbow.

"It's okay." Bright red tinges her cheeks. "I'm happy you

two are back together. Even if that means I have to deal with your loud moans and endless fucking."

I stick my tongue out at her. "You're just jealous."

"Of you banging Gavin?" She scoffs. "No." A sad smile curves her lips. "But it's a vivid reminder that I'm not getting any."

"I'm sorry, Lily." I rest my hand on her knee and give it a comforting pat. "Whatever happened with that cowboy you were talking to online?"

"He's halfway across the country." She hides her face behind her mug. "As if I would hook up with a guy I've never met before."

"True. That's not your style, but it sounded like you two hit it off."

"We did." Lily sips her coffee.

Gavin pauses the game and sets aside the controller. "Did he cross the fucking line, Lily?"

"No." Her eyes widen when she shakes her head. But that tell-tale blush is back with a vengeance. "We've spoken on the phone, but it's always platonic. There's never been any talk of us meeting in person."

"Good." Gavin straightens and cracks his knuckles. "You let me know if he pushes you around."

Lily rolls her eyes. "Don't overreact, Gavin. We're both adults. I can take care of myself."

"I don't want anyone to take advantage of you." He scowls. "Sometimes you're too trusting and I'm afraid you're going to get hurt."

I rest my hand on his thigh. He's tense. I can feel it vibrating through him. The worry he's harboring for Lily. "We want to be sure you're safe."

"I can handle this." She shifts uncomfortably.

"I just don't want to see it affect your work. Remember what happened to Jen?"

"Yeah." Lily heaves a heavy sigh and pinches her eyes closed. "I know. Mr. Roberts caught me chatting on Discord and told me to keep it on my own time."

"Mr. Roberts caught you flirting with the cowboy online?" I smother my laugh behind my hand.

"Not exactly. But he reminded me to save my phone time for outside of work hours and lunch breaks."

"Isn't your boss in his fifties?" Gavin asks.

"Late forties, I think." Lily harumphs. "What does that have to do with anything?"

He pauses, almost like he's calculating in his head, before replying. "He's old enough to be your dad, Lily."

Her humor vanishes instantly. "Don't compare Mr. Roberts to my father."

"Okay. I'm sorry. I'm just pointing out the fact that he's older and he's probably looking out for your best interest because you're his employee."

"Or," I add with a devious grin. "He's secretly jealous and wants to keep you all to himself."

Lily's face goes from pink to ash white and back to flaming cherry red in the space of a breath. "Mr. Roberts is my boss. He would never—he's not like that."

"Like what, Lily?" Gavin wraps his arm around me. "Not interested in you romantically?"

"Yes." She sniffs and glances away.

"But you've thought about him, haven't you?" I fan the escaping flames.

Lily squeaks in protest, but no words come out of her mouth.

"Admit it, Lily. I hear you and Jen talk about this stone-cold silver fox all the time." Her blush deepens as I continue. "You're telling me you've never thought about him bending you over his desk and having his wicked way with you?"

"Oh, God." Lily hides her face in her hand and groans. When she finally looks up, I see the truth burning in her eyes.

"You have." I laugh. "You saucy little vixen. Do you dress up just for him?"

"I always dress up." She glares at me. "And he has never been anything but completely professional at work."

"But you want him to be *un*professional, don't you, Lily?

Admit it." I push her, enjoying the twitch of her eye when she finally realizes the precarious situation in which she finds herself. Toying on the edge of professionalism with a man in a position of power can be a heady aphrodisiac indeed.

"Fine. Okay. Yes, I want Mr. Roberts to do all kinds of deliciously naughty things to me, but that's not going to happen because I need this job!" Her eyes wild, she nearly spills her coffee. "Damn it."

"Lily. It's okay. You're normal." Gavin reassures her, giving me a squeeze as if to tell me to ease off. I relax against him.

"I'm sorry, hon." I take her hand. "I can't stand to see you all twisted up over some guy who lives in Wyoming while fighting this attraction to your boss."

"I can't help it. I'm hopeless." She slumps back against the cushions. "I like Mr. Roberts, but if I fuck this up and end up without a job because of it, I'll never hear the end of it from my father. I can't go crawling back to him. I won't."

"You're not daddy's little girl anymore, Lily. You're a successful, beautiful woman. You have nothing to prove to him." Gavin's words soothe her, and I nod in agreement with his sentiment. "If something happens, you can always come work for us."

Lily blinks twice. "What do you mean 'work for us'?"

I jab him in the ribs and he winces. "We were waiting until after my meeting on Tuesday to confirm the details, but Gavin and I are looking at starting our own business together."

"Don't you have enough side gigs, Gavin?" Lily scowls at him. "The arcade, the programming, the web merch store?"

"This would combine them all together though." Gavin's voice quivers with excitement. "We're going to call it Rebel Tech Alliance, where gaming and innovation unite."

Lily beams. "This is a big step. A merger on both fronts with a wedding and a combination of both your strengths toward a common goal. Congratulations!"

"Thanks, hon." I shiver with a mix of apprehension and excitement. "I have a meeting on Tuesday with FreeWheel Games to discuss projects and funding."

"Good luck." Lily laughs. "Not like you'll need it." Her expression sobers. "What about Solus?"

A ball of dread settles in my stomach. "Well, I'll have to make that decision when the time comes, I guess."

"I'm so proud of you." Lily's eyes fill with tears.

"Thanks." I hug her tight.

She breaks free to hug Gavin, and he kisses her cheek. "We're proud of you too."

"I didn't do anything." Lily shoves him aside. "I'm going to miss you. I would offer to let you both live here, but honestly, I don't think I could stand hearing you two banging every night." She shakes her head and a lock of blonde hair tugs free from her bun. "You're quite vocal during sex, Maggie."

Gavin's laughter echoes through the room.

"That's not a bad thing." Lily tries to clarify but ends up laughing right alongside Gavin.

"You just don't want to hear it." I cross my arms. "Yeah, I understand."

"We'll look for a place next week." Gavin sits up and wipes the tears from his eyes. "I promise we'll keep the kinky shit for when we're at her place."

"Deal." Lily takes her coffee and heads for the door. "Love you guys."

"Love you, hon." I blow her a kiss.

"Ditto," Gavin says as he picks up his controller and restarts the game.

Lily disappears into the hallway, leaving us alone once more. I settle down beside him on the couch as he selects a new battle.

Gavin hands me the controller. "Care to show me how I should have died?"

I blow a raspberry. "I'll show you how a master avoids certain death."

When the horde of Bantou Beasts charges toward me, my muscle memory clicks into action. Even as I battle, Gavin's heat sinks into my skin where we're pressed together. I'm hyper-aware of his presence.

Even though I'm invested in the game, it reinforces my

focus. We're partners. Teammates. Friends. Lovers. Competitors. Enemies. We are inseparable. With our goals in alignment, there's nothing we can't do, and I'm up for whatever challenge comes next.

CHAPTER TWENTY-SEVEN

When I arrive late to the office on Tuesday, I'm floating on air. Nothing on the entire planet could steal away the elation coursing through me. Well—*almost* nothing.

Ben's sitting in my office, and he doesn't look happy.

"Good morning, Ben." I hang up my coat and set my purse on the shelf beside my radiant violet.

"It's nearly noon, Maggie. Where the hell have you been?"

"I sent a message to you and Evan telling you I had an important meeting this morning." As I settle in my chair, I take measure of his stormy expression. "Didn't you get it?"

"Oh, I got the message." He unfolds his arms and leans forward. "I was more concerned about the fact that we had a meeting with Mr. Kennedy at eight and you weren't here."

"I informed Andrew of the necessities for that meeting on Friday." My pointed look shifts to the room beyond the window facing the rest of the office. "Did he not handle the task well?"

"He handled it just fine." Ben's scowl deepens. "But you are the office manager. It is your responsibility to make sure things are in order. Not Andrew's."

Uncertainty twists in my gut. Pushing back in my chair, I knock on the wall connecting my office to Evan's. Within the space of a heartbeat, he appears in my doorway.

"Hey, Maggie. You knocked?" Mr. Sunshine beams at me. The perfect complement to the thundercloud sitting in the chair beside him. He and Ben exchange a confused look.

"Yes, would you close the door?"

Evan pushes it closed and leans against it. "What's up?"

"I want you both to know that I will be tendering my resignation this afternoon." I ignore the way their eyes bug out of their heads and press forward. "I have enjoyed my time here at Solus and will do my part to ensure Andrew, or whomever you hire, is up to the task of running the company with the same efficiency as I was."

"You're leaving?" Evan stammers for a moment, trying to find the right words. "But why?"

Ben slowly rises to his feet and fixes his tie. He says nothing, but I can see the storm clouds forming around his head. Shit.

"I know you both sent me to the gala to represent Solus, but you also sent me at Gavin's request. Don't give me that look, Evan. I know he contacted both of you before the event."

Evan's mouth snaps shut. Ben has the good sense to look suitably chastised for his part in it.

"I'm not upset about it. I'm grateful. It presented me with an opportunity I wouldn't have had otherwise. So, thank you." I twist a pen between my fingers.

"What opportunity?" Ben asks, his brow raised in curiosity.

"Gavin asked me to marry him."

"You're going domestic?!" Evan's jaw hits the floor. "Plot twist!"

I want to smack him as much as I want to laugh. "No, he's asked me to join him in creating and promoting our own company. We pitched one of my ideas to a prominent media investor, and they're willing to fund our startup."

Ben and Evan stare at each other for a long moment before responding.

"So that's it. After ten years you're just going to pick up and leave us?" Evan pouts. "That's cold, Maggie."

"You can't guilt-trip me, Evan. It's been a good run here at Solus. I've learned a lot and I'm proud of what we've accomplished. But it's time for me to move on and chase my dream."

"And that dream is Gavin?" Ben looks skeptical.

"He's part of it, but our relationship is more than that. He's offered me a chance to build something I've wanted to create for a long time." I smile at the thought of the opportunities lying ahead. "We're partners, and I'm ready for a change of pace."

Evan stuffs his hands into his pockets. "Are you sure we can't keep you on part time? You know, until your replacement figures things out."

"I'll help in any way I can. But you can't hang on to me forever." I'm touched by their grief over my departure. "You'll be fine without me."

"I doubt it," Ben mutters under his breath. "But we'll make it work." He straightens and offers a tight smile. "I'm happy for you, Maggie. Truly. We wish you the best in your future endeavors."

"Thank you, Ben."

Evan's about to break into a hundred pieces. "Don't leave, Maggie."

"Oh, Evan. You'll be fine. We'll see each other. It's not like I'm moving across the country."

"But Ben will be miserable without you here to keep him in line." Evan nudges his best friend.

Ben rolls his eyes toward the ceiling and I can almost hear him muttering a prayer of serenity. He turns to Evan. "Just tell her you'll be happy for her and let her live her life, damn it."

Evan chuckles and turns to face me. "I am happy for you, Maggie. You deserve all the best things in life. Thanks for sticking it out with us for as long as you did. I know we aren't the easiest people to work for."

"It's been a…well, I'd say pleasure, but it was more of a steep learning curve with random moments of levity and camaraderie." I beam. "So yeah, it's been an honor."

"All right, enough of the sentimental drivel. Back to work." Ben pauses in the doorway. "Don't worry about finding a replacement. We'll take care of it. Just…don't be a stranger, okay?" He smiles, and I nearly fall out of my chair.

"Thanks." I blink twice after he leaves the office and meet Evan's sad blue eyes.

"I can't believe you're leaving us." He pouts like a two-year-old.

"Evan, don't start with me."

"I'm just teasing." He pulls me from my chair and hugs me. "We will miss you, but I'm glad you're off to find new adventures. Oh, and that you're finally getting some quality nookie on the reg."

I shove him away with a growl. "You had to ruin the moment, didn't you?"

He lifts his hands and backs away, laughing. "Always."

"Tell Gavin congrats," he calls out before leaving my office.

I glance around at the familiar space and inhale deep, trying to gather my wits. I have things to do. Once I get everything organized, I call Andrew in and show him the ropes. He can hold down the fort until Ben and Evan hire a replacement.

Andrew's disappointed as well, but I can tell he's excited at the opportunity to move up in the company. Over my last two weeks at Solus, I'll teach him all my tricks. It'll be like I never left. He grasps the opportunity with both hands.

At four-thirty, I grab my coat and my purse. The bounce in my step lingers from the meeting with Julia and Vivien this morning. They loved my Gamer Girl app and the other ideas I threw on the table. I can't wait to get home and tell Gavin about it.

When I reach the landing outside my apartment, I smell the savory aroma of sauteing veggies and roast chicken. I can't tell which apartment the temptation is coming from. Whoever's cooking, I hate them.

I swing the door open and the smell wraps around me like a loving embrace. Gavin spins around from his spot in front of the stove.

"Hey. I was just about to call you." He gestures to the table. "Dinner will be ready in five if you want to set out plates and silverware."

I drop my coat and purse on the couch before crossing the room and wrapping my arms around his waist. "I fucking love you."

Gavin chuckles. "I love you too." He kisses my head and nudges me aside so he can remove the skillet from the stovetop.

I admire his grace as he moves. "I gave my notice at Solus today."

He nearly drops the pan holding the roast chicken. "You did? How did they take it?"

"They understood. Wished me the best." I skirt around him and pull two plates from the cabinet.

"I take it that means the meeting with Julia and Vivien went well?"

"It was amazing." I grab glasses from the cupboard. "Not only do they want to fund Gamer Girl, but they want us to come up with more ideas to foster interest in gaming and innovation with computer software."

"That's amazing." He grabs me by the waist and kisses me. I melt into him. "I knew you were a genius." His words brush against my lips, and I shiver at the husky tone of his voice.

"Are you sure you want to do this?"

"Do what?"

"Marry me? Start a business together? All of it."

Gavin hooks his finger beneath my chin and our eyes lock. "Listen to me very carefully. I'm only going to say this once."

I hold my breath and my heartbeat pounds in my head.

"I. Want. You. Only you. Forever. Do you understand?"

I nod and lick my lips.

"Rebel Tech is ours. I started it for you. I want to create amazing things with you." He grips the back of my head, and I moan at the firm touch.

"If you do that again, dinner will get cold."

"Do what?" I feign ignorance, but desire courses through me. It's his fault. He wrecks every defense with a single touch.

"Moan." He leans close. His breath tickles the hair at my nape when he whispers in my ear. "I will fuck you right here. Don't tempt me."

My stomach looses a mighty growl. Gavin bursts into laughter and pulls away.

"Food first." He arches a brow with sensual promise. "Then I'll fuck you."

"Promises. Promises."

"Sit down before I change my mind."

"Yes, sir." I salute him before pulling out a chair and slumping into it.

Gavin shakes his head. "You need to learn some manners.

I mean, we can't have your new employer filing complaints with HR about your behavior."

"Good thing I'm fucking the boss then, isn't it?" I wink and pour some wine from the open bottle on the table.

His lips quirk into a lopsided smile. "The perks of being a small business owner."

"To working from home." I lift my glass.

"To the beginning of a beautiful partnership." He clinks his glass to mine.

"I'll drink to that."

After our toast, he sits down and cuts the chicken. Silence fills the space between us and I dig into my vegetables with gusto. They melt in my mouth. So delicious.

"I didn't know you enjoyed cooking."

"You never asked." Gavin chuckles and places a chicken thigh on my plate.

"Anything else I should know about?"

"Yeah, we have dinner with my parents on Saturday night. So wear something nice. Dad's taking us to Fabrizio's."

My fork clatters to the plate. "Your parents want to meet me?"

"Yeah, that's typically expected when two people get engaged." Gavin cuts his chicken breast before stabbing it with his fork. "Is there a problem with that?"

"Not at all. I just didn't think about it before." I cock my head. "What if they don't like me?"

"They'll love you."

"Does this mean I have to introduce you to my parents too?"

Gavin's laughter fills the apartment. "I mean, if you want to, that would be wonderful, but I'm not going to force you." He sobers. "Are you nervous about meeting my parents?"

"A little." I take a deep breath. "But it'll be fun. I can't wait to meet them and tell them how amazing their son is."

"Flattery don't charge these batteries, ma'am."

"You're full of shit."

"Eat your dinner, so I can have dessert." He winks and

wipes the back of his hand across his mouth.

Whatever remained of my panties is now gone, disintegrated by that feral look full of hunger and promise. Damn it. I love this man.

We finish dinner in record time. Dessert was orgasmic.

CHAPTER TWENTY-EIGHT

One month later…

Ten. That was the number of people at our wedding. Lily, Jen, and Shaun were the only friends in attendance. The rest were family. My mom, stepdad, and two brothers. Gavin's parents and his grandmother. We met outside the courthouse and the whole affair was over in ten minutes.

Everyone should get married like this. No stress. No fuss. Just two people starting fresh without fanfare. I've never been one to follow tradition, so our wedding day came as a surprise to no one. Cheers fill the air as we kiss in front of the Justice of the Peace.

Gavin helps me out of the car after the ceremony. He hired Cyril's to drive all of us into the city for the wedding reception. I stare up at the arcade building and grin.

A huge banner hangs across the front of the brick façade. *Congratulations, Maggie and Gavin!*

"Perfect touch," I compliment the brazen announcement and take Gavin's hand.

"If you like that, wait until you see the inside. Lily and Jen spent all week working on it." He opens the door for me, and the familiar sounds of pinball machines and video game intros wrap me in a warm embrace.

"I can't believe they wouldn't let me help decorate." I pout as he leads me to the stairs at the back of the room.

"They wanted it to be a surprise."

I ascend the staircase careful not to rip the hem of the gown Lily created for my special day. The vintage game print fabric was hard to find, but Lily worked her magic and created the perfect wedding dress for me in less than two weeks. She's a wizard, that's for sure.

Gavin stops at the top of the steps, his hand resting on the door handle. "Close your eyes."

I close them and a shiver of excitement wracks me. I lick my lips when I hear the door open and he ushers me inside.

Warm air brushes over my face. "Can I open them?"

"Not yet." He leads me deeper into the room and I can almost feel the anticipation ripping my heart apart. "Okay, open."

I gasp, clapping my hands over my mouth. Teal and purple balloons and streamers hang from the ceiling and along the wall. The tables have deep purple cloths. Crystal vases sit in the center of the tables filled with a variety of purple chrysanthemums, white roses, and teal tulips nestled in a base of ferns and dyed baby's breath.

A buffet table stands against the far wall where servers stand at attention. There's a small bar against the neighboring wall and a DJ, standing behind his setup playing the soft strains of 80's rock. My eyes fill with tears, but not because of the decorations or the ambiance.

No. It's the loving faces of my family and friends who fill the room that tips me over the edge. I laugh as the tears spill free.

Lily steps forward and hands me a handkerchief. "Do you like it?"

"I love it," I reply just for her. Then I turn my attention to the guests who gathered to celebrate our union. "Thank you all for coming at such short notice to celebrate our marriage." I take Gavin's hand in mine and glance up into his handsome face. "We're so happy to share this day with all of you!"

Cheers, catcalls, and shrill whistles fill the room. I laugh and cheer with them.

Gavin pulls me close, kissing me thoroughly in front of our guests.

"Get a room!" Someone yells from the back, and I bet a hundred bucks it's Evan. Laughter meets his comment.

Gavin pulls away and takes the two glasses of whiskey Shaun offers. He hands one to me and winks.

Shaun raises his drink aloft along with the rest of the guests. "To Gavin and Maggie!"

"Cheers!" The guests all counter in unison and drink their health and happiness.

"Let's get this party started!" Gavin shouts.

I hold Gavin's hand as we make our way through the crowd, greeting friends and family members. His mom kisses my cheek and compliments my gown. I tell her how wonderful her son is because it's the truth. Gavin squeezes my hand.

After the food and the pleasantries, we dance. Then we game.

No one has ever been to a wedding reception at a cabinet, or what most would call an arcade. We're so untraditional it hurts. From the moment we met, Gavin and I have turned expectations upside down. It's almost comical to see my mom trying to dance battle my stepdad. They might sprain something.

All around us, our guests are laughing, dancing, mingling, and playing games without a care. That's how life should be. Opportunities for everyone to let loose and have fun are rare if you don't make the time for them. I'm glad Gavin reminded me how precious that connection is.

After a few intense rounds of *Mortal Kombat II*, Gavin sneaks me up to the rooftop. He wraps his jacket around me as we step out into the cool October evening. The sun set long ago, and I can almost taste winter on the crisp night air.

From this height, we can see part of the cityscape with her bright lights flickering in the distance. The bustling sounds of New York City surround us, and I lean back into his warmth as he wraps his arms around me, resting his chin on my head. For several long moments, we linger wrapped up in each other.

"How did they do?" His question breaks the comfortable silence.

"Who? Lily and Jen?"

He nods.

"Amazing." I sigh. "I couldn't have done it better. In fact, I doubt I could have done it at all. Those two have a talent, that's for sure."

"You should see the cake." He chuckles. "You're going to lose your shit."

"Seriously?" I wrap my arms around his waist. "Did they put sex toys all over it or something?"

"No." His laughter reverberates off the neighboring buildings. "That's something you would do."

"Then what?"

"It's *Zelda* themed."

My eyes bug out and my jaw hits the rooftop. "No fucking way."

"Yeah, they even found a Link and Zelda cake topper." He boops my nose with his fingertip. "They certainly know you well."

They remembered. I'm going to hug those two so hard they burst. My eyes fill with tears again, and I swear under my breath.

Gavin lifts my chin until our eyes meet.

Shit. I don't think I'm ever going to get used to calling this man my husband. It feels like a dream ripped from the pages of a sappy romance novel. I love him so much that it makes my heart ache.

"I love you, wife."

It's like he can read my mind. "I think I prefer baby girl."

He laughs and hugs me tight. "Come on. I'm sure they're all looking for us."

"They probably think we snuck off for a quick fuck."

Halfway to the door, Gavin grabs my hand and slowly backs me against the brick wall beside the entrance leading inside.

"Maybe we did." His lips caress my throat and I moan. My panties are fucked. I'm not far behind.

"Gavin. The neighbors. They'll hear us." I gasp when he bites me softly. "See us." I melt against him when his hand slides along my thigh and delves between my slick folds. He teases me and I cling to his shoulders.

He groans. "I don't care."

After fumbling with his pants and hiking my skirt around my waist, he slides his cock over my pussy, coating it in my desire. Fuck the neighbors.

As if sensing my desperation, he pushes up into me. My heart and my pussy are full. When he retreats and drives deeper, my cries echo off the brick buildings surrounding us.

He takes me fast and hard. My heart thunders in my chest. I claw at his back, arching against him, needing more. Faster. Harder.

Gavin complies without relenting. He kisses me and presses his fingers to my clit. I gasp and a loud moan rips from my throat as he tips me over the edge.

His kiss swallows my keening cries of pleasure. I'm lost in the depth of it and collapse against him, weightless and sated, as he finds his release, filling me.

When he finally pulls back to look at me, he's practically glowing. Slowly, he lowers me to my feet and helps me fix my dress before he takes care of himself.

I chuckle as we try to make some semblance of order out of our chaos. "Do I look all right?"

He smirks. "You look thoroughly fucked."

"Good." I pat my hair. "I'd hate to ruin their expectations."

"Like you give a fuck what anyone thinks."

"Exactly." I wink. "Now, let's go. I need dessert after my dessert."

Gavin laughs and opens the door. "After you, my lady."

"Thank you, kind sir."

He slaps my ass as I cross the threshold. My cheeks—both sets—warm at the touch.

"Behave, baby girl."

"Never."

They say gaming has no future. I say it led me to a pretty fucking good one.

THE END

Kirsten S. Blacketer
Confessions
of a
Glamour Girl

CHAPTER ONE

First Day at Valentina's

I might as well be wearing a flashing neon sign over my head that says *New Girl.* After suppressing the urge to retreat, I take a deep breath and ignore the curious glances. Lifting my chin high, I cross the lobby, savoring the click of my kitten heels on the marble tile.

Staring is rude, but that's exactly what they're doing. Gawking. Not that I can blame them. The cherry print swing dress with the red petticoat always turns heads. Probably not the best choice for my first day working in a corporate position, but I don't care. This is me, and I refuse to dim my shine to conform to ridiculous contemporary fashion standards. I readjust the purse strap over my shoulder, cursing the soft cashmere of the bolo sweater.

A glance at the clock on the wall calms my nerves. I have fifteen minutes until I have to be on the forty-fourth floor. I skipped my morning coffee to ensure I would be on time, but the lack of caffeine has undermined my confidence.

This is my first major step toward financial independence. After five years in college and six years working at a boutique downtown, I am still dependent on my father. He has paid for everything to get me to this point. My college degree. My wardrobe. My hobbies. Everything. Hell, he owns the Brooklyn Heights brownstone where I live with my three roommates. We pay rent, but still, I have my dignity. I'm tired of being daddy's little girl, living on his charity.

Which is why I applied to Valentina's. If I want to make my mark on the fashion industry, I need to understand how it works. College didn't prepare me for that, but this will. Valentina's is the largest high-end department store in the country, and I fully intend to learn everything I can.

With a yearly salary and room to advance, this job will give me the advantage I need to break free from my father's controlling grip. He might be the most wealthy, powerful man in New York City, but he's far from generous. He never invests in anything that won't guarantee him a return. Me included. He'll be pissed when he finds out my long-term goals don't include him.

I'm relieved to see there's a café in the lobby, and I step in line behind a tall man in a dark gray suit. While I wait, I admire the expensive fabric and the custom cut of the jacket. As a designer, I take in every detail, noting the polished brown leather oxfords and expertly tailored suit. Whoever this guy is, he knows exactly what to wear to make an impression.

He steps up to the counter and orders his drink. "*Doppio.* Two sugars." The deep, confident cadence of his voice leaves me breathless. He steps to the side, glancing to the left and giving me the perfect view of his profile.

Holy shit. Silver fox alert. I'm not normally attracted to older men—unless they're Cary Grant or Gregory Peck—but dark hair threaded with silver at the temples is my kryptonite. Something inside me whimpers.

But it actually escapes my lips and he turns toward me. Oh. My. God. I look away and fidget with my purse.

"What can I get started for you, hon?" The petite barista raises a brow in question. She's kind enough to not say anything about my gaffe.

"Cappuccino with caramel drizzle, please."

She rings up my order and takes my money. I step off to the side to wait for my coffee, joining the sinful silver fox, who looks like he just stepped out of a vintage noir film set.

His attention remains on the newspaper in his hand when I stand beside him. Who is he? Does he work here? The thought of working alongside this man on a daily basis has my body thrumming. How the hell would I get any work done? I'd be distracted all the time.

The barista sets his drink on the counter and calls out his

order. I manage to tamp down my disappointment when he takes the cup and walks away.

"Cappuccino with caramel drizzle." She sets mine down on the counter. I grab it, making sure the lid is tight before I head for the elevator. I step into the full car right before the doors slide closed. When I reach for the button for the forty-fourth floor, it's already lit.

It stops a few times on the way up, and by the time we reach the thirty-second floor, there is only one other person in the car with me.

The silver fox. He's still reading his paper. I hold my breath and close my eyes.

"Please don't be on the same floor," I mutter.

"What number?"

Oh, shit. He heard me. I clear my throat and turn with a smile. "Forty-four."

He looks up from the paper and I'm pinned in place by his ice blue eyes. "Hmm. You must be the new hire." He folds the paper beneath his arm and takes a sip of his coffee.

"Yes, sir." I'm so screwed.

"What's your name?"

"Lily Astor."

His brow knits momentarily, accentuating the firm set of his jaw, but his expression quickly relaxes. "Ah, yes. Miss Astor." He holds out his hand. "Mr. Roberts."

I shake his hand. His firm grip conveys strength and confidence, and it takes all my effort to mirror it.

The elevator comes to a stop on the forty-fourth floor, and I sway at the sudden halt in motion. His hand grips my elbow, steadying me. Before I can speak, the doors slide open.

"If you will come with me, Miss Astor." He gestures for me to exit first.

I do, but the moment I'm out of the cloistered space, I step to the side and allow him to lead me down the hallway. We make our way through the maze of cubicles and hallways lined with offices. I keep my attention focused on his broad shoulders and curse myself for not looking up the staff I would be working with before I arrived.

"Good morning, Mrs. Foster." Mr. Roberts nods to the woman sitting behind a desk outside a row of large offices facing the southern tip of Manhattan.

"Good morning, Mr. Roberts."

He pushes open the door and steps into the office beyond the secretary's desk. "Come in, Miss Astor."

I nearly stumble over my heels but manage to compose myself quickly. Mrs. Foster casts me an encouraging smile before I follow him into his office. I glance at the door in passing and gasp when I see his name and the title beneath it. *Vice President.* Mr. Roberts closes the door behind me.

Oh. Sweet. Hell. I've been lusting after the vice president of the company. I take a fortifying sip of my cappuccino and hiss when it burns my lip.

"Please, sit down." He gestures to the leather chair beside his desk.

Maintaining some semblance of decorum, I gently sit on the edge of the chair, careful not to mush the crinoline skirts, and cross my ankles.

He rounds the desk and unbuttons his jacket before sitting. "Well now, Miss Astor. I have a few questions before I let you get settled in."

"Yes, sir. Of course." I clear my throat and pray my voice sounds stronger than my confidence.

He pulls a file from the corner of his desk and opens it. "It says here you have a degree in fashion design from NYU." He sets the file aside and meets my gaze with an intensity that leaves me simmering.

"Yes, sir."

"Tell me, Miss Astor." He steeples his fingers together and leans back in his chair. "Why Valentina's?"

"Valentina's is the oldest, most successful department store chain in the country. I want to learn all I can from the leader in the industry and be instrumental in reviving vintage fashion."

"Interesting." The corner of his mouth lifts, betraying his amusement. "Why work for us? With your family connections,

I'm sure you could cast your influence with a much larger shadow."

"I'm sorry?" I feign ignorance, but inside I'm cursing myself for not changing my name. Of course, they would run a background check before they hired me. My father once again asserts his influence without effort.

"Surely you don't need to work when your father is one of the wealthiest men in the country."

"In all transparency, sir, I may be the daughter of Monroe Astor, but our connection is in name alone." I straighten my shoulders and keep my jaw from trembling.

"The tabloids once painted you as a daddy's girl searching for her prince charming."

"The tabloids print lies and fabrications to suit their own ends." I pin him with a confident stare. "I am not a *daddy's girl* any more than I am a media darling. I applied to Valentina's in an effort to step out from under my father's shadow and cultivate a name for myself. Now, do you have any other questions, or may I be permitted to do the job you have hired me to do?"

"Of course, Miss Astor. Please, forgive me. I did not mean to pry into a sensitive subject." Mr. Roberts rises from his seat. "I look forward to having you on the team."

"Thank you, sir. I'm excited to be here."

He reaches the door before I can and opens it. "Mrs. Foster, will you please show Miss Astor to her desk?"

"Of course, sir."

Mr. Roberts turns to me. "If you need anything, Miss Astor," he smiles, and my heart shatters at the charm he carries with such ease, "please do not hesitate to reach out. My door is always open."

"Thank you."

Mrs. Foster leads me down the hallway, but the tension between me and Mr. Roberts remains like a nagging itch in the back of my mind. This will either be the best experience of my life or a waking nightmare.

One thing is for sure. I can't indulge in vivid fantasies about my boss. Mr. Roberts might be the modern equivalent of Cary

Grant with Paul Newman's eyes, but I can't let that distract me. His assertion about my father was accurate. I could have just batted my eyelashes and my father would have hung the moon for me. But that's not what I want.

I'll do it myself. I'll show every last one of them how tough I really am. I'm more than a rich man's daughter with a pretty face and expensive taste.

One day I'll have my own vintage line with staying power like Gucci and Versace. But it won't be my father's name they see—it'll be mine.

Lily Starling.

CHAPTER TWO

Three years later

The bright shiny future I envisioned once upon a time has taken a back seat to reality. A glance at the clock on my screen tells me it's almost four thirty.

A shadow falls over my desk, and I look up in time to see Mr. Roberts walk past. He nods to me in greeting and my heart flutters. I smile. Once he disappears down the hall, I exhale and press my hand to my chest.

Even after three years working at Valentina's, I still get flustered when I see him. He's gotten hotter if that's physically possible. I'm half convinced he's a time traveler from the Golden Age of Hollywood.

I shake the fantasies from my mind and focus on finishing the spreadsheet entry before saving and closing the file. As I gather my items together, I catch sight of Jen talking to Shaun, the newest member of the marketing team. Those two make such a cute couple.

My heart aches at the sight. Even though I'm happy for Jen, I can't help but feel a twinge of jealousy. Not that I need a man. I don't. But seeing love blossom around me leaves a sinking feeling in the pit of my stomach.

Three years at Valentina's, and I have nothing to show for it. My career hasn't taken off like I hoped it would. I'm still in the same position I was when I started. Even though there have been opportunities for advancement, I've fallen into a comfortable rut. The only goal I've achieved is financial independence from my father.

Part of my fear might be because climbing the ladder would put me in direct daily contact with Mr. Roberts, and I'm not sure if I can handle that kind of pressure. Not unless I can get over this infernal crush. I want to impress him. I want him to like me. But worse, I want way more than that.

I want him to tell me I'm a *good girl.*

Oh, God. What the hell is wrong with me? I do not need his praise. Just because I have issues with my father doesn't mean I should go running to the nearest authority figure and beg for tiny scraps of affirmation.

I should be pouring all my focus on the sketches for my winter line and creating the sample dresses. My goals haven't changed. But this job has certainly commandeered a lot of my creative time.

My coworkers slowly filter from the office. I stand and grab my coat from the wall rack.

"Miss Astor, might I have a word?" Mr. Robert's voice cuts through the silence behind me.

I jump and spin around. "Yes, of course, sir."

The office is empty except for the two of us. I drape my coat over my arm and smile, waiting for him to continue. Desire skims over me, but I shake it free. Focus.

He shoves his hands in his pockets and regards me carefully. His suit jacket is gone. The sleeves of his dress shirt are rolled up to his elbows. My mouth waters at the veins trailing beneath his muscular forearms. I redirect my attention to his handsome face, but that does nothing to aid my distress.

"You've been working hard over these past three years, Miss Astor." He smiles. "I commend your attention to detail and dedication to the company."

"Thank you, sir." My face warms at his praise. Shit, I shouldn't be enjoying that anywhere near as much as I do.

"I was wondering if you would be interested in taking on a special project for the Christmas season."

Mental math is not my strong suit, but Christmas isn't for, what, another seven months? He continues as if reading my mind. "I realize this may seem premature, but I wanted to be sure you had all the time necessary to complete the project."

"What did you have in mind, sir?"

"Mrs. Bradshaw has expressed an interest in adjusting the

holiday marketing plan for the year." He rubs his jaw and grins. "I was hoping you might have some creative ideas to contribute."

"The holiday marketing? That's not exactly my specialty, sir."

"No, but I feel you have the creativity to contribute some ideas." He raises a brow. "Are you interested?"

"Of course!"

"Very good." His smile rewards my enthusiasm. "I'll send you the details in an email, and we can get started on Monday."

"Thank you, Mr. Roberts." I reach out my hand.

He shakes it. Warmth engulfs me, and the desire rekindles into a flickering flame.

"Have a good weekend, Miss Astor."

"You as well, sir."

It's not until he steps out of sight that I'm able to move again. As if in a trance, I pull on my jacket and grab my purse from beneath my desk. What just happened? Why would he ask me to work on this project when he has a whole crew of marketing experts on the floor below ours? Part of me wants to ask Shaun, but since Mr. Roberts didn't mention his name specifically, I don't want to bring it up.

Somehow I manage to make it to the subway and across town without incident. I unlock the front door and step over the threshold of the brownstone.

"Lily?" One of them shouts from the living room.

"Yeah!" I call back.

"Come on!" I hear James protesting and shake my head.

I lean against the doorway and stare at the three grown-ass men I share a house with. "Is this all you guys do all day?"

"No." Gavin glances up from his laptop.

James and Michael shove each other as their avatars battle on the 80-inch screen. I roll my eyes. *Gamers*. I'll never understand the fascination with virtual reality.

Gavin sets his laptop aside and stands. He's so damn tall. Gone is the lanky teenage boy I met in seventh grade. He's filled out in every way. Handsome and charming, his computer skills are the cherry on top. He flicks the curl on my shoulder as he passes.

"How was work, hon?"

"It was fine." I follow him down the hall toward the kitchen, peeling my coat off as I walk. Leaning against the archway leading into the kitchen, I watch him retrieve a bottle of water from the fridge. "Mr. Roberts asked me to work on a special project."

Gavin straightens and arches a brow. His Shemar Moore smolder game is strong lately. I keep hoping Maggie will snatch him up before someone else does. Those two deserve each other.

"Like a special project or a *special project.*" He winks for emphasis.

"Seriously?" I stumble into the kitchen and sit on the bar stool at the island counter. "In three years, he has never once made an inappropriate comment or sexual innuendo." I scoff. "He's far too professional to indulge in an office flirtation."

"Don't sound disappointed or anything." Gavin takes a sip of water to wash down the sarcasm.

I stick out my tongue.

He chuckles and sets the bottle aside. "Listen, Lily. I've known you for years. You're the sweet girl next door, even though we both know you'd absolutely wreck someone if they fucked with you."

"Or someone I know." I blow him a kiss.

Gavin rolls his eyes at the reminder. "True. But still, when people look at you, they're not going to see your fierce inner tiger. They see the cute little kitten."

I wrinkle my nose at his assessment, but deep down, I know he's right. "But this is *me.* I'm not changing how I look on the outside to match how I feel on the inside."

"No one is asking you to change, Lily." He rests his hand on mine. "We just want to make sure you're safe and loved."

My heart warms at his words. "Thanks, Gav. I just..." I groan and bite my lip. "I spent my whole life being daddy's little girl, and the moment I have the opportunity to break free, I end up stuck in a rut."

"I'm proud of you for breaking free from your dad, but Lily, give yourself a break. You don't become a rich, famous designer overnight. It takes time."

"You're right. I know you're right." I nod and return his warm smile. "Maybe this project is just what I need to show Mr. Roberts my potential."

"It could be a great opportunity for that." He smirks. "Or it's an excuse to get you alone so he can show you all those erotic fantasies he's been having about you."

"Don't even joke about that." It's like he can see inside my darkest desires.

"It's what you want, isn't it?" Gavin's soft laughter makes me squirm. Why does he have to be so damn observant?

"That's not the point."

"That's exactly the point, sweetheart." He leans closer. "You want him to take you into his office and bend you over his big desk..."

"Gavin!" My cheeks flame hot. "Don't give it a voice. If you put it in the universe, then it'll ruin everything."

"Will it?" He grins and takes another drink.

His words take root in my mind. Thoughts of Mr. Roberts fill my brain, and my imagination runs free. His deep voice telling me to bend over. The splay of his large hands across my bare ass. Oh, shit. No. I need to stop this.

"I forgot to tell you." Gavin interrupts my train of thought completely derailing it.

"What?"

"I finished your site." He motions for me to follow him. "Come here."

"Wait, my designer site?" It takes a few seconds for my brain to shift gears from fantasyland to reality.

"Yeah." He climbs the stairs and I follow him into his room. Gavin sits at his desktop and brings up a website. "Here, check it out." He stands and offers me his chair.

I sit down and take the mouse in my hand. The website on the screen calls to me. The vintage fonts with chrome and deep jewel tones combine in a magical portal transporting me back to the 1950s. At the top of the screen is a header with the name of the site.

The Victory Vixen
featuring the original styles of
Lily Starling

Tears fill my eyes as I scroll through the page and click on the links. Images of my designs and previous collections pop on the screen.

"How does it look?"

I turn to face him and wipe the tears away. "It looks amazing."

He looks concerned for a moment but grins at the compliment. "Take some time to go through it and let me know if you want any changes made."

I launch myself off the chair and into his arms. He hugs me tight and I bask in the comfort of his hold.

"Thank you, Gavin." I kiss his cheek, leaving red lipstick smeared on his skin.

"Anything for you." He presses a kiss to my forehead. "One day you're gonna be famous. Just wait."

That's the problem. I've been waiting. Maybe it's time I take some action. I may look like a daddy's girl, but they have no idea how hungry this tigress really is.

CHAPTER THREE

I'm not drunk. Fuzzy and feeling good, but not wasted. The scowl on Maggie's face tells me she disagrees completely. I giggle at the cards in my hand and take another sip of sangria.

I'm in complete control of my faculties. Why is she being such a downer anyway? This is supposed to be a fun night playing inappropriate card games with friends.

After my conversation with Gavin last night, I feel better. More confident. Back on track. The website certainly helped bolster my determination. But still, the uncertainty lingers in the back of my mind. Damn that imposter syndrome.

Tonight, I'm not worrying about Valentina's, the website, my goals, or the sinful Mr. Roberts. I'm going to enjoy time with my friends and drink my delicious sangria.

Jen's distracted by something on her phone, and Gavin gives her a nudge with his elbow. "Jen. You're up."

"Oh, yeah." She sets the phone aside.

"Who's got you so distracted?" Maggie teases her. "We know it's not Shaun. That's why I made him sit over here instead of beside you."

"Ya gotta keep 'em separated." The words burst from my lips without thought and I giggle at the connection. Both Jen and Maggie eye me suspiciously before glancing at the half-empty glass in my hand.

Gavin's close to laughing. Shaun's trying hard not to break. His shoulders shake as he hides his face behind his cards.

"Who's blowing up your phone?" Maggie launches into her inquisition.

"No one." Jen's face turns bright red.

Maggie snatches the phone from her grasp and reads the notifications. "Oh...and who is Madre?"

The name rings a bell. "Isn't she the moderator of the *Space*

Vendetta blog you emailed a few months ago?"

"Yeah." Jen picks at the table cloth. "We chat once in a while."

"There's like twenty missed messages here," Maggie says.

"You're into *Space Vendetta*?" Gavin commandeers the direction of the conversation.

"Yeah. I mean, not deep into it, but I enjoy the films." Jen points to her boyfriend, who's sitting beside me. "Shaun's read the books."

"Have you played the video game based on the series?" Gavin has successfully distracted Maggie, which is no easy feat.

"There's a game?" Jen glances at Shaun.

"Yeah. PlayStation, I think. I never got into it, but it's supposed to be good." Shaun flexes the cards in his hand.

"Can we get back to this Madre person?" Maggie interjects with a frown.

"What about her?" Jen tries to play it off, but she's fidgeting. Maggie's like a dog with a bone when she's worried.

"Honey. You're spending an awful lot of time chatting online with someone you never met. Do you need an intervention?" Maggie's half-serious. We've been friends long enough for me to recognize that tone.

Jen laughs. "Come on, Maggie. Like none of you have ever had extended conversations with someone on the internet." She fixes each of us with a stare. I bite my lip, guilty. "Exactly. This is the digital age."

"Just be careful, okay." Maggie returns her phone. "It's easy to get caught up in the online drama."

"Thanks for the warning, but I got this covered." Jen doesn't look convinced, but Maggie lets it slide.

"What app do you use to chat?" Gavin asks.

"We started on Tumblr and then moved to Twitter." Jen puts her phone away.

"You should try Discord. All the gamers use it. There are groups for everything on there. It's like Reddit, but more conversation-friendly." Gavin taps his fingers on his glass before taking a drink.

"Thanks. Now, can we get back to the game?" Jen shakes it off with a nervous smile.

"Yes, please." I shift in my chair eager to divert our attention to more neutral ground.

"You're cut off." Maggie removes the glass from my hand. "Drink some water."

I stick out my tongue. She's definitely in mom mode today. I frown and cross my arms.

"Okay, children," Jen interjects. "There's one *blank* in the *blank*. Make it count."

Shifting through my cards, I select two that fit the category, but they're not really funny. I lay down my cards.

When did game night turn into a lecture on internet safety? I know Jen's struggling with finding a balance with her newfound obsession and her handsome boyfriend. Shaun's a great guy, and she's lucky she found someone who understands her little crush. I hope she sees it too.

Gavin's watching Maggie over the top of his cards. The tension is thick between these two. After her little victory dance the first night they met, I'm stunned Gavin's even willing to play a card game against her. But the way he's eyeing her across the table, I'm willing to bet he's imagining that dance going in a very different direction. Those two have more in common than they're willing to admit.

It always feels like I'm the odd one out. Aside from the people in this room, I really don't have any other friends. Growing up the way I did, I avoided making friends. At first, people seemed sincere, but once they found out who my dad was, they only wanted what I could get them. Money is a powerful motivator.

Maybe I should find an online group to join. A place where I could be anonymous and build some networking for my clothing line. The internet is the one place I can be myself without having to confess my connection to Monroe Astor.

"Really?" Jen laughs. "There's one *Sugar Daddy* in the *Space Vendetta Universe*." She slams the cards face up on the table. "Who had these? You win, hands down."

"That'd be me." Gavin takes the cards. "Thank you."

"Are you serious?" Maggie gapes at him and pouts. "Mine was better."

"Sugar daddy?" I repeat the phrase and scrunch my nose up. "What the hell is a sugar daddy?"

Everyone at the table turns to stare at me. I slide deeper into my chair.

"Are you serious, Lily?" Gavin's lopsided smile does nothing to soothe my rising irritation.

"Why would I ask if I knew what it meant?" Maybe I should know what it means, but I'm not up to date on current trends and slang. I stick to what I know. Designing clothes, fashion, and all things vintage.

"A sugar daddy is a rich man who's typically older and likes to spoil a younger woman by buying her things and giving her spending cash." Jen clarifies when no one else replies.

"Oh." Well, that's definitely not what I was expecting. The idea leaves a sour taste in my mouth. Sounds far too much like a spoiled rich girl who gets everything she wants from her actual father.

"I'll be right back." Maggie clears her throat and retreats from the room.

I seize the opportunity to stretch my legs and grab a glass of water from the kitchen. Unsteadily, I rise to my feet and slip through the pocket doors leading to the kitchen.

Maggie's there with two glasses of water in her hands. I take one and sip it at her insistence. When I ask if there's something going on between her and Gavin, she bristles and evades my question in all her defensive splendor. It hurts because I only want what's best for both of them. If that means they should be together, then so be it. But she's adamant there's nothing there. Conversation over.

We return to the dining room and the game continues, but my mind is still bothered by this whole *sugar daddy* thing. Later that night, after we've cleaned up and Shaun, Jen, and Maggie have left, I retreat to my room and grab my laptop.

I open a search for design groups and find a few on Reddit.

There are a few on Discord too. I remember Gavin mentioning it during the game, so I create a new account using my designer name, Lily Starling. This is my first foray into creating an online presence, so I want to be as professional as possible. I also set up a Twitter account and link my Instagram to my Lily Starling Facebook page.

The alcohol has long since dissipated from my system thanks to Momma Maggie cutting me off, but I'll thank her in the morning. Hangovers in my thirties are worse than they were in my twenties.

I request to join a few Discord servers dedicated to pin-up style and vintage design. Thank God for the internet. All the networking I could ever want at my fingertips.

Curiosity burns in the back of my mind. I open a new window and search the term *sugar daddy*. My eyes widen at the results as I scroll through the countless pages. Now I know why it was funny when Gavin laid down that combination of cards. I curse my ignorance.

The thought of an older man giving me money leaves me in a cold sweat. I hated being tied to my father financially, but the idea of tying myself to a stranger in such a way leaves me nauseated. Then I see it.

Oh, damn. It's a sexual thing? I slam the laptop closed and toss it aside. That's a big ol' nope for me.

I grab my towel and head to the shower determined to wash the ick off after uncovering a kink I didn't even realize existed in the world. It might be something other people enjoy, but not me.

As I step beneath the hot spray, my thoughts swirl in a kaleidoscope of color and possibilities. If I can get my social media accounts running, it will push traffic to my website. I need to make some notes on content and scheduling, but if I pour a little effort into it now, I should start seeing growth over the summer. Of course, it will take time. I might be able to steal a few moments at work during my breaks to make posts and updates. That would leave my nights and weekends open to the actual design and creation process.

Unbidden, an image of Mr. Roberts pops into my mind. I

brace my hand against the wall and close my eyes. What happens if Mr. Roberts catches me working on my little side project while I'm on the clock? I can almost imagine his look of disappointment. Isn't it bad enough he torments me with his presence? Now he shoves his disapproving scowl into my personal thoughts.

Even though I want to banish him, I allow his image to linger a moment longer. From the first moment I met him, there was a gravitational shift in his direction. Perhaps it was fate that led me to this specific position under his watchful eye.

When Jen and Shaun started dating, it ignited hope. Dating a coworker was typically frowned upon, but Mr. Roberts seemed unbothered by their relationship, so long as it remained professional during work hours. When Jen told me about it, I nearly fell off my chair.

Not that it mattered, of course. Mr. Roberts never mixed business with pleasure. His personal life remained enshrouded in secrecy. He never spoke of his life outside the office. No one knew him outside the office and why would they? He's the vice president. Aloft and untouchable.

With a sigh, I turn off the shower, wrap up in a towel, and retreat to my room. I throw on a pair of comfy silk pajamas and slide into bed to download the Discord app. Once I log in, I set the phone aside to charge. I'll begin networking in the morning.

Mr. Roberts haunts my dreams in black and white.

CHAPTER FOUR

"You did what?" Jen whips around and stares at me. Her voice echoes through the room, catching the attention of several of our coworkers.

"Shhh." I hush her and lean closer. "After you guys left on Saturday, I got an idea to boost my new website through social media. I signed up for Discord and joined a few vintage designer groups."

"Why?"

"You know, networking." I smooth my hands over my skirt and fidget with the pleats running along my thigh. "I have no idea what I'm doing. I need to find other designers who are open-minded and driven to get me back on track."

"Makes sense." Jen nods. "Have you met anyone yet?"

"Not really. I mean, I was accepted into a group yesterday and introduced myself, but I haven't really put myself out there yet." I pout. "And no one has responded."

"What's the Discord group called?"

"Vintage Pin-Up Designers. It's not a catchy title, but they seem legit."

"Ladies, please continue your conversation during your lunch break." Mr. Robert's voice echoes behind me.

A bolt of equal parts fear and need shoots through me. I straighten and turn to face him. His blue eyes steal my breath.

"Yes, sir." I duck my head and skirt around him. Safely seated behind my desk, I glance at Jen whose wide eyes follow Mr. Roberts as he heads down the hallway toward his office. She meets my gaze. I offer a smile, which she returns, but deep inside, guilt tugs at me.

I dislike being on the receiving end of Mr. Roberts chastisements. The people pleaser part of me kicks into high gear when there's even a remote chance I've disappointed someone.

It does nothing for my mental health. My therapist tells me I should work on finding balance and accept my mistakes, but I can't ignore the fear that I've done irreparable damage to my relationship with the person I've failed. Obviously, I need to work on my boundaries and accept the reality that not everyone will like me.

Shaking the worrisome thoughts from my mind, I return my attention to the computer screen where I have the spreadsheets open for Valentina's monthly orders. By the time lunch rolls around, I've successfully pushed the incident from my mind.

Jen and I grab something from the café downstairs in the lobby. She's in full support of my new endeavor, but I can tell she doesn't truly understand the depth of my passion and my drive to make it a reality. We're still relatively new friends, and she doesn't know a lot about my past. I think she still operates under the impression I was born and raised in Brooklyn. I don't have the heart to correct her assumption. Honestly, I like the status of our friendship without my father's presence hovering like a ghost over my shoulder.

When I return to my desk, I check my new social media accounts. There's not a lot of content to entice interaction yet, and it'll take time to build a following. After a quick glance around the room, I open Discord.

There are a few comments under my introduction post. Most are individuals welcoming me to the group and asking simple questions. I skim through them and respond quickly. Another message pops up in response to mine.

Vintage Cowboy. Images of a sexy, shirtless cowboy slick with sweat pop into my mind. Holy shit. I shake the thought from my mind and glance at the icon by his name. A man with a hat pulled low to cover his face.

Vintage Cowboy: I'm new here too. Do you have a website for your designs?

I bite my lip and type out a quick response. The rules of the group specifically say no marketing to other group members, but it didn't say anything about private messages. As long as I don't give him a bunch of personal information, I'm safe. That's how the internet works, isn't it?

I open a private message to the mysterious cowboy. *Yes, I do. Here's the link if you want to check it out. Are you a designer?*

My toe taps nervously as I set my phone next to my keyboard. I see the icon. He's responding. When it pops up on my screen, I suppress my excitement and pretend to read the document beside my phone.

VintageCowboy: Not a designer. I'm more of a scout. I look for designers with talent.

He sounds fishy. I scrunch up my nose and close the app. Maybe Maggie was right, the internet can be a dangerous place. I ignore the urge to make a snarky comment and block him. What if he's telling the truth? I groan and indecision fills me.

The phone at my desk rings, interrupting my thoughts.

"Miss Astor, would you please join me in the conference room?" Mr. Roberts brings me back to reality.

"Yes, sir." I hang up the phone. Shit. In all the chaos of the weekend, I completely forgot about this special project he wants me to help with.

Frantic, I grab my notebook, a pen, and my phone and scurry toward the conference room.

Mr. Roberts glances up from the paper he's reading at the head of the table. "Please, join me." He gestures to the seat next to him.

His scent surrounds me as I slide into the chair beside his. The warmth of his body combines with the cologne he's wearing, and I'm transported to the first day we met. Trapped in the elevator, praying we weren't working on the same floor.

I set my stuff on the table, resting my phone on top of the purple notebook. Self-consciously, I straighten my skirt and brush my hair over my shoulders.

A squeak escapes me when Mr. Roberts grabs the armrest of the rolling chair and pulls it closer to his. His fingertips brush my elbow.

Startled, and a bit shaken by his proximity, I bite my lip to keep from speaking first and saying something ridiculously stupid.

"Now then. That's better." He gestures to the files on the table. "These are the records of every holiday promotion we've run over the past twenty years. I need a fresh perspective on the upcoming holiday season promotional campaign."

"You have an entire department dedicated to marketing and design. Why ask me to work on it?"

Mr. Roberts leans back in his chair and strokes his jaw. "You have a distinct flair for style, Miss Astor. While everyone flocks toward the popular and safe, you march to the beat of your own drum." A smile splits his lips. "I admire your confidence."

Heat spreads across my cheeks and I am unable to maintain eye contact. "I appreciate the compliment, sir, but it doesn't explain why you want me to take on such an important project."

His low chuckle fills me with desire. "Allow me to elaborate, Miss Astor." He leans forward. "I have chosen you for this task because you are the only person in this company who can bring my vision to life."

My heart stops. Words fail me. Before I can attempt to wrangle my brain into motion, he pulls a file off the top of the pile and removes the paper tucked inside.

"When Valentina's first opened, it was the epitome of modern fashion."

I take the paper and glance down at it. It's a photograph of a woman wearing a 1950s evening gown with a fur stole wrap. "This is a vintage holiday ad for Valentina's." Slowly, his vision becomes clear. "You want me to recreate a vintage holiday."

"Very good, Miss Astor," he replies. "Do I have your undivided attention now?"

The silken tone of his voice slides across my skin, wrapping me in a comforting embrace. I ignore the suggestive meaning I've gleaned from his words and smile. "You had me at vintage."

His eyes sparkle. "Shall I show you some of my ideas?"

"Yes." I lean closer and his shirt brushes my bare arm as he opens his notebook. Following his lead, I open mine and pick up my pen.

He launches into a brief summary of his vision for the holiday season promotional. It's glorious but vague. He's a big picture person. After a few minutes, I realize he needs me to be his compliment and focus on the details to bring the whole project together with a bright red bow.

I scribble notes as he speaks, being sure to ask questions and clarify any details before jotting them down. After an hour, he finally draws a deep breath and relaxes in his chair.

"If there is anything you require for the project, please don't hesitate to ask. I'm more than happy to help." He tugs at his tie, loosening it a fraction.

The action leaves me breathless. "Of course, sir." I clear my throat and gather the files into a pile. "Would it be possible to gather some of the original documentation for the early ads you wish to emulate in this project?" I point to the photo he showed me earlier of the woman in the red evening gown. "Like this."

Mr. Roberts nods. "I'll see what I can find. It was difficult to come up with this one." He sighs and rakes his hand through his perfect hair, mussing it. "It seems there was a fire in the seventies that destroyed a lot of the files. A shame, truly, to lose so much of the company's history."

"There must be an online archive of the information somewhere. Not the originals, unfortunately, but collectors and such who have gathered items from the company over the years."

"Clever girl." He slowly stands. "I knew you were the right candidate to take charge of this project."

My confidence soars at his praise. Why does that feel so damn good? I rise to my feet and gather the files into a large pile. He pushes my hand away.

"Allow me." He gathers the stack of files and lifts it with ease. "After you, Miss Astor."

He follows me down the hall to my desk and deposits the stack neatly beside my computer.

"Thank you." I glance around and notice my colleagues have disappeared. "What time is it?"

"Five o'clock." He shoves his hands in his pockets. "My

apologies, I must have lost track of time." Concern furrows his brow. "I didn't mean to keep you this late. I'm sure your boyfriend will be concerned."

I nearly choke. "No need to apologize, sir. My roommates won't be concerned at my absence."

He lifts a brow but says nothing in response to my assertion. "Shall we meet once a month to discuss your progress?"

"That sounds good." I retrieve my purse from beneath my desk and pull my coat from the hook on the wall. "I look forward to working with you."

"Likewise, Miss Astor." Mr. Roberts turns to leave. "Goodnight."

"Goodnight, sir."

He vanishes down the hallway and I retreat in the opposite direction. Inside the elevator, I lean against the wall and take several steadying breaths. Finally some momentum. First with the website and my designs, and now this project to give me the experience I've been waiting for. Things are looking up. And working directly with the boss is a bright red cherry on top.

On the subway, I open Discord and check for any updates. There's an unread message from *Vintage Cowboy*. I take a deep breath and click it.

VintageCowboy: I promise I'm not lurking to try and steal your identity or lure you into something nefarious. Your designs are unique and refreshing. I'm genuinely curious. Where do you draw your inspiration?

I close the app when the train comes to a stop. When I get home, I make my way upstairs to change. My gaze lingers on the phone sitting on my desk. Should I respond?

It's an innocent conversation, right?

Once I pull on my lounge pants and shirt, I grab the phone and type out a response.

Curiosity killed the cat, sir. I shall sate it only if you agree to answer my questions in return. My inspiration comes from old Hollywood glamour and pin-up couture. Now, it's your turn. What is a cowboy really doing in a retro fashion design group?

I tuck the phone into my pocket and retreat downstairs to make dinner. I'm starving, and unfortunately, food isn't the only thing I find I have a hunger for.

CHAPTER FIVE

"Seriously, I'm over him." Jen hands me a tray of cookies to set on the coffee table. "We can watch whatever you guys want."

"Are you sure?" I snag a chocolate chip cookie off the top of the pile and set the tray down. "I mean, it was only a few weeks ago we had to stage an intervention for your villain obsession."

This summer has been a hell of an adventure. Not only did Jen tumble down the rabbit hole and nearly lose her job—and her boyfriend—over her fangirl obsession with an actor, but Maggie has been keeping her cards close when it comes to her newfound flirtation. She hasn't even told us she's seeing someone, but I can tell by the dewy shine radiating from within that she's getting laid on the regular. She hasn't mentioned it yet, but I know. Not only do I know she's getting some, I know who she's getting it from. Doesn't take a rocket scientist to figure out that my best friend is sleeping with my roommate.

"Yeah, I know." Jen's face turns pink at the reminder. "I appreciate you guys stepping in and helping me through that whole mess. I couldn't have done it without your support."

"Sometimes we all need a wake-up call." Maggie flops down on the couch and grabs a cookie. "Are you and Shaun getting serious yet?"

"Yeah." She grabs the remote and turns on the television. "I mean, I could definitely see myself with him forever."

"Ooh, maybe he'll propose soon! Wouldn't that be fun?" My heart swells at the thought. "You could have a Christmas wedding."

Jen laughs. "That might be too soon. I'm thinking spring might be better for everyone involved." She takes a cookie. "My mom asked me to wait until May."

"That would be a great time for a wedding." I nibble on my

treat. "If you need any help planning, let me know. I can make a few calls."

"Thanks, Lily. I may take you up on that—*if* he proposes." Jen selects the streaming service. "Oh, that reminds me. How's work since you took over the account I fucked up?"

"You didn't fuck it up." I wave my hand in a halfhearted attempt to brush it off. "I was able to get it straightened out. Mr. Roberts assured me there was no harm done. He was more concerned about you."

Her face turns red again. "I feel like such an ass failing like that. I'm sure he thinks I'm a complete slacker."

I shake my head. "Not at all. He speaks quite highly of you."

Over the last few months, I've been working closely with Mr. Roberts on the holiday promotion. Taking on Jen's neglected account added to my workload, but Mr. Roberts assured me there was no expectation to continue if I wasn't able to handle it.

Truth is, I can handle it because I don't have anything other than my designer dreams to occupy my time. Even with the launch of the website and my social media for the label, it's been a slow grow to gain traction. I really need to do more research on marketing and find those niche groups who want the designs I have to offer.

I heave a heavy sigh. Between my friends and Mr. Roberts, I really don't speak to anyone. Well, not including *Vintage Cowboy* on Discord. But his messages are sporadic and he still hasn't told me much about himself.

"You've been spending a lot of one-on-one time with Mr. Roberts lately," Maggie says with a wink to Jen. "You sure there's nothing funny going on behind his closed office doors?"

Her comment pulls me from my thoughts. "What? No." I shake my head vehemently.

"Maybe there should be." Jen grins. "He's hot, and we know he's not totally against workplace relationships."

"He may have supported you and Shaun." I pick at the lint on my sweater. "But he's far too professional to indulge in something like an office romance."

"Office romance?" Maggie snickers. "You've been reading far too many of those racy paperbacks again."

"Don't you dare attack my romance novels." I scowl at her. "Just because you like to wallow in your misery doesn't mean the rest of us do. We all need a little escape. You have your games. I have my novels."

"Does Mr. Roberts know you read those on your lunch break?" Maggie teases me.

"He's asked her what she's reading," Jen adds with a chuckle. "She doesn't even bother to hide the covers anymore."

"I'm not embarrassed by my selection of reading material. I'm an adult and I enjoy love stories with high heat. Sue me." I stick out my tongue and cross my arms.

"Maybe he's trying to see what you're into."

"Whatever."

"We're just teasing you, Lily." Jen rests her hand on my knee. "We love you and want you to find someone who will take good care of you." She winks. "You should put yourself out there. Maybe you'll meet someone who has similar interests."

I bite my tongue to keep from mentioning *Vintage Cowboy*. We haven't spoken a lot, but there's something about his messages that have me hooked. He seems honest and sweet, but I haven't really pushed beyond general conversation to get to know him more. Maybe I should. But I can't tell Jen and Maggie about him. Not yet.

"I don't need a man to make me happy." I pull a pillow into my lap and hug it. "Life is good."

Maggie nods. "Okay, movie time."

"Oh, let's watch a western."

"Lily, you and your cowboy kink." Jen chuckles and shakes her head. "Fine. A western it is. How about Clint Eastwood?"

"Yes, please." I lick my lips.

"Not only does she like cowboys, she likes older men." Maggie howls. "Maybe you should just ask Mr. Roberts out. I bet he'd wear a cowboy hat if you asked him."

The thought of Mr. Roberts in a cowboy hat, jeans, a button-down flannel, and cowboy boots has my mouth watering.

Oh, God. That image is burned into my mind. My face heats but I refrain from fanning myself.

"I think she likes the idea." Jen nods toward me.

"Just start the movie." I gesture to the screen where Clint in a cowboy hat is looking like a goddamn three-course meal.

Later that night after I get home and take a shower, I'm still thinking about the conversation with the girls. Maybe they're right. I can't keep daydreaming about a man who doesn't exist. Jen has Shaun. Maggie has Gavin. And me? Well, I don't have anyone.

Lying in bed, I unlock my phone and open Discord. *Vintage Cowboy* hasn't messaged me in a week. I scroll through our past conversations and smile. He asked a lot about me, but I don't see much about him.

Are you sleeping? I send the message.

No. His response came through almost immediately. *I was thinking about you.*

My heart warms and I bite my lip. This feels weird. *Are you really a cowboy?*

Yes, ma'am. He replies. *I own a small ranch in Wyoming.*

Pictures? I hit send and then realize I didn't specify what I wanted pictures of. Before I can clarify, two photos appear. One is of a log cabin with pine trees and mountains far off in the distance. The other is of the rolling flat plains and the sun setting on the horizon. Both make me smile.

Does this satisfy your curiosity? His message makes me laugh.

It looks like heaven. It must be lovely to live there. Are the winters harsh? I chew on my fingernail while he types out a response.

Winters can be harsh, but they're lovely. The perfect time to curl up with a good book and a warm woman. He adds a winking emoji. Is he flirting with me?

Sounds wonderful. Your wife is a lucky woman. This could be a bad idea, but I follow the trail nonetheless.

If I had one, she would be. He's still typing so I wait before responding. The words glare at me from the screen in bright neon green. *Do you have someone to keep you warm?*

Oh, this is dangerous territory. As sweet as he is, he's still a stranger. Granted, he's never made any perverted or overt sexual gestures before and we've been talking on and off for a few months now. He's harmless—isn't he? Maggie would have a fit if she knew.

No. I send it and wonder what the hell I'm doing. I'm playing with fire. Every warning bell in my head is ringing, and I don't care. The soothing image of his cabin and the wide-open space on his ranch has my imagination running wild. I want to know more. More about him. His hopes, his dreams, his goals.

He told me his sister was a fashionista. It's how he got interested in scouting for new designers. He helped his sister find her footing and wanted to do the same for other new designers. With every conversation, my heart and my curiosity get the better of me.

Lily, I like talking with you, but my penchant for being direct sometimes gets the better of me. If I ever make you uncomfortable, tell me.

I read the words several times before I respond. He seems sincere. Even if nothing comes of this, whatever this is, then it won't matter because he doesn't know my name or any details about my personal life. I may be a little reckless, but I'm not irresponsible.

Okay. Butterflies take flight in my stomach as I work up my courage. *Can I ask you one favor?*

Whatever you want, sweetheart.

Can you send a photo of yourself? I'm curious to see if it fits what I see in my head.

A few tense minutes pass and I worry I crossed a line. Then an image appears. A man wearing a dusty brown cowboy hat pulled low concealing his face. His gloved hand holds the corner of the hat, and a blue work shirt pulls tight across his broad chest. I recognize the faint glimmer of a belt buckle at the bottom of the photograph. He's strong. Work worn and tough. He deliberately left off his face. Smart man. I chuckle.

Tease. Giving me a glimpse, but not the whole picture. I wait for his response.

Well, I didn't want to scare you off with my haggard face.

I doubt it would scare me. Do you look like Clint Eastwood in Hang 'em High?

Ahhh, so you have an affinity for middle-aged cowboys? Maybe there is hope for me after all.

I laugh and snuggle deeper beneath my blankets. Talking with him is refreshing. *Maybe. Perhaps I'll send you a picture in return.*

I would love that, but there's no pressure to send me a picture if it makes you uncomfortable.

He truly is a gentleman. I smile fondly and tell him goodnight. When sleep does come, it's Clint who greets me in my dreams, wearing a dusty brown hat and a blue shirt.

CHAPTER SIX

"You look like you could use a pick-me-up." Jen hands me a coffee cup from the café downstairs.

"Oh, you're a gem." I set it beside my keyboard. "I'm dragging today."

"It's Monday, hon, everyone's dragging. I'll let you get back to it."

"Thanks for the coffee." I wave as she retreats to her desk.

I cradle the cup in my hands and take a sip. The sweet caramel blends perfectly with the espresso and cream, wrapping me in a warm embrace. Even now, the flavor transports me to my first day at Valentina's. The day I first saw Mr. Roberts.

With a sigh, I check my phone. No messages. *Vintage Cowboy* hasn't messaged me since our conversation on Saturday night. I wonder if I shifted the dynamics of our relationship too quickly.

A message pops up in the bottom corner of my computer screen. I straighten the moment I see it's from Mr. Roberts.

Please come to my office at three o'clock to discuss the final details for the holiday special.

I glance at the clock. It's two forty-five. Damn. Quickly I save what I was working on and close the windows. I retrieve the stack of files and my notebook from the top drawer of my desk.

At first, the project intimidated me, but once Mr. Roberts explained his vision for the holiday promotion, I found my stride. Whether it was his confidence in my abilities or the comforting way in which he laid out the details and expectations, his words helped me find the strength I needed to work on the project. I completely forgot today was the deadline for my proposal. With three months until Thanksgiving, he wants to be sure the details are finalized with plenty of time to prepare any changes or adjustments. Good thing I finished early last week.

I quickly down the remaining coffee in an effort to boost

my energy. My stomach flutters at the thought of working beside him again. Our monthly meetings have become something of a treat. Being near him gives me a kick of adrenaline.

Jen and Maggie weren't far off in their assertions. If I knew Mr. Roberts was the type of man who indulged in office dalliances, I would certainly consider it. But his professional demeanor never falters, much to the chagrin of the single—and some married—women in the company. He's a rock of conviction when it comes to his reputation. I admire that about him, even though it leaves me longing for something forbidden.

Gathering my files and notes against my chest, I stand and take a deep breath. The moment of truth. What if he doesn't like my designs? What if my ideas are stupid? I banish the negative thoughts and smile at his secretary.

"Go in, hon. He's waiting for you."

"Thanks." I knock on his office door anyway.

"Come in." His voice echoes through the wood. When I open the door, he glances up from behind his desk. "Ah, Miss Astor. Right on time. Please, close the door and have a seat."

I shut the door and take a seat across the desk. The files rest in my lap as I wait for his instructions.

He sets aside the papers he was reading and clears a space on the desk. "Show me what you have."

I place my notebook on the chair beside me and the files on his desk. I can't lay them out properly from a seated position, so I stand to organize them for his perusal. His gaze drops from my face to my neck before resting on the folders. My face warms when I realize my mistake.

The sweetheart neckline I thought looked cute with a pearl necklace gapes as I lean forward giving him an eyeful of my cleavage. I snap upright and clear my throat.

"I was able to locate much of the original advertising from the forties and fifties through an online archive for prominent American companies over the twentieth century." I gesture to the stack of ads I printed and used as references. "The high-resolution scans were perfect for getting a better glimpse of the vintage vibe you had mentioned."

He looks through the files and sets them aside with a nod. His gaze holds mine. "Good work finding these."

I flush at his praise. "Thank you, sir."

"I trust you were able to use them as adequate inspiration for your own designs." He rests his hand on one of the photos of a Rockwellesque cottage decorated with lights and covered in snow.

My mind shifts to the photograph *Vintage Cowboy* sent me of his ranch in Wyoming. Longing shoots through me as my thoughts wander.

"Miss Astor?"

"Sorry." I smile and ignore the heat rising in my neck and flooding my cheeks.

"Tell me about your design."

I launch into the carefully crafted design I've curated over the past several months. Fortunately, I had outlined my ideas and included a detailed report. He follows through the document, nodding, and interjecting several times with questions. When I finish, he counters with a few ideas of his own that enhance my design with a more masculine flair. He seems to like it.

"Now, tell me about the timeline and cost."

"Oh, they should be there." I gesture to the document in his hands.

"I don't see them."

With a sigh, I round the desk and come beside him. He slides his chair back and relinquishes the document when I take it from his hand. I carefully flip through page by page until I locate the section in question. Folding it open, I lay it on the desk.

"Here it is. I've included a detailed report of the estimated cost and the timeline for implementation."

He leans closer, bringing us side by side. Far closer than we've ever been. I hold my breath and study his profile as he reads. My heart flutters at the smattering of gray woven through the dark hair at his temples. He oozes confidence.

I shouldn't let my crush on Mr. Roberts distract me from the task at hand. His professional demeanor never slips. He's oblivious to the effect he has on me.

"I stand corrected, Miss Astor. You've certainly considered everything in your design."

"Thank you, sir. I've worked hard on the project and I'm quite proud of it."

"You should be." He pushes his chair back and stands, rising over me. The action isn't intimidating, but it leaves me even more flustered when he faces me. "You've risen to the challenge. I'm impressed with your dedication and your creative, unique designs."

I sway at the words of praise. He has no idea the effect they have on me. "I'm honored you trusted me with the project."

A slow smile steals across his sensual lips. "No one else would have done it justice."

I hold his gaze and my breath catches in my throat. My heart pounds in my chest. "Is there anything else I can do for you, sir?"

"Actually there is." He gestures to the files on his desk. "I would like you to continue with the project and see it through to completion."

"Really?"

"Yes. Whatever you need, it's at your disposal. If you encounter any issues, just let me know." He grins, and my heart damn near explodes. Why does he have to be so damn handsome and charming? The full package of perfection and completely off limits.

"Well," I hedge, uncertain of my own capabilities. "I need you." His brows rise at my statement. I shake my head and clarify. "I mean, since this was originally your idea, I would feel better if we worked together on implementing the project." I blunder forward. "If you aren't too busy, that is, sir."

He runs his hand over his jaw and ponders my request. My hand trembles where it leans against the desk. "I am quite busy, but I may be able to spare a few hours during the week."

"Perfect. I appreciate your insight. I would hate to make a mistake and ruin it all."

"I don't think that's possible." He clears his throat and gathers the files together onto a pile, keeping the proposal packet off to the side. "You're much more capable than you think."

"I appreciate you saying so, sir." I heft the stack of files into my arms and head for the door.

"Oh, and Miss Astor."

"Yes?" I ask, ignoring the cloud nine feeling lifting me from the ground.

"Please limit the time you spend on your phone to emergency use only."

My face must be the same shade of red as my cardigan. "Yes, sir."

"Have a good evening."

"You too." I step out of his office and into the cool air of the hallway. His secretary gives me an encouraging smile as I pass.

I spend the last half hour of the day wondering what prompted his parting comment. I rarely spend time on my phone while I'm at work, but I have been spending more time on it lately. Not only for my social media accounts but also for checking my Discord messages.

I pick up my phone and glare at it. There's a Discord message. I bite my lip and open the app. It's *Vintage Cowboy.*

I was thinking about you. I hope you're having a productive day.

My heart melts at the thoughtfulness of his comment. I need to be careful. Such a man could easily sweep me off my feet. My thoughts turn to Mr. Roberts, and his admonishment lingers in my mind. I tuck my phone into my bag.

He's right. I need to focus on work. I shouldn't be daydreaming about some man a thousand miles away. I have work to do, and the last thing I want to do is disappoint Mr. Roberts. But is that the only thing I want?

CHAPTER SEVEN

By the time Friday arrives, I'm ready for a break. Jen stops by my desk at lunch.

"Hey, Lily, you want to grab something to eat with us?"

Shaun comes up beside her and rests his hand on her waist. "You've been working so hard lately. Come on. My treat."

I set aside the spreadsheet in my hand. "Sure. I'm at a stopping point anyway."

Shaun leads the way to the elevator, and Jen links her arm through mine. "I wanted to apologize." She leans close, her voice low. "I feel like I've neglected you since Shaun and I got together."

I squeeze her arm when we step into the elevator. Shaun smiles at us both and directs his attention to the numbers over the door.

"It's okay. You're happy and I'm happy for you." I lean my head against her shoulder. "You're caught up in the moment, as you should be." I drop my voice to a whisper. "Shaun's a good catch. You're a lucky woman."

Shaun chuckles. Obviously, I wasn't as quiet as I thought.

When we reach the café in the lobby, we order and find an empty table. Normally it's busy at lunch, but it looks like we beat the rush.

"So, I've been dying to ask." Jen pulls my attention back to her. "Do you think there's something going on with Gavin and Maggie?"

"Oh my lord, yes. Twenty bucks says they're already dating."

Shaun snorts. "You'd win that bet. When do you think they're going to tell us?"

"If it were up to Maggie, probably never." I smile at the waiter when he delivers our drinks. "But Gavin won't be able to keep it a secret for long. We've been friends for years."

"How did you two meet anyway?" Jen takes a sip of her iced tea.

"We went to school together." I stir some sugar into my tea and smile at the memory. "The first week he started, one of the jocks decided to have some fun harassing Gav, and I set him straight." I grin. "We've been friends ever since."

"You guys seem close," Shaun says.

"We are. He's like a brother to me." I shrug. "All three of my roommates are." I sigh and set the spoon aside. "They're far too protective of me, though."

"Like brothers should be." Shaun laughs. "I would know. I have three sisters."

"That's awesome. I'm sure they miss having you around."

"No, they really don't." Shaun loops his arm over the back of Jen's chair. "Although they're excited to meet Jen. I'm sure they'll find a way to embarrass the hell out of me."

Jen's face turns red. "He's taking me home to meet his family over Thanksgiving. I'm freaking out a bit."

"They'll love you, babe." He kisses her temple.

The gesture is so natural, so sweet. I crave the same connection, but my sheltered upbringing and overprotective roommates have made dating a damn near impossibility.

I glance up as the door of the café swings open. Shaun and Jen follow my gaze as I watch Mr. Roberts walk toward the counter.

"You've been working closely with Mr. Roberts lately. What's going on in that office, Lily?" Jen winks.

My face heats. "Nothing." I clear my throat and shift in my seat, steering my attention away from the man in question.

"It's not nothing, Lily." Shaun's statement makes me blush harder, and he turns to Jen. "He's asked Lily to head up the holiday promotional. She's done an amazing job with the designs."

Shaun continues, lifting his glass in my direction. "Mr. Roberts sent over the details this week. Bravo, Lily. If you ever want to come over to the marketing division, just let me know.

You've certainly got an eye for design and composition."

"Of course she does. She's a fashion designer." Jen beams. "I didn't know Mr. Roberts asked you to work on the holiday promo. That's amazing! I can't wait to see it."

"You're going to love it. She definitely tapped into the vintage nostalgia with her design."

Warmth fills me at his words. It feels good to know my hard work and effort are both noticed and appreciated. "Thanks, Shaun."

I glance up as Mr. Roberts passes by the table. Our eyes meet.

"Miss Astor."

"Sir."

He takes a seat in a booth near the door. I know because I can see it clearly from the corner of my eye. He pulls out his phone.

"Uh, what was that?" Jen asks.

"What was what?" I twist the glass in my hand nervously. "I was being polite."

"Is there something you're not telling us?"

"No. Why?" I feign innocence.

"Mr. Roberts never comes to the café for lunch." Shaun's voice drops low when the waiter appears with our food. He waits until the man leaves before continuing. "He always eats in his office."

"Really?" I pick up my sandwich and shrug. "I haven't noticed."

That's a lie. I have noticed. For over three years, I've watched and waited, hoping he would come to the café while I'm here. I would fantasize about him asking to join me and us sharing a quiet lunch together. He would never do that because it would spark a flurry of speculation and gossip throughout the building. But I still imagine it in vivid detail.

"I wonder what made him change things up?" Jen asks between bites of her Cobb salad.

"Who knows." Shaun nudges her with his elbow. "Maybe he's keeping an eye on you."

"I doubt it." Jen snorts. "He's probably making sure no one flirts with Lily."

I nearly choke on my bite of club sandwich. "Seriously?"

"You're a catch, Lily." Shaun grins. "I'm sure he's now realized how talented you are and he doesn't want to let anyone else get their hands on you."

"Haha." My snarky response falls flat. I sneak a peek at Mr. Roberts who seems entranced by something on his phone. He sets it aside when the waiter arrives with his lunch. "I'm pretty sure he was just tired of being cooped up in his office all day and needed a change of scenery."

"Yeah, one with a view of Lily." Shaun winks.

"Stop teasing her." Jen jabs him in the ribs. "Eat your lunch."

We continue eating in silence. When my phone vibrates in my purse, I pull it out and glance at the messages. There are three from *Vintage Cowboy*. I smile and tuck the phone back in my purse. Jen and Shaun take no note as they're engaged in a friendly debate about the new *Space Vendetta* cartoon series.

I finish the last of my sandwich and wash it down with the remaining iced tea in my glass. "I'm going to head back upstairs. Thanks for lunch, Shaun."

"You're welcome, Lily,"

"Game night tomorrow, right?" Jen asks as I stand up.

"Absolutely." I wave and head toward the elevator.

The moment I'm out of sight, I pull my phone from my purse and unlock the screen.

I've been thinking about you all day.

The elevator opens and I step into the carriage, leaning against the wall and cradling the phone in my hands.

I'm driving myself crazy wondering what you look like. What your voice sounds like. I inhale sharply at his words. *Can I call you tonight? I promise I'll behave.*

"You forgot to press the button, Miss Astor."

Mr. Roberts steps in and presses the button for the forty-fourth floor.

"Oh. Yes." I force a smile my mind still reeling from the

message from *Vintage Cowboy.*

The doors close and Mr. Roberts takes up the space beside me. His scent, a combination of the wickedly familiar cologne mixed with his heat, surrounds me.

"You seem distracted." His voice sends a bolt of need straight to my core. "Good news, I hope."

"Just a message from a friend." I straighten and discreetly tuck my phone away. "How was your lunch, sir?"

"Delightful, thank you. And yours?" He sways when the carriage launches into motion. My shoulder brushes his arm.

"It was delicious." I pull the lip gloss from my purse and twist off the top. My focus remains fixed on our reflection in the paneling along the wall as I slide the balm on my lips. He glances at me, and my heart stops.

"Indeed."

How can a single word wreak such havoc on my whole body in such a manner? I replace the cap and tuck the gloss back into my purse.

"You look lovely today, Miss Astor." He leans close when the car comes to a stop. "Red is most definitely your color."

My hand grips the pleats of my victory red skirt when the door opens on our floor. "Thank you."

He nods and steps out of the elevator. "Have a lovely weekend, Miss Astor."

"You as well, sir." My voice drifts after him as he disappears around the corner.

I manage to drag myself out of the elevator and to my desk without collapsing. After five minutes, I'm finally able to focus on the orders on my screen.

What just happened? First, the message from *Vintage Cowboy* left me disoriented, then Mr. Roberts complimenting me that way? What did he mean? *Red is most definitely your color.*

My body warms at the memory of his voice, the cadence of his words. I swear I felt his breath on my neck when he said it. Or was it my imagination? What is wrong with me?

I shake the distracting thoughts from my mind and try to focus on the computer screen. I barely register when the rest of my coworkers return to their desks. The flurry of motion and noise around me fades into the background as my mind replays the encounter in the elevator, and I'm left sitting in a pool of my own need. Why must he torment me so?

It takes a valiant effort, but I manage to refocus my attention on the task at hand and the orders I need to place before the end of the day.

During my coffee break at three, I pull out my phone and type out a response to *Vintage Cowboy. I'll call you at nine EST.* Before I can stop myself, I hit send.

Oh, have mercy. What have I done? I hang my head at the desperation driving me to chat with a perfect stranger on the other side of the country when the man I want is down the hall in his office.

CHAPTER EIGHT

The clock on my nightstand says eight fifty-nine. My hand trembles when I open Discord. I must be crazy.

I've never done anything like this before. I mean, I've talked to complete strangers on the phone, but not in a let's-get-to-know-each-other kind of way. My father was always super strict about who I spoke to online or who I hung out with outside of school. Since I broke free from his controlling grip, I've been slowly taking steps toward experiencing the things I've been purposely sheltered from.

This is one of those things. I feel like the most naïve person on the planet. But isn't this more than naivety and inexperience?

A message pops on the screen. *I'm here. You still want to call? No pressure.*

Swallowing the uncertainty lodged in my throat, I connect my earphones and hit the start call button.

"Howdy, Lily Starling." His deep voice filters through the line, and I grip the phone tighter in my hands.

"Hello, *Vintage Cowboy*." My voice sounds strained, muffled by the headphones, but the soft chuckle from his end of the line distracts me. I wrinkle my nose.

"Sam." He pauses for a long moment. "Call me Sam."

"I think I like *Vintage Cowboy* better. Gives you an air of mystery." I tease with a laugh. "Sam sounds like you have an epic handlebar mustache and flowing silver hair."

"Someone's been watching Roadhouse." Amusement taints every word as it leaves his mouth. "A classic film, for the record." He clears his throat. "However, I do not sport a world-class mustache, nor do I bear a resemblance to the quintessential cowboy in question."

"Sam Elliot is a national treasure," I add with a grin, slowly falling into the comfortable conversation.

"On that, we can agree." He pauses. "I'll admit I wasn't expecting you to have such a sexy voice."

"I was thinking the same thing." Warmth swirls in my stomach. "I like your accent."

He laughs again. A low deep rumble I feel to my bones. "I didn't realize I had one."

"I guess it's not really an accent. More of a cadence." I lay back on the bed and set my phone on the blanket beside me. The headphones let me savor every syllable as he speaks. Like this, I can imagine it's just the two of us having an intimate conversation. "New Yorkers all speak fast. It's like we're in a hurry to get the words out. Am I going too fast now?"

"Not at all."

"Good." I sigh and close my eyes trying to picture him in my mind. All I can see is the photo he sent. The slow twang of his drawl is different from what I'm used to, but I can't seem to get enough. It's strange but comforting.

"How was work today?"

"Productive." I smile at the thought of lunch with Shaun and Jen. "I had lunch with my friends. That helped me get through the day."

"Sounds like your job is stressful."

"It can be." I sigh. "Lately it's been a bit overwhelming. Nothing I can't handle, but it doesn't leave me much time to work on my designs."

"That's not good." I hear the smile in his voice. "I like the ones you have on your website."

"Thanks." His compliment wraps around me like a warm, safety blanket.

"Aren't you working on a winter line?"

"I should be." I frown. "But my boss asked me to take care of a special project on top of my overburdened workload. It was such a great opportunity, I would have been crazy to turn it down."

"Why didn't you tell him the truth?" Sam asks, his voice tender.

"At the time, I thought I could handle it." I tug at the hem of my pajamas. "I enjoyed the challenge. It was fun. But there was a lot of other stuff going on. Personal stuff."

"Boyfriend problems?"

"No boyfriend." I smile at the offhand way he asked the question. "My friend was struggling with some addiction issues, and I had to take over for her temporarily at work."

"Hmmm." Sam's response rumbles through the phone like a growl.

A shiver wracks me. I shouldn't have such a sensitive response to his voice.

"Sounds like your boss trusts you can handle it." He takes a breath. "Or he expects you to tell him if you can't. Communication is important."

"I know." My thoughts drift to Mr. Roberts. "You're right. I should have been more honest with him about the stress of everything weighing down on me."

"This project he asked you to work on. You enjoyed it?" Sam groans and my body tenses at the flood of need coursing through me.

"I did. We're still working on it. It allows me to use the creative side of my brain for a change. I typically look at spreadsheets all day." I brush off the growing attraction and focus only on the words.

"We?"

"Yeah, the boss is helping me with the implementation of my proposal." My face heats at the memory of his comment in the elevator. "We make quite the team."

"Is that so?" He groans again. "Sorry, been a long day in the saddle. Can't seem to get comfortable. I'm not as young as I used to be." He chuckles.

"How old are you, if I can ask?" I bite my lip. Most of the conversation has been focused on me. I want to know more about him.

"Oh, darlin', you don't want to know how old I am." He laughs. "Probably old enough to be your dad."

A chill washes over me at the mention of my father. "I doubt that." The change in my tone must have been evident because he sobers instantly.

"I apologize if I offended you."

"It's okay." I sniff. "My dad and I, well, we're not exactly on the best terms right now."

"Bad blood?"

"Something like that." I exhale and try to relax again. "He was very controlling when I was growing up and expected me to follow his rules to the letter."

"Sounds like an asshole."

"Yeah. A rich asshole." I scoff. "They called me a spoiled daddy's girl. I learned quickly to distance myself from any association to my father."

"I'm sorry to hear that, Lily." His apology soothes my agitation. He exhales sharply. "To answer your question, I turn fifty next year."

My mind spins at the mental calculations in my mind. "Sixteen."

Sam chokes. "You're sixteen?"

I laugh outright. "No, you're sixteen years older than me."

"Damn it, you nearly gave me a heart attack." His rumble of laughter leaves me weak and wanting. "I thought I was about to be on Dateline or something."

"I promise I'm not catfishing." I smother my laugh behind my hand.

"I think you and I have very different definitions for that term. Because it means something very different out west."

"It's when—"

"I know what catfishing is. I may be fifty and live on a ranch, but I'm not completely unglued from modern society." He chuckles again.

"Sam." My curiosity burns bright and hot. I have to know. "Why did you really message me?"

"Do you want the savory answer?" he asks in a teasing manner.

I smile even though he can't see me. "I want the truth."

"I saw your first post and visited your website. You're incredibly talented." He responds with slow, thoughtful words.

Even though he teased me at first, I can tell he's sincere.

"But why reach out to me?" I'm glad he did, but I can't shake the nagging questions in the back of my mind.

"My sister was a designer when she was younger." He sighs. "She had an eye for it. Truly. I helped her get on her feet when she started out. She trusted my opinion. I picked up a lot from working alongside her."

"That's so sweet of you." My heart melts into a puddle of emotions and mush. "Does she still design?"

"No, not anymore. It didn't really pan out." He shifts away from the topic quickly, and I can hear the pain in his voice. "I like to help out where I can, offering support and advice."

"So you weren't completely honest with me then."

The line goes silent for the space of a few heartbeats. "What do you mean?"

"When we first started talking, I asked you why you were in a designer group. You said you were a talent scout." I clarify, wondering if he forgot to tell me that little detail.

"I didn't lie. I'm always looking for new designers with talent. But up until now, I hadn't found any." Sam pauses. "You remind me of my sister when she was first starting out. I wasn't able to help her succeed, but I can help you."

"What are you proposing, Sam?"

"I want to invest in your design company." Sam continues, "You have such potential, Lily. I want to make sure the rest of the world sees how truly gifted you are."

"Sam." I sputter for a few moments unable to string together enough coherent words to serve as a response. "That's sweet of you, but you hardly know anything about me."

"I know you're a talented designer. You're driven and dedicated." His voice drops nearly to a whisper. "My sister failed because she didn't have the funds she needed to get off the ground. We were dirt poor. I couldn't help her then and it wrecked me." He takes a breath. "I have the money now. Let me pay it forward, Lily."

Guilt twists in my gut. The thought of taking money from anyone leaves a bitter taste in my mouth. It reminds me too much of being under my father's thumb. I don't want to have money be the influence that crushes my creative process. But the reality is, I'm not making nearly the amount of money I need to truly give my design company a chance to grow and blossom. I bite my lip, deep in thought.

"Can I think about it?" The question spills from my lips before I can stop it. I cringe at my inability to walk away from such a tempting offer.

"Absolutely. Take your time." Sam sounds disappointed, but he quickly recovers. "There's no rush. I'm not going anywhere."

"Thanks, Sam. I appreciate the offer."

"Of course, Lily." He sounds tired.

"Sounds like you need a vacation. Maybe you should take some time to rest."

"There's no rest for the wicked, darlin'." His rough laugh is familiar and comforting. "It sounds like you need a vacation though."

"I wish." I moan at the thought of escaping the city for a much-needed break.

"Well, you're always welcome to visit the ranch if you need an escape."

"Really?"

"Of course. There's plenty of room. I have a guest cabin. You'd have it all to yourself if you like."

"That sounds like heaven. Thank you, Sam."

"The offer stands." He yawns. "Well, I should hit the hay. Thanks for keeping this old man company."

I shake my head. "You're not old."

"Tell that to my body."

"Okay, thanks for chatting with me. I enjoyed it."

"Me too." He draws a deep breath. "Goodnight, Lily."

"Goodnight, Sam." I disconnect the call and pull the headphones out of my ears.

The conversation replays in my mind as I turn off the light and crawl beneath the covers. Any remaining concern I have about *Vintage Cowboy* melts into the darkness. Sam. What a sweet man and such a sexy voice.

I look at the photograph he sent me one last time before I drift off to sleep. Strong and capable. Sweet and compassionate. A cowboy. It's like he's been pulled out of my dreams and placed directly in my path.

CHAPTER NINE

Working alongside Mr. Roberts isn't as distracting as I thought it would be. In fact, I find his presence soothing. For the last three weeks, we've been working closely on getting the holiday promotion organized and putting the plan into motion. Every Friday, I spend my afternoons in his office finalizing the details with his help.

I gather my file and notebook, preparing myself mentally.

Jen stops at my desk on her way back from the break room. "Off to Mr. Roberts's office?"

"Yeah. Our deadline is November first, so I'm trying to get these last kinks ironed out." I cradle the file against my chest.

"Kinks, huh?" Jen winks conspiratorially and my face warms.

"Jen," I murmur in warning. She can't say stuff like that in the office or everyone will think there's something going on between me and Mr. Roberts.

"Fine." She chuckles. "Oh, and don't forget to ask him about the Halloween party."

"I won't. Catch you later." I skirt around her and head for his office.

My stomach twists in knots as I approach the secretary's desk. She glances up.

"Hi, Lily."

"Hi, Gladys. How's the family?"

"Great." Her smile dims. "Mr. Roberts isn't back from his one o'clock meeting yet. Go on in and get started. I'm sure he'll be back any minute."

Inside his office, I set my things on his desk. Being in his space without him feels almost sacrilegious. I'm afraid to touch anything. My gaze skims over the gray sofa against the far wall, the floor to ceiling bookcase laden with books and binders, and the massive desk near the large window overlooking the city.

The sun hides behind the nearby skyscrapers, and the buildings cast long shadows across the city streets. I creep closer and lean against the glass, taking in the view. It's not nearly as nice as the view from my father's penthouse apartment on Park Avenue, but it doesn't matter. Any window affording a view of the city is better than nothing.

"I see you're hard at work."

I spin around and meet Mr. Roberts's bemused smile. "Sorry."

"I should be the one apologizing, Miss Astor." He removes his jacket and hangs it from the hook on the wall. "I trust you weren't waiting long."

"Not long at all." I return to my seat opposite his, brushing past him as I maneuver around the oversized desk. His scent teases me.

"Let's dive in, shall we?" He clears his throat and sits down. "Tell me what loose ends we still need to tie up."

I slide my chair closer to the edge of the desk and open the file. "Well, everything seems to be in order. We have a few other items to purchase, but if I put the request in on Monday, they should arrive ahead of schedule." I hand him an itemized document with an attached budget spreadsheet.

"Anticipating problems?" He scans the papers.

"Not at all. But I would rather have a buffer of time and resources available to me instead of leaving things to chance." I fold my hands in my lap. "I would hate for all of our hard work to be ruined by a delay in shipping or delivery that could have been avoided."

"How astute of you, Miss Astor." He signs the bottom of the file and hands it back to me.

"Thank you, sir." I tuck the documents back into my folder.

He leans back in his chair and strokes his hand across his jaw. "Walk me through your plans for implementation again."

This time I'm confident and precise in my presentation.

"Excellent work. It sounds like you have this well in hand, Miss Astor." He smiles, and my heart flutters. I can't tell if it's from his charm or his praise, but it doesn't matter. I let it infuse me with confidence.

"Thank you for trusting me with this project."

"Of course." He nods. "Will you be needing any more assistance from my quarter?"

"No. I should be able to have Mr. Townsend and the marketing department help me with the rest."

"What about the department displays?" He rocks forward and rests his elbows on the desk interlocking his fingers.

"I've already spoken with the department heads and given them a detailed outline for them to use in the decoration of their specified areas."

"I stand corrected." He chuckles. "Your skills well surpass your current position. Perhaps I should make you my assistant."

My head snaps up. "Your what?"

"My personal assistant. Gladys is growing tired of being at my beck and call." His eyes sparkle as he studies me. "Would you be interested in the position?"

"I'm flattered, sir." My heart races at the thought. But my mind can't stop playing the sordid variety of fantasies such a position would provide. "I would have to think about it."

"I understand." He slowly rises to his feet. "There's no rush."

"Thank you." I gather my things and stand.

"Is there anything else I can do for you, Miss Astor?" he asks, shoving his hands into his pockets.

"Yes, actually. Would it be possible to have an office Halloween party this year?"

"A Halloween party?" His eyes narrow. "We're already having a Christmas party. Is that not sufficient?"

My heart drops at his tone. "Well, yes, but everyone has been working so hard this year, I thought it would be a nice way for us to gather after work and relax."

"Is that so?"

I bite my lip.

"Very well." He wags his finger at me. "But nothing extravagant, and keep the cost to a moderate budget. Do you understand?"

"Yes, sir." I bounce on my toes as excitement fills me. "Will you come?"

"To a costume party with my employees?" His eyes flash with amusement. "I don't think that would be appropriate."

I pout but it transforms into a smile. I can't suppress my enthusiasm. "You'll miss out on all the fun."

"I'm sure I will." He presses his hand to his heart. "I will email you the budget for both the Halloween and Christmas parties by Monday morning."

"Thank you, Mr. Roberts."

"Oh, I meant to ask you about the holidays." He stops me with a wave of his hand.

"Yes?"

"Will you be spending Thanksgiving with your family?"

I lick my lips, unsure of how to answer his question without going into a huge explanation of my family history. He knows who my father is, but since the first day we met, he has never again mentioned it. Not even in passing.

"No." I shift my weight from one foot to another. "My father and I...we're not on the best terms right now. I typically spend Thanksgiving with my roommates, but they'll be out of town this year. So I'll be spending it alone."

"Oh, I'm sorry to hear that." He offers a warm smile. "Guess that makes two of us."

"Was there something you needed over the holiday, sir?"

"Nothing that can't wait." He walks me to the door. "Have a good weekend."

"You too, sir." I make my way back to my desk and grab my phone to send a message to Jen with the good news about the Halloween party.

There are three unread messages from *Vintage Cowboy. Sam.*

Been thinking about you all week.

I hope you're doing well.

Call me tonight?

The last message just came through.

I grin when I type out my response. *Sure. 9 p.m.*

Without waiting for a response, I put my phone in my purse and respond to one urgent email from Shaun about the holiday project.

Jen meets me by the elevator five minutes later. "He said yes?"

I nod.

"You're amazing." She hugs me tight.

The elevator arrives and we step inside the car. "Isn't Shaun leaving?"

"He's working late." Jen adjusts the strap of her bag. "I'll go home and make dinner. We're starting a new series tonight."

"Sounds like fun." I fake a smile, but inside my heart aches. I wish I had someone waiting for me at home. With Gavin and Maggie getting married and moving in together, I'm stuck trying to find a new roommate. The last thing I want to do is short my father on the rent. It's bad enough he owns the brownstone. I could find my own place, but I don't want to live alone. I like having people around me.

Jen chatters about Maggie's wedding tomorrow, but I'm lost in thought. The Halloween costume party. Why won't Mr. Roberts come? It would be fun to see him cut loose a little.

"You want to meet early tomorrow morning to finish decorating the arcade?" Jen's question cuts through my wandering fantasy.

"Oh, yeah. Sure." I step out of the subway and onto the sidewalk. "I need to finish up Maggie's dress tonight. Want to meet at my place at seven?"

"That works for me." Jen hugs me. "See you tomorrow."

I wave and walk in the opposite direction toward home. The meeting with Mr. Roberts replays in my mind. Why would he ask me about my holiday plans? Maybe he has something else he needs me to do at work. We'll both be spending Thanksgiving alone. Part of me wishes I had the nerve to invite him over and we could celebrate together, but I know he'd turn me down. It would be inappropriate.

At least I have a cowboy waiting for me tonight.

CHAPTER TEN

This month has left me emotionally exhausted. Between Maggie and Gavin's wedding and the finalization of the vintage holiday promotion I spent half a year working on, part of me wants to cry, but the rest is clamoring for a chance to let loose.

Jen, Shaun, and I spend all Friday afternoon decorating the office and transforming the break room into a spooky buffet of finger foods and beverages.

I had hoped Mr. Roberts would change his mind and join us for the celebration, but he left early after sending me a note requesting my final summary and the contracts for the holiday project to be delivered by the end of the day. Sure, I'll get right on that—*after* I finish getting the party ready.

When I finally glance at the clock, it's five. My coworkers have already flipped the switch from work to party mode. They're wearing various levels of costumes, and I admire their creativity. The rhythmic pulse of music fills the office. Jen and Shaun appear, wearing *Space Vendetta* costumes. Shaun cuts a dashing, strangely accurate Commander Colton, and Jen looks perfect as the deadly Space Ranger Lynnea Stark. I chuckle. These two were made for each other.

"Where's your costume?" Jen shelves her hand on her hip. "The party has already started." Her voice carries over the eighties flashback track playing over the speakers.

"Sorry, I have to print this for Mr. Roberts first."

"Just email it."

"He wanted a hard copy." I wave my hand. "It'll only take a minute."

"I'll print it for you." Jen groans and nudges me aside. "Go change, then you can take it to the boss."

I shove away from my desk and grab my duffel bag. In the bathroom I peel away the layers of Professional Lily, replacing them with the sleek pleather catsuit I made a few years ago. I've never had an opportunity to wear it, but after watching Michelle Pfeiffer rock it, I had to have one. Forgoing the full head covering, I slip on a headband with cat ears and a black domino mask. A little red lipstick finishes the ensemble and I rejoin the party.

Shaun whistles low when he sees me cross the room. "Geezus, Lily." He turns pink. "Are you sure that's appropriate for the office?"

"What?" I run my hands over the suit clinging to my curves. "Too much?"

Jen stares, open-mouthed. "Uh, not too much, but I wouldn't recommend wearing that in the subway after dark."

"Thanks." I toss my bag under my desk. "I need a drink." I've been working too hard lately. This is exactly what I need to relax.

"Yes, please," Jen agrees.

"I'll get them." Shaun ducks toward the break room.

Jen leans against the desk beside me. "You doing okay?"

"Yeah. I'm good."

"You've been working hard, Lily." Jen takes my hand in hers. "Don't forget to take some time for yourself and recharge."

I lean my head against her shoulder. "Thanks. I'm trying. But there's always something that needs to be done."

"I know, but you're not a superhero."

"No, but tonight I can play the villain." I wink.

"Wearing a Catwoman suit does not change who you are, Lily." She pats my hand. "I don't think you have a wicked bone in your whole body."

"This good girl image is getting old." I frown. "Maybe I should be bad from here on out."

Jen laughs. "What evil ideas are you plotting?"

"I don't know. Maybe I'll take a page from your book and go meet someone I found online."

"Are you seriously considering going to meet that cowboy you met in a chat group?"

"Why not? He's been nothing but sweet and

understanding." I sigh. "Plus, he has the sexiest drawl."

"You've spoken to him on the phone?"

"Several times."

Jen stares at me like she's never seen me before. "You don't find it a little suspicious? His sudden interest in you?"

"No, should I?" Her concern leaves me a bit unsteady. Of course, I thought about it before, but it's been months and he's never asked anything of me. He's just been there. Supportive and sweet.

"I mean, with your family ties, I would be extra cautious." She bites her lip. "What if he lures you out to his ranch and holds you ransom?"

"How would he know who my father is?" She has a point, but there's no way he knows who I am. I'm extremely careful in the details I put online.

"I don't know." Jen's brow furrows. "But be careful, please."

"You went to a comic con and met online friends. Nothing bad happened."

"You're right. I wasn't kidnapped or held ransom by a lunatic." Jen rests her hand on my shoulder. "But my father isn't Monroe Astor. Promise me you won't do anything crazy."

"Fine." I heave a dramatic sigh. "I won't do anything crazy, like run off to Wyoming."

"Ladies." Shaun reappears bearing drinks. I take one from his hand and sip it. The pungent flavor of fruit punch and vodka hits me hard.

"Woo, that's strong." I sip it again.

"Good." He hooks his arm around Jen's waist as another classic eighties jam ramps up. "Let's dance."

"You two go." I shoo them away with a wave of my hand.

The flash of the impromptu strobe lights creates a club atmosphere where we've cleared some of the desks. I laugh as Jen and Shaun pull our coworkers onto the makeshift dance floor.

Taking another drink, I rest back against the desk and knock a file onto the floor. The documents for Mr. Roberts.

"Shit." I set my drink down and gather the papers into the folder. With a quick glance through the documents, I nod, satisfied they're all there.

I head down the hallway toward Mr. Roberts's office. This side of the building is dark. I rest my hand on the wall as I walk. There's a glimmer of light ahead, coming from his office. The shaft of light shines through the cracked door.

When did he come back? My hand trembles when I knock.

"Yes." His voice drifts through the gap.

When I open the door, he glances up. "Miss Astor?"

"I'm sorry to disturb you, sir." I cross the room and lay the file on his desk. "Here are the documents you requested."

Mr. Roberts ignores the folder. Instead, his gaze remains fixed on me, dropping down briefly before returning to meet mine. Then I realize why he's staring at me in such a way. I'm wearing a pleather catsuit and fuzzy ears.

"Oh." I brush my hair back away from my face suddenly self-conscious. "I should get back to the party."

"You look..." He swallows. "Lovely."

"Thank you." I warm at his compliment.

He stands, and before I can respond, he's rounded the desk. "Did you make this?" His finger trails down the outside of my arm.

The breath I was holding chokes me. I can only nod.

"Are you looking for trouble, Miss Astor?" His touch falls away.

"Excuse me?" I turn to face him. Surely I misheard.

His gaze drops down the length of me and back again before he licks his lips. "I hope you have more sense than to wander around the city wearing something this—" He inclines his head, studying me as he searches for the right word. I arch a brow, daring him to continue with his sexist remark, but it's hidden behind the mask.

"This what?" I push beyond propriety and call him out.

"Distracting." He smiles, but it doesn't reach his eyes.

"Well, if it's distracting, I should leave." I turn, my heart hammering in my chest. How dare he treat me like I'm wrong for wearing a costume at a Halloween party. His opinion doesn't matter to me. I'm an adult. Perfectly capable of making my own decisions concerning my wardrobe and my body. Fury pours off me as I stride toward the door.

His grip around my wrist brings me to a stop. I stumble on my heels and nearly trip, but he catches me, pinning me against him. Oh, shit. He's strong. Warm and welcoming, but firm and steadfast. I brace my hand against his chest as he helps me find my footing.

"I apologize, Miss Astor." He clears his throat and gently relinquishes his grip. "Forgive me. I overstepped."

"Damn right you did." I straighten my ears and glower at him. "What I do outside designated work hours is none of your damned business."

"You're absolutely correct." He doesn't blink. "Again, I apologize."

His calm demeanor leaves me confused and only infuriates me further. I take several deep breaths in a wasted attempt to calm down. But being in his presence, having him this close to me and being torn between professionalism and pure desire has me twisted in knots.

I jab my finger in his chest. "You're the kind of man who likes his women silent and submissive."

He swallows hard, his blue eyes darkening to steel gray. "You have no idea what kind of man I am, Miss Astor." His hand takes mine and he smooths his thumb across my knuckles.

I whimper at the touch and bite my lip. "You're right." My voice sounds weak and breathless. He's close. Closer than he's ever been. It would take one step to put us within kissing distance. All I want is one taste. One forbidden taste of his sensual lips. Then I'll behave. I promise.

He lowers my hand and releases it, breaking the spell between us. "Go enjoy your party."

I can't even respond. I retreat from his office and close the door behind me.

In the darkness of the hallway, I lean against the wall and hold a hand to my racing heart. Holy shit. What have I done? I press my eyes closed and breathe deep.

Shaking off the lingering effects of his touch, I paste a smile on my face and head back to the party to retrieve my drink. Once I down the contents, I join the dance floor where Jen and Shaun are leading the conga line.

Am I looking for trouble? I wasn't before, but I sure as hell am now.

Chapter Eleven

A week after the Halloween incident, nothing has changed. I don't understand. How could Mr. Roberts react in such a way and then brush it under the rug like it never happened? The intensity of his reaction lingers in the back of my mind and I can't shake it.

But I have to. If he can move on, then I can too. It does nothing to quell the need inside of me. Damn him.

The holiday promotion is live, and it looks amazing. Everything is flowing smoothly and the feedback is overwhelmingly positive. I'm on fire and nothing can ruin this high!

I take my lunch break and head down to the café in the lobby. I brought a sandwich from home, but I'm dragging and need a caramel cappuccino to get me through the day. While I'm waiting for my order, my phone buzzes in my skirt pocket.

It's my father.

"Hi, Dad." I keep my voice low and steady.

"Lily." He clears his throat. "Are you coming for Thanksgiving? I need to let the caterer know how many to expect."

"Sorry, Dad, I have plans this year. I won't be able to make it." My teeth grind at the impassive way he addresses the event. He doesn't want my company, he wants my presence. I refuse to grant him the satisfaction of giving in to his deluded vision of familial bonding.

"Very well." He continues without asking about how I'm doing or what my plans are. It's disheartening, but I've come to expect it from him. "Don't make any plans for Christmas. Violet would like you to join us this year."

Violet. Dad's third wife. Mom died when I was fourteen. He loved her, I'm fairly certain. But he said the same of Mimi and Violet too. I sigh and bite my lip. I can't tell him I've already got plans, he'll know I'm lying. But I don't want to go. Violet's nice enough, but I really have no interest in spending time with my father. He cares more for his money and his reputation than his daughter.

"I'll think about it." The barista calls my order. "I gotta go, Dad."

"Okay. Text Violet if you change your mind about Thanksgiving."

"Will do." I end the call and grab my coffee.

My mood sours with every step I take toward the elevator. What does he want from me? I'm not interested in playing happy family with him and Violet. I cut ties for a reason. The paparazzi, the unrelenting media coverage of every event my father hosted—it was hell. I left and it was the best decision I ever made.

Lying about my plans for Thanksgiving felt drastic. I should have been honest with him. But truth is, I want to have plans with my friends and roommates. James and Michael are visiting family for the holiday. I tried inviting Maggie and Gavin last week, but they're celebrating with his family this year. That's good.

When I reach the forty-fourth floor, I search for Jen. She's standing by the far window talking to Shaun.

"Hey."

"Hey, Lily." Jen turns with a smile. Shaun nods in greeting.

"You guys still going out of town for Thanksgiving?"

"Yeah. We're flying to Iowa to spend the week with Shaun's family. I'm nervous about meeting them."

"They'll love you, babe," Shaun reassures her.

"Of course, they will." I back him up, but my heart sinks. Looks like I'll be spending Thanksgiving alone. Damn it.

"Do you have plans?" Jen asks.

"No, but it'll be a great opportunity to catch up on my design projects." I smile, but inside, my heart is aching. I hate cooking a feast for just me.

"That's a great idea. I'm excited to see what you've got

planned for your spring line."

"I may need a model, so be prepared." I wink. "I'll catch you guys later."

I settle at my desk and take a sip of coffee. My phone pings when a message drops in from Discord.

It's Sam. *Hey, darlin'. Sorry I've been MIA. Work has me running around like a chicken with my head cut off. How's your day?*

We haven't spoken for nearly two weeks. I was starting to worry about him. I type out a quick response, but it transforms into a massive purge. I shouldn't burden him with my shit, but he's so easy to talk to. So understanding. I pour my heart into the message.

It was okay until my father called and wanted me to come home for Thanksgiving. Let's just say I'm not interested in reigniting any drama with him right now. All my friends have plans and I'm stuck celebrating alone. Which sucks, but it'll give me time to work on some designs and catch up on my neglected marketing content.

Oh, and I made a complete fool of myself in front of my boss at the Halloween party last weekend. I'm pretty sure he thinks I'm insane, and I'm convinced he's one of those men who want to control absolutely everything. Chauvinist. But I may have pushed him over the edge with my Catwoman costume. Now he's acting like nothing happened. I'm so confused.

Sorry, didn't mean to dump all that on you, but you did ask how my day was. Thanks for listening, Sam.

I hit send before I can overthink it. The moment it hits the internet, a sense of calm washes over me. Purging these thoughts feels good. I like having someone I can talk to who isn't connected to my real life. It's liberating in a strange way.

Shoving my phone aside, I take a deep breath. There's plenty of work to keep my brain occupied. The last thing I need is Mr. Roberts chastising me for being on my phone.

"Is everything okay, Miss Astor?" Mr. Roberts comes to a stop in front of me.

It's like I summoned him from the darkest voids of my mind. How does he do that? I banish the scowl forming on my face and force a smile. "Yes, sir. Just distracted by the upcoming holiday."

"I trust you've made plans to celebrate with friends." His voice is low, carrying between the two of us, but I can feel the curious gazes of my coworkers.

"They all have plans already."

"And your family?"

"I'd rather spend the day alone." The response slips from my lips without thought. Quickly I turn the conversation to him. "Do you have plans?"

"No." He straightens his tie. "Oh, and I wanted to extend a personal thank you from Mrs. Bradshaw for the excellent work on the holiday promotional. It's a smashing success."

"Thank you." My mood brightens at the high praise.

"I'll let you get back to work." He taps the desk with his fingers and retreats down the hallway toward his office.

Stunned, I stare into the vacant space where he stood only moments before. Why would he show me any concern after what happened on Halloween?

Later that night, a wild plan hits me, but it takes two weeks for me to work up the courage to act on it. I spend two hours making a handwritten invitation, and three days convincing myself to deliver it.

The Friday before Thanksgiving, I knock on his door.

"Come in."

"Am I interrupting?"

"Not at all, Miss Astor." He sets his pen aside, giving me his undivided attention. "What can I do for you?"

I close the gap between us and lay the invitation on his desk.

"What is this?" He opens it, and his carefully curated expression falters. He arches a brow and a smile curves his lips. "Are you inviting me over for Thanksgiving?"

"Yes, sir." I grasp my hands firmly before me to keep them from fidgeting with my skirt. "If you don't have any plans, that is."

"No. I don't have plans." He sets the invitation aside.

"I figured we could celebrate together." My face flushes with warmth. Why is this so damned hard? "I mean, there's no point in spending the day alone."

"I wouldn't want to impose."

My heart jumps as he stands and walks around the desk. "It's no imposition. I hate cooking for one."

He chuckles and the sound leaves me weak in the knees. "Well then, I accept your gracious invitation. Is there anything I can bring?"

"Wine would be nice," I murmur, unable to trust my own voice.

"I believe I can handle that. I look forward to it. Thank you, Miss Astor."

"You're welcome." I turn to leave, but he calls out as I reach the door.

"It would be prudent if we didn't broadcast our plans. I wouldn't want to feed any rumors, would you?"

I shake my head.

"Good." He returns to his seat. "Enjoy your weekend."

"Thanks." I slip out of his office and return to my desk. Did that really just happen?

Jen catches my eye and waves. I wave back and guilt festers deep in my chest. I can't tell her. At least not yet, I want to keep this all to myself and the last thing I need is this blowing up in my face.

He started it. His comment about my costume and the tension between us left me aroused and angry. I fully intend to uncover this darker side to Mr. Roberts, and if I have to play dirty to get it, I will.

He thinks I'm a good girl who doesn't know her own mind. But he doesn't know me as well as he thinks he does.

CHAPTER TWELVE

Are you awake?

I stare at the message from *Vintage Cowboy* for five minutes before I respond. *Yeah.*

I lay in my dark room, staring at the ceiling. My alarm clock warns me how close it is to midnight. But I can't sleep. I've been trying to for the last two hours.

I've been twisted in knots since I invited Mr. Roberts over for Thanksgiving dinner. What the hell am I thinking? I'm not going to magically unravel all the mystery surrounding him in one evening. But worse than that, what if the events at the Halloween party were one huge misunderstanding?

I scowl harder at the dark ceiling. My phone dings as a message comes through.

Are you up for a chat?

Sure. With a deep sigh, I grab my earbuds and connect them to my phone.

The call comes through a moment later. "Hi, Sam."

"Hello, Lily." His deep voice soothes me.

"Where've you been?" I ask, closing my eyes and picturing him on his ranch.

"Busy. Sorry I've been MIA." He sighs. "Life's been a little crazy lately."

"I understand." My body sinks deeper beneath the blankets. "It's been crazy here too."

"What's going on? You sound tired. Aren't you feeling well?"

I smile at his concern. "I feel fine. Well, physically at least."

"What's wrong, kitten?"

I gasp at the nickname.

"Sorry, I shouldn't have called you that."

"It's okay. I kinda like it."

His soft chuckle makes my body tingle with awareness. "Want to talk about what's wrong?"

"Everything." I inhale deep unsure where to start.

"Let's start with what's on your mind right now."

"You."

A low growl emanates from the phone. "What about me, kitten?"

"Are you single?"

"I wouldn't be talking to you if I wasn't."

I smile at the response. "Good answer."

"Why are you wasting your time talking to an old man instead of finding a nice guy to take you out on the town?"

"Who says I want a nice guy?" I keep my voice low so the whole house doesn't hear my confessions, but it comes out sounding breathy and laced with need.

"Ahh, the good girl wants herself a bad boy, huh?"

"Why does everyone assume I'm a good girl?" I frown even though his words ignite a fire inside me.

"Aren't you?"

"No."

"Let's find out, shall we?"

"Fine." I bite my lip. This could be dangerous. But I need to see where this leads.

"Do you flirt with men with no intention of following through if they show interest?"

I pinch my eyes closed and think hard. "Sometimes. It depends on the guy and who I'm with."

"Have you ever broken the rules and not had immediate regret?"

"No," I admit bashfully.

"What's the most wicked thing you've ever done?"

My breath hitches. Thoughts of my vivid fantasies involving Mr. Roberts fill my mind. Him taking me hard and fast on his desk. Him seducing me in the elevator. Him sitting beside me at a fancy dinner with his hand between my thighs as he talks to the other guests. I shake the smoldering images from my head.

"I…" I pant as the heady desperation lingers. "I've never

done anything wicked."

"But you've thought about it, haven't you, kitten?"

"Yes," I murmur.

"Who do you imagine when you think of being wicked?" His words unlock the pent-up frustration I've let simmer on the back burner since the first day I met Mr. Roberts.

"My boss." I clap my hand over my mouth. Why did I say that? I've never told anyone about my crush on Mr. Roberts. Not a soul.

"Oh, you are a wicked girl, aren't you, Lily?" His growl reverberates through the line. "Tell me, sweetheart, do you think about me the same way?"

A guilty flush consumes me, and I'm thankful for the darkness hiding my shame. "Yes."

"Ohhh, kitten," he groans. "Now we're getting somewhere."

I hear the rustle of movement on the other end of the line. "Sam?"

"Yeah, sweetheart. I'm here. Just getting comfortable."

A vision of him wearing jeans that do nothing to hide his bulging cock springs to mind. I swallow my reservations and push forward. "Can I ask you a question?"

"Anything."

I lick my lips. "Have you thought about me...when..." I can't bring myself to say the words. I want to, but it's like a filter is firmly affixed in my brain that keeps me from voicing my desires.

"When I stroke my cock?" he finishes the sentence with a low groan. "Yes, kitten. I have."

Oh, shit. Desire courses hot through me.

"Do you want me to tell you what I imagine?"

"Yes," I manage to get the word out. My hand releases its death grip on the phone and slides beneath the blankets.

"You remember that red dress you posted on your site?"

"Mmhmm."

"You're wearing that when you show up at my ranch." He moans, low and slow. "You find me sitting on the porch watching the sun set."

The image forms in my mind and my breath quickens when my fingers delve inside my pajama bottoms. I'm slick with need.

"You curl up on my lap and we watch the sun slowly sink beyond the horizon." Desire unravels his accent and the drawl fades as his breath hitches. "I slide my hand beneath your skirt and find you wet. Are you wet for me, kitten?"

"Yes," I moan as my finger slides across my clit in tight circles. "So wet."

"Good girl." The words send a pulse of heat straight to the spot I'm touching. "I lift my fingers to my lips and taste you. You're sweet. So fucking sweet."

"Oh, God." I quicken my pace and the orgasm builds in tandem with his story.

"I bury my face in your hair, wanting to wrap those fair locks around my fist and force you to your knees." He chuckles. "But I don't. Instead, I slide two fingers deep inside you and slowly fuck you with them while my thumb caresses your clit. Do you like that, kitten?"

"Yes, please," I gasp as the pressure builds.

"Do you want to come for me?"

"Fuck, yes," I pant, desperate to find release.

"Then come for me, kitten."

His command breaks something inside me. My orgasm hits hard making me moan and pant. I bite my lip trying to keep quiet, but the intensity of the sensations overwhelms me. Fireworks ignite behind my eyelids and every part of me trembles as the waves of pleasure wash over me. Holy shit. I've never come that hard by myself. Technically I'm not by myself, and the thought sobers me.

"Sam?" I ask hesitantly.

"I'm here." His soft laugh fills the silence. "That must have been one hell of an orgasm. I wish I could have been there to see your face."

I cover my face with my hand. "I'm sorry."

"For what, sweetheart?"

"For ending it before it started."

"Don't apologize. It's unbelievably hot hearing you get off

to my voice."

Disbelief at my own actions leaves me self-conscious. "I guess I'm a bad girl now, huh?"

"Nonsense." He scoffs. "You're a very good girl."

Those words reignite the heat between my thighs once more. I shove aside the rising need. "What about you?"

"Oh, don't you worry about me, sweetheart. I've already taken care of it."

I frown. Part of me wanted to hear him moan and grunt as he stroked himself. "Well, that's not fair."

"What's not fair?"

"Nothing."

"No, tell me."

"I wanted to make you come."

"Oh, sweetheart, you made me come the moment your orgasm hit. All those breathy moans and desperate gasps made me wish I was buried deep inside you. I came so hard I saw stars."

I love hearing him talk like this. It should be awkward and strange, but it feels natural. There's something about Sam's voice that's familiar and comforting. I could listen to him all night. A yawn strikes me.

"I'm going to let you get some sleep."

"Okay." I snuggle deeper into my mound of pillows. "Goodnight, Sam."

"Goodnight, kitten." He disconnects the line and I move the phone to the nightstand.

My last thoughts before drifting off are of my cowboy and my boss. I want them both, and yet both are a million miles away. Too far out of reach. Loneliness joins me, wrapping me in a tight embrace as I fall asleep.

CHAPTER THIRTEEN

By seven on Thanksgiving morning, I have the turkey in the oven. It's the smallest one I could find, but I'm pretty sure the boys will be eating the leftovers for two weeks. Both James and Mike left yesterday afternoon. So I utilized the quiet evening to make pumpkin pie. I promised myself I wouldn't go overboard with the meal since it's only two of us.

My whole body tingles at the thought of spending the afternoon alone with him. I can't tell if it's excitement or guilt. After the unexpectedly steamy call with Sam on Saturday night, I feel as though I'm cheating on him by having Mr. Roberts join me today.

But I'm not in a relationship with Sam. We just relieved a little tension over the phone. No harm in that. He had no expectations. Even his sweet message the following morning stated as much. He doesn't want to pressure me because he knows the reality of our situation. I'm in New York and he's in Wyoming. Long distance isn't something either of us wants.

That leaves my one-sided crush on Mr. Roberts. I don't know what to think about him anymore. His actions vacillate between personal interest and professional inquiry. And I still can't forget that night when he chastised me for my Halloween costume. Today, I fully intend to find out if there's something there or if I'm imagining things. I just hope it doesn't leave me without a job come Monday morning.

I prep the side dishes and set them on the counter. Traditional dressing, green bean casserole, and homemade cranberry sauce. All adaptations of my own creation tweaked from recipes I've found online over the years.

Once all the heavy lifting is done, I head upstairs and take a shower. The long blonde curls cooperate for once when I wrangle them into victory rolls and I cheer at the small triumph.

I keep my makeup simple with winged liner and cherry red lip gloss. After affixing my stockings with the garter clips, I pull on the auburn and green plaid swing dress, fluffing the skirt to cover the red petticoat. A glance in the mirror tells me I'm ready. I tug at the three-quarter sleeves and slide on my black pumps before heading back downstairs.

The timer goes off before I can tie on my apron. I finish the haphazard bow and grab my oven mitts. The turkey looks done. I check the temperature and set it aside to rest. Then I slide the casserole and dressing into the oven and reset the timer.

The doorbell rings twenty minutes later. Oh, crap, he's here already? I glance at the clock. It's ten till twelve. The invitation said noon. I take a deep breath and open the door.

Mr. Roberts is standing on my doorstep with a bag in one hand and a bouquet in the other, looking like he just stepped out of a nineties rom-com. "Hello, Miss Astor."

"Lily." I correct him. "Just call me Lily today. Please, come in." I open the door and step aside.

He crosses the threshold and proffers the bouquet. Calla lilies and dahlias surrounded by sprigs of baby's breath. I cradle them and inhale the sweet fragrance.

"They're lovely. Thank you, sir."

"Jackson." His response confuses me for a moment. "If we're being informal, you might as well call me Jackson." A smile curves his sensual mouth. "Although if you want to continue calling me *sir*, I certainly won't mind."

Heat shoots through me like a bolt of lightning. Before I can respond, he glances around the foyer. "You have a lovely home."

"Thank you." I clear my throat. "I need to get some water for these." Halfway down the hall, I glance over my shoulder. He's following carefully, taking measure of the space around him.

In the kitchen, I find a vase and fill it with water. Turning back to the bouquet on the counter, I suck in a breath at the sight of Jackson as he shrugs out of his coat.

"Something smells divine." He smiles warmly and part of

me melts.

"Did you have any trouble finding the house?" I ask while arranging the flowers in the vase of water. Anything to keep my hands busy and my mind occupied. His presence in my home overwhelms me with need.

"Not at all." He drapes his coat over his arm.

"Let me hang this up." I reach for it, brushing my hand across the sweater covering his forearm. He's wearing khakis and a gray cardigan with a blue button-down shirt beneath it.

I step from the kitchen and fan myself. I've never seen him outside the office or in casual clothing. He's delicious in a three-piece suit, but that cardigan makes him more approachable and softer. Dangerous, in other words. I manage to hang up his coat and return without incident.

"Oh." I stop short when I see him with the mitts on standing in front of the open oven.

He pulls out the casserole followed by the dressing and sets them on the heat-resistant pads sitting on the counter. "Your timer went off." His lopsided smile steals the breath from my lungs. "Figured I could give you a hand."

"That's sweet of you."

"It's the least I can do." He glances up. "You certainly outdid yourself."

"It wouldn't be Thanksgiving without all the staples."

"You have a point." He gestures to the bag. "Would you like some wine?"

"I'd love some." My mouth waters when he pulls a bottle of Italian Cabernet Sauvignon from the red bag.

"Ever since my trip to northern Italy, I can't seem to stomach any other wines." He chuckles. "Do you have an opener?"

"Yeah." I grab the corkscrew from the drawer and hand it to him. Our fingertips brush and I suppress a moan. Damn it. Calm down.

While he opens the wine and allows it to breathe, I retrieve glasses from the cabinet and set them on the counter.

My mind blanks and instead of fumbling for conversation,

I spring into motion and set the table in the dining room. Jackson helps carry the food to the table. I reach for the knife to carve the turkey, but he rests his hand on mine.

"Allow me."

I relinquish control and pull my hand away from his searing touch. Is he immune to whatever this heat is building between us? Am I the only one who can feel it? I must be because his expression never wavers.

My gaze lingers on every movement as he cuts the turkey with precision.

"Breast or thigh?"

I nearly choke on my own spit. "Uh, thigh, please."

He carves it from the bone and lays it neatly on my plate. I busy myself with the other side dishes. When I offer them, he accepts graciously. The gentle flow between us lulls me into a sense of complacency. I like this. His company. His help.

Once he resumes his seat, Jackson lifts his wine glass. "*Salute e buon appetito.*"

The soft clink of our glasses echoes through the dining room. "You speak Italian?"

"A little. I spent some time in Italy and learned some basics." He sips the wine, and his eyes close in appreciation at the flavor. I can't help but wonder if he savors everything with such deep reflection.

"Oh." I manage before taking a drink. The vibrant flavors hold me captive. "That's delicious."

"I knew you'd like it." He smiles and gestures to the heaping plate before him. "Shall we?"

I tame my overzealous nod and take a bite of turkey. He goes right for the green bean casserole. We eat in silence, enjoying the meal and each other's company.

My mind wanders. A million questions rush to the forefront of my mind. I want to know more about him, but how do I ask without seeming nosy?

"Your roommates don't know what they're missing," he says between bites. "This is fantastic. Best Thanksgiving meal I've had in years."

"Thank you." I blush at his compliment. "They know exactly what they're missing. I cook for them all the time."

"Well, they're crazy to pass this up." He finishes the last bite on his plate. "If you cooked like this for me every day, I'd never let you go."

My stomach flips at his statement. I'm sure he meant it as an innocuous comment, but it leaves me aching in ways I can't examine too closely. I invited him over out of the goodness of my heart, didn't I? Not to twist every word he says into some sexual innuendo or declaration of love.

I manage to finish the food on my plate without making a fool of myself. When I stand to collect the dishes, he beats me to it and grabs mine from my hand.

"I'll do the dishes." His eyes hold mine, challenging me to argue.

"We can do them together." I carry the turkey into the kitchen with him behind me.

As he fills the sink with water, I retrieve the rest of the food from the dining room.

"Sorry, I don't have a dishwasher."

"It's fine. I'm used to doing dishes the old-fashioned way."

"There's something soothing about washing them by hand." We banter as I finish putting the leftovers in the fridge. I stack any remaining dishes by the sink and come beside him.

"I'll wash, you rinse?" He sways against me, nudging my arm with his elbow.

I hold my hand out in response. He places a sudsy plate in my grip.

"Why aren't you married?" The moment the question leaves my lips, I'm mortified.

Jackson chuckles. "I never found someone worth investing that level of commitment in." He glances at me. "Why are you still single, Lily?"

My body tingles at the way he says my name. I ignore it and focus on rinsing the next dish. "I haven't found anyone mature enough to handle me."

"Is that so? It has nothing to do with who your father is?"

"My father has no say in my life. We may share blood and a surname, but I am my own woman."

"I can see that." He hands me the silverware one piece at a time as he cleans them. "I apologize. I didn't mean to upset you."

"I'm not upset. I've spent a long time trying to make a name for myself devoid of any ties to my father. People always change when they realize I'm related to Monroe Astor."

"You're a talented woman, Lily." He hands me the remaining dish and drains the water. "It takes courage to step out on your own and put your heart out there. Life is cruel."

"Thanks. It does suck, but there has to be hope."

"So trusting and optimistic." He turns and leans his hip against the counter beside me.

"Would you like some pie and coffee?" I offer, unable to bear the tension drawing me closer to him. If I stay like this, I'll do something stupid. Like kiss him.

"Sounds delightful."

As I brew the coffee, he cuts the pie and sets it on the small plates. I hand him the whipped cream to put on top before I add a splash of bourbon cream to both coffee mugs.

"Grab the pie." I motion for him to follow me.

In the living room, I set the mugs down on the coffee table. He hands me a plate and we sit side by side on the oversized couch. A fire flickers on the television and soft music filters through the speakers as we eat our pie.

He sets his empty plate aside and picks up the coffee to wash it down. "That was amazing."

"Thanks for keeping me company today. I really don't like spending the holidays alone."

"I appreciate the invitation." He sips thoughtfully before setting the mug aside and leaning closer. "Don't move. You have a little something..." His voice drifts off as he reaches out and brushes the corner of my mouth with the pad of his thumb.

My heart stops beating. I watch as he lifts his finger to his mouth and licks the whipped cream from the tip.

"Oh. Thanks." I set my plate aside and grab my coffee. Did he really just do that?

"Lily." I'm humming with need, and he's close. So damn close.

"Yeah?"

"Is everything okay?" He takes the mug from my trembling hands and sets it aside. There's nothing between us but air and heat.

I lick my lips. "Everything's fine."

"Then why do you look like you'll shatter into a thousand pieces?"

"Because I feel like I will."

"Why?"

"Being with you makes me unsteady." I inhale deep, and his scent intoxicates me. "Like I'm made of glass and falling."

"I'll catch you." His murmured confession lingers between us. I barely register the implication of the words before he captures my lips in a searing kiss.

A moan rips from my throat as his soft lips punish mine. He wraps his hand around the base of my neck, threading his fingers in my hair. He drags me across his lap, my thighs brushing against the cotton of his khakis, his insistent erection pressing against my hip.

My arms link around his neck, holding me firmly in place as he devours my mouth. Clove and coffee with a hint of bourbon pull me deeper. I'm lost in Jackson's embrace and I don't want to be saved.

One hand holds my waist firmly, while his other cups my cheek. He's warm and strong while his kiss leaves me breathless and drowning. This man is everything I knew he would be and more.

I whimper as he draws back to search my face. His brow furrows even though I can see the hunger in his eyes. I trace my fingers along his jaw. It tenses beneath my touch and his eyes drift closed.

"Jackson?"

He gently sets me on the couch and stands. "Forgive me, Lily."

"For what?"

"I crossed a line." He rakes his hand through his hair. "I should go."

"Wait. Jackson..." I race after him and grab his arm before he reaches for his coat. "What just happened?"

His jaw clenches tight before he responds. "Nothing."

"Bullshit." I rest my hand on his cheek. His expression softens briefly before he steels his gaze.

"It doesn't matter." Jackson steps from my reach, grabs his coat, and opens the door. "Thank you for everything, Lily."

I stand on the landing outside and watch him walk toward the nearest station. When he disappears around the corner, it hits me.

Jackson wants me as much as I want him. Why is he fighting it? We're both consenting adults. I shiver at the biting cold breeze and retreat into the house, slamming the door behind me.

CHAPTER FOURTEEN

The Monday after Thanksgiving, Mr. Roberts doesn't show up for work. He doesn't come in all week. When he finally reappears the following Monday, he's aloof and professional. The quintessential boss greeting his employees.

Heat burns my face at the memory of his kiss. His touch. How can he act like that never happened? It fucking happened.

By Friday, I'm convinced it's a figment of my imagination. Did I imagine having him over for dinner? The comfortable comradery we shared? That scorching moment of explosive sexual tension culminating in the best fucking kiss I've ever experienced? I must be insane because Mr. Roberts treats me no differently than he did before I knew what his sinful mouth tasted like.

I tried to reach out to Sam, but my messages went unanswered. Surely he wouldn't ghost me—would he? My mood takes a dive, and by five o'clock, I'm stewing in misery.

"Hey, you want to come over for dinner?" Jen is standing by my desk wearing a radiant smile.

"I can't tonight." I pout, knowing full well I'm lying. I just don't want to spend the evening watching Jen and Shaun make eyes at each other. My heart can't handle it. "We still on for movie night tomorrow?"

"Yeah. My place at four." Jen waves before she retreats.

"Sounds good." I slowly gather my things and wait until I'm sure Jen and Shaun have left before I head for the elevator. I love them, but I'm really not in the headspace to be with couples at the moment.

The office is completely empty by the time I leave. I step inside the elevator and press the ground floor. As the doors close, a hand appears between them, forcing them open.

Jackson steps into the carriage. I pointedly keep my gaze

forward despite the magnetic pull drawing my attention to him. He's an arm's length from me, but I can smell his familiar cologne. I bite my lip to keep from saying anything. If he wants to act like nothing happened, fine. Two can play that game.

"You're upset with me, Miss Astor."

I refuse to respond. My silence should speak clearly enough. He glides his fingers through his hair.

"You have every right to be angry." His tone softens. "I took advantage of your hospitality. You invited me into your home and I crossed a line."

My jaw clenches and my desire to remain silent erodes, exposing the tender nerve. "I invited you to my home because I *enjoy* spending time with you. I wanted to know more about the man you are outside of the office." I press forward. "You can't kiss me like that, apologize, and pretend it never happened."

"I have to. I'm your boss, Lily." The excuse is weak on his tongue. His faltering smile confirms the truth. He knows it's a pitiful defense.

"No shit." I shelve my hand on my hip. "The first moment I saw you in the lobby three years ago, I wanted you, Jackson. But when I found out you were the VP, I hid it because I'm a goddamn professional."

His feral growl echoes in the small space. Before I can react, his hands are on my waist and I'm pressed against the wall. His gaze is intense. Hungry. His strength surrounds me and I'm tired of fighting it. I'm tired of hiding how I feel about him.

"You and your dainty cappuccino have haunted me for years." His breath ghosts over my lips, and I want him to kiss me. To end my suffering. Instead, his mouth twists with amusement. "I knew exactly who you were. From your application. The tabloids."

"Don't." I try to push him away, but his unrelenting grip tightens. He presses his body against mine. He's hard in all the places that matter.

"Whatever I was expecting, it wasn't the woman who swanned into my office that morning. The woman who has stolen my breath every day for the past three years."

"What are you saying, Jackson?"

"I've heard the whispers around the office. I know the effect my presence has on people." His hand glides higher until his thumb brushes the curve of my breast. "I've worked hard for years to ensure there was never any opportunity for gossip concerning my personal life. My love life. But your presence makes it hard to maintain my professionalism."

"Wha..."

"I'm tired of fighting this." He cups my cheek, and I lean into the touch. "I've spent the past two weeks in torment over that kiss. Tell me I'm not too late."

His words hit with the force of a well-placed jab. Too late? Is it too late? The elevator stops and the doors slide open. The lobby is vacant, but I suddenly feel exposed, vulnerable. Uncertain. I gently pull his hand away.

"I need time to think."

"Of course." He takes several steps back and drops his hands to his sides. "Have a good weekend, Miss Astor."

"Sir." I nod and exit the car, barely able to contain my rioting emotions as I head toward the revolving doors. I want to rush back into that elevator and kiss him senseless. I want to tell him exactly what I want. But I can't. I won't. I need a few days to process this.

By the time I make it home, I'm composed enough to fake my way through a conversation with James and Mike before excusing myself and hiding in my room. I end up spending all night working on designs. Somewhere around dawn, I crash.

When I wake up at two, it's a mad dash to get ready for movie night with the girls. Should I cancel? If I bail, they'll know something's up. Shit.

I'm a jumbled ball of nerves. The walk to Jen's place clears my head a bit, but I need to talk this out. It's about time I came clean to Jen and Maggie. They'll understand.

"Lily!" Jen hugs me and pulls me into her apartment. Sealed boxes lay stacked against the far wall.

"When's your last day in the apartment?" I ask, hanging up my coat.

"The thirty-first." Jen retreats to the kitchen and I follow. "Want a drink?"

"Please." I lean against the counter and watch her pour a mug of mulled wine. "Where's Maggie?"

"I'm here." Maggie emerges from the hallway.

I give her a half hug, careful not to spill my wine. "How's married life?"

"It's nice. I highly recommend it."

My heart warms knowing my two friends found happiness in each other. "I'm so happy for you guys. How was Thanksgiving with his family?"

"It was great." Maggie picks up her drink from the table. "I'm sorry we left you all alone this year." She frowns. "How was it?"

"Uh." My gaze shifts from Maggie to Jen. "Well, I wasn't alone."

"Wait, what?" Jen stares at me in disbelief.

"Yeah, back that trolly up a minute." Maggie narrows her gaze. "Who did you...?" Her eyes widen. "Did your cowboy daddy fly in to spend Thanksgiving with you?"

"No." I bite my lip remembering our sexy conversation before he went radio silent.

"All right, girl." Maggie pulls me toward the couch. "Spill it. What's going on?"

I take a fortifying sip of my mulled wine and set it on the coffee table. Jen and Maggie stare at me in anticipation.

"His name is Sam, not Cowboy Daddy." I wrinkle my nose at the nickname. "He's been very supportive and sweet. But he's been quiet lately."

"What happened? You two have a fight?" Jen asks, fully invested.

"No, we…well, we were chatting and…things got a little steamy."

Jen's eyes are as big as dinner plates. Maggie's shit-eating grin does nothing to offer me comfort.

"You had phone sex with Cowboy Daddy?" Jen's jaw hangs open.

"His name is Sam." I sigh. "And yes, I guess I did."

"Get some, girl!" Maggie cheers. "Good for you."

"Well, then what happened afterward?" Jen pushes for more information. "Did he come visit you over Thanksgiving?"

"That's the problem. I haven't heard from him since." I worry my lip between my teeth. "Do you think I scared him off?"

"You never know. Maybe something came up and he's been busy." Jen tries to comfort me.

"Yeah." Maggie strokes her jaw. "But if the cowboy didn't spend Thanksgiving with you, then who did?"

I pinch my eyes closed. "Mr. Roberts."

Two extremely high-pitched squeals fill the apartment. I wrench my eyes open when my whole body rocks back and forth. Maggie's got me by both shoulders, shaking me. Jen's completely frozen with shock.

"You invited your *hot boss* over for Thanksgiving dinner and didn't TELL US?" Maggie's voice rises exponentially. "Did you fuck him?"

Heat consumes me from the roots of my hair to my toes. Jen and Maggie share a look before fixing me with matching incredulous stares.

"You slept with Mr. Roberts?" Jen manages to get the question out without choking.

"No!" I grab Maggie's wrists and pull her hands from my shoulders. "I didn't sleep with him."

Disappointment crashes over my friends.

"Start from the beginning," Maggie says. "Don't skimp on the details."

"He didn't have anywhere to go, so I invited him to join me. We had a lovely meal, he helped me with the dishes, and we had our pie and coffee in the living room."

Maggie's gaze narrows. "And that's it?"

"He kissed me." I press my fingertips to my mouth.

"Holy fuck." Jen gasps. "He kissed you."

I nod.

"Then what happened?" Maggie interjects, wanting all the nitty gritty details.

"He left," I explain in detail and include his odd behavior for the past two weeks.

"Asshole." Maggie folds her arms across her chest. "Kissing you like that and acting like nothing happened."

"I'm sorry, Lily." Jen rests her hand on my arm. "I knew you looked off yesterday. Why didn't you tell us before?"

"I couldn't. I was just going to forget it until he cornered me in the elevator after work yesterday."

"Wait, what now?" Maggie's interest perks again.

"We were the last two in the office." I swallow and press forward, distracted by the vivid memory of his bold declaration. I launch into a recap of what happened in the elevator.

"Girl, he's got it bad," Jen says, leaning back with her hand over her mouth. "I mean, I always knew he favored you, but now it makes sense."

"What did you tell him?" Maggie licks her lips like a lioness creeping up on an unsuspecting deer.

"I had to think about it." I throw my hands up. "He can't just dump that on me after kissing me like that and then leaving me to wonder what the fuck I did wrong."

"You're absolutely right." Jen agrees with a firm nod. "At least he was honest with you."

"He could've been honest with me on Thanksgiving instead of making me stew in it for two fucking weeks."

"So, let me get this straight." Maggie taps her jaw. "You and Mr. Roberts have a little thing going on."

"I guess."

"And you're having a semi-flirtatious relationship with some cowboy in Wyoming via the internet."

I clap my hand over my mouth. "Oh, God," I mutter between my fingers.

Maggie's eyes gleam. "You're gonna have to make a choice, sunshine. You can't have phone sex with a cowboy and make out with your boss too."

I groan. "What the hell am I going to do?"

"Be honest with them," Jen suggests, earning a reluctant nod from Maggie.

"I'm in it for the delicious drama, but she's right." Maggie relents. "You're going to have to be honest with both of them up front."

"I know. Ugh! Why does this have to be so difficult?"

"I'm sorry, Lily. I know it sucks," Jen apologizes. "You'll figure it out though."

"*How?*"

"Well, maybe you should give Mr. Roberts a chance. He's right here in front of you, not halfway across the country." Maggie picks up her mug and takes a drink.

"I agree with Mags on this one." Jen offers a comforting smile. "Sometimes it's best to focus on what's right in front of you."

She's right. They both are. "You guys are the best friends. Thank you."

"Any time." Maggie settles back against the cushions. "Now then, when do I get to meet this sexy stud muffin of a boss?"

I clap my hand over my face.

"Let her talk to him first before you go butting into their love life." Jen laughs.

"Enough about me and my problems." I cradle my mug in my hands and look at Jen. "I want to hear all about your visit to Iowa. How was it? Did his sisters love you?"

The conversation turns to Jen's adventure in the Midwest with Shaun's family, and a sense of relief fills me. Why did I wait so long to be honest with my friends? We're our own little family, helping each other out and giving the push the other needs.

I'm a lucky girl. Things are finally coming together.

CHAPTER FIFTEEN

It's nearly four and I haven't seen him all day.

When I got to work this morning, Jen gave me a supportive thumbs up from across the room. After the conversation we had on Saturday night, I was ready to have an open and honest conversation with Jackson. The problem is, I can't do that at work. There are too many eyes and ears.

So I wait for my opportunity and do what I was hired to do. Which is good, because I need the distraction. I even took my lunch to the break room in the hopes he might find me there when he passed by. But he never did. The only communication I've had from him is an email requesting a rough draft of the end-of-year report I should be working on. He wants it on his desk by the end of the day. Of course, he does.

I could email him back and tell him I need to speak to him, but using our interoffice network for that seems shady. This would be so much easier if I had his personal number. A simple text could have cured half the anxiety swirling around inside me. All I can do is wait for the perfect opportunity to catch him alone in his office. At least I have an excuse to interrupt him.

At four thirty, I'm in the middle of proofreading the document when Jen stops by my desk.

"Working late?" she asks, but I see the gleam in her eyes.

"Yeah, I need to finish this before I head home."

"Don't work too hard." She winks. "I'll see you tomorrow. Text if you need anything." Her voice drops low. "Good luck."

After she leaves, I wait for the rest of the office to empty. Slowly my coworkers vacate their desks and head for the elevator. The moment Gladys passes me wearing her coat and hat I make my move.

I print the document and put it in a new folder. With a deep breath, I make my way down the hall toward his office, my heart pounding in my chest.

With a nervous glance, I check my reflection in the mirrored panel running along the wall. I'm wearing red trousers paired with a cream blouse and a dark green cardigan embroidered with a poinsettia. With Christmas right around the corner, it felt natural to spread some holiday cheer. Now I wish I had worn something a little sexier.

One knock on his office door earns me a summons. Jackson glances up from his desk, peering over a pair of dark-rimmed reading glasses. He takes them off when I step into his office.

"Miss Astor." He sets the paper aside, along with his glasses. "To what do I owe this pleasure."

My face warms at the inflection of his voice when he says the final word. "I have that report you requested, sir."

He stands and rounds the desk. I offer the file as he approaches. He takes the folder and sets it on his desk.

"And here I thought you missed my company."

"I did."

"Have you considered our previous conversation?"

"I have." I put my hand up when he takes a step closer. "But there's something I need to tell you first."

"Very well." Jackson gestures to the chair beside him. "Would you like to sit down?"

I shift my weight from one foot to the other. "No, thank you."

"Please, speak freely."

The confidence I felt earlier disintegrates under the heat of his steady gaze. He devours me with a single look, and I'm not sure I can withstand the torment a moment longer.

"There's someone else." What sounded good in my head transforms his curiosity into something darker. More possessive.

"Is that so?"

"Yes." Shit, I'm screwing this up. "But it's nothing serious. We're not in a committed relationship or anything." I laugh at the absurdity of the whole situation. "I've never even met him in person."

Jackson's left brow rises.

"I met him a few months ago. We've been chatting online. He's shown interest in us forming something more than friendship." I twist my hands together. "But he's halfway across the country, and..."

"And what, Miss Astor?"

"He's not you." I lick my lips. "Sir."

Jackson stalks closer with purpose and confidence in every step. "Why are you telling me this?"

"Because I want to be honest with you." I meet his gaze and my world spins. There's nothing but us at the center of this mad universe.

"What do you want, Lily?" He brushes his finger along my jaw.

"I—" My breath hitches. "I want you, Jackson."

His hand slides around the base of my neck, and I melt into the pressure of his grip as his fingertips slide through my hair. He's solid and strong. Relief and arousal flood me when he closes the gap between us and kisses me.

It's hard and possessive. His free hand wraps around my waist and draws me against him. The memory of his previous kiss is nothing compared to this moment. I breathe him in and let his scent pull me deeper into senseless abandon. He teases my lips apart and tastes me. When he moans, my resolve snaps. I'm his in every possible way, consequences be damned.

I grip his lapels, wanting him closer. My fingers slide across the soft cotton of his dress shirt. Why are there so many clothes? I want to feel his skin against mine. It's been far too long since I've been intimate with anyone.

"Jackson," I murmur, breaking the kiss. "There's...something...you need to...ah...know." I gasp the words as he kisses along the column of my throat.

He pulls back, his eyes dazed with desire, his lips kiss-bruised and gleaming. "Do you want me to stop?"

"No." I cup his cheek in my palm. "But you should know, I've never...fuck, this is going to sound stupid."

"Tell me."

"I've never gone all the way." The lame euphemism does

nothing to ease the conversation.

"Are you telling me you're a virgin?"

"I've been with men before," I murmur in a pitiful defense. "But I never let them fuck me."

Jackson's soft chuckle leaves me stunned. I try to pull from his embrace, but he holds me fast.

"No, sweetheart, you're not getting out of this that easily." He backs me up until my back hits the wall. His arms cage me against it.

"I shouldn't have told you."

He hooks a finger beneath my chin and drags my attention up until our eyes lock. "You think I wouldn't have figured it out?"

"No." I muscle through the shame. "I'm quite comfortable with my sexuality, and I'm not as innocent as you think I am."

"I have no doubt that you're in touch with your desires, Lily." He leans closer, his breath brushing over my lips. "Are you sure I'm the one you want?"

"Yes." I hold his gaze. "Please."

"If I cross that line, you're mine." He kisses my neck. "Do you understand?"

"Yes."

"Good girl." He unfastens my trousers and slides his warm hand beneath the fabric. I cling to his shoulders as his questing fingers push aside my soaked panties.

"Oh, God." I moan, collapsing against his chest when his fingers brush my aching clit.

"Is this for me?" He growls and delves deeper, sliding two fingers into me.

"Yes." The sound his fingers make as he thrusts them in and out is obscene and so fucking hot. I open for him, giving him as much access as my clothes and our position allow. My grip on his arms tightens as he strokes me higher, using his thumb to massage my clit in firm circles.

I rock my hips as he quickens his pace. He palms my breast in his other hand and squeezes.

"That's my girl." He purrs in my ear. "I want you to come

for me, sweetheart."

A strangled cry rips from my throat as my brain overloads. He's playing me like a maestro plays the violin. All I can focus on is his talented fingers working black magic on my body as my climax builds.

"Look at me." His hand cradles my cheek. "Come for me. Now."

Gasping and panting, I'm boneless as the orgasm radiates through my body. He holds me against the wall and continues fucking me with his fingers until I collapse forward against his chest and bury my face in his neck. When he slowly withdraws his touch, I'm ruined.

Not only my panties and my trousers, but me. No one has ever touched me in a way that's left me completely speechless and sated like this.

When I meet his gaze, he licks his fingers clean. "So sweet." Before I can respond, he refastens my trousers and straightens my blouse.

"What are you doing?"

"Sending you home." He presses a gentle kiss to my cheek.

"Why?"

"Because I won't have your first time be in my office, Lily." He readjusts the front of his pants where his erection presses prominently against the fabric.

"But you're..." I step forward, but he holds up his hand.

"Don't worry about me, Lily." He smiles and rakes his hand through his hair. "I'll be fine."

"But I want to help you."

"You can help me by going home and getting some rest." A smirk plays on his lips. "I'll see you tomorrow morning, Lily."

"Yes, sir." I rise slowly and turn to leave. I glance over my shoulder. His gaze follows me, dropping to my ass. "Good night, Jackson."

He resumes his seat as I close the door behind me. *You belong to me, Lily.* Jackson's words filter through my memory, and a satisfied smile curves my lips.

That went better than expected.

Chapter Sixteen

I've made my decision, and for once, I'm confident I made the right one. Now, I need to tell Sam. He'll understand, won't he? He doesn't reply to my message until Friday. I see the notification at lunch, but I don't open his response until I get home from work.

I grab some leftovers from the fridge and heat them up. While I wait, I open my notifications and smile.

*I apologize for my absence. Work has been overwhelming lately, but it's no excuse to ignore such a lovely woman who deserves my undivided attention. *winking emoji**

A second message is below the first. *I miss you.*

Guilt pierces my heart. I pull my plate from the microwave and sit at the counter. While I eat, I ponder what to say. There's no point in prolonging the inevitable. I've already chosen Jackson, it would be unfair of me to lead Sam on any longer. I finish my impromptu supper and clean the dishes. Once I finish, I grab my phone and retreat to my bedroom.

With a sigh, I collapse on my bed and type out a response. *I miss you too, Sam. Can we talk? I have something important to tell you.*

I change into my green and red plaid flannel pajamas while I wait for his answer. My phone pings.

I'm just sitting by the fire having coffee. Call whenever you're free.

I work up the courage to press the call button. Sam deserves the truth. Within half a heartbeat, he answers.

"Hello, gorgeous." His drawl leaves me weak.

"Hi, Sam." I lay back on the bed and let his voice wash over me. "It's been a while."

"Yeah, I'm sorry about that, kitten." He uses the nickname with ease. "But I'm here now. How are you?"

"I'm fine."

"Something wrong? You sound like you've got something

on your mind." It's like he reaches into my brain and tugs on the thread keeping my thoughts bound together.

"Oh, Sam. I'm sorry. I feel like I've led you on." The truth spills from me in a rush. "I've enjoyed our conversations and I really like you, but I've recently started seeing someone."

The silence on the other line gives way to a heavy sigh followed by a soft chuckle. "You have nothing to apologize for, kitten. We had a little fun. There's no harm in that."

"I know, but I feel bad." I pinch my eyes closed. He's taking this well and it's leaving me awash in guilt.

"Now, now. Don't you dare feel bad about making that choice." He soothes me with his tone and his words. "We're both adults. I'm glad you felt comfortable enough to tell me."

"I couldn't lead you on. That's not who I am. You're so sweet and kind, and you deserve to have someone who can be there with you."

"That's mighty considerate of you, Lily. I appreciate your honesty." He inhales deep. "I won't lie, my pride is singed, but I'll survive."

"Oh, Sam. I'm so sorry."

"Don't apologize for following your heart, Lily. You don't owe me a thing. It was fun while it lasted."

I pout, unable to form a response. Tears prick at my eyes.

"This man you found. If he doesn't treat you right, you call me. I'll make sure he understands what a treasure he has."

I sigh. My romantic nature finally gets the best of me. "Damn it, Sam. Do you have to be so wonderful?"

"Of course. My mother would have my head if I wasn't the gentleman she raised me to be."

"She did a wonderful job."

"I'll be sure to tell her." He laughs. "But I'm serious, Lily. If it doesn't work out with this guy, I'll be here. You're more than welcome to call me any time. And if you need an escape, you can come visit the ranch whenever you want."

"Oh, I couldn't impose like that." My soul relaxes at his kind invitation.

"It's not an imposition. It's a standing invitation." I can hear the smile in his voice when he reiterates.

"Thank you, Sam."

"Remember, Lily. You're not alone. I'm here if you need a friend—or more." His voice deepens. "My Mamma raised me to be a gentleman, and I know exactly how a woman should be treated. Treasured." He growls. "Loved."

My heart pounds. "Don't tease me."

"I'm sorry. You're right." He clears his throat. "I won't keep you any longer."

"Have a good night, Sam, and Merry Christmas."

"Merry Christmas, Lily."

I set my phone aside and let the tears fall. Sam was kind enough to let me go without a fight. But part of me wanted him to push, to fight for me.

I grab my pillow and bury my face in the soft fabric to muffle my scream. When I pull the pillow away, my makeup is smeared on the white fabric. Damn it.

After replacing the pillowcase, I head for the bathroom and remove my makeup. I brush out my hair and tuck it into a net before retreating to my bedroom.

With only a week until Christmas, I begin making plans for the holiday. Will Jackson accept my invitation? Will he finally give me the release I crave? Total surrender lies wrapped like an oversized gift beneath my Christmas tree and I wish to give it to him complete with a bright red bow.

I settle into bed and retrieve the romance novel I started a few months ago. Tonight, I'm going to read. A reward for making such a tough decision. I'm halfway through the fifth chapter when my phone rings.

"Hello?"

"Good evening, Lily." My father clears his throat. "Violet and I would like you to join us for Christmas luncheon."

"Oh." I scramble to find a valid excuse. "Well, I have plans already."

"Who could be more important than your family?"

Everyone, I want to say, but I bite my tongue and offer a more diplomatic response. "My boyfriend, actually."

A click of disapproval comes through the line. "Bring him along. I should meet the man who thinks he's worthy of my daughter."

I want to rip into him. To tell him I'm not his little girl anymore. That he cannot tell me what to do and that I am the mistress of my own life. I should let it pour out and end this charade once and for all, but I can't seem to muster the strength to fight him. Not after such an emotional day.

"We'll see."

"Very well. Luncheon starts at twelve-thirty. Don't be late."

I don't even say goodbye before I end the call. How *dare* he make demands of me and belittle the man I want to spend time with!

Jackson. Oh, God. I haven't even asked if he'd spend Christmas with me, and now I'm scared to offer it. My father will put him on trial. He'll crucify him.

On the other hand, Jackson is the vice president of a prestigious company. A mature businessman. I've seen him face down investors and infuriated customers with grace and aplomb. My father might be intimidating, but if anyone could hold their own against him, it would be Jackson.

I have two days before I see him. Two days before I have to issue the invitation. I'll simply compose myself and ask him. Just like I did when I spoke to Sam. I'm an adult. I can do this.

But that doesn't stop my mind from spinning over the possibilities of a monumental catastrophe when I arrive at my father's penthouse on the arm of a man who's sixteen years my senior. I can almost feel my father's disapproval like a disturbance in the Force.

I *was* looking forward to Christmas. Now I just wish it was over.

CHAPTER SEVENTEEN

"Want to grab some lunch?" Jen's question makes me jump. "Oh, sorry. I shouldn't have snuck up on you."

I press a hand to my racing heart and spin around to face her. "It's okay. Lunch sounds great. I need a break from this mess."

Jen steps to the side as I grab my purse from my desk drawer and we head toward the elevator. I've been on edge since I got to the office this morning. Christmas is four days away and I haven't worked up the courage to ask Jackson the big question.

"Everything okay?"

"Yeah, it's just my father." I lick my lips and focus on the numbers descending over the door. "He's invited me to come home for Christmas."

"I take it you're still not on the best terms with him?"

"No. I've been able to avoid his invitations for a while, but at some point, I'll have to face him."

The doors open and we head for the café. There's an open table along the far wall. I steer us there through a maze of hungry employees.

Jen settles in across from me and slides her chair a little closer. Her voice is low when she speaks. "Did you get a chance to talk to Mr. Roberts and your cowboy?"

I nod and smile when the waiter delivers our drinks. The moment he vanishes from sight, I catch Jen staring at me.

"Well? What happened?"

The story pours from me in a rush. The encounter with Jackson in his office after hours. The honest conversation with Sam. I spared very little detail in my recounting. I'm sure the blush on my cheeks complimented my red cardigan and cherry lipstick. Then I add the bonus bombshell of my father's invitation to Christmas luncheon. When I finish, Jen's wide green eyes blink twice before she exhales sharply.

"Sounds like a hell of a predicament." She goes silent when the waiter appears with our soup and sandwiches. "At least you straightened out everything with Mr. Roberts and the cowboy."

"Yeah." I take a bite of soup letting it warm me through. "But I'm going to miss talking to Sam."

"Honey, you have Mr. Roberts eating out of the palm of your hand." Jen chuckles. "Most of the women in this office would love to be in your position."

"You're right," I reply between nibbles. "I was going to invite Jackson over for Christmas. Just the two of us." My excitement falls. "But my father insisted I come for luncheon. I can't keep putting it off."

"Take him with you, then." Jen's smile borders on evil. "Maybe if your father sees that you have someone in your life who's successful and stable, he'll back off and leave you alone."

I scoff. "My father will only see it as a challenge to torment Jackson without reason."

Jen laughs, covering her mouth with her hand after garnering stares from neighboring tables. "Sorry." She clears her throat. "I'm not laughing at you or the situation, but I think Mr. Roberts is more than capable of handling an afternoon meal with your family."

"You don't know how critical my father can be. He's brutal and trusts no one." I sigh and take another sip of the creamy chicken soup. "He never let me date and limited the time I spent with friends. When I finally left home and moved in with the boys, my father ran extensive background checks on all of them and made them sign contracts to ensure my safety."

"Holy shit, Lily." Jen's smile falters. "I'm sorry."

"He's controlling and borderline abusive." My voice catches and I take a drink of warm tea. "I don't want to drag Jackson into the lion's den. We've only just reached an understanding. I don't want my father to ruin it."

"Do you really think he'll try to ruin your new relationship on Christmas?"

"I wouldn't put it past him." I finish the soup and set it

aside. "Maybe I shouldn't invite him to the luncheon and have him meet me for dinner instead."

"Lily." Jen takes my hand in hers. "You're a strong, vibrant woman. Do what you want to do. But ask Mr. Roberts what he would prefer before making the decision for him." Her smile softens my apprehension. "He's not some simpering teenager or a fresh-faced twentysomething who's still trying to figure out his place in the world. Mr. Roberts is the most powerful man in this company."

Pride fills me at her observation. "You're right. If anyone could face down my father, it would be Jackson."

"Exactly." Jen picks up her sandwich.

We finish eating and head back upstairs. When we step out onto the forty-fourth floor, Jen hugs me.

"Whatever you choose to do, it'll work out."

"Thanks." I sneak into the break room and refill my water bottle.

My phone pings notifying me of a text. *Christmas luncheon. Twelve thirty. Don't be late.*

I stuff my phone into my purse, grumbling under my breath.

"Bad news?" Jackson's standing in the doorway with his hands in his pockets. I melt when he smiles.

"Not exactly." I shake my head and step closer. "I was wondering if I could speak to you alone."

Jackson's brow rises, but he says nothing and steps aside, gesturing down the hallway toward his office. The scent of his cologne and the heat of his body teases my senses as I brush past him.

What if he says no? What if he says *yes*? Oh, God. I bite my lip as we move closer to his office.

Gladys offers me a friendly smile when I pass her desk.

Jackson opens the door to his office and motions for me to enter. Inside, I'm transported to the week before when he had me pinned against the wall with his fingers buried in my pussy. Heat washes over me at the vivid memory. When I turn to meet his gaze, I can't tell if he's thinking the same thing I am.

His face is a mask of professional curiosity. Handsome and regal. No bullshit. No nonsense.

"Is everything all right, Miss Astor?" Even with the door closed, he's professional and courteous. Damn him for keeping such a firm grasp of his composure.

"Yes, I'm fine."

"What did you want to talk to me about?" he asks, gesturing to the couch.

Being close to him makes it difficult to focus now that I know what he tastes like and how easily he can make me climax with one talented hand.

"I...uh..." My words jumble together when I meet his eyes. "Yes, well, I wanted to ask if you would be interested in spending Christmas Day with me?"

"I would be honored."

He splays his hand over his thigh and my thoughts scatter. I pinch my eyes closed. "Before you agree, you should know, my father has requested I join him for luncheon. I promised him a brief visit, citing other plans for the day. We can meet afterward and..."

"I would much rather spend the *whole* day with you."

"Yes, but I'm not sure you would enjoy my father's company."

"On the contrary, I would relish the opportunity to meet your family and tell your father what an amazing, talented daughter he has." Jackson cocks his head and smiles. "Unless you would rather I do not attend by your side."

"Yes. I mean, no." I growl in frustration. "What I mean to say is that my father can be a particularly stubborn man. I would hate to have our day ruined because he cannot hold his tongue."

"It sounds like you need my companionship even more." His sinful mouth leaves me breathless as it curls into a devastating smile.

"You do not know my father. He is—"

"Lily." He rests his hand on mine, interlacing our fingers together, and I forget how to breathe. "I know exactly who your father is." He brings my hand to his lips and kisses my knuckles.

"Trust me. Monroe Astor does not intimidate me in the slightest."

"Jackson."

"I love the way you say my name."

His breath brushes over my cheek as he leans closer. "Like a whispered prayer and a veiled curse twisted together."

"We shouldn't. It's not appropriate. Work—"

"You're right." He draws back and relinquishes his grasp on my hand before standing.

"Would you please send me your parents' address?"

"Why?"

"So I can pick you up on Christmas morning and escort you to luncheon." He pulls his phone from his pocket. "Here. Put your number into my personal phone."

I take the phone and add the information he requested, labeling it as Lily before handing it back.

"Is there anything else you wish to discuss?" he asks, his hungry eyes devouring me from head to foot in a brazen perusal.

"No, sir."

His eyes darken with need. "Very well, Miss Astor. That will be all."

I turn and retreat from the room, heading directly for the bathroom to press a damp towel to my overheated skin. "You're completely smitten," I mutter to my reflection.

Once I gather my wits, I return to my desk, retrieving my water bottle from the break room along the way. It takes me a few minutes to find my routine once more.

An hour later, my phone dings. Unlisted number. Curious, I open the message.

It's Jackson. Another message follows the first. *I can still smell you. Christmas can't come fast enough.*

A rush of desire pulses through me, leaving me wet and aching. Jackson has no idea how much his words—his very existence—affect me. Part of me wants to cancel luncheon with my father and keep Jackson all to myself on Christmas.

But my father is relentless. It's better for both of us if we dispense with this pleasantry and move on with our lives. The sooner my father realizes I'm no longer his child but a grown woman with desires and passions of my own, the better off I will be. Perhaps allowing Jackson to join us will provide the perfect way for me to show my father the truth. I'm not his little girl anymore.

I type out a reply. *I look forward to it, sir.*

After I turn off my ringer, I tuck my phone away and focus on work. The weekend can't come fast enough. Because I know this year, my Christmas wish will come true.

CHAPTER EIGHTEEN

On Christmas Eve, I couldn't sleep. My subconscious churned for hours, playing through all the possible outcomes of the Christmas luncheon with my father and Violet. It conjured a horrifying variety of possible disasters.

I must have drifted off at some point and woke to the sound of my alarm at eight a.m. Exhausted, I drag myself into the bathroom to shower. It revives me, but does nothing to calm the nervous energy coursing through my limbs. I apply my makeup and pin my hair into a simple bombshell wave.

With deliberate care, I select an emerald-green swing dress from the closet and pull it over my head. Paired with a ruby petticoat and seamed stockings, it looks quite festive. I slip on my gold kitten heels and finish the ensemble with a pearl necklace and earrings.

It's nearly ten. I glance at the gift sitting on my desk, wrapped in gold paper and topped with a small red bow. It was impulsive, stopping to buy Jackson a present on the way home from work yesterday. It wasn't expensive, but I saw it in the window of the jewelers down the block and couldn't resist.

A knock on my door pulls me from my indecision. I open it to find Mike wearing sweats and a t-shirt.

"You look fantastic!" He whistles low in appreciation. "Your date is going to flip when he sees you. He's downstairs waiting."

"He's here already?"

"Yeah."

I grab my coat and purse before heading down the stairs.

"Have fun and call us if you need anything," Mike yells after me.

Jackson turns when I enter the living room. The brief flash of need in his gaze dims as he assumes his professional demeanor. He steps closer. "You look lovely."

"Thank you." I take in his broad shoulders emphasized by his well-tailored pinstripe suit. "So do you."

He chuckles and takes my coat, holding it open. "Shall we go? I don't want to be late and make a bad impression."

"Of course." His fingertips brush the nape of my neck as he lifts my hair out of the way. If we remain here a moment longer, I won't be able to restrain myself.

When I walk toward the door, he follows, stepping forward at the last moment to open it for me. There is a black town car parked on the curb, and a driver standing at the ready.

Once I'm seated, Jackson slides in beside me. He doesn't speak until we're over the bridge and halfway uptown.

"Are you well?" he asks, studying my profile.

My body's alight with awareness. Of his presence. His scent. His heat. I want to kiss him, ruin his perfect hair, tear that suit off those tempting shoulders. My mouth goes dry. I lick my lips, and the storm in his eyes darkens.

"Just a bit nervous."

Jackson takes my hand and holds it between his. "There's nothing to worry about. I doubt Christmas luncheon can match the corporate meetings I've had to attend."

"You've never met my father." I sigh and squeeze his hand. "Please don't take anything he says to heart. He's just overprotective."

"Nothing he could possibly say will affect me."

"I wish that were true."

"You are mine, Lily." His thumb brushes across my lower lip, creating a riot in my mind. "As my girlfriend, you are mine to protect. Not his."

My breath catches at the sincerity of his words and the intensity of his expression. "Your girlfriend?"

His devastating smile wrecks me. "Yes, sweetheart. Isn't that what you want?" He leans close, his breath brushing my ear. "To be mine?"

I nod, unable to form a single coherent thought.

"Good girl." He pulls me against him.

I want to stay here, nestled to his side, safe and warm. But the car comes to a stop. When I glance out the window, I see the familiar stone entrance to my father's building.

"We've arrived."

Jackson presses a tender kiss to my forehead and steps from the car. When the driver opens the door, Jackson is waiting, hand outstretched in offering. I take it and smile. Confidence infuses me as we approach the lion's den.

Inside, I'm struck at the changes Violet has made to the décor. It still looks familiar, like it did when I was a kid, but it's also evolved with time and taste. Much like I have.

The butler instructs us to follow him to the living room. Violet turns from the window when we appear in the doorway.

"Lily, I'm so glad you could make it." She crosses the room and presses featherlight air kisses to each cheek. "You look radiant."

"As do you." I step aside and introduce Jackson. "This is my—boyfriend, Mr. Jackson Roberts." The word feels foreign on my tongue, but not unwelcome.

Violet's eyes brighten. "Lovely to meet you, Mr. Roberts." She shakes his hand.

"Please, call me Jackson, Mrs. Astor."

"Oh, Violet, please." Her cheeks pinken at his attention.

I stifle a laugh. Violet is only a few years older than I am. She seems as smitten with Jackson as the rest of the female population at Valentina's.

He smiles politely and glances around the room. "Your home is lovely, Violet. Thank you for extending such a generous invitation."

Violet waves her hand in dismissal with a soft laugh. "Oh, it's no trouble at all. We missed seeing Lily at Thanksgiving. I'm pleased she's found someone so handsome and charming."

Jackson and I share a look. I can tell he's also thinking of our Thanksgiving meal for two.

I clear my throat and turn back to Violet. "Where's father?"

"Probably taking care of last-minute business. He's in the process of selling some of his properties." Violet instructs the server to offer drinks.

"Which ones?" He's mentioned on several occasions his intention to sell the brownstone in Brooklyn. So far I've managed to stave him off, but perhaps my desire for independence will come at a price.

"You'll have to ask him yourself. You know he never discusses business with me." She lifts her champagne in toast. "To the lovely couple."

Jackson clinks his glass against mine. I sip the bubbly concoction out of politeness. I'm not a fan of the fizzy drink.

"My apologies." Father's voice booms as he steps into the room. "There were some unexpected issues with the realtor."

He comes closer and wraps me in a hug. "You look pale, Lily."

"Hello, Father." I force a tightlipped smile. "May I introduce my boyfriend, Mr. Jackson Roberts." I gesture to Jackson by my side.

Father clasps him in a firm handshake while sizing up the man who dares lay claim to his daughter. His gaze narrows.

"Sir, it's an honor to meet you." Jackson's attempt at polite conversation is met with cold indifference.

"So you believe yourself worthy of my daughter, do you?" He squints, eyeing Jackson from head to foot before relinquishing his grip.

"Your daughter has excellent, discerning taste, sir. I would never question her decisions. She's quite capable of making educated, informed choices." Jackson meets his stare on level ground. To anyone else, the response would sound diplomatic and flattering, but all I can hear is the tense undercurrent beneath the pretty words.

"Hmm." Father regards him carefully. "How old are you, Mr. Roberts?"

"I turn fifty in a month," he replies without missing a beat.

"Doesn't that make you a bit old for my little girl?"

"There's no more difference in our ages than there is between you and Violet, Father."

"That may be the case, but you are still my only child and I will not have anyone off the street lay claim to you." He sneers at Jackson.

My hand clenches into a fist, but Jackson's hand covers mine, easing my fist open and interlacing our fingers together.

"Your daughter is perfectly capable of making her own decisions."

My father scoffs. "And you think I'll allow her to waste her time with someone like you?"

"Lily is the most dedicated employee in my company." The edge to Jackson's voice bites deep. "She's brilliant. A true visionary. And she most certainly does not deserve to have her wings clipped because you deem her boyfriend unacceptable."

I tug on his arm trying to get his attention, but he's locked in a furious battle with my father.

"Your employee?" Father arches his brow. "Ah, yes. I knew your name sounded familiar. The vice president of Valentina's." He scowls. "Do you make it a habit to date all your lovely, young employees, Mr. Roberts? Or just my daughter?"

"This isn't about you," I snap at my father. "It's never been about you. Jackson knew I was your daughter the moment I started at the company and never capitalized on the connection. Ever." Fury laces my words with venom. "For three years, Jackson has treated me with nothing but professional courtesy. This—" I step closer to Jackson and soak up his strength "Is my choice. No one forced me to do anything I didn't want. I chose Jackson because he's a gentleman."

"I'm sure you believe that. You always were a hopeless romantic." A sneer steals across my father's lips. His handsome, familiar face contorts with rage. "But if you continue on this path, I will be left with no other alternative than to cut you off completely."

"Finally." I hold his gaze, unflinching in my declaration. "Let's go, Jackson. I can tell we've overstayed our welcome."

My father's voice echoes behind us.

"If you walk out that door—"

I turn just enough to see his reddened face and Violet's quivering form behind him. "Do what you must. I have made my choice." I nudge Jackson into motion. We head for the front door walking past the bewildered staff.

"Lilian Grace Astor!" Father's voice shakes the chandelier overhead.

Jackson opens the door and ushers me out of my father's house and into the Christmas chill. Snow drifts down from the sky, and the city is coated in pure white. He escorts me down the street to a small café near the park.

Inside, he orders me a caramel cappuccino and leads me to a small table by the front window.

"I'll be right back. I need to make a call." Jackson smiles and steps outside.

I sip my cappuccino and watch the snow fall through the glass. I thought I had cut ties with my father already, but I see I was only lying to myself, trying to make myself believe I was truly an independent woman. I shake my head and wipe away a stray tear.

Outside, Jackson paces along the sidewalk as he speaks on the phone. He must think I come from a family of lunatics. What if he decides to walk away? What if he realizes I'm not worth this hassle?

He defended you, my mind whispers. My heart warms at the memory of his impassioned declaration.

Jackson enters the café and joins me. "The car will be here shortly."

"Thank you. For everything."

"No need to thank me." He takes my hand and squeezes.

By the time the car shows up, I'm ready to just go home and change into something comfortable. I knew better than to accept my father's invitation. He never could leave well enough alone.

Neither could I. I am my father's daughter, after all.

Chapter Nineteen

The ride home in the town car with all its plush comforts does nothing to improve my mood. I stare out the window as the snow accumulates on the trees lining the street and the sidewalks.

Jackson remains silent as if sensing my need to collect my thoughts. While I appreciate his thoughtfulness, it only makes my anxiety spike. Surely he doesn't want to spend Christmas with me. Or pursue this relationship any further.

When we arrive at the brownstone, he exits the car and opens the door for me. The snowflakes gather on the sleeves of my coat and kiss my face, melting upon contact. Jackson's soft touch rests on my elbow as he leads me up the stairs to the front door.

"I'm so sorry." I spin to face him when we reach the snow-covered welcome mat. "I ruined your Christmas."

Jackson slides his thumb along my jaw. "You did nothing wrong, Lily. I shouldn't have aggravated the situation further. But I had to defend you."

"Why? I mean, we barely know each other, and my father is not one to back down from a confrontation."

"I told you before, your father doesn't intimidate me in the slightest." He cradles my neck in his hand and warmth floods me despite the cold encircling us with a halo of snow. "I care for you, Lily. There's nowhere I would rather be than here with you."

His kiss sends me into a whirlwind. I wrap my arms around his neck and drag him against me. This is exactly what I need.

He draws away, panting, his eyes dark with desire. "Tell me what you want, Lily."

"You," I respond, breathless and desperate.

Jackson waves to the driver who pulls away from the curb.

I seize the moment and fish my key from my pocket.

His arms wrap around my waist as I unlock the door. His warm lips seek out my neck. The moment the door closes behind us he pins me against it and kisses me hard.

His hand rests on my hip as the other wraps lightly around my throat. I moan as the pad of his thumb caresses my racing pulse.

"Sweetheart," he whispers, nuzzling my neck. "If you keep that up, this will be over before I have a chance to explore every inch of you."

"Oh, God." I lick my lips. "Please."

He takes my hand and pulls me into the living room where the Christmas tree sits in the corner by the front window. The lace curtains are drawn and the lights from the tree cast a festive glow on the room.

Before I can speak, Jackson captures my face in his hands and kisses me again. His mouth moves with slow precision, searching for the perfect pressure, the precise angle. When he finds it, I sink into his embrace.

A growl rumbles from deep in his chest when I slide my hands beneath his coat. We break apart long enough to remove our outer garments and toss them onto the recliner. His pinstripe jacket joins the pile.

"Jackson." I grab his tie and slide it free of the tidy knot. He unfastens his cufflinks and slides his sleeves up, exposing his strong forearms.

"Yes, sweetheart." His voice is rougher than I've ever heard it, hoarse with arousal I feel to my core.

"Unzip me." I spin around and brush my hair to the side. His touch is featherlight as he grasps the zipper and draws it down. I shiver as his fingertips trace my spine.

When I step from the gown and petticoat, I can feel the heat of his gaze burning through to my soul. I turn and drape the gown over the back of the nearest chair.

He snatches me by the waist and drags me back against him. One hand holds me firmly in place, while the other slides down over my lace panties. I'm wet and the fabric is completely soaked.

His fingers nudge it aside and glide between my slick folds.

"Oh, Lily, I've wanted this for so long," he murmurs.

I grind my hips back against the hard ridge of his cock still tucked inside those expensive trousers. He groans and his grip tightens.

"Please, Jackson." I rest my hand on top of his where it rests against my sex, applying pressure to my clit. "I need you."

"Hmmm." He releases me and steps away. I steady myself on a nearby recliner. When I recover, I find him on his knees. He glances up at me and licks his lips before parting my thighs. When he presses a light kiss to my aching pussy, I nearly collapse.

"Jackson, don't tease me." I grip the recliner tighter and open wider.

His wicked smile transforms as he devours me. I thread my fingers through his hair as he feasts and rock my hips against his talented tongue. Pleasure spirals higher and higher until I think I might explode.

Sinful and deliberate, he holds my gaze as he draws back, wiping his mouth with the back of his hand before rising to his feet and nudging me toward the wingback chair near the tree. He settles down and pats his lap.

Still wearing my thigh-high stockings and underwear, I straddle him, careful not to get his tailored suit messy. He snatches me by the waist with his strong arm and I'm pressed fully against his cock.

"I don't want to ruin your suit."

"I want you to ruin it." He leans forward and takes a lace-covered nipple in his mouth. "Ruin me, Lily."

I run my fingers through his hair, savoring the attention he's bestowing on one breast, then the other. My satisfied moans echo through the room. What little experience I've had with intimacy in the past pales in comparison to his confident touch. He unclasps my bra and tosses it aside.

While his hands explore every bare inch of me, I unbutton his shirt, exploring him with equal enthusiasm. I spread it open and lean down to run my tongue over his skin. My teeth rake over his nipple.

"Lily." It's a warning. He pushes me back and takes a deep breath.

I toy with his belt, slowly unfastening it. "I need you inside me."

His brilliant eyes drink me in as I unwrap him like a present beside the tree. He shifts enough so I can free his cock before tearing my underwear from my hips, ripping the delicate lace. "I'll buy you another pair." He glides his hand over my bare ass. "I'm all yours, sweetheart."

For years, I've imagined my first time, but I never anticipated the rush of emotions now pulling me underwater. He guides my hips into place and fits himself against me.

"Look at me," he speaks softly.

I comply and brace my hands on his shoulders. He lowers me onto his cock. What should feel like an invasion melts into a gentle exploration. It's tight and full, but he holds me steady until I'm fully seated with him deep inside me. He releases his hold to cup my face with one hand.

"Good girl." He rocks his hips and pleasure shoots through me at the combination of his words and the movement. The sensations build with every gentle sway. "Now, take what you want."

Gripping his crisp white shirt, I move my hips, riding him like I've seen women do in movies. It's new. Different. Exotic. Jackson's soft moans mingle with my panting breaths. He gently rests his hands on my hips, not to guide, but to restrain himself. I quicken my pace and grind my hips against his.

"Fuck." He bites his lip and closes his eyes and I revel in the power I wield over him. "That's it, sweetheart. Ride me."

Desire courses hot through my body. I chase my pleasure with him gently encouraging me. The handsome face I've admired from afar for years is flush with erotic bliss. I cup his face in my palms and kiss him hard. He opens for me, his tongue delving between my lips and returning my kiss with reverence.

He grips my ass and pushes deeper, moving his hips in tandem with mine. I feel my orgasm building, spiraling higher with every stroke, making me crave it. Harder. Faster.

When he pushes me over the edge, I shatter in his arms. Pleasure consumes me straight to my soul. Nothing matters except Jackson and this moment. I collapse against his chest. He stills beneath me, stroking my back and pressing kisses to my shoulder.

"That was amazing."

He chuckles. "Let's get you cleaned up."

I climb from his lap, careful not to trip. He steadies me before sweeping me into his arms.

"What are you doing?"

"Taking you upstairs." He kisses my forehead.

"Why?"

"So I can clean you up and fuck you properly." He heads for the staircase.

I finally find my voice when we reach the top of the stairs. "Second door on the right is the bathroom. My room is the last door on the left."

With a nod, he carries me to my room and places me on my bed. He retreats and I carefully remove my stockings and shoes. When he returns with a washcloth, I'm naked, standing in the middle of the room.

"Fuck, Lily. You're gorgeous." He cups my pussy with the warm cloth. It soothes the ache, but I don't want him to treat me like a delicate flower. I want him to unleash the beast I know he has harnessed within. I nudge his hand away.

"Are you okay?" he asks softly.

"Better than okay." I pull his shirt off and toss it aside.

"We should take it slow." His words play at odds with his actions as he slips his shoes off and pulls down his dress pants.

My hand glides down his abs and wraps around his cock. "I don't want it slow, Jackson. I'm not going to break."

He growls and moves forward, pushing me down onto the bed. Hunger burns in his eyes. He's far from done with me. This time when he slides his cock deep, I welcome him with a breathy sigh of satisfaction.

He kisses me hard and fucks me harder. His pace quickens as he teases my clit with his fingertips.

"Come for me, sweetheart."

My orgasm hits just as strong as before, but he drives deeper, prolonging the pleasure. He pulls out and comes on my stomach. I pout at the mess he's made of me.

He exhales a shaky breath. "I left my condoms at home."

"I have some." I gesture to the drawer beside my bed.

"I thought—"

"It's good to be prepared in case of all eventualities." I wink.

"Clever girl." He kisses me, and we sink deeper into each other's embrace. I could drown in him, in the contented bliss.

"Are you hungry?" he murmurs against my neck.

"Starving."

"You take a shower. I'll order Chinese food for delivery." His soft kiss lingers against my lips. "Then I'll join you."

I nod and stumble toward the bathroom. The spray of the water washes away the ache, but the memories remain fresh and simmering in my mind. When Jackson joins me in the shower, he takes me hard against the wall.

Twenty minutes later, we're wrapped in bathrobes eating lo mein and kung pao chicken in the living room. I admire his mussed hair and lopsided grin.

Merry Christmas to me.

Chapter Twenty

My sexy boss looks so peaceful tucked beneath my velvet bedspread fast asleep. Who would ever have imagined this happening? I chuckle as I quietly slip from my bed and into my robe.

As much as I want to kiss him, I don't want to disturb him. I did that a few times throughout the night. Waking to find myself entwined in his warm embrace left me desperate. The first time, I slid beneath the blankets and took him in my mouth. He swore and drew the covers back so he could watch me pleasure him. It took a moment to find a rhythm, but when I did, Jackson's litany of curses empowered me. Before I could make him come, he flipped me beneath him and fucked me until we both found release. The second time I woke to his fingers buried inside me, stroking until I fell apart trembling in his arms. Then he made love to me soft and slow.

I tiptoe down the stairs and head for the kitchen. There's no one here but us. Mike and James won't be back until tonight. Gavin and Maggie are at their new place. It feels good to have the house to myself. To be able to imagine it as my home with Jackson, if only for one night.

As I put together a hashbrown quiche for breakfast, I hum softly. While the sausage cooks, I whip up the eggs and set them aside. I thaw out the spinach and grab the shredded cheese from the refrigerator.

My phone pings in my pocket. I pull it out and unlock the screen. A message from Jen to our little group chat.

Merry Christmas! Love you.

Maggie chimes in. *Merry X-mas. Hope you all got laid! *wink emoji**

I shake my head and smile. If they only knew. I'm about to respond when an incoming call fills the screen. Shit. It's my father. I shouldn't answer. I should let it go to voicemail or block his number completely, but I don't.

"Yes?" My voice is clipped.

"That's not a very nice way to answer the phone, Lilian." My father's brusque tone sinks its claws into my already delicate psyche.

"I thought you were done with me. Cut me off without a thought." I pull the skillet with the sausage from the stove.

"Is *he* there with you?"

"Not that I owe you a response, but yes, he spent the night."

"Damn it, Lilian." He swears beneath his breath and I miss the colorful imagery. "That man is using you."

"I have spent my entire life trying to live up to your warped, unattainable expectations. Whomever I choose to spend my time with is of no concern to you. Not anymore."

"You will end whatever farce you're playing with that man and quit that position immediately. Do you understand?"

"Jackson is a good man. He treats me well and honors my decisions. Unlike you." I huff as the fury builds. "I have spent years building my reputation and my skills at Valentina's. I will not throw it away because you demand it."

"A good man?" My father scoffs. "He is your superior. The vice president of the company. Do you think he chose you because he values your talents in the office? Are you delusional enough to believe he *loves* you?"

My heart pounds like a stampeding herd of horses in my chest, trampling my remaining reserves of strength. "I have spent years trying to prove myself to you. To the world." I sniff, holding back the tears. "I didn't have to prove anything to Jackson. He asks nothing of me. He wants me not because of what I can give him. Not because I'm your daughter. He wants *me.*"

"Stupid, naïve girl." He hisses. "That man is lying to you."

"You don't know him!" I shout and realize I will surely wake Jackson if I continue at this decibel.

"Neither do you." His tone is measured once more.

"I know him better than you do."

"Do you?" He almost sounds amused. "Tell me what you know of his past?"

"I—" My throat closes. I don't know much other than the small glimpses he's shown me through conversation, which isn't much. I don't really know much about him beyond his work at Valentina's.

"I thought so." My father's silky reply ignites a tempest within me. "Would you like to know what breed of viper you've brought into your bed?"

"What are you talking about?"

"Jackson Roberts." He pauses for emphasis. "The name sounded vaguely familiar, though I haven't heard it in nearly thirty years."

"What?"

"Twenty-eight years ago, a young man came to me, begging for a loan. He had nothing. No collateral. No assets. No connections. Nothing." He sighs dramatically. "When I denied him the loan, he vowed retribution for my shortsightedness in singling him out with my blatant bias."

"No." Surely my father was mistaken. "You lie."

"After you left yesterday, I verified my suspicions with my records at the bank." He presses on. "Jackson Roberts, age twenty-two, requested a business loan of one hundred thousand dollars." He chuckled. "I admit, the request took guts, as futile as it was."

"What does it matter? That was years ago."

"Tell me the truth, Lilian. Did he know who you were when he hired you?"

The memory of our first meeting rises in my mind. He knew exactly who my father was. Who *I* was. It can't be possible. He wouldn't do that. He wouldn't use me to get to my father—would he?

"Lilian."

"Yes. Okay, is that what you want me to say?"

"He's using you to get to me," my father says. I glance up and see Jackson standing in the doorway wearing a white robe. He steps forward and I hold my hand up. "You cannot trust him,

Lilian."

I end the call. Emotion chokes me. Indecision, uncertainty, and fear strangle whatever hopes I had for us.

"What's wrong, Lily?" Jackson's eyes soften with concern.

"You met my father before yesterday." It's not a question. He regards me for a moment before answering.

"Yes. Years ago." Jackson straightens, preparing to take the brunt of my attack. "I went to him for a loan, which he denied." The response is calm but laced with venom, even after all these years.

"Why didn't you tell me?" I keep distance between us as he steps closer, backing around the island.

"I should have told you." He reaches out a hand. "I was wrong to keep it from you."

"This." I gesture between us. "Is it a lie?"

"No." Sincerity rings in his voice.

"Did you hire me because of my father?"

"Partially." The honest response sets me reeling.

I grip the counter to keep from throwing something. Was I ever good enough for anyone? I swallow the question and bury it deep. "Were you using me to get back at my father for what he did to you?"

"At first, I contemplated it." Jackson sighs and drops his hands to his sides. "But that was before I met you, before I knew *you*, Lily. Before I saw how hard you worked and how much you cared about your coworkers, your job, your ethics."

"Don't." I shake my head vehemently. Part of my hair tumbles free and I push it behind my ear. "You don't know me."

"That's not true, Lily." His voice remains soft as though he's trying to comfort a startled animal. "I know exactly who you are. You love fashion design and all things vintage. You're a loyal and devoted friend. You're smart and capable. Funny and charming."

"Stop." I whimper, unable to bear the torment. His words rip open a part of my soul I managed to keep together with denial for years. "You lied to me by withholding the truth."

"You're right." Jackson's expression falters. He looks

vulnerable and exhausted. "I knew if I told you the truth, you would look at me in the same way you are right now. Full of distrust and pain."

"Did you orchestrate this as a way to get back at my father?" I draw further into myself. "I told you of my family. Of the rift between me and my father. It brought you pleasure to rub it in his face, didn't it? To show him how you possessed the one thing he lost?"

"No, Lily." He shakes his head and rakes his hand through his hair. "I never intended to pursue you. I vowed I would leave you alone. Over three years of torment, I succeeded in keeping my distance." Jackson's stormy gaze holds mine. "I love you, Lily. I've loved you from the moment I saw you in that cherry print dress in the lobby with your ridiculous cappuccino."

"I don't believe you."

"You struck me in that moment, Lily, and I dreamed of you every night after." He rests his hand on the counter. "Please, believe me. I never intended for it to come out this way. I should have been honest from the start."

"Yes, you should have." I straighten, unable to trust my words or my body's response to his presence. Pretty words after such wounding lies. "But it's too late."

"Lily." His entreaty rips at my heart.

"I need time to think."

"Of course. I'll go." Jackson flexes his hands. "I'm sorry, Lily. Truly."

When he turns to leave, my heart breaks. As much as I want to chase after him, I need time to think and evaluate these new circumstances. I collapse against the counter and let the tears flow.

Five minutes later, the front door closes. I type out a quick S.O.S. message to Jen and Maggie before I let the waves of grief drag me under.

CHAPTER TWENTY-ONE

The day passes in a haze. Between unrelenting tears and the pressure of heartache, I manage to finish making breakfast and eat a few bites before abandoning the dirty dishes in the sink and returning to my room. Seeing my rumpled bed breaks me a second time as the memories come rushing back. I retreat to the bathroom to take a long, hot shower.

But Jackson haunts me there as well. I can't escape him. His imprint is on everything. My home, my job, my heart.

After dressing in a warm sweater and leggings, I head downstairs and turn on some fantasy television show about a monster hunter and stare blankly at the screen for a few hours until I drift off to sleep.

Reality is waiting like a specter in the shadows when I wake. I glance at my phone. Three missed messages from Jen. Five from Maggie. I skim through them and a smile cracks through my sadness. They're on their way.

Maybe I should send Jackson a message. No. I can't. Everything is still too fresh in my mind. The wound still bleeding and raw.

The knock at the door shakes me from my thoughts. I wrap a blanket around my shoulders and wander into the hallway. Jen and Maggie launch themselves across the threshold and hug me the moment I open the door.

"What the hell happened?" Maggie asks.

Emotions rise from deep in my chest and the tears break free once more. Jen wraps her arm around me and leads me into the living room. Maggie grabs the remote and turns off the television. She sits on the coffee table facing Jen and me.

"Was it Mr. Roberts?" Jen asks, softly, stroking my back in rhythmic motions.

I nod.

"What the hell did that bastard do to you, Lily?" Fury flashes in her eyes. She's a force to be reckoned with and heaven help Jackson if she ever confronts him.

With a deep breath, I pull back and dab my eyes with a tissue. "We went to my father's for Christmas yesterday."

Jen and Maggie exchange looks but say nothing. I explain the events as they unfolded at my father's and what happened after. When I get to the part where Jackson and I hooked up, they don't press for details, and I don't offer any more than I feel comfortable with. But I can tell by their wide-eyed expressions, it's more than they expected.

By the time I tell them about the phone call from my father that morning, I could see the rage building in Maggie and the horror in Jen.

"He didn't tell you?" Maggie launches to her feet. "That sneaky bastard."

Jen shakes her head in disbelief. "So he had a distant history with your father. Do you really think he would use you to get back at your father for not giving him the loan?"

"I don't know." I sniff and wipe my nose. "Maybe? I don't know anymore. I can't trust anyone." Jen and Maggie stare at me. "I mean, aside from you both. And Gavin. Maybe James and Michael."

"What happened after you confronted him?" Maggie asks. "I hope you ripped him a new one and kicked his ass out."

Typical Maggie. Such a fighter. "No, I let him try to explain." The conflicting emotions choke me once more. "He told me he loves me." I hiccough and cover my face with my hand.

"He said those words?" Jen seems surprised.

I nod slowly. "What am I supposed to say to that?"

"Not a damn thing," Maggie interjects. "You don't owe him anything, Lily."

"But I love him." Frustration bubbles to the surface making my hands tremble. "I wanted him for so long. I finally had him, and he loves me."

"He lied to you, Lily." Maggie takes my hand in hers. "I

know it hurts and you want him. But he chose to keep the truth from you for years. He had his opportunity, and he blew it."

"I know."

"What did you say to him after that?" Jen rests her hand on my shoulder.

"I told him I needed time to think." I bite my lip when the pain consumes my heart again. "Then he left."

"Good." Maggie squeezes my hand. "I'm proud of you."

"What do I do now? I can't go back to the office. I'll have to quit and start over somewhere else."

"Maybe this is a good thing. You can take time to focus on your website and your own designs then." Jen brightens at the possibilities, but I don't share her enthusiasm.

"My father is selling some of his properties." I blink back the fresh tears. "I think he's going to sell this house. James and Michael can find a smaller place, but my father cut me off. I barely make enough to cover the rent he charged me here. How am I supposed to find a new place?"

"You can come stay with us," Jen offers immediately.

"Gavin and I would never leave you stranded either, Lily." Maggie hugs me. "You can stay with us as long as you need to if it comes to that."

"Thanks, guys. But I can't intrude on you indefinitely."

"We'll help you find a place that works with your budget." Maggie's brimming with certainty. "It'll all work out, trust me."

I hug them both tight. "Thank you. I knew I could count on you both to make sense of all this chaos."

"You're welcome." Jen nudges me gently.

"And if you need to find a new job, I can check with Ben and Evan to see if they have any openings at Solus," Maggie offers. "I mean, it's not in the fashion industry, but it's a steady paycheck. You're already well qualified with spreadsheets and data entry. Should be a simple enough transition."

"I appreciate your offer, but I haven't decided what to do yet." I collapse against the cushions. "What am I going to say to him on Monday?"

"If I know Mr. Roberts, he won't treat you any differently

than he does any other day."

"But what if it *is* different?"

"Change can be a good thing." Maggie stands and puts her hands on her hips. "A lot has changed this year, and we're stronger than ever."

"You should take some time and focus on yourself." Jen pats my thigh. "Do what you want to do. Fuck your dad and Mr. Roberts. You don't need a man to define you."

Her words ignite a fire deep in my belly. She's right. For too long, I've worked to please Mr. Roberts, to please my father. It's about damn time I did something for myself.

"Thanks, ladies." As I think on their suggestion, I'm able to slowly climb from the floundering sadness that seemed so futile just a few minutes ago. It won't be easy. I'm not sure I can make it, but I need to try.

"Feeling better?" Jen asks.

"Yeah." I clutch a pillow to my chest and exhale steadily.

"Good." Maggie snatches the remote off the coffee table and turns on the television. "Now, let's watch a little Jeralt."

"Yes, please." Jen settles deeper into the couch beside me. "He's delicious."

"Don't tell me you're obsessed with him now?" Maggie teases her.

"Maybe a smidge, but it's not like it was with Ransom. I swear." Jen crosses her heart.

With a chuckle, I snuggle with my best friends and watch the new episode start. As the show plays, Jen and Maggie throw out comments and observations. I've missed this. Maggie's right, things *have* changed this year. I don't think I realized how much until this point. But it's comforting to know that no matter how much we change, we're still here for each other.

I rest easy in the knowledge I'm not alone. No matter what happens next, I have my friends to keep me grounded.

CHAPTER TWENTY-TWO

The Monday following the Christmas fiasco Jackson was not at work. The day after New Year's, I still hadn't seen him. By the end of January, there were whispers around the office when he still hadn't shown up.

On February first, an interoffice memo circulated announcing Mr. Roberts would be taking an extended leave of absence and a temporary replacement would be filling his position. Did his disappearance have anything to do with what happened between us on Christmas? Or worse, did my father have something to do with his sudden departure?

One evening in early March, I arrive home to find a letter pinned to my door. An eviction notice. It seems my father finally followed through with his threat. He sold the house, effectively cutting me off.

Shit. What the hell am I going to do now? Jen and Maggie both invited me to stay with them should this happen, but I don't want to be a burden.

I stumble into the house and close the door. Gunfire echoes from the living room. Inside, James and Michael are playing *Space Vendetta: Armada.* They pause the game when I enter the room.

"Lily, what's wrong?" James asks, setting aside his controller.

I hold up the paper, unable to say the words aloud.

"What's this?" Michael takes the paper and scans it. "What the hell? Is he serious?"

James grabs it. "Shit." He glances up at me. "Is your dad selling the place? Why didn't he give us a warning?"

"This is the warning." Michael rolls his eyes. "Guess we'll have to start looking for another place."

"Yeah." James runs his hand through his hair. "What are you going to do, Lily?"

"I don't know." I sink down onto the couch and bite my nail. Tears form at the corners of my eyes and I blink them away.

"You're always welcome to live with us in a new place," James offers with a charming smile.

"Yeah, Lily. We'll find a new place." Michael sits beside me and wraps his arm around my shoulders. "Don't worry."

"Thanks, guys. But this is all my fault." I wipe the escaping tears with the back of my hand. "I fucked things up at Christmas and now he's punishing me."

"Would your father really be that spiteful?" James asks.

"You have no idea how spiteful he can be." A derisive laugh escapes me. "This was the final tie that bound us, and he's cut it."

"That should be a relief, right?" Michael holds me tight. "You're free now. You can do whatever you want. Go anywhere you want. The sky's the limit."

"Easy for you to say." I sway against him. "You and James are set with your investment portfolio."

"We can set you up too, Lily." James kneels to my level. "Do you have anything saved?"

"A little, but I was going to use that to get my design company off the ground." They exchange a confused look. "Last year, I started working on putting my own designs online, see if I could get my company some followers." I sniff and drop my gaze. "But I got distracted and it just fell to the wayside."

"Well, it's never too late to get back at it." James takes my hand. "We'll help you."

"Yeah. Do you have a website set up?" Michael jumps in.

"I do. Gavin built it for me last summer. It's beautiful."

"Good. Then we have a starting point." James rubs his jaw. "Maybe we should create a Kickstarter campaign and blast it on social media to get some traction and build some funds?"

"You guys are the best." I wrap my arms around Michael's neck and hug him tight. James joins in, making it a group hug. I'm surrounded by love, and it eases the ache in my chest.

James pulls away and turns off the television. "I'll go get my laptop and we can brainstorm a bit."

"We also need to look for a new place." I pout and glance at the paper laying on the coffee table. "They want the house empty by the end of the month."

"No problem. I have a friend who's got some rental properties she manages. She'll hook us up," Michael adds with a wink and pulls his phone out of his pocket.

I can't help but notice the faint blush on his cheeks when he mentions this friend. But I don't say anything because I'm just happy to see he's finally taken an interest in something other than his video games and work.

"I'm going to change quick." I stand and head for the stairs.

James passes me on the fifth step and gives me a high five. How did I get so lucky? Anyone else would have abandoned me at the first sign of trouble, but these two thrive on a challenge. It's one of the reasons I love them.

Maybe it's time I broke free from Valentina's and found something that better suited my talents. If James and Michael are successful in building a platform for my design company, then there's hope I can finally invest my time into something I'm passionate about.

When I return to the living room, Michael and James are arguing about something, but they go quiet when I walk in.

"Problems?"

"Nope. James won't admit when he's wrong." Michael grins and scoots over so I can sit beside him. "So, Peggy has a few places that might fit our needs. I can schedule a day next week to look at them."

"That sounds wonderful. The sooner the better." I ignore the work conundrum in the back of my mind. Honestly, I might not even be working by that point if I put my notice in. But I don't voice that part.

"What's your website address?" James asks, giving me a soft nudge in the ribs.

When the site pops up on his screen, memories flood me. Mostly of all the hard work I put into creating the designs on the page, but also the haunting compliments from *Vintage Cowboy*. Those early conversations where he encouraged me to pursue my dreams.

I bite my lip. I wonder how he's doing.

With a sigh, I push aside thoughts of Sam and Jackson and focus on the task in front of me. James and Michael help me work through the details of building a campaign. We brainstorm ideas and goals. They even take the time to help me build a business plan and set some attainable goals, both short and long term. My confidence builds as the conversation deepens.

We order pizza and work well into the night. It's midnight by the time they relent, satisfied with our progress.

I take a shower, wash my face, and brush my teeth. Life doesn't feel so overwhelming anymore. Maybe I *can* do this. There's no better time for me to spread my wings and take flight. At least if I fail, I have my friends to soften the blow. They've encouraged and supported me more than my own family. I don't know where I'd be without them.

My body sinks into the mattress when I climb into bed. I set my alarm on my phone and plug it in. My finger hovers over the Discord icon. I open the app and pull up the chat box between me and Sam. His words from before Christmas stare back at me.

I type out a message.

Hey, Sam. Sorry I've been distant. It's been a rough couple of months. The other guy, well, we split, and I'm being kicked out of my home by the landlord who's selling the house. Everything is up in the air right now and I don't know what's going to happen next. It's frustrating. Anyway, I just wanted to make sure you're doing well. I miss our conversations.

I hit send and set the phone aside. When I reach for the light switch, a response pings on my lock screen.

Hello, lovely Lily. I'm sorry life is hard right now. Do you want me to break his legs for you? You deserve to be cherished and loved. I hope you find what you're looking for. Thanks for thinking of me.

My fingers trace over the cowboy hat icon. Why is he so sweet? Why do we have to be so far apart? I know I promised Jen and Maggie I would take time for myself, but I can't ignore the draw Sam has.

Thanks, Sam. I appreciate your kind words, but I'll be okay. I'm working on myself right now. It's better this way. Having someone to share my successes with would be nice, but I'm thankful for the time to love myself first.

I watch the dots move next to his icon as he replies. When he finally sends the response, it makes me smile.

That's very mature of you. I'm proud of you for taking care of yourself first. That's truly important. If you ever want to visit Wyoming and get away for a while, you let me know.

Oh, the temptation is there, bold and bright. I want to reach out and grab it. But I have things to take care of before I can indulge in a little trip. Maybe as a reward, once I get my life in order.

I may have to take you up on that. I hear Wyoming is beautiful in the summer.

A picture comes back in response. The sunset from the front porch and a pair of cowboy boots propped up on a barrel. It looks like heaven.

It is. Here's the address if you decide to come. I'm here if you need me, Lily. Send me a message any time. I'll give you the world, all you have to do is ask.

Those words infiltrate my soul. All my life, I've wanted to be seen, respected, and loved. My father did a shit job when it came to my emotional care. Sure, I had access to the best schools and the most lavish experiences, but I would have given anything to have a family that loved me unconditionally. Even if it meant we lived in a cabin in the Wyoming wilderness.

Thanks, Sam. Goodnight.

Goodnight, Lily.

I turn off the app and set my phone on the nightstand. Curled on my side, I close my eyes and dream of all the possibilities spread before me like a banquet. Even though my heart aches for someone to share my life with, I'm content, knowing I can do this on my own if I need to.

First thing in the morning, I submit my resignation to Valentina's.

CHAPTER TWENTY-THREE

Two months later

"There's no way I can talk you out of this?" Maggie's voice filters through the speakers of the car.

"Nope. I'm an hour out. There's no turning back now." I readjust my sunglasses and scan the desolate road stretched out before me.

"Shit." She grumbles beneath her breath. "Okay, but keep your tracker on and call me if he tries anything stupid." Jen's voice echoes in the background. "Yeah, and call us when you get there. If we don't hear from you by eight, I'm calling the cops."

"Don't worry." I chuckle. "I'll be fine. It's just a little getaway."

"A getaway to cowboy daddy's ranch." Maggie snorts, her distrust evident. "I wish you would have let us come with you."

"Now, you know I couldn't ask you guys to come. With Jen's wedding next month and your launch coming up, you both have enough on your plates. You don't need to babysit me. I can handle this."

"Uh-huh." Maggie doesn't sound convinced, but she relents. "Remember, you need to be back by the fifth. You can't decide to stay in Wyoming and leave us here to celebrate without you."

"I'm not going to stay in Wyoming." I roll my eyes. She's so dramatic. "I have orders to fill and a fall line to finish."

"Then why are you running off to the middle of nowhere?"

"Because I promised myself a treat for meeting my goals." I beam with pride in my achievements. After my father kicked us out of the brownstone, James and Michael followed through on their promise. They let me crash with them, but even better, they helped me get my Lily Starling line off the ground.

The Kickstarter campaign raised nearly five hundred thousand dollars in three weeks. I had emails flooding my inbox from companies who were interested in investing and partnering with me to get my line into production. My social media stats went through the roof with a little creative marketing help from my friends. I'm still working out the final details, but come the new year, I will have my own line of vintage pinup-inspired dresses on sale at boutiques nationwide.

It's a dream come true, and I couldn't have done it without the love and support of my friends. Last year was difficult for all of us, but we came through it stronger than before. Even though I don't have a special someone to share my victory with, I know I made the right choice in doing it on my own. I'm that much stronger for it.

"I'm proud of you too, but I still don't see the appeal of running off to a ranch in Wyoming to celebrate your success." Maggie sighs heavily, adding to the drama.

A sign for Guernsey alerts me to my upcoming exit. "I gotta go. I'm almost there."

"Okay, call me as soon as you're settled. Love you!"

"Love you too." I disconnect the call and the music resumes. The eighties playlist makes for great road trip music. The closest airport with a direct flight from Newark was Denver. Upon research, I realized it would be easier to rent a car and drive from Denver to Guernsey than get a smaller flight to Cheyenne. I'd still have to rent a car, so it didn't matter.

Even though I've had my license since I was eighteen, I've never had the opportunity to drive. Living in the city there was never a need. Everything was a cab ride or a subway stop away. Once I left the city limits, my confidence behind the wheel increased. Wyoming is a straight shot north on I-25. The traffic is nothing compared to the city. A girl could get used to these wide-open spaces.

After a quick stop in Cheyenne for lunch and fuel, I got back on the road. Maggie called me shortly after that. Now that I've addressed her concerns, I can focus on the task at hand: finding the ranch.

The address Sam gave me leads me past a state park and down a long dirt road. I slow considerably, careful not to cause any damage to the rental car. The landscape looks flat, but there's a gentle roll to the countryside dotted with sporadic patches of trees clustered in the valleys.

I jump out of my skin when a small group of animals darts in front of the car. I stop and watch in awe as these deer-looking creatures bound across the road in a small herd. Some of them sport black goatlike horns. They look fluffy and cute, but in a flash, they're beyond the ridge and dipping into a valley. Definitely not something you see at home, that's for sure. I make a mental note to ask Sam about them when I arrive.

The entrance to the ranch should be the next right according to the GPS on my phone. Service seems pretty solid for not being close to a major city. I just hope it holds out until I get to my destination.

Sam seemed surprised and excited when I asked if I could come visit. I'm not sure what to expect when I arrive. I've never sent him a picture, so I'm sure he's just as curious as I am. During the flight, I reassured myself he wasn't a stalker or a serial killer who wanted to harvest my organs or sell me on the black market. Maggie and Jen both know my location and the contact information should I fall off the face of the earth. Am I worried about Sam being a psycho? Not really, but better safe than dead.

The next right turn has a sign hanging between two large poles flanking the driveway. Black Water Ranch. I creep down the driveway and as I crest the hill, several buildings come into view on the horizon. A cluster of smaller cabins sits around the main cabin, which faces the sun as it starts its descent on the horizon.

I made decent time. It's nearly five-thirty. Sam said they eat dinner at seven. My stomach rumbles in protest at the sad drive-through meal I had in Cheyenne.

As I stop near the main cabin, I notice the trees and shrubs. Sparse and simple, they complement the landscape perfectly. I feel like I've stepped into the wild west.

When I get out of the car, a gust of wind catches my skirt,

lifting it like Marilyn Monroe's infamous white dress. I manage to wrangle it into submission and make my way toward the porch. The moment I reach it, a woman opens the door.

"Hi!" I call out with a grin.

She smiles back. "You must be Lily." Her weathered face shows her age, but she's beautiful. Her dark hair is pulled back in a bun and she's wearing a pair of jeans and a blue button-down shirt. "Sam's in the barn. I'll go get him."

"No, that's okay. I don't want to interrupt you." I gesture to the potato and the peeler in her hands. "Just point me in the direction and I'll find him."

"In those shoes?" She laughs. "Honey, at least put these boots on." She toes the boots off her feet and kicks them toward me.

My face warms. I came woefully overdressed for the occasion it seems. Sitting on the bench beside the door, I sigh and remove my kitten heels. Her boots are a bit big, but they're sturdy and solid.

"Thanks."

"Follow that path there and it'll take you to the barn. Don't mind the dogs, they're all bark." She winks. "Good luck, honey."

Before I can ask her what she means, she disappears into the cabin and the screen door closes behind her with a slam.

Straightening, I muster up my courage. I've come this far. There's no reason to run now. The narrow path leads away from the cabins and down toward the barns.

In the corral beside the barn are a half dozen horses. Their coats glisten in the sunlight. The deep blue sky stretches overhead meeting the rolling hillsides of the high plains desert. It's beautiful. Strikingly so. My heart flutters when I see a man wearing a cowboy hat step out of the barn leading a black horse.

He ties the lead rope to the fence and returns to the barn. I wander closer and the black horse turns when I approach, giving a soft nicker. I stop ten feet away and admire the horse's silky coat and curious eyes.

"What's wrong, Rocket?" The cowboy emerges from the barn again, and I sidestep to catch a glimpse of him.

No...It can't be...

Jackson runs his hand over the horse's rump as he steps closer. For every step he takes toward me I take one in retreat. *What is he doing here?*

"Where's Sam?" I stutter, tempted to turn and run.

Jackson stops just out of reach. "Oh, Lily. Don't tell me you haven't figured it out yet?"

"Figured *what* out?" My voice dies in my throat as the realization slams into me with the force of a hurricane. "Oh, God. No. Please tell me you didn't lie to me about this too."

"I never lied to you, Lily." He shoves his hands in his pockets. "My full name is Samuel Jackson Roberts."

"This is a joke, right?" Disbelief and fury rip through me, threatening to shred my heart into tiny pieces.

"No, it's not a joke, Lily." He scuffs his boot in the dirt, taking a half step closer.

I back away and put my hands up.

"Please let me explain."

My head shakes in defiance. My tongue ties in knots at the sight of him. A hundred emotions flood me. Pain, frustration, fury, lust, confusion, love. I missed him so damned much. When he disappeared after Christmas, I counted it as a learning experience. It was painful, but it gave me the push I needed to step out on my own. I owe him thanks for that, but I don't owe him one more moment of my time.

"I can't." The words finally break free. "I shouldn't have come."

I turn to run up the path back to my car. If I leave now, I can make it back to the airport before ten and catch a red-eye back to New York. Maggie was right, this was a mistake. I should have known. The way he spoke to me. The way he made me feel. I should have known Sam was Jackson. Stupid. So fucking stupid.

I break into a run. The moment I do, I hear his boots crunching in the gravel behind me. Never turn your back to a predator. That's what I read in that magazine about the animals in the west.

There's no denying it. Jackson is a predator, and I'm his prey.

Chapter Twenty-Four

Jackson catches me by the waist as I reach a row of trees near a small cabin. I twist against his hold and claw at his hands.

"Let me go."

"Just listen. Five minutes. Please." His scent, his heat, his voice sinks into me, dispelling the fight, and I go still in his embrace.

I close my eyes and lean against him. My breath comes in short bursts and I struggle to breathe. It's the elevation. That's it. It has nothing to do with the effect this man has on me. In an instant, I remember everything and it hits me hard. I've missed him. Damn him, but I did.

Jackson turns me in his arms until I'm facing him. The familiar scent of his soap and his skin hides beneath the earthy scent of horses and leather.

"What do you want from me, Jackson?"

He pulls off his hat and rakes his hand through his hair. "Same thing I've always wanted. That's never changed."

"My father cut me off. You can't take your revenge through me."

"You really think so little of me?" He braces his hands on his hips and stares at the sky for a long moment. When he meets my gaze again, he steals my breath. "I fucked up. I'll admit that. I should have told you about my past, about your father and the loan, and yes, I should have told you that I was the cowboy you spoke to with such passion." He sighs. "But I couldn't because I knew it would drive you away."

"Why?"

"Why what?"

"Why did you think it would drive me away? Did you think you couldn't be honest with me from the start?"

"When I first saw you, I knew I was lost. I restrained myself from engaging with you as long as I could." He leans against the nearest tree. "You're smart and talented. Yes, I knew who your father was, but I didn't care. Not when I saw how dedicated you were to your friends and your job."

"How did you know about my Discord account?"

Jackson's cheeks flush with color. I don't think I've ever seen him blush, but he's red. He rubs his hand across his jaw. "I overheard your conversation with Miss Ashcroft. It didn't take long to find you."

"Why didn't you just tell me who you were?"

"I didn't want it to affect our professional relationship." He looks almost sheepish. "I wasn't sure how you felt about me. I fully intended to tell you, but then you seemed so comfortable with this newfound friendship, I didn't want to ruin it. I loved our honest conversations."

"Only they weren't honest, were they?" I glare at him. "Omitting the truth is still lying. You led me on. Made me feel something—for Sam *and* you."

"I may have hidden behind the anonymity of the internet, but every word I said was true." His serious expression makes me pause.

"You own this ranch?"

"Yes."

"What about all that bullshit you sold me about scouting for designer talent? About your sister? Your promise to help aspiring designers?"

"All true."

I narrow my eyes, searching for a sign of deception. But I can't find anything but open vulnerability in his handsome face.

"I can't play this game anymore, Jackson." Tears fill my eyes. "I'm exhausted and fed up. I have to go."

"Don't leave. Not yet. Please," he pleads, taking two steps toward me.

Holding my ground, I take a deep breath. I've come so far. Both literally and metaphorically. I had such high hopes for this trip, and now I wonder if Maggie and Jen hadn't been right to question my decision to come. Somehow, *they* sensed the danger waiting for me. But *I* should have known. *I* should have figured it out. I was stupid and naïve to trust someone I'd never met. But it was even more stupid for me to trust someone who held a position of power over me.

"I love you, Lily." He brushes his fingertips along my jaw.

My eyes flutter closed at his touch, his words. "Jackson, please don't...my heart can't take it."

"I was a fool. For all my years and experience, when it came to you, I acted like an ass. You deserved honesty from the start, and I failed miserably." He cups my cheek in his warm palm. "Can we try again?"

"I already made a fresh start. Without you." I step out of reach, even though it kills me to do it.

"You found someone?"

"That's just it. I don't *need* anyone. Not my father, and certainly not a man who couldn't be honest with me or himself."

Hurt steels across his face. "I deserve that."

"I'm not a vindictive person, but I learned something valuable from all of this." I straighten to my full height. "I don't need validation from anyone. I'm enough. My ideas and goals are worth investing in. I was so concerned about pleasing everyone around me, I forgot to take care of myself."

Jackson nods in agreement, leaving me stunned. "I'm glad you found yourself in the middle of all of this chaos." He steps back and shoves his hands in his pockets. "If you want to go, I won't stop you. But you're welcome to spend the night. Viv should have dinner ready soon. You can leave tomorrow—" He gestures to the scenery around us. "But you've come so far, at least take some time to relax. I'll leave you alone."

Stunned, I'm rooted to the spot. Jackson's sad smile is the last thing I see before he turns and heads back down the path toward the barn. I press my hand to my chest and close my eyes.

He's right. It would be a shame to waste such a beautiful retreat. I *should* leave, but he promised to leave me in peace. But is that *truly* what I want?

I pout and slowly walk up the path toward the main cabin. On the porch, the woman from before is leaning against the post smoking a cigarette.

"You find him?" she asks, regarding me with kind eyes.

I nod.

"Come on then. I'll show you to your cabin." She steps from the porch and waits for me to retrieve my bags from the car.

We walk in silence. When we reach the nearest small cabin, she fishes a key out of her pocket and unlocks it. Stubbing out the cigarette, she blows the smoke to the side and pushes open the door, gesturing for me to enter.

Inside, it's a one-room setup with a bed on the far wall. On the opposite is a small kitchenette with a café-style table and two chairs. It's homey and comfortable. I love it.

"Bathroom is through there." She gestures to the door at the back of the room. "If you need anything, just let me know."

"Thank you," I fumble for her name and realize she never told me what it was. Jackson did though. "Viv, is that right?"

"That's what Jackson calls me." She extends her hand with a laugh. "You can call me Vivian."

I shake her hand and notice the similar bone structure in her face. "Are you related to Jackson?"

"Only by blood." She releases her grip and grins. "He's my brother."

"You're the designer?"

"No, that was my sister Julia." Her smile fades. "She died ten years ago."

"I'm sorry." I stumble over my thoughts, trying to find the right words. It occurs to me too late that I don't know much about Jackson's family or his past.

"Nothing to apologize for." Vivian eases back into conversation obviously noting my discomfort. "Jackson said you were sweet, but he neglected to tell me how stunning you were."

"He told you about me?"

"Yeah." She slides closer and winks conspiratorially. "You've had him in a twist for years, missy. I'll never understand what you see in him, personally, but I can say that because he's my brother."

"Of course."

"I'll let you get settled in here. Dinner is at seven. Don't knock, just come on in." Vivian crosses the room and pauses in the doorway. "Make yourself at home."

I don't know anything about Jackson, aside from what he shared with me online as Sam. That's if he was even telling me the truth about being honest. But in the depths of my soul, a still, soft voice reminds me of my feelings for Jackson. Is it love? Or am I clinging to the desire I felt—and still feel—for him?

I retreat to my bag and unpack my toiletries. I might be overdressed today, but I didn't come completely unprepared. The rest of the items in my bag are jeans and comfortable shirts. However, the sneakers I brought won't work. I may have to find myself a pair of boots unless Viv is willing to let me steal hers for a week.

I take a quick shower to wash off the travel dust and fix my hair into a low ponytail. After throwing on some jeans and a t-shirt, I pull on the borrowed boots. They fit better with thicker socks. My stomach grumbles with impatience and I glance at my phone.

Five to seven. I text Jen and Maggie, letting them know I'll call them tomorrow with a full update. They're going to freak the hell out when I tell them Sam is Jackson.

Am I crazy for staying? Maybe. But somewhere in the back of my brain, I hear my conscience telling me I'll regret it if I don't see this to its full conclusion. Even if Jackson doesn't deserve me, he does deserve a chance to explain what happened between us and why he kept the truth from me. I deserve closure at the very least.

But what if this backfires? What if he convinces me to abandon everything I've worked so hard for? I bite my lip and shove the negative thoughts aside. I'm stronger than he thinks. It'll take a lot more than sweet words and pretty promises to win me over after what he did.

He could always seduce you, the voice whispers in my mind. Desire courses hot through me. My heart beats wildly as I step from the small cabin.

Whatever happens, I'm determined to remain steadfast in one thing: being true to myself.

CHAPTER TWENTY-FIVE

The moment I step into the main cabin the scent of roasted potatoes and pot roast hits me. The savory aroma has my mouth watering before I close the door.

Vivian looks up as she sets the final plate on the table. "You're just in time." She gestures to the chair beside her. "Have a seat."

The cabin is quaint, homey with gingham curtains around the kitchen windows. The kitchen and living room are combined in one large, welcoming space. A wood-burning stove sits along the far wall opposite a worn sofa and two recliners.

"Thank you. You have a lovely home," I murmur as I sit where she indicated.

"Thanks, but this is Sam's place. I live in one of the smaller cabins."

"Oh."

"I just take care of all the housekeeping and the cooking." Vivian smiles kindly. "Don't tell him, but I stay here when he's out of town. It has a huge bathtub." She winks.

"Can I help with anything?" I ask, desperate to change the subject. I'm not sure if she's assuming there's something between her brother and me, but I'm not about to unpack it all at the dinner table.

"Nope. You're our guest. Just enjoy." She spears a few pieces of roast and places them next to the potatoes on my plate.

"Sam!" She calls down the hall before retrieving the veggies from the stovetop.

Jackson appears, his hair wet and slicked back. He's wearing a form-fitting cotton t-shirt and wranglers that hug his thighs. I can only imagine what they do to his ass.

"You settled in?" he asks, sitting across from me at the table.

"Yes."

"Good." He lays his napkin across his lap. "It's not a five-star resort, but it's home."

"It's lovely." I force a smile. Why am I irritated by his comment? Does he assume I'd rather be anywhere but here? He's not wrong, but he's not right either. Part of me wants to repair this damage between us even if it means I walk away in the end.

"Let's eat before it gets cold." Vivian takes a bite of potatoes before asking me about myself.

It seems Jackson has told her a little about me, but not the whole story. I'm careful of how I respond. It's easy to be polite with Vivian. She's kind and listens intently when I tell her about my design company and my upcoming projects.

Jackson says nothing during the meal, but I know he's absorbing every word I say with interest. I've seen that look before in boardrooms and quarterly meetings. He's feigning polite disinterest, but I can see the wheels turning in his mind.

"Are you planning to expand in the future?" Vivian asks, clearly intrigued by the direction of the conversation.

"I might. Right now I'm trying to focus on what's in front of me before setting my sights on anything bigger." I sip my iced tea.

"I'd love to see your designs sometime." Vivian's attention shifts to Jackson for a split second before a sad smile crosses her lips. "Julia was such a talented designer."

Her comment tugs at my heart. I remember the conversation I had with Sam, where he mentioned his interest in fashion because of his sister's passion for design. The connection makes me wonder if he had been telling me the truth the whole time, even though he concealed his identity from me for a year.

"I'm sorry for your loss."

"You two would have been fast friends." Vivian slowly stands and gathers the plates.

"Let me help."

"Not a chance." Vivian shoos me with her hand and turns to her brother. "Why don't you two go out and enjoy the sunset?

I can handle this."

Jackson slowly rises to his feet. His eyes plead, but he's too proud to beg. Instead, he turns and walks toward the door. With a nod, he encourages me to exit first.

The sun is settling over the expansive landscape. The orange rays of light branch through the fluffy clouds on the horizon. It looks surreal, like a painting hanging in an art gallery, not real life.

I recognize the scene before me as the photo he sent months ago. The one of him sitting on the porch watching the sunset after a long day in the saddle.

"Sit with me."

He takes me by the wrist and an alarm goes off in my mind, but the warmth of his touch seeps into me, dispelling any reservations that remain. He sits in a rocker and gently pulls me onto his lap.

The moment I'm nestled against his strong chest, all the fight goes out of me. I inhale and savor the familiar scent. I missed it. I missed him. We sit silently, my attention fixed on the sun as it descends beyond the hills in the distance.

His touch lingers on my hip while the other hand remains encircled around my wrist. His thumb brushes against the pulse of my heartbeat, stroking in a gentle rhythmic pattern.

"You don't know how long I dreamed of this moment, kitten. Holding you like this while we watch the sun set. Away from the noise and chaos of the city."

I can't speak. If I turn, it'll bring us eye to eye, mouth to mouth. I can't trust myself not to take what he freely offers.

The sun slowly sinks and shadows appear over the plains, throwing the hills into stark relief.

"Why did you keep the truth from me?"

"I was scared."

"You? Scared?"

His handsome face transforms with refrained amusement. "Contrary to the rumors about me, I am not made of stone."

"I've seen you face down irate customers without flinching. Displeased employees without missing a beat. You take everything in stride and handle it with professional decorum." I lean back and shift my weight to better study him.

It's as though he can see into my soul. "This is why I found it so hard to be honest with you from the very beginning." A blush creeps into his cheeks. "For three years, I struggled with my attraction to you. I knew my reputation within the office would disintegrate the moment I approached you."

"You believed they would respect you less if you showed anything less than professional behavior."

"I heard the rumors. The whispers about me. Silver fox CEO." He smirks and shakes his head with derisive laughter. "If I would have shown anyone the slightest favorable attention, there would have been chaos. Whatever influence I had would have been lost in the scramble for my affection."

"You think so highly of yourself."

"I was thinking of my position and the importance of maintaining a professional work environment." He pauses. "I am not averse to interoffice relationships, but as the vice president, I couldn't allow myself to indulge merely because of my position. Too many would view it as abuse of power."

"I understand."

"I longed to speak with you on many occasions. For months I waited for my opportunity to bring you closer, to learn more about you." He heaves a deep breath. "When I saw your flair for design, I recognized your potential for the Christmas promotional and took my chance."

"Why didn't you tell me then of your interest?" I soften against him as he tells his story.

"Because you're young and beautiful and talented. Why would you want an old man like me?"

I scoff. "You're not old."

"When I overheard you talking to Miss Ashcroft about joining an online community, I saw my chance." He smooths his fingers over my knuckles. "It was the perfect opportunity to show you who I was outside of work."

"But why hide? You could have told me exactly who you were. I wouldn't have judged you for wanting to keep your personal life separate from work."

"I wasn't sure you even liked me, Lily," he admits quietly. "It was selfish and sneaky. I was stupid."

"You should have told me sooner." I shake my head. "I felt guilty for weeks over my feelings for two men."

"I wanted to tell you the week before Thanksgiving. But things escalated, and I couldn't bring myself to ruin the moment."

Memories of our steamy conversation that night make my cheeks heat.

"After what happened with your father on Christmas, I couldn't tell you." He slides his fingers through his hair. "Then…I didn't want to tarnish such a beautiful evening."

I cup his cheek.

"I woke alone and realized I needed to be honest with you if we were going to make our relationship work." He shifts me in his lap, his grip firm around my waist. "When I came into the kitchen, I was prepared to tell you about everything."

"But my father beat you to it."

Jackson nods. "I knew I fucked up. There was nothing I could have said to fix it. I had to show you."

"How? By making me fly across the country?"

"By quitting my position at Valentina's. By readjusting my priorities before I reached out to you again." The pain in his voice tugs at my heart. "After Christmas, I knew I couldn't go on as I had been before. I changed. You altered the course of my life when you walked into the lobby that day."

"Oh, Jackson." I blink away the tears. "You can't just expect me to act like everything is fine and it's all water under the bridge."

"I don't expect you to forgive me." He brushes his fingers along my jaw. "But you deserve to know the truth. All of it."

Shadows play over his features as the sun vanishes completely, casting us in darkness. "Why am I here?"

"Because you needed to get away from the city." He sighs. "And I needed to show you the part of me that no one sees before you decide whether to walk away forever."

Damn him. He knows exactly what to say to put me at ease. "What do you want from me?" I repeat the question from earlier that afternoon.

"I want all of you, Lily. You complete me in ways I never imagined another person could. You bring sunlight and joy into my life. I can't fathom the rest of my life without you in it."

"Jackson." He's breaking down the barriers between us, and I want to hate him for it. But I don't. I love him.

"You don't have to figure it all out now." He slowly nudges me to my feet and stands, wrapping his arms around me. "Sleep on it."

"And tomorrow?"

"Tomorrow I'm taking you on a tour of the ranch." He grins down at me. "On horseback. So get ready to cowgirl up."

"Really?!" An unexpected squeal of excitement bubbles from deep in my chest. It's been so long since I've been riding. I've missed it. At least this eases the sting of not knowing if I made the right decision. The tension sags from my shoulders.

"Come on, I'll walk you to your cabin." He takes my hand and we wander down the path wrapping around the house. When we reach my small cabin, he stops on the top step.

"Goodnight, Jackson." I open the door. The moonlight illuminates his face.

"Goodnight."

Once I'm alone inside my cabin, I collapse against the door. I'm glad he didn't push me into responding to his declaration. It'll be hard enough to face it in the sunshine, but wrapped in shadows, I nearly surrendered to the need pulsing through me.

Love shouldn't be this complicated.

CHAPTER TWENTY-SIX

The next morning I'm up before the sun rises. The sky outside takes on a brilliant violet-blue as dawn approaches. I curl beneath the blankets and cradle my phone in my hands.

Jen and Maggie blew up my messages while I was at dinner. Chewing my lip, I contemplate the easiest response I can offer them without having to launch into an hour-long explanation of the situation in which I'm currently mired.

After our conversation last evening, I can say in total honesty I know why he chose to keep the truth from me. It doesn't make it right, and I certainly don't condone his technique. But no matter how much I want to be angry with him, the feelings I have for Jackson run deeper than I anticipated, and I'm unprepared to handle the fallout of discussing this in person.

Sincerity echoes in his actions and his words. Do I really believe he would use me to retaliate for some past slight by my father? Or that he would purposely mislead me online to lure me into a situation where I would expose myself to open ridicule?

My ties to my father are gone. Yet Jackson still wants me. Those conversations we shared on Discord were private, intimate discussions. He could have easily used them against me. Yet he didn't.

He loves me.

I burrow deeper into the blankets and stare at my phone. Opening the group chat, I form a clear response to Jen and Maggie's desperate messages from the night before.

Busy all day. I'll call you later. Don't worry about me.

Without elaborating, I close the message and tuck my phone aside. I wish Jackson were here beside me, holding me close and telling me not to worry. Everything will be fine, he'd whisper in my ear before seducing me with his firm kiss and persistent touch.

Shaking the thought from my mind, I throw off the blankets and sit up. If I can't sleep, then I'm getting up. There's no point in prolonging the inevitable. I wonder if Jackson and Vivian are even awake.

By the time I dress, streaks of red and orange are painting the sky as the sun creeps up over the horizon. I pull on my NYU hoodie and the borrowed boots. There's a chill in the air when I step out onto the porch, but the morning sun warms my face with a sweet kiss of her comforting rays.

When I reach the house, I pause mid-knock and instead open the door. Vivian told me to make myself at home, so I do just that.

The scent of bacon and fresh coffee teases my senses.

Vivian glances up from the book she's reading at the table. "Good morning. I wasn't sure if you'd be up this early. Trouble sleeping?"

I nod. "It's too quiet."

"Sam says the same thing. City slickers." Viv laughs and sets her book aside. "Well, come in, have a seat. Can't send you out on an empty stomach."

"Thanks." I admire the efficacy with which she fries two eggs on a hot skillet and slides them onto a bed of hashbrowns before topping it off with a few slices of thick bacon. She sets the plate in front of me.

"Coffee?"

"Yes, please."

She places the coffee mug beside the plate. "Dig in."

Vivian leaves me to my breakfast. I can tell she wants to talk, but she's holding back. I wonder if Jackson told her what happened.

After I finish the last bite, I wash it down with the strong, black coffee. "Thanks for breakfast, it was delicious." I cradle the cup in my hands. "Is Jackson still asleep?"

"Nope. He's at the barn. Left before dawn." Vivian lifts her mug in salute. "Better get moving."

I carry the dishes to the sink and head for the door.

"Hey, Lily."

"Yeah?" I turn around and Vivian closes the distance between us. She draws me into a hug. I'm stunned for a moment, but it feels good. Comforting and warm.

"I don't know what happened between you two, and I don't need to know. That's your business." She draws back and smiles. "But I've never seen my brother light up the way he does when you walk in the room. That's gotta count for something, right?"

My response catches in my throat, so I nod instead.

"Have a good ride." She winks and shoos me out the door.

The sun is warm on my face as I walk down the trail toward the barn where I found him the day before. When I approach, there are two horses tied to the corral fence. A black gelding and a blood bay mare.

Jackson emerges from the barn and his lips curve into a charming smile. "Good morning."

"Morning." I stop before I reach him and shove my hands in my pockets. "Can I help?"

"Do you know how to saddle a horse?"

"Of course." I throw my hair back over my shoulder. "I've only ridden English, but it can't be that much different."

Jackson shakes his head and chuckles. "Here, let me show you."

I watch intently as he saddles his black gelding. It takes all my effort not to stare at his strong hands or the way his shoulders flex beneath his button-down shirt. I nod with confidence when he finishes and steps aside.

"Got it?"

"Yes, sir." I saunter past him and collect the saddle pad from the fence. Aware he's watching me, I take my time saddling the mare and manage to get all the tack in place without any problems. When I step aside, he comes beside me to check my work.

"Looks good. You ready to ride?"

"I was born ready." The banter comes easily with him, and I slowly relax when he hands me a cowboy hat from the post.

He unties the mare and leads her away from the fence. I follow and he boosts me into the saddle. It's wider and more comfortable than the English saddles I'm used to, but it feels natural. I gather the reins in my hand and twist around to find Jackson.

My mouth goes dry when he pulls himself up onto his horse. His hat casts his face into shadow. The photo he sent me on Discord all those months ago flashes into my mind. How could I not see it was him? He gave me all the tools I needed to figure it out. Was I truly so blind and trusting?

With a nudge of his heels, he urges his gelding forward. I barely tap my mare's flanks and she takes her place behind him.

We follow a wide trail as it weaves around the buildings and corrals. The gentle sway of the horse beneath me and the calm breeze drifting over the plains lull me in a way nothing in the city can. There's a peace here I was never able to find back home. I could get used to this.

Jackson steers us toward a small forest area in a deep valley. The horses manage the trail easily, and I grip the horn as we venture down the narrow path.

A stream runs through the valley hidden by tall trees swaying in the breeze. The moment we venture beneath the canopy of trees, the temperature shifts and a chill shoots through me.

"Look." He points ahead to a small cluster of the same animals I saw yesterday on my drive to the ranch. There are a few with horns wandering around the thicket. The moment my horse steps into view, they bound off into the distance.

"What are those?" I ask, watching their retreating fluffy white butts disappear over the ridge.

"Pronghorns." He laughs. "Like a deer, but not. More like a goat. Makes tasty meatloaf."

"You eat them?"

"Yeah. In fact, I think that's what's on the menu for dinner." He chuckles and urges his horse deeper into the trees.

After a few minutes, we reach a small clearing where the stream widens into a small pool swirling and bubbling. I glance into the water and see the flicker of movement beneath the surface.

"Fish!"

Jackson nods and dismounts his horse. "Trout. My grandpa used to bring me here fishing when I was a kid."

I slide out of the saddle and pull the reins over the mare's neck. "It's so peaceful."

"It really is."

With a deep breath, I survey the small oasis. The sound of the creek and the shade provides a perfect escape.

"It's beautiful, like something out of a dream."

"Yeah, you are."

"Jackson..."

He closes the gap between us. The moment his hands rest on my hips, I'm lost.

"I know I promised to give you space, to let you think things over," he murmurs against my cheek. "But I can't stop thinking about you. These last few months have been pure torture."

Before I surrender completely, I grip his biceps and push gently. He draws back and searches my face.

"When you disappeared—" I search for the right words. "It crushed me. I didn't know what happened to you."

"I'm sorry. When you said you needed time to think, I couldn't bear the thought of seeing you at the office. I had to leave." He smooths his fingertips over the small of my back, drawing me closer.

"We had things to work on individually. Distance was the best thing for both of us." I cup his scruffy cheek in my hand. "But I missed you every day."

"Not seeing your face each morning almost broke me." He swallows and covers my hand with his. "But I had business to finish before I returned."

I blink away tears. "I love you, Jackson." My soft words are nearly lost in the sound of the flowing creek behind us. "Heaven help me, but I love you."

His mouth is hot on mine when he kisses me. I collapse in his embrace as he pulls me against him. Everything inside me vaporizes into dust on the Wyoming breeze. Every fear, every desire, every moment of anguished torment. My hat tumbles to the ground when he pulls me away from the water's edge and backs me against a tall tree.

"Tell me again." He pulls off his hat and a grin splits those sinful lips.

"I love you."

CHAPTER TWENTY-SEVEN

I welcome the onslaught of his kisses, savoring his invasion. His body pins me against the tree while his hands delve beneath the fabric of my top. I arch my body into his touch. I need more.

My moan echoes through the valley when he unfastens my jeans and slides his hand between my thighs. Those talented fingers delve into my embarrassing wetness. I bite my lip to stifle my cries.

"No, kitten, I want to hear every whimper when I take you," he whispers against my ear. "There's no one around for miles in any direction." Two fingers plunge deep.

"Oh, shit." My voice echoes off the rocks, dissipating into the sound of the rushing water.

He strokes deep and kisses my throat until I'm clawing at his shoulders and bucking my hips into his hands.

"Please, Jackson. I need—" His hand closes over my breast and squeezes.

"What do you need, kitten? Tell me." He draws back and meets my eyes. I'm lost in a torrent of need and desperation. I'll tell him whatever he wants as long as he finishes what he started.

"I need you to fuck me." I grab his belt and pull it free. "Now."

His mouth covers mine. Hands fumbling, I manage to free his cock. He tugs my jeans down, wraps an arm around my waist and hoists me up, pinning me against the tree.

He sinks his cock deep, groaning against my throat. I cling to him, savoring the fullness of both mind and body. It's been so long since Christmas.

"I missed you."

I gasp at the sensations he unleashes with a single thrust. He speeds up, driving deeper, harder, faster. The tree's bark digs into my back, but Jackson holds me close with every stroke, saving me from the brunt of it.

Our mingled breath and panting moans echo around us. The valley erupts into a live erotic symphony. His touch ignites a wildfire inside me. I can't get enough of him. Of this.

When he shifts his hips, he brushes my clit, sending me into a spiraling climax. Jackson grasps me tighter as my orgasm flashes through me like pockets of firecrackers igniting against the darkness.

His release follows, and I hold him against me as his breath brushes my neck. Kisses pepper my skin. He pulls back and his satisfied smile steals my breath. He's so damn handsome it hurts.

He lowers me to my feet and pulls a handkerchief from his back pocket to tenderly clean the mess from my thighs before helping me dress.

My body aches in the best way. Once he fixes his belt, I grab his shirt and pull him in for another lingering kiss. He cups my cheek and tastes me. I melt like a snow cone in July.

"I belong to you, Lily." He strokes my cheek with his thumb. "All of me."

"Oh, Jackson…"

With a kiss, I draw back. The heat of our encounter cools in the shade of the cottonwood trees. I nudge him playfully. "Is the tour over?"

"Not at all." A mischievous grin overtakes his smolder. "You able to ride after—"

I scoff and step around him. "It's gonna take a lot more than that to keep me out of the saddle."

"Challenge accepted."

"Later." I untie my mare and pull myself into the saddle with ease. My body twinges in protest at the movement, but I ignore the pleasurable ache he left between my thighs.

Jackson frees his gelding and mounts the impatient horse. "I'm holding you to that promise, kitten."

I blow a kiss and urge my horse forward. The moment we reach the open plains, I kick my mare into a run. We gallop over the ridges. Jackson follows behind, his horse keeping pace with mine. I laugh and urge her faster. The wind rushes through my hair, nearly stealing my hat, and I embrace the exhilaration of the moment.

Everything falls to the wayside. My father. My fear. My uncertainty. There's only open sky and unending possibilities.

Jackson's gelding passes us. He flashes a handsome smile and tugs his hat down as he takes the lead. I let him. I have no idea where I'm going, and this is supposed to be a grand tour of the ranch.

As we crest one of the ridges, he slows to a walk and I come alongside him. Our horses take a break, their breathing hard and hot.

Jackson gives me a glimpse into the ranch's history, the boundaries, and his family.

"Wait, you're telling me your great-grandparents met on a train?"

"No. They worked for the duchess long before the whole train incident."

"Then what does the train have to do with it?"

"That's where they realized they were in love." He winks.

"A Russian bodyguard and a German maid fall in love on a train traveling through the Alps?" I shake my head and scoff. "Sounds like the plot of a historical romance novel."

"It does, doesn't it?" Jackson laughs. "But it's the truth. Their oldest daughter is my grandma. She married my grandpa, the son of the neighboring rancher. Their families were close, and eventually, they merged ranches."

"So how did you end up with it?"

"After my grandparents died, my mom didn't want the inheritance and passed it on to me instead." He stares off into the distance. "She moved to the city to marry Dad. They had a small shop in Brooklyn for years. She hated Wyoming."

"So, you're a city slicker *and* a country boy." I nod with appreciation. "You seem suited to both."

"I learned to adapt." He points to the horizon in the distance. A cluster of buildings appears beyond the hill. "We're almost home. We'll grab a late lunch."

"Sounds good to me."

By the time we reach the corral, I'm confident in my ability to recite Jackson's family history, but I still haven't learned much about him. I guess that's part of the process when you spend time with someone. Uncovering all those little details that make them interesting.

"I'll take care of the horses if you want to head up to the house and scrounge up some food." He takes the reins from my hand and presses a kiss to my forehead.

"Okay."

The kitchen is empty when I stumble into the cabin. Vivian must be busy with other work. I whip up a few sandwiches and grab some fruit from the counter. When I glance out the window, I see Jackson crossing the front porch.

I manage to balance the plates and open the door. He grabs one from my hand and closes the door behind me. The cool breeze in the shade of the porch soothes my overheated skin.

We eat in silence. He steals glances between bites.

"What?" he asks, wiping his hand across his mouth. "Do I have something on my face?"

"No." I chuckle and my face heats. "I was just admiring your scruff. I think I like this better than your serious VP look."

"You must have liked that side of me too."

"I do, but I think there's more to you that I haven't seen yet."

He wags his brows. "Kitten, you've seen me naked. I don't think I can reveal more than that."

"You know what I mean."

"You're right though. I'm sure there's a lot we still have to learn about each other." He rests his hand on my thigh. "If you're willing to find out more?"

"I am."

"I won't rush you into anything, Lily, but I want you with me always." He takes my hand. "No more secrets. No half-truths."

I interlace our fingers. "I have plans, Jackson."

"I expect nothing less." He kisses my fingertips. "I shall follow you to the ends of the Earth. Whatever you want to do,

I'm game."

"Are you serious?"

"As a heart attack." His expression brightens. "I've wasted too much time chasing things that give me no fulfillment. When I met you, I lived for my work. Nothing else mattered."

"And now?"

"Now, nothing matters but you." His words sink deep, leaving a puddle where the ice surrounding my apprehension has melted. "As long as you're by my side, I'm content."

"Jackson. We barely know each other."

"I'm not in a rush. I just want to spend time with you." He tugs my hand, drawing me closer until I collapse against his solid chest. "Where you lead, I'll follow."

A thousand thoughts bombard me, but one question shines brighter than the rest. "Anywhere?"

"Yup." His breath ruffles my hair.

"What are you doing the week after next?"

"What do you have in mind?"

"A wedding."

Both his brows shoot into his hairline. "*What?*"

I laugh when I realize he thought I meant *our* wedding. "Jen and Shaun are getting married next week. Will you come with me as my date?"

He relaxes, but I see the disappointment in his eyes. I can't blame him, the thought of marrying him has my body humming with delight. For now, though, I think we should take it slow.

"I'm not sure how they'll feel about me crashing their wedding, but if you want me to accompany you, then I will."

I launch myself into his lap and kiss him. He grips me tight as he explores every inch of me. We manage to make it to his bedroom before we concede defeat on the porch. I could only imagine Vivian's face if she caught her brother having his way with me in full view of God and country.

Jackson makes love to me twice before dinner, and even though he assured me I wasn't too loud, the stain of pink across his sister's cheeks tells me that was a complete lie. But she's happy for us. I'm happy for us.

Here's to a fresh start with the man of my fantasies.

CHAPTER TWENTY-EIGHT

Two weeks later

"I look ridiculous."

"You look fine," I murmur and nudge him to pay attention. Jen and Shaun are in full *Space Vendetta* cosplay standing in front of the ordained minister at the head of the room.

My heart soars. The time I spent helping Jen create the perfect Ranger Lynnea Stark dress to compliment Shaun's Commander Colton uniform was worth it. Even though I'm not a fan of the books or the film series, I appreciate the dedication these two have to their fandom and each other.

Tears fill my eyes when they exchange vows before their small collection of family and friends. I'm honored to be part of their special day. Shaun and Jen's respective families seem perplexed by the theme of the wedding, but no one says a word. This is their wedding, and if anyone tries to ruin it, I'll duct tape them to a chair in the closet.

A rousing cheer fills the garden area when they share their first kiss as husband and wife. I dab my tears away with a handkerchief. Jackson takes my hand and squeezes it.

The congregation rises as the bride and groom make their way down the aisle. Jackson wraps his arm around my waist and holds me tight. The faux leather I used for his jacket pulls tight against his arm.

When he agreed to attend the wedding with me, I managed to throw together a quick ensemble for him that would complement mine. My dress was inspired by a side character from the films—a sexy alien with teal skin who manages a trading outpost near the galaxy's edge. I always had a soft spot for her, especially when she would interact with a handsome rogue who frequented the outpost and occasionally teamed up with Captain Ransom to thwart Commander Colton. They don't have an on-screen romance, so using him as inspiration for Jackson's clothes allowed me to play out the fantasy pinging around in my mind.

Jackson doesn't know this, but I fully intend to enlighten him later tonight.

We returned to the city together and spent the entirety of the past three days locked away from everyone. When Jen and Maggie realized I had returned, they demanded to see me. Jackson invited them over for lunch and sat beside me while I told them everything.

Maggie nearly launched herself over the coffee table at Jackson when I revealed he was really Sam, the cowboy I'd been talking to online. Jen's expression of stunned disbelief turned to hysterical laughter at the reveal. By the end of the conversation, all our cards were on the table, and neither of my friends attempted to dissuade me from remaining with Jackson.

Jen wished us all the best, while Maggie vowed retribution on Jackson should he lie to me again. The threat left Jackson visibly stunned, but he took it in stride.

Jackson takes my hand and leads me through the crowd as we follow Jen and Shaun into the hotel ballroom. Maggie's former bosses were able to pull some strings and reserve one of the nicest hotels in Brooklyn for Jen and Shaun's special day.

Their lovely garden ceremony leads into the expansive ballroom decorated in a stunning, stylish *Space Vendetta* themed reception. Maggie and I helped with the planning and decorations. I made a few calls to ensure my best friend got the wedding of her dreams. It might not be fancy or traditional, but it suits them right down to the miniature spaceship centerpieces on each table.

When we reach Jen, she throws her arms around my neck. "Thank you so much. Today wouldn't have been as special without you!" She turns to Jackson and opens her arms.

"Congratulations, Mrs. Townsend." He hugs her.

"We're practically family now." She beams. "Call me Jen."

Shaun pulls me in for a hug. "Thanks, Lily. We couldn't

have done this without you."

"You're welcome." I kiss his cheek.

Shaun's grin fades when he sees Jackson's arched brow and he extends his hand. "Sir."

"Jackson." He takes Shaun's hand and smiles. "Congratulations."

"We'll catch up with you later," I murmur and take Jackson's arm.

We weave through the room and find our seats near the head table. I glance at the cards even though I know who else is sitting with us.

Maggie and Gavin arrive as we take our seats. After exchanging greetings, Jackson offers to retrieve drinks from the bar. Gavin joins him. Maggie sits beside me and sighs.

"You okay?"

"Perfect." I grin. "What about you?"

"I'm good." She relaxes, but her gaze remains fixed on my face. "You sure about this?" She gestures to Jackson. "About him?"

"Yes, Mags. I'm sure."

"I just don't want to see you hurt. You're taking a big chance on him."

"I know." I rest my hand on hers. "But life's more fun with a little risk."

"You're right, but I'm serious. If he pulls that shit again, I will unalive him without hesitation. Just say the word."

"Thank you for your concern, but I'm sure I won't need your services."

Jackson and Gavin return with our drinks.

"How was Wyoming, Lily?" Gavin asks before taking a sip of his old fashioned.

"Different, but beautiful. How's the company coming along?"

"Great. We sold two more apps." He wraps his arm around Maggie's shoulders. "We're on a roll."

"I'm so proud of you both." We chat about their flourishing business, and I tell them all about my plans for the upcoming release of my Kickstarter fashion fundraiser.

The longer we chat, the easier the conversation becomes. Jackson even joins in. He and Gavin hit it off quickly. My heart warms at the way our lives intertwine.

After the bride and groom take the floor with their first dance, Jackson takes me by the hand.

"Dance with me," he whispers in my ear and pulls me to my feet.

I melt into his embrace when he grasps my waist in one hand and my glove-covered palm in the other. The familiar strains of an eighties love ballad plays over the speakers as couples slowly fill the dance floor.

His eyes sparkle in the flashing lights of the disco ball overhead. "You look beautiful, Lily."

"Thank you. You look quite dashing yourself."

"I have a good tailor."

"That suit looks good on you." I lean closer. "But it'll look even better on my floor."

"Keep talking like that, and you won't get any cake." He growls. "I will haul you over my shoulder and carry you to our hotel room right now."

"That sounds like something he would do."

"Who?"

"The character I modeled your costume after." I lick my lips. "I'll show you later."

"Kids these days." He shakes his head. I jab him in the ribs. He laughs and pulls me tighter against him.

I rest my head against his shoulder as the music continues. This is exactly where I want to be. We dance in blissful harmony until he speaks again.

"What did you say?" I ask, uncertain I heard him correctly over the music.

"I sold my penthouse."

I pull back and meet his gaze. "Wait, why?" My eyes fly wide. "Are we moving to Wyoming?"

He kisses my forehead. "No, kitten. We're not leaving the city yet."

"Then why sell the penthouse?"

"Because I found a better place for us." He spins me around in a wide circle as the music changes tempo.

"Where?"

He presses his lips to my ear and whispers the address I've lived at for the last eight years.

"No! Really?"

"Really." He vows, crossing his heart.

"I can't believe you bought the brownstone. When?"

"February."

It takes a moment, but the realization hits me like a brick to the side of the head. "You're the reason we got kicked out of the house."

When I try to pull from his grasp, he tightens his hold. "Lily." His tone warns me I'm overreacting but I don't care. He lied again.

With a sigh, Jackson leads me off the dance floor. We find a quiet corner near the windows. The sunlight streams through the glass, illuminating his face.

"The day after Christmas, after you asked for time alone, your father called me." Jackson holds my hand, and his thumb strokes my knuckles. "He threatened me and then tried to bribe me. The longer I resisted, the more desperate he became. When he let it slip that he intended to sell the brownstone, I called him a selfish bastard and ended the conversation."

I stare at him in shock. "But how did you convince him to sell it to you?"

"I called in a favor from a friend who's a realtor. She pulled some strings and had an offer in by the end of the week." He cups my cheek. "The house is yours, Lily."

"How?" Tears blur my vision. Jackson retrieves his handkerchief and wipes them away.

"Your father's a businessman. He was liquidating assets and trusted his associates to follow his direction. They never asked for the details of the purchaser, aside from corporation name and verification of payment." He tips my chin up. "I put the house in trust to you once the sale went through. It's yours."

"Why didn't you tell me?"

"I wanted to surprise you." He lifts a shoulder. "But I just got the confirmation today from my legal team. We can move in next week."

I throw myself at Jackson and wrap my arms around his neck. He instinctively catches me and buries his face in my hair.

"I love you, Lily. I want you to be happy." He draws back and searches my face. "Are you happy?"

I nod, my smile wide and heart so full it might burst. "I love you too."

He wipes the remaining tears from my cheeks.

"Am I smudged now?" I fan my face.

"Not at all. You look beautiful." He kisses me and the world around us dims to muffled background noise.

Passion bubbles up from the well inside me and I moan against his mouth when he slides his tongue across mine.

"Behave, kitten," he murmurs low and deep. "I wouldn't want you to miss the festivities because I couldn't wait to get you back in my bed."

With a groan, I remove myself from his embrace, knowing one more moment in his arms and I'd surrender completely.

"Lily!" Jen calls when she spots us by the window. "Come over here. I want a photo of all of us together."

I grab Jackson's hand and together we weave through the tables toward the small dais where Jen and Shaun are standing together. Maggie and Gavin join us. Three couples pose for a very prom-like photo before falling into fits of laughter.

The photographer snaps a few mementos and throws his hands up in defeat.

Jen and Maggie crush me in a hug.

"I love you guys."

"Ditto," Maggie says with a lopsided smile.

"Always." Jen gives us one last squeeze. "Who's ready for cake?" she shouts for the crowd.

A chorus of cheers goes up from the guests.

Jackson pulls me into a hug. "After cake, you're mine." His whispered promise lingers in my ear.

I shiver with anticipation. God, I love this man.

CHAPTER TWENTY-NINE

One month later

"Stop." I push his hands away. "They'll be here any minute."

"Come on, kitten. Just one taste." Jackson purrs in my ear. "I promise I'll behave the rest of the night."

"You'd better behave, regardless." I whip around brandishing the spatula like a sword.

Jackson takes a step back and licks the chocolate icing from his fingertips. "I just offered to make sure it wasn't poisoned."

"You think I would waste perfectly good brownies with chocolate ganache to poison someone?" I scoff and finish scooping the squares from the baking pan.

"Well, they would eat the whole thing."

I finish plating the brownies and carry them into the dining room. Jackson follows behind carrying the small stack of plates. I set the brownies next to the rest of the snacks on the buffet and nod with satisfaction.

"This should be enough."

"You could feed an army, Lily. It's more than enough."

"I can't be a good hostess if I don't feed my guests." I rise up and kiss him on the lips.

Jackson seizes the opportunity and wraps his arms around my waist, holding me tight. He deepens the kiss as I savor the taste of ganache on his tongue. I'm about to concede defeat to his relentless siege when the doorbell rings.

"They're here!"

Jackson sighs in disappointment. "Fantastic timing."

"Be nice." I swat his arm before retreating to the front door.

"Lily!" Jen bursts over the threshold and hugs me. Shaun nods at me over her shoulder.

"Hi! Come in." I step aside and let them enter the house. It's changed a bit since the last time we all got together here.

Jackson had the whole house cleaned from top to bottom and freshly painted before we moved in. He let me decorate the house however I wanted. I leaned heavily on my eclectic retro taste.

"The place looks amazing!" Jen spins around in the entryway and admires the new décor.

"Thanks. It's nice to finally have my own space." I spy Maggie and Gavin climbing the porch steps.

"Hey!" Maggie joins the fray, hugging me.

"Hey, Lils." Gavin squeezes me tight. "Are Michael and James coming tonight?"

"I invited them, but those two are always busy." I close the door and herd them into the dining room.

Gavin and Shaun gravitate toward Jackson, who welcomes them with a warm smile and a firm handshake. Beside those two, Jackson looks his age. But that doesn't bother me. I like my mature silver fox exactly the way he is.

"Want something to drink?" I ask, grabbing a glass and pouring some sangria.

"Only if you promise it's not a million proof like the last time." Jen winks.

"No, it's not that strong. I promise."

Maggie accepts hers without hesitation. "So, how's life with your cowboy daddy?"

"It's good. Really good." My face warms. "He's set up the spare bedroom as an office so we can both work from home, which is really nice."

"Easier to get some afternoon delight, huh?" She's not wrong, but I'm not going to bolster her ego by confirming her suspicions.

"How's your new place coming along?" I ask, changing the subject.

"It's good. Finally got the shop downstairs set up the way we want it. I like having the workspace downstairs and our living space upstairs." Maggie takes a sip of her sangria.

"She's getting sex on the regular now too, which is a relief for all of us." Jen laughs.

"Ha ha. You should be a comedian." Maggie turns to her. "How was the honeymoon?"

"Fantastic." Jen sighs dreamily. "London was amazing. I walked so much my feet nearly fell off. Shaun surprised me with tickets to see Nicholas Hughes' new play, *Redemption*."

"How did that go?" I ask, curious to see if Jen lapsed into her obsessed fangirl habit.

"Great. The play was wonderful, and we had a lovely dinner at a pub near Hyde Park afterward."

"I'm glad you both had fun." I glance at our men huddled at the far end of the table having what looks like an animated discussion. "Shall we get this party started?"

"Yeah, if we don't wrangle them now, they'll wander off." Maggie crosses the room and snags her arm through Gavin's.

Settling down at the table, I glance at Jackson. His mouth is puffed up like a chipmunk's. I scowl at the chocolate smeared on his upper lip. He gives me a wan smile and chews.

As he slides into the seat beside me, I nudge him in the ribs. "Couldn't wait, could you?"

"No. They're so good."

Maggie bursts into laughter, and Jen smothers her mouth behind her hand.

"Her brownies are orgasmic," Gavin vows, snatching one for himself before sitting down.

Shaun joins in the fun, grabbing a square before taking his seat. He nods furiously after the first bite and stuffs the whole thing in his mouth.

"You guys are worse than kids."

"What do you put in these things? Crack?" Jackson licks his lips.

I hum innocently. "Guess you'll never know."

Everyone bursts into peals of laughter. I grab the cards from the center of the table. Another wonderful game night full of inappropriateness and shenanigans. Life couldn't be better.

Jackson takes the cards from my hand and deals them for

me. "I got this."

"Have you ever played this game before?"

He winks. "Guess you'll never know." He kisses my cheek and deals the starting hand.

The room lapses into silence as we read through our cards, and I steal a moment to study everyone around me.

Jen and Shaun side-eye each other, and she blushes when he mouths something only she can see.

Maggie and Gavin kick each other under the table. The heat from their looks nearly sets my curtains on fire.

Jackson rests his hand on my thigh. His touch burns through my wiggle skirt. I glance up to find him watching me, his blue eyes sparkling. He leans close and kisses my cheek.

"Behave," I murmur under my breath.

"That's impossible when you're this close to me." He nips my ear.

"I'll switch seats with Jen if my presence distracts you."

Jackson takes my drink. "Don't you dare, kitten."

I squirm in my seat, unable to bear the intensity of his attention. "Who—" I clear my throat and turn away from him. "Who's first? Shaun?"

Shaun snaps to attention and draws a question from the pile.

With that, we're drawn into the companionable and irreverent game. Three hours pass before we realize snacks are waiting for us.

I had my reservations when I offered to host game night. My friends never really had the opportunity to see Jackson in the same light I had. They knew him from my stories or from working for him at the office. But here, in this light, Jackson transformed in the best way.

Gone was the staunch professional. The unapproachable boss. In his place sat a man who laughed and loved with the same passion as the rest of us. The longer we spend together, the more my friends see the man I fell in love with.

It might have been love at first sight for both of us, but that time spent apart gave me the opportunity to find myself and my passion.

With Jackson by my side, I'll reach my goal: fashion week in Milan. If the pre-sales for my Kickstarter are any indication, there's a thirst for a vintage-inspired line for real women. Lily Starling will soon be a competitive brand.

The best part? I did it on my own with the support of my friends and Jackson. He saw my potential and nurtured it. Yeah, our start was rough, and it took time to overcome those obstacles. But we're both stronger for it. We're right where we need to be.

Surrounded by those we love and chasing our wildest dreams.

THE END

About the Author

Kirsten S. Blacketer is a multi-published indie author of both historical and contemporary romance. When she's not writing, she homeschools her two children and enjoys time with her family. In those moments of freedom, she devours romance novels while sipping a glass of wine. Age has only shown her that writing villains can be just as fun as heroes. Her next life goals are to write a New York Times Bestseller and one day have Adam Driver play a starring role in a film version of one of her books. A girl can dream, right?

Read more at **http://kirstensblacketer.com.**
Also Writes as Jen Bradlee

OTHER BOOKS BY KIRSTEN S. BLACKETER

CRAVING 1985 SERIES

When I Found You
Can't Fight This Feeling
She Gives Love a Bad Name
Owner of a Lonely Heart
Just What I Needed

HISTORICAL

An Irresistible Shadow
A Shadow's Kiss
Mississippi Moonshine
Deceiving the Earl
Jewel of Winter
At Winter's Demand
Under Winter's Control
Seducing Winter's Gentleman
Stealing the Widow's Heart
Seduction on the Alpine Express
Temptation on the Alpine Express

CONTEMPORARY

A Lockdown Love Affair
A Holiday Love Affair
Mistletoe and Mistakes
Confessions of a Fangirl
Confessions of a Gamer Girl
Confessions of a Glamour Girl
The Cosplayer
The Artist
The Bodyguard
The Director
The Author

FANTASY/FAIRYTALE

Curse of the Huntsman's Jewel
The Huntsman's Revenge

PIRATE FANTASY/HISTORICAL

Queen Takes Hook

Paranormal Historical Monster Romance

Death and Desire

The Society of Wanton Widows

The Duchess Pursues Her Pleasure
The Viscountess in Bloom
The Marchioness Makes a Bargain
The Countess Keeps a Secret

A Series of Late Victorian Romance
Coming 2026 from Dragonblade Publishing

www.ingramcontent.com/pod-product-compliance
Lightning Source LLC
Chambersburg PA
CBHW030341310726
48979CB00001B/139

9781966905189